First published in Great Britain in 2022 by
Bannister Publications Ltd
118 Saltergate, Chesterfield, Derbyshire S40 1NG

ISBN: 978-1-909813-85-4

A catalogue record for this book is available from the British Library

Typeset by Bannister Publications Ltd
Cover design by Harry Kenyon

Printed and bound in Great Britain

This book was self-published by Bannister Publications.
For more information on self-publishing visit:
www.bannisterpublications.com

HOLDFAST

HOLDFAST

STEVE KENYON

WITH THANKS

- Wendy – the sine qua non of the imaginary world of Kirk Aeppel and of my life.
- Harry – the grand and brilliant illustrator and IT rescuer.
- Margaret and Brian – editors and encouragers par excellence.
- ThirdSpace – my weird and wonderful "with-breaders" – forever feasting and fasting.
- To all the dogs who have comforted and cheered my journey.
- Rob Bannister – always cheerful, positive and encouraging.
- Kitty, Parker and Vicki - for inspiration, calligraphy, encouragement and lockdown fellowship.
- Mike and Patti - on whose roof top terrace in Kathmandu this book was started and whose generous hospitality and wonderful company I have enjoyed over many years.

To Wendy – "to love another person is to see the face of God."
Les Miserables.

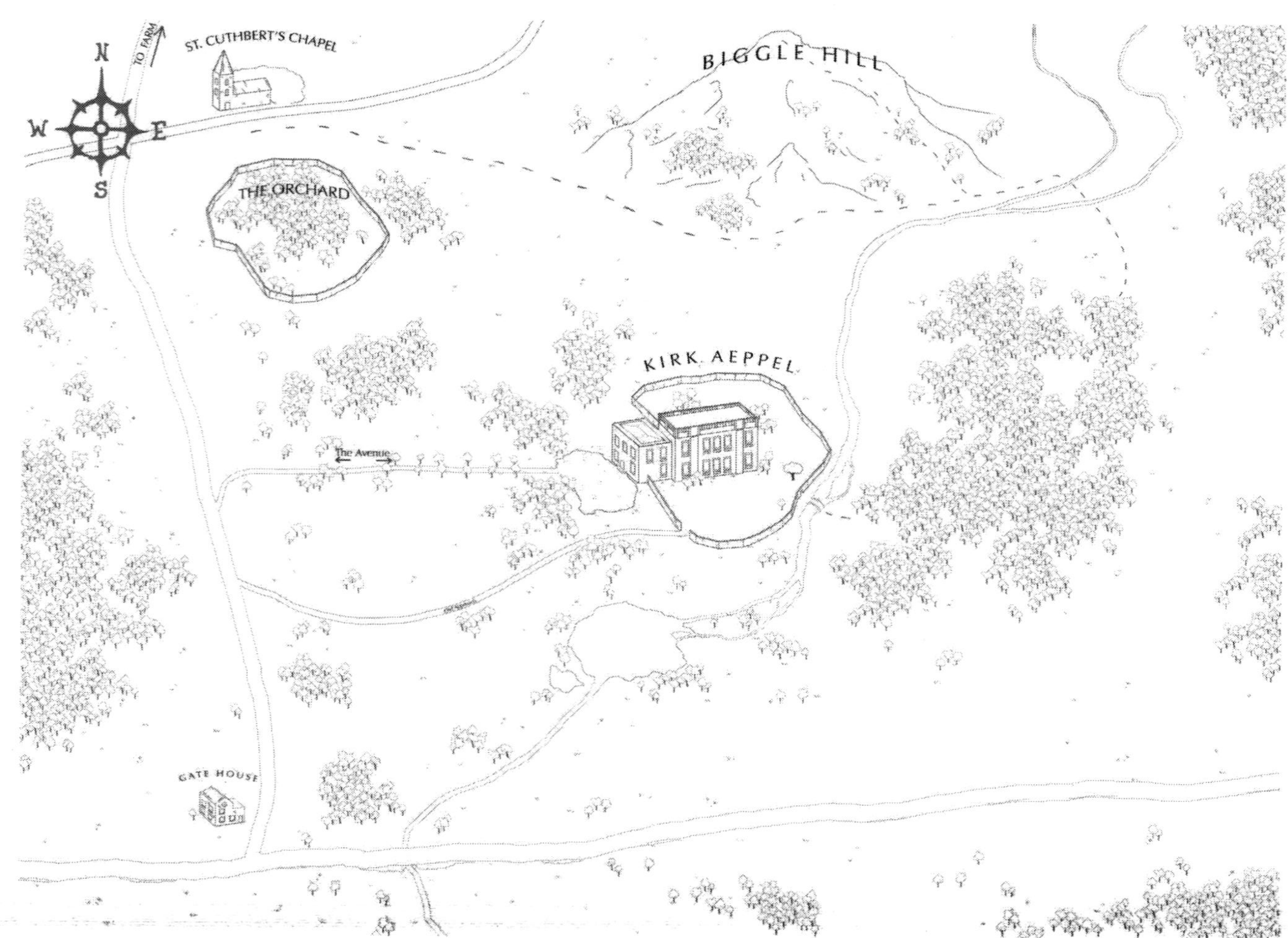
TO FARM
ST. CUTHBERT'S CHAPEL
BIGGLE HILL
N
W
E
S
THE ORCHARD
KIRK AEPPEL
The Avenue
GATE HOUSE

CONTENTS

PREFACE 1 – HH – October 2013 – the commissioning of the diary.

1. This is not my idea. It's Tanushi's idea. She thinks this will raise money for the repair of the roof. I doubt that. Still it's worth a go, I suppose.

2. We both share (along with Beatrice) editorial control to select and clarify but not change content. This is something I will monitor carefully.

3. She has persuaded me not to enter temperature, wind and precipitation details for each day. She says that no one would be interested. Really?

4. I suppose I ought to introduce myself. My name is Henry Havard. I am 53 years old. I own Kirk Aeppel. My family have lived here since 1673. I live here with the four dogs.

i. Ribble – the matriarch – 6 year-old Giant Schnauzer bitch.
ii. Tywi – 4 year-old Wired-haired Vizsla bitch.
iii. Brook – 4 year-old castrated Spinone.
iv. Tiffey – 1 year-old male Glen of Imaal Terrier

(And Nith – Jack Russell. Died 4th August 2012 – see first diary entry.)

5. You will be introduced to the various estate workers through the diary.

6. It's "EYEPULL" by the way.

7. Things have happened in the last year or so – changes – and that's often not a good thing.

PREFACE 2 - TANUSHI - October 2013 - Tanushi's idea

Hi everyone! This is Tanushi here! I am the new "Preservation and Procurement Officer" here at the amazing Kirk Aeppel* estate. It's a great job and as part of the Kirk Aeppel team, may I welcome you to this bullet-journal-diary.

We have now "agreed" that the book will be called "Holdfast" – taken from the family motto "Obtineo, Obtineo, Obtineo" which is variously translated as "to get hold of, to hold fast, to maintain." This has taken some negotiation!

*As many who love this part of Derbyshire will know, there is some controversy as to how to pronounce Kirk Aeppel – is it "Eepull", "Apull" or "Eyepull"? I'll let you decide.

There's so much work to be done at Kirk Aeppel (I say "Apull" by the way) and I thought I'd introduce the team who are dedicated to preserving this wonderful building and estate. There's the amazing Ted and Jane who have lived here pretty much their whole lives – Ted as head gardener and caretaker and Jane as head cook and housekeeper. I have been told I can describe them as being in their senior years! Then there's their son Roger and his two children – Samantha 26 and Jimmy 23 who run the estate farm. And I'm the latest recruit to the team. You'll also be hearing from Timothy who's the son of Charles and Beatrice. But more of them later.

Enjoy!

xxxxxxxxxxxxxxxxxxxxxxxxxxxxxxxxxxxxxxxxxxxxxxxxxxxxxxxxxxxxxxxxxxxxxxxxxxxxxxxxx

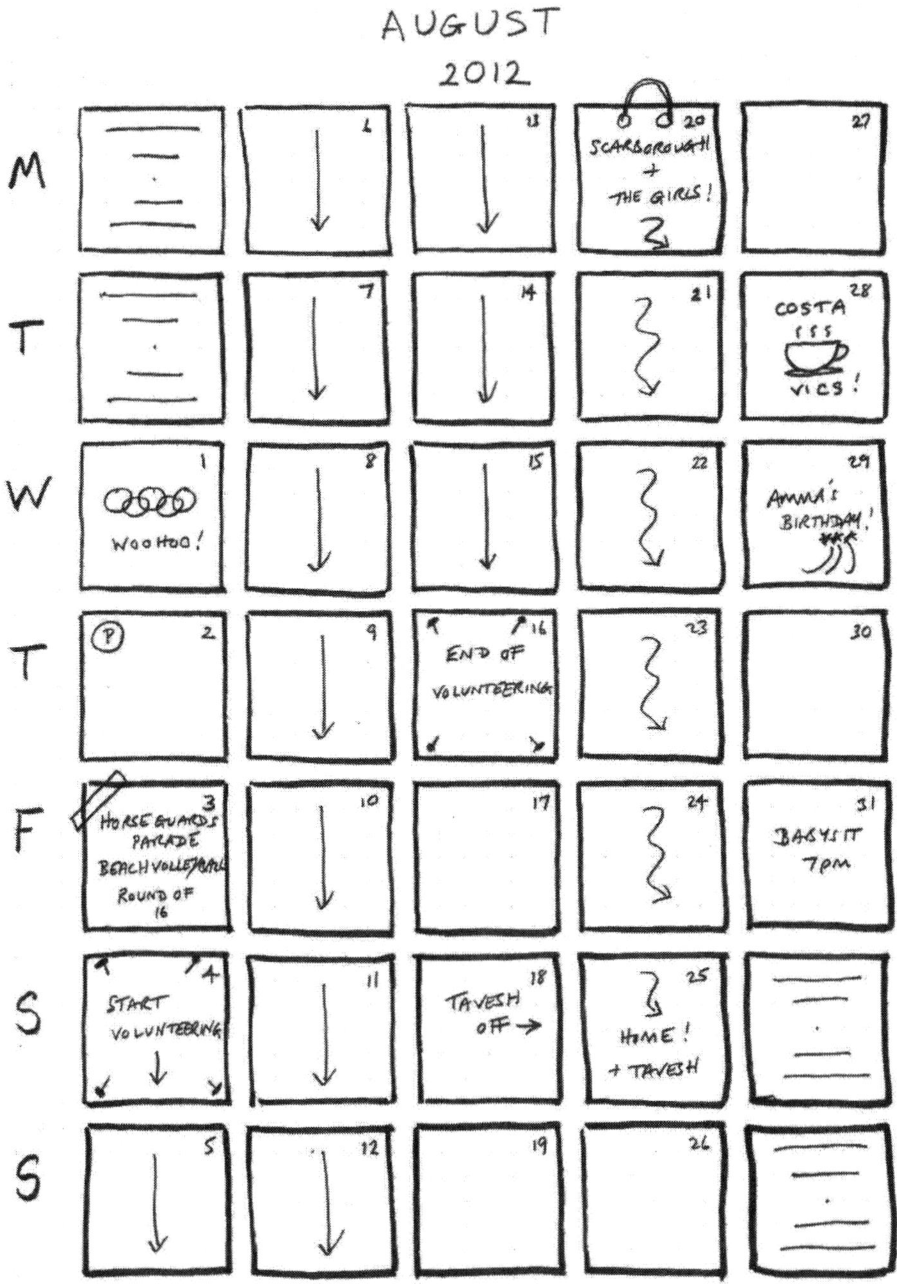
AUGUST
2012
M
T
W
T
F
S
S
6
13
20
SCARBOROUGH
+
THE GIRLS!
27
7
14
21
28
COSTA
VICS!
1
WOOHOO!
8
15
22
29
AMMA'S
BIRTHDAY!
2
9
16
END OF
VOLUNTEERING
23
30
3
HORSEGUARDS
PARADE
BEACH VOLLEYBALL
ROUND OF
16
10
17
24
31
BABYSIT
7pm
4
START
VOLUNTEERING
11
18
TAVESH
OFF
25
HOME!
+ TAVESH
5
12
19
26

Saturday 4th August 2012

1. A bloody awful day – and they're already calling it Super Saturday (not for me).

2. Started fine – off with the 4 dogs at 5.40 – glorious breaking dawn. All seemed well. I knew Nith was not in the prime of life – 14 for a Jack Russell – certainly collecting his pension. But you wouldn't have known it.

3. Out, across the stream, through the woods, up Biggle Hill.

4. The plan was to finish the one remaining tray of beetles sent last month. No surprises in this lot. And then settle down with the dogs to watch the Olympics.

5. It was Ribble – of course – who noticed, came over, pulled my shirt, tugged it, not to be ignored. She showed me to Nith in discomfort, breathing hard, lying motionless. Dear God.

6. Rang Ted. Rang Vet. Ted took me in. Long and short – he had to be put down. I whispered into his ear as the injection went in: "Terra Integrata" – "renewed earth" old boy. You can have whatever stick you want. Holdfast!

Sunday 5th August

1. Plates bad of course. (Ed: This refers to the metal plates at the side of Henry's head which are the result of a bad accident when he was just 11 years old.)

2. 5.40 am off with the 3 dogs. They were lost. I could tell. I was. We skirted the woods to look where we should bury dear old Nith. Vet is delivering him tomorrow. I marked with twigs where I wanted Roger to dig.

3. Nith had a party trick – I've seen other dogs do this – he'd get hold of a stick and challenge you to get it off him. You could pick him up and he'd hang there like a fruit bat. Never let go! Not even Ribble – the big, bold Giant – could prize him off a stick.

4. First Sunday of the month – communion at St Cuthbert's. The usual there. Revd. Dorothy presiding. Good.

5. Olympics couldn't distract. I invited Ted and Jane to our little service 11.00am tomorrow.

6. When someone dies, you consider your own mortality afresh. I've been here before. What will you leave? What contribution of any significance and to

whom? And what of Kirk Aeppel? Surely it is worth fighting for? One more generation at least...

7. Charles came in the evening as per usual arrangement. He brought a bottle of cask strength Lowland – Littlemill. Not had that before. Excellent.

8. All at sea and Charles' presence helped. A dear man. And the whisky started my tongue wagging.

9. Was it too late to provide an heir for the estate? How could this possibly happen? And could something of value – that had a functioning roof – be handed down? Given my disabilities in every relevant department, the solutions were not clear. Charles said he would think on. He apologised for not being there tomorrow for the funeral.

10. Brook had a soft spot for Charles – reciprocated – and the Spinone climbed on the settee and sat on him. Ha!

11. Murray beats Federer for gold. Good show.

Monday 6th August

1. Plates bad overnight.

2. The deed is done. We have buried dear old Nith. Stone – yet to be engraved – in place to stop the foxes. I hadn't invited Revd. Dorothy – I thought she would think it was beneath her. But she turned up. Assume Jane told her. Good for her. So there was Roger who I'd asked to dig the hole – but of course he'd made Jimmy to do it. Lazy bugger. And Jane and Ted, Samantha and Jimmy and Revd. Dorothy. I said some words, we popped Nith in. I dropped a stick in for him, covered him up and put the stone on top. Then Revd. Dorothy blessed us and we went back to the house for a nip of sloe gin at the Big Table. They went on their way.

3. A good job done. Vet – she did her bit. Vicar turned up. Nith sent on his way with proper process.

4. Examining beetle genitalia is, without question, fascinating. There's always the hope that this one – encased in some museum unstudied for a 100 years is a new species. But it does leave you time to ponder.

   Rebirth? Resurrection? Recycling? One dimension? Two? More?

Wednesday 8th August

1. No-one in 25 years has shown the slightest interest in the beetles. No-one. Revd. Dorothy came round unannounced. Found her way in. Must have spoken to Jane. Said she wanted a tea and started to speak to me about beetles – extraordinary. I took her around the specimens table as best I could. "350,000" she repeated, when I told her how many beetle species there were. "The good Lord must have an inordinate love of beetles, mustn't She?" And she looked directly at me and smiled. Didn't know what to say. Fortunately, Jane brought the tea in.

2. There was some controversy earlier this year when she was appointed. Rural parish – all very traditional. I'm not worried about gender – except in beetles – seems wasted energy to worry about such a thing. Theologically irrelevant.

3. Charles confirmed Sunday and said he'd had some thoughts.

4. No golds today.

Friday 10th August

1. Each morning we visit Nith. I think the dogs get it. They were there when we laid him in the ground. They take their turn to sniff at the stone. Brook even cocks his leg.

2. Apples and pears both looking promising at this stage. Ted's done miraculously in the walled garden – as usual – works wonders. Season of perfect salads and veg. I have much to be grateful for. If only we could sort the roof.

Sunday 12th August

1. Evening. Charles came round early clutching papers. I dug out the 15-year-old Edradour we'd started earlier in the summer. It seemed appropriate.

2. He asked about Nith's send off.

3. Then he launched straight in. His first question was, "Are you really committed to providing an heir to Kirk Aeppel? I mean really committed, Henry?" He leaned forward and looked at me. I'm not often called Henry. Jane calls me Henry which she sometimes shortens to Hen – from when she first looked after me in the nursery. Otherwise, I'm known as Mr Havard – or HH for some reason.

4. He pinned me with his eyes. Yes. "Are you prepared to do what it takes? To have to undergo things you don't like thinking about?" I was uncomfortable. Only from Charles. I grabbed Ribble and pulled her close. "You see, I need to know Henry, before I go on. You've always said that you were disinterested in women – or men for that matter. Asexual you called yourself. An evolutionary dead end."

5. Steady on Charles. "ARE YOU COMMITTED?" Loud.

6. I said nothing for a long time. He was right of course.

7. I looked at him. Charles had lost his hair but still had that youthful open optimistic face of when we first met on day 1 at Jesus – 8th October '79. (Ed: Jesus College, Cambridge.) He was my friend then and now. I trusted him.

8. I held Ribble by the scruff. Yes. "Can you produce sperm? If so, we need to get it sent off to make sure it's functional. Then we need to consider Artificial Insemination – and" (he paused here) "how to get hold of the appropriate woman. No point in starting this process if you're firing blanks." No.... Absolutely.

9. We then had a discussion about the ethics of surrogacy. For me there are practical considerations which need careful handling but apart from that – as long as the two contracted parties are content – there are no ethical concerns at all. Charles always liked to play devil's advocate in such debates – always probing to tease out any lurking dilemmas. As long as one avoids emotional entanglement, which goes without saying, procreation is a very simple and effective mechanism. Biologically beautiful.

Monday 13th August

1. Awful night. Troubled dreams. Relief to hear shipping forecast.

2. Went down with the dogs. Opened front door. Perfection. Turned east – the sunlight glancing through the trees. Caught the early resurrection rays. Paused to remember Nith.

3. Worth passing this place on. Holdfast. The vigour of the dogs at play fortified me.

Tuesday 14th August

1. No point asking Roger to do anything. He is the essence of idleness. So, Jimmy – with whom there is actually a decent chance that he'll do something – is checking the orchards. Always been Roger's task – part of the rent. Each evening, checking for signs of disease etc. What does Roger actually do up there? Apart from silage? Cows are gone. He keeps a handful of pigs. Jimmy seems to juggle whatever college stuff he does with actual work. How Roger managed to bring forth Jimmy…it fills me with hope.

THE HISTORY of Kirk Aeppel (1) 1000-1400

Kirk Aeppel is first mentioned in the Domesday Book 1086

KIRK AEPPEL
HUNDRED: HAMSTON
TOT POP: 26 HOUSEHOLDS
TAX: 3.5 UNITS
LORD: KING WILLIAM
VALUE TO LORD: £7
HOUSEHOLDS: 18 HOUSEHOLDS
7 SMALLHOLDERS
1 PRIEST
60 ACRES OF MEADOWLAND
5 ACRES OF WOOD
1 CHURCH
1 MILL
1 GALENA MINE

The name Kirk Aeppel came from the profitable apple orchard – apples thought to have been brought to these shores by the Romans. Kirk refers to the newly built Norman church – built over what is thought to be a Saxon church. Some of the stone from the Saxon church has been reused. Interestingly, a 10thCentury Celtic cross survives intact. Its origins are unknown.

Life and death and lead mining, cider-making and cider drinking, sowing and reaping continued in this tiny, isolated area. The Black Death took its toll but not with the same ravaging intensity as in the urban populations.

Sunday 19th August

1. I have to go to a hospital and submit a sperm sample in a pot. It is then tested. The results follow. Charles has made the arrangements already. THURSDAY. Dear God – what have I agreed to?

2. We tend to leave the Islay malts for winter and in the summer it's Highland or Lowland and Speyside spring and autumn. No reason really – it's just evolved that way. And so Charles produced a speciality Auchentoshen Heartwood. A real hit with both of us. MUCH better than the Springwood.

3. Conversation returned inevitably to the future. Assuming (and I'm not assuming) that all is well with the sperm count, what then? Charles obviously had already thought about it.

THIS IS HIS ASSESSMENT:

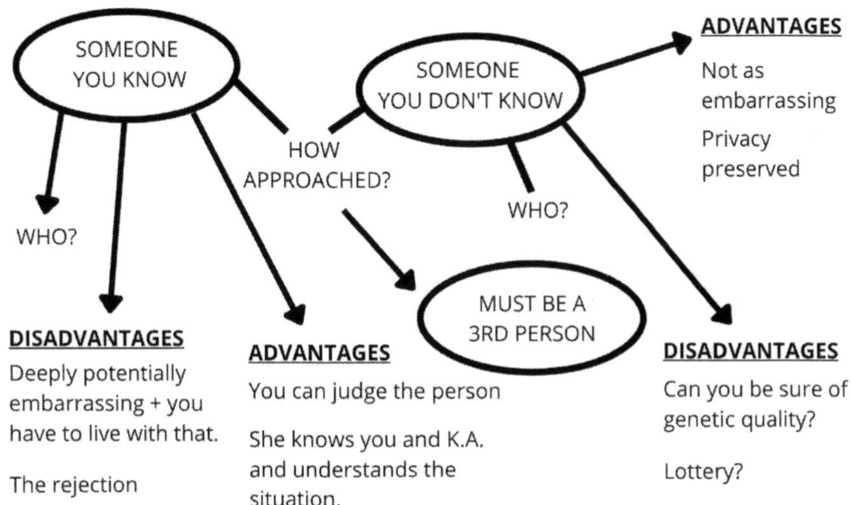

How then can we get hold of someone we do not know, but do know will be young, healthy and intelligent (my only 3 requirements)?

Monday 20th August

(Plates playing up)

1. Don't know quite what Roger does with the pigs – re slaughter etc. Anyway, he pops round and gives me a fine-looking lump of pork. Out of the blue. Accepted. Jane has popped it in the larder for Saturday. What goes on up there?

2. Later walked up Biggle Hill with dogs contemplating how to replace the irreplaceable Nith. Pack of dogs must be 4, minimum. Mustn't compromise. Out of the question. Small terrier for balance.

3. Met Revd. Dorothy, would you believe, with a female parishioner she introduced me to. Small mousey woman. Eating a picnic – it was 1:30 pm – appropriate therefore. Revd. Dorothy invited me to join their little communion. Dogs showing interest of course – I retreated as quickly and decently as I possibly could. Unexpected social contact is not my thing.

4. Let me describe Revd. Dorothy – must be mid-40s – on the larger side of medium – 5ft 6" – dark hair. Confidently assertive – quite disconcertingly so. I try to avoid eye contact – too much. Assume she's a lesbian. They mostly are.

   Thursday looms – plates bad all week.

Thursday 23rd August

1. Hospital. Job done. Results anticipated. Ghastly. Thank God that's over. Stag beetles rule OK as I think they say.

2. Jimmy very faithful in tending orchard. I'm impressed. He follows not his feckless father. Jimmy will want paying in cider no doubt. Happy with that.

Sunday 26th August Decision – tentative:

I am tending towards a Glen of Imaal Terrier

1. 8.30 am last Sunday of month brief communion in St Cuthbert's. Having mourned Nith, having hurdled first of many barriers, having chosen terrier breed, went feeling quite positive. There was Revd. Dorothy with her mousey friend . Good of her to turn out twice in a month for the tiniest of congregations. No homily. But tries out new liturgies from time to time - Creation spirituality she calls it. Interesting.

2. Charles turns up with Timothy in the evening . Nice young man - always got along .Bright chap, like his father. Continued with Auchentoshen Heartwood. Timothy started the meeting. He had a suggestion: let's select from the brightest - a young and healthy recipient. Let's invent an estate job. Let's get her here to KA then tell her the deal. She gets to stay and live at KA with the offspring, raise him / her as the heir to the estate as your son / daughter. She is not committed to HH (absolutely no question of sex) but she is committed to the estate and to her child and his / her destiny here. He suggested advertising / selecting at Cambridge several potential applicants. He'd only left Cambridge 3 or 4 years previously so he knows how to go about this. It'd be completely discreet.

3. At that point Timothy retreated to the Big Table downstairs. This seemed like a plan. I was won over. Charles was not so convinced - who at the age of 23 or so would sign away her life? The power of evolution is what will win the day, I suggested. And it will be a legal nightmare trying to draw up any sort of half - convincing, half - legally applicable contract between the two of you.

4. And finally before they left - "Are there any additional unstated requirements?" I suspected I knew what was being hinted at. So I said, "I believe firstly in God and secondly in Genetics. We are all made equally in the image of God. Racism is thus theologically and morally indefensible. And there is every evidence that a diversity of genetic profile is beneficial (as opposed to the perpetual interbreeding of first cousins). Racism is thus biologically indefensible. A young, healthy, Cambridge University student. That's it."

Results this week, I think.

Monday 27th August – Bank Hol.

1. Weather surprisingly benign for a Bank Hol.

2. Slept well. No troubling dreams. No worries about the outcome of results. Today was a good day. A break from the beetles.

3. I pottered all morning in the orchard, joined Ted and Jane for lunch in the walled garden. Jane asking questions, sensing something. She knew of course about the hospital visit – I rarely leave KA and it is an event when I do. She knew – God knows how – that Timothy had visited the previous evening with his Father. She may be 70 something but she's a keen observer – knows me better than I know myself I wouldn't wonder. "How's the plates?" she probed. "All well? Good. That's good Henry. So concerned all those years ago when you returned from the hospital. 11 and a half you were. I was so concerned about you. Who could have known you'd turn out so well?" She laughed and put her softly calloused hand onto mine. She is the only person allowed to touch me. She stroked my hand and then smacked it with some vigour. She looked me in the eye, "All well Henry? You sure?"

4. Jane has always mothered me. She'd been my saviour after the accident. She'd always treated me as her own. More than my own Mother if I'm honest. But that's another story.

Wednesday 29th August

1. All tickety-boo. High motility. There you go. Phoned Charles to tell him the news. Expected a more enthusiastic response.

2. New tray of beetles arrived. Had been buried deep in some museum in Bradford, Blackburn or Bolton. Excited to get started.

3. Jane will have noticed the stamp on the letter – Derbyshire Dales NHS Trust. She'll be twitching to know.

SEPTEMBER

2012

M		3	10 PRE-RAPHS PREP	17 FINALISE PRE-RAPHS POWERPOINT!	24 LECTURE 10am
T		4 BOOK CLUB ST M's PRIMARY	11 BOOK CLUB ST M's	18 BOOK CLUB ST. M's	25 FEMINIST ART HISTORY 2:00 pm
W		5	12 PRE-RAPHS PREP	19	26
T		6	13 PRE-RAPHS PREP	20 HAIR 12:30pm	27 ART AS PROPOGANDA 1:00 pm
F		7 CINEMA + VICS	14 PRE-RAPHS PREP BABYSIT 7:00pm	21 SHOP FOR UNI!	28 RENAISSANCE + INDIAN ART 10:00 am
S	1 BABYSIT 6:30pm	8 PICNIC! ALEXANDRA PARK 1:00pm	15 → CENTRAL + THE GIRLS!	22 → CAMBRIDGE + FRESHERS' FAIR	29 BABYSIT 7:00pm
S	2 (P)	9	16	23	30 (P) TAVESH ARRIVES

Saturday 1st September

1. Roger's pay-day. Twice a year we have this performance from Roger. Nearest Saturday to 1st Sept and 1st March. "Been a troubled year weather-wise Mr 'Avard and what with the electricity needing re-doing and the elements have been very costly and the rats have done their worst" etc.

2. This time inexplicably different. He comes in and slaps the money on Big Table – in full, in real cash, no promissory notes. Cash – grubby £20 notes.

3. He then, all confident, starts a conversation about dogs – "knowing how you're looking to replace... not that you can replace" etc. He can get hold of a labra-doodle-poo or maybe I might want a spronger-poodle-doo or maybe a Shit-poo and aren't these new "breeds" ever so nice?

4. I do not say: Bugger off you work-shy lump of **** (Ed: deleted). Don't try to sell me your tartified mongrels.

5. I do say, "How's the orchard coming along this year Roger? Good crop?" "Oh I think Jimmy's got that covered Mr 'Avard – working ever so 'ard he is." Indeed.

Sunday 2nd September

1. First Sunday – brief communion at St Cuthbert's. Reminded that the next service there at the end of the month would be the little harvest service. Revd. Dorothy making the arrangements. Mousy friend not there.

2. Upon leaving she held her hand out to be shaken. Not done this before. Jane from behind me, seeing the situation, clutched my arm and asked if I could help her over the porch step – she was feeling a bit wobbly she said. Situation averted. Dear Jane.

3. Definitely a Glen of Imaal. It's a decision.

4. Charles and Timothy in the evening. We follow the equinox. A few more Highland/Lowland. I dig out an Old Fettercairn. Chewy and satisfying.

5. Timothy – all keen and dew fresh – makes his report. He'd done some research, got an advertising plan, suggested a title: "Preservation and Procurement Officer to a small Northern estate." We argued about Northern or North Midlands and

he'd set a time and a place for the initial interviews at Christs (his College) 9.00 am Saturday 8th December. He showed us the job description – all suitably vague. Northern will put off the pompous southerners – and that's all to the good. "Domesticated curating" will put off the men – and that's all to the good. What could go wrong?

6. Charles remained cautious – not wishing to expunge my eagerness and yet doing exactly that.

NEW DIARY ENTRY – TIMOTHY PARKER

Sunday 2nd September

Exciting and a little nerve-wracking all at the same time. Just imagine if this scheme – my scheme – actually works out and solves the inheritance issue at KA. So, I have done all the necessary research. HH seemed very impressed. He was up for it (probs the wrong phrase!) Father reserved his judgement. Exciting though.

Jobs to do:

1. Check venue, time, cost.
2. Sort advertising.
3. Finalise job description.
4. Book hotel Friday 7/8 Dec.
5. Draw up potential questions.
6. Draw up details for the next round @ KA.

I love KA – I have always loved it – playing there with my sister on Sunday evenings in the summer as Father chatted away to HH. I just loved the place – the enchantment of the walled garden, the little wood, Old Oak, the "lake". For me it is another place altogether. I must get this right.

THE HISTORY OF Kirk Aeppel (2) 1400-1700

And so we meander towards the end of the late medieval era. Popery banished almost. Passing records of the lead mines in this part of the world are the only historical notes. Until the purchase of what was to become the Kirk Aeppel estate by a Mr Gwyn Havard formerly of the county of Pembrokeshire. The Havards made their money out of building ships along the mouth of the Nevern at Parrog, Newport.

A family fall out of some sort led Gwyn Havard to seek a patch of land on which to build and display his considerable fortune and Kirk Aeppel was ripe for the plucking. And so, in 1673 he completed his manor house with copious amounts of south facing glass and of course a lead roof.

And he worked on the land. Our records show the replanting and rejuvenation of the orchards; the construction of the walled garden; the digging of the trout "lake" and the landscaping to bring all that about. Mr Gwyn Havard brought with him a small retinue of domestic and rural workers all housed in the newly built estate cottages. We even have a record of his planting and nurturing of Old Oak with a Welsh sessile acorn he brought with him.

Wednesday 5th September

1. What would we do without the internet? I email all beetle classifications to Cambridge to a chap in the Zoology department – there when I was an undergrad – just stuck around and refused to move on – now has ascended to some incredibly junior post. He sends me the beetle specimens to classify. Marvellous really. Good for him I say.

2. And I have found a breeding Glen on line – producing in a week or two. Rare as hen's teeth. Can I have a puppy? Preferably a dog? Yes, if all goes to plan. Marvellous.

3. Trouble is the pups are in east Cambridgeshire. At some distance therefore. And an expedition will need to be mounted – with ancient Ted at the wheel – or maybe Jimmy. I shall sit in the back with eyes covered and music in my ears. We'll do that.

4. Revd. Dorothy turned up – unannounced again. I swiftly (and neatly I thought) stepped to the far side of the specimen table. "Now then Mr Havard, am I to call you Mr Havard or Henry or HH like everybody else?" So confrontational! "And do stop calling me Reverend Dorothy – Dorothy will do!" She smiled.

5. She's going to call me Henry apparently. "We need to discuss the Harvest Service. Can I invite you to the Vicarage? It's in Elton, so a bit of a trek I'm afraid." Jane arrived with tea. I spluttered and demurred and equivocated until Jane suggested she could rustle up some sandwiches and Revd. D would be welcome to join us at the Big Table in 20 minutes or so. Splendid.

6. Tywi (Ed: the wirehaired Vizler) wandered over to "Dorothy" (as I am now to call her). Did the usual sniffing about, sat at her feet and looked up. Not many win Tywi's heart.

7. Around the Big Table: Ted, Jane, Dorothy, me and 3 hopeful dogs. She got her Tablet out and started asking questions – have we ever done this or that? Might this be possible? Don't get me wrong – all reasonable suggestions but all a change in previous practice and I'm not at all sure I'm the one to be talking to about change.

8. Tywi hadn't left her side even when all the food had gone and that was curious. Dorothy looked down with a lump of cheese she had secreted in her hand. "Can I?" she asked looking directly at me. I nodded.

Wednesday 12th September

1. This time Dorothy emailed ahead of time. Arrived and straight into questions. No time for tea. "Which dog would you take to the Harvest service – if you could choose?" Ribble – but then Charles would want Brook and I think you might want Tywi? She smiled.

2. 25 people maybe 30 max can fit into the chapel. She's wanting animals too. "It's a Franciscan thing. I want to do a Franciscan service thanking God for all of sentient Creation – Brother Sun and Sister Moon – or vice versa preferably! You can't do that and keep the dogs out." Fine by me I said.

3. She is ever so slightly bonkers I have concluded – though interesting theologically.

4. Timothy emails every day with updates about what he's been doing. They're all headed "Operation Preservation and Procurement." Very keen.

5. Litter born – 3 dogs, 4 bitches and they should be ready in 7/8 weeks. Mark calendar.

6. Suddenly life seems pregnant with possibilities!

Thursday 20th September

1. Annual check-up on my plates. Usual palaver – x-rays etc. Each year the same questions. Do you have any recollection of how this happened? No I don't. I was told at the time I fell down the stairs at Prep School. Blood pressure, headaches, overall health checked.

2. I am declared fit to continue. "Just don't take up rugby Mr Havard!" I smiled thinly at the doctor – who incidentally looked about ready to take his O' Levels or whatever they're called these days.

3. In truth the only thing I do remember from Prep School is loving rugby and never being allowed to play it again after the accident. A shame.

Sunday 23rd September – Autumnal Equinox – Speyside

Saturday 29th September

ROOF DAY: Even if everybody turns up – which they don't and even if everybody works in a planned and coordinated way – which they don't, this is a testing day. Shifting and cleaning tarpaulins, pouring goo in the appropriate places.

Re-installing those tarpaulins. I hate it. Not my idea of a day well-spent. But it's got to be done. I've banned Ted from the roof. Jane provides the tea and sandwiches. Roger turns out with various feral associates. This year suddenly he swaggers, full of himself, gives the orders. Cannot work out why. He even stands the first round at the Peacock (traditionally my role).

This year went as well as any other. Hopefully more or less waterproof for another year.

Sunday 30th September

1. I took all three, Ribble, Tywi and Brook in the end. This was a Harvest service like no other. Jimmy and Samantha came down with a rook they had discovered fallen from the nest in the spring and had hand reared. Now as tame as a teapot. Various animal life there – but not Roger of course. Ted had decided not to bring their cat for obvious reasons.

   Dogs remarkably well behaved. The service a riot of laughter and joy. I liked it even though I suppose I knew or thought I knew I shouldn't have. Ted and Jane had decorated the church beautifully as usual. Revd. Dorothy the source of much of the hilarity. Interesting. I have come across the St Francis' Canticle of Creation somewhere before. Can't remember for the life of me where or when.

3. All back to the Big Table for the cutting of Jane's amazing harvest loaf. Butter, sloe gin and sherry on offer.

4. Sometimes in carrying on tradition, in maintaining what has been handed on, in marking the cycle of the seasons – there is great solace and meaning I find.

5. Later spoke to Charles about the Canticle and he immediately remembered where we had come across it. I had had a platonic dalliance with a vet at Cambridge – Helen. Still exchange Christmas cards. She'd given it to me in my graduation card. Interesting.

OCTOBER
2012

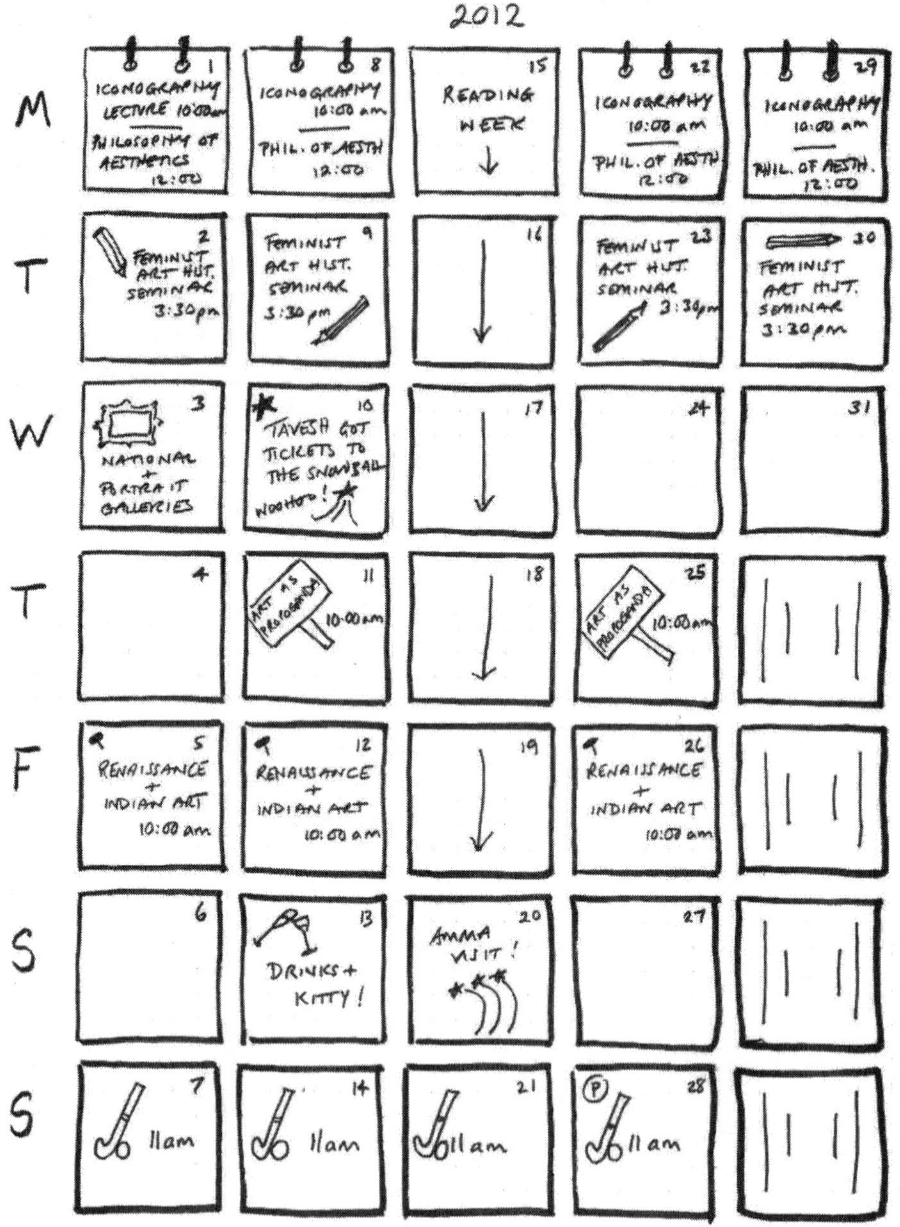

Monday 1st October

1. It seems to me that dogs should be bred for a reason, to fulfil a purpose – a good honest purpose (this precludes fighting and the like for the amusement of Neanderthals). So scenting, herding, guarding, retrieving, ratting, burrowing, hunting – these seem noble callings in the dog/human relationship. These are activities in which the dog earns its keep. There is an exchange of value. Dignity is maintained. NOT so the designer mongrels one comes across up Biggle Hill from time to time. Their sole breed quality is cuteness. Ugh! I've stopped enquiring what breed such and such a ball of fluff might be. Depressing. Interestingly Ribble equally dismissive of such hybrids.

2. Ted and Jane still effusing about the Harvest Service. Excellent – all down to their amazing display say I. No – I am corrected – it's Revd. Dorothy.

3. Puppies all healthy (4 bitches and 3 boys) and one can be collected after Bonfire night. Must phone prior to confirm arrangements. Speak to Ted re journey. He suggests Jimmy. Fine. I'll speak to him + apple/pear pressing timings and logistics. Is it really that time of year once again?

4. Timothy is going to advertise in the Tab and the Varsity for the last 4 weeks of term. He seems happy with that. All arranged.

Tuesday 2nd October

1. Meeting Jimmy each morning now in the orchard at 9.00 sharp for the apple/pear harvest – shaking each tree, collecting the fallen. Jimmy takes them all to the barn. I follow him up to the farm. He's already cleaned the press and made it ready. Good show.

2. No sign of Roger at all. I enquire of Jimmy as to his whereabouts and he is suitably vague. I rarely visit the farm. I notice they seem to have installed solar panels on the southern facing roof of an outbuilding. "Oh, I think my Father is thinking of expanding the pigs." What? Does that make any sense? "It's for the young'uns." Jimmy suddenly asking my advice about the pressing. He'd thought of asking the Revd. Dorothy to say a blessing at the start.

3. Many years ago, my Mother had introduced and conducted a wassailing ceremony for the apple and pear harvest. It hadn't survived her. What harm could there be in asking the vicar along? Jimmy is to take care of it. Seems to like the Revd. Dorothy.

Thursday 4th October

1. Dentist rang to confirm what has been fixed in stone for the past four years. In on Friday 19th October – out on the Saturday. Some new private facility he can access. Marvellous.

2. The apples and pears will distract. All fixed and arranged for weekend of 13/14th October. We'd need a final stripping of the trees on the Friday.

3. I suggested to Jane she invited the Revd. Dorothy for a meal along with Jimmy and Samantha partly to thank her for the Harvest Service and partly to discuss her proposed cider/perry wassail involvement. We shall see. Twyi will be pleased if nothing else. Have to be this Sunday. Perhaps with Charles and Beatrice as well.

Saturday 6th October

1. Ribble picked up a thorn into her front left paw. Managed to patch it up without recourse to the vet. Must stop her licking it. Jane has come across this clever evaporating anti- bacterial liquid which we used on the cut.

Sunday 7th October

1. I am exhausted but strangely content.

2. 6.00 pm meal including Jimmy and Samantha, Charles and Beatrice, Timothy, Ted and Jane and Revd. Dorothy. Round the Big Table and Jane got out the fine crockery and flatware. Good show.

3. Dorothy had somehow learnt the rules and kept her distance but in all other ways seems part of the fabric now. She entertained the troops. Beatrice (Ed: Beatrice, married to Charles, is a Head Teacher of the small local private school) told some extraordinary, horrific stories about parental incompetence and special-pleading and this is at a Private School! I suddenly had to consider the remote possibility that this might in the future be relevant to me.

4. Samantha and Dorothy seemed to have conducted some wassail research and were discussing a plan for the Friday night prior to pressing which was getting altogether out of control. Still I was feeling benign and was reluctant to pour cold water on their enthusiasms.

5. Jimmy is a surprisingly impressive young man. Finished one course and now off on another – carbon-neutral farming. Seemed a contradiction in terms. No doubt he will keep me informed. Jane and Ted so proud of him. Quite touching. Grand-parental pride. What does that feel like?

6. The dogs took their places. Ribble at my side, Brook attentive to Charles, Twyi with eyes fixed on Dorothy. I could tell she quite liked this distinction and so she should.

Tuesday 9th October

1. Samantha dropped in. Thoughtfully, she had told her Grandmother to forewarn me. She reported on her plans for the Friday night Wassail. Did I approve?

2. Samantha is a sweet and gentle girl. She takes after her Mother. Very crafty with her hands. She is making hand held torches. Dorothy has sourced the right words. We are circling and thanking the apple gods and goddesses. Would I dig out some suitable cider vinegar from last year's harvest? To sprinkle and ward off evil. Then we're off to the press barn for hot chocolate.

3. I can cope with that just about. Invitations have gone out.

Wednesday 10th October - TANUSHI

OMG Brother has got two tickets for the Selwyn Snowball 7th Dec. Finally, Tavesh is useful! DRESS!!!! SHOES!!!! There are going to be Reindeer there!!!! Living the dream. Can't wait to tell Amma.

Not helping me write about Renaissance art and its use of Judaeo-Christian creation motifs. Aaaaargh!!

Friday 12th October

1. Apples collected.

2. Quite a do put on by Samantha. Spirits not dampened too much by persistent drizzle. Flaming torches a little lethal but lessons can be learnt. Samantha had invited some "reliable" children from the local Primary. There's a link between the theatrical and vicaring worlds. They all like dressing up and being the star of the show. Revd. Dorothy in her element.

3. All in all – ready for tomorrow.

Saturday 13th October

1. Exhausted.

Sunday 14th October

1. Exhausted.

Monday 15th October

1. Exhausted.

2. The apples and pears are pressed. A good amount this year despite the early drought, plenty of rain latterly and some autumnal sunshine.

3. Apple juice distributed.

4. Jimmy working to some new-fangled ideas he's researched on the internet – from the fenlands. We'll see.

5. So, this year we have:
   - One batch dry cider
   - One batch medium cider
   - One batch perry/cider mix
   - One batch perry

   Not convinced about the apple / pear mix. We'll see. Jimmy seems very confident.

   The pressing – always my mind goes to my Father and the only thing he ever did for the estate – quite uncharacteristically. He squandered and never invested. He destroyed and never rebuilt. Hence the present difficulties. Except once. 1967 – the screw cracked. It had faithfully pressed apples and pears for going on 130 years. Cast iron – Sheffield cast. And my Father replaced it – at some expense and with significant difficulty. I have no idea why. His drink was never cider. But he must have felt some affinity. I don't know. Just before I was sent off to Prep School.

6. Cameron has stitched up a deal with Salmond re Scottish referendum. Nationalism. Here we are within 12 years of the end of the Twentieth Century and some bright spark thinks, "Oh I know, let's give Nationalism a go. Not tried that before. Bound to go well." Do they know NOTHING?

Tuesday 16th October

1. Revd. Dorothy called in on Jane... then me, to wish me all the very best at the Dentist this Friday. How on earth did she know? What goes on? I don't need to account for going to the dentist. Spoke to Jane – snottily.

2. Glad to be left in peace with the Beetles.

3. Then made to feel dreadful when Jane came to apologise for speaking to Revd. Dorothy about my going to the dentist. Dogs don't have these difficulties.

4. Everything on the news is historical child abuse. What goes on? Everyone is accused it seems. Entertainment, Church, Politicians, Schools.

Saturday 20th October

1. Over for another two years. Cost a fortune. Money gets sorted first of course - **** (Ed: delete) dentists. And he always starts with how difficult it is these days for him to use anaesthetic and he's not sure if he can keep on with the present arrangement. Money tends to be persuasive - **** (Ed: delete) dentists. Not that I said that in the moments before he put me under. Check-up, clean, de-scale. No fillings needed. Front teeth remain a problem. As always.

Monday 22nd October

1. Wrote little card for Samantha to say thank you for her Wassail efforts.

2. Thought I'd do the same for Revd. Dorothy but sufficiently irritated by her Dentist comments that I thought better of it. Communion this coming Sunday...

3. Roger turned up talking animatedly with Ted as he was pegging back the Wisteria for winter. A right racket. Who knows what that's about? Ted said nothing. Jane looked flustered when she brought the tea in.

Monday 22nd October – TIMOTHY

I have been over everything again and again. I've checked the ads – all well. I have decided not to use the Premier Inn. Duncan still at Christ's – final year of his PhD. He's said he'll put me up for the night. I think that'll be best; then I can walk to Christ's the next day to set up early for the interviews. I know I have to play everything by the book and get this right.

Thursday 25th October

1. Always a frisson of excitement when I think I have found a new species or even a sub-species. Ceylon turn of the C20th. I have sent it off to Cambridge. And I might just get to name it –within the accepted parameters – obviously. Related to Coptops Leucosticta but I think not the rustica... We shall see.

Sunday 28th October

1. Early Communion.

2. Climbed Biggle in shirt sleeves. Last time of the year I should think.

3. Glad to see Charles. He brought a 15 year-old Glen Grant – much the best from that distillery that we've supped.

4. He shared my excitement about the Coptops. Then he started to press – once this woman turns up for interview, how are we going to actually raise the issue of bearing a child? Is it a "real" job we are offering this woman? What of salary? What can she profitably do apart from provide an heir? Difficult. Pretty sure I am the last person on God's good earth who should be attempting to speak to a young modern woman. And we're all men.... there are difficulties.

   Can't get Jane. What of the omni-competent Beatrice? Or get Samantha to show her around and provide a sweet aspect to Kirk Aeppel. She'd know what to say.

5. There's plenty to be done in the House – or out in the grounds. She can be useful if she's a grafter. The Georgian rooms haven't been touched or most of them even entered for years. Who knows, she might enjoy that.

6. And where might she be housed? Charles identified two possibilities – my Mother's old bedroom – part of the Georgian wing not now frequented. Bathroom will need fixing. Or there's the gatehouse. Habitable, water-tight, can be heated but again needs money spending.

7. I gain the impression that some of Timothy's enthusiasm for this project may be rubbing off on Charles! Maybe.

8. Must arrange to go around the Gatehouse with Jimmy.

9. And we need at some stage to tell the troops about the appointment of this Preservation and Procurement Officer. Hmmm....

Monday 29th October

1. Ring up breeder – a Mrs Ashworth. Seems a good sort. Agreed to come across Tuesday 6th Nov. I will have the pick of the boys. Given directions and postcode.

2. Pass the above on to Jimmy. We meet at Gatehouse. Dogs desperate to explore the garden. Turns out to have fox den. Recently used but cubs have left.

3. The house is as I remember it when I was nursed there and not in bad shape, though even I acknowledge it does need a modern shower and decent kitchen. A lick of paint should complete the preparation.

4. Jimmy asking what for, why, who etc. All will be revealed.

5. So, Jimmy, upon whom I am increasingly relying – in the apparent absence of Roger – is going to make enquiries re getting the Gatehouse sorted out. Quotes etc.

6. If it doesn't work out, we can rent it out? Two bedrooms. Vital income.

NOVEMBER
2012

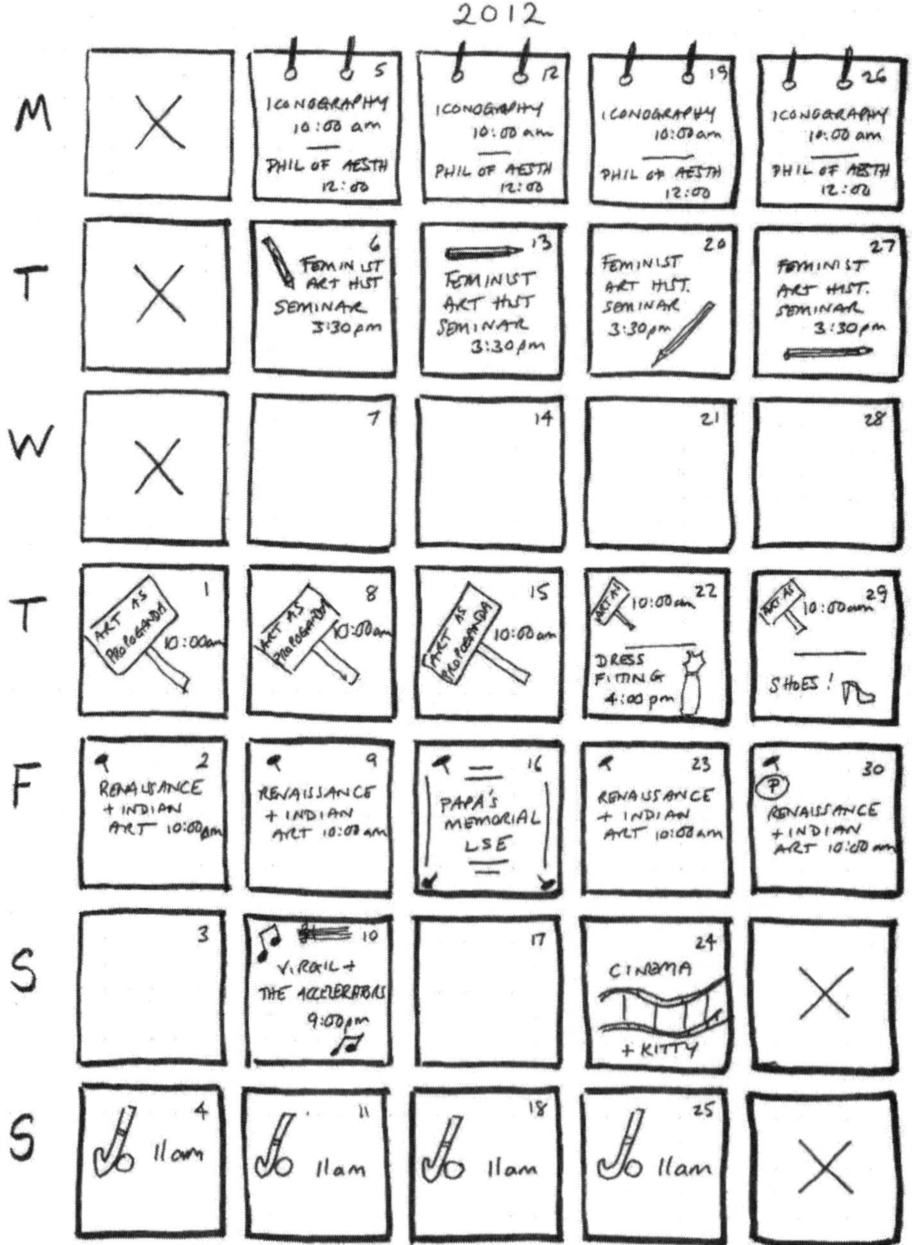

Thursday 1st November - TANUSHI

Amma has instructed me to write down my thoughts about the future (getting a husband she means). What are my hopes and dreams, my skills and abilities? What can I do to secure the future (she wants)?

It's OK for Tavesh to go full out on his medical career. The girls will flock to him because he'll be a qualified doctor by the time marriage beckons. So as long as he "steps out with" a Tamil Christian, Amma will be happy with her ideal son. (Yes really – "steps out with"!)

For me, the academic "also-ran" of the family, my only hope is to find that rich doctor – a consultant with property or with the firm prospect of property ownership. It's all about land. Having a stake. And that's why she has agreed to make my dress for Selwyn Snowball. Something classy, exotic, modestly alluring. My looks will be my strongest suit and not anything else.

I get it – I really do. We're immigrants in a foreign land. She left a prosperous life in Sri Lanka. Started at the very bottom all over again in Harrow and without our Papa. In grief for everything lost and so violently and unjustly. And so she grafted for us to survive and has poured her life into her two children hoping for their material security which she lost so suddenly in 1995.

But it's not as if she is some backward-looking little woman. She got an engineering degree! Yes, Papa was the real intellectual powerhouse, but he chose an equally well-educated woman in Amma to be his wife. He had thoroughly progressive attitudes to social change and women's education. And yet she seems to have reverted since coming to the UK. At least with regard to me.

So here's what I am going to give her:

Strengths:
Intelligent Creative Spiritual Imaginative Artistic
Good with people A team player Confident and assertive Flexible

Weaknesses:
None

Ideal job – working in the Fitzwilliam in archive, restoration, artefact preservation, curating – or something like that.
Papa will be laughing in heaven! I like to think. I can only just remember him now.

I was 5 when it happened. We have photos. Two just with him and me together. I remember him teaching me to draw the Anuradhapura Cross. We would practice it together… and he would explain, again and again and again, its meaning… as if he knew he had limited time.

We will join Amma on the 16th Nov. – to remember him.

Friday 2nd November

1. I have finalised everything with Jimmy regarding travel. I have printed the route from AA. He tells me he has a satnav and not to worry. Jane will have sandwiches prepared the previous evening. Samantha will lend me her musical device with headphones and a pre-prepared selection of classic jazz. And she will have instructed me on how to use it. I have a blindfold. We are setting out at 5.00 am to minimise traffic delays etc.

2. It turns out that the breeder is not a million miles from Cambridge (Little Downham) and I was briefly tempted to drop in on the Zoology Dept. but quickly thought better of it. No parking on Downing St. of course.

Sunday 4th November

1. Communion. Despite the turmoil in my life at the moment – the change and threats of change – I was strangely warmed within the chapel – the prayer-soaked stones will outlive us. Revd. Dorothy struck the right note.

Tuesday 6th November

1. A very satisfactory day.

2. Arrived at the place by 7.30 am – far too early. Jimmy found a café in Little Downham. Offering every sort of bizarre germinating seed imaginable. Extraordinary what people eat these days. Had a bacon cob – outdoor reared local producer. Very commendable. Brown sauce.

3. Turned up to meet Mrs Ashworth at 8.35 am. Turns out she was up and about and saw us at 7.30 am!

4. Listened carefully to what she had to say about the 3 male pups. Observed them at play and with food. Inspected Mother. Made my choice. Mrs Ashworth

approved. Did the finances and health/microchip/kennel club business.

5. We'd taken a crate. Popped Tiff in there. Next to me on the back seat. A little whining and a deposit of vomit. Otherwise all well.

6. A new life – exciting. Just a wee little thing.

Wednesday 7th November

1. Life revolves around Tiff for the time being. Inevitable. The stairs are too much for him and he needs lifting and fetching. I have given him to Ribble – she immediately started to lick. Marvellous. Could not be more proud. Tiff now knows who's in charge.

2. Ted went up to the farm for the best part of the morning. Said he needed a chat with Roger. Said he'd found him. Suitably ambiguous. Returned with some pork chops. Otherwise unforthcoming.

Friday 9th November

1. All well with Tiff. Beginning to learn the routines. The dogs will teach what's needed.

2. Cider and Perry bubbling away nicely apparently.

3. Ted has become even more taciturn than normal since his visit to the farm. Jane making up by being over fussy.

4. Preparing for accounts day. Charles likes it all to be done properly and then we know where we are and where the estate is. I rather dread the whole thing.

Sunday 11th November

1. Walked into village take part in the remembrance parade. Managed not to talk to anyone.

2. Decided to press on with the Craigellachie. I like it more than Charles. He says it's thin.

3. All ready for Wednesday's accounts.

4. Still getting regular updates from Timothy. Really not sure what about except he's very keen to make this all work. I suspect he feels somewhat responsible for having suggested the mechanism by which a future might be secured.

5. Charles worries for him. No sign of a girlfriend. And he's a little otherworldly apparently. (Something I said I admired.) Good at his job – thorough, hardworking – but clients find him somewhat effete. Charles doesn't think he's homosexual.

6. Beatrice thinking of packing it all in. Parental incompetence (in a private school at that) making the job increasingly impossible.

Wednesday 14th November

1. Accounts. A day when Charles and I have the potential to fall out. His job is to attempt to convey the seriousness of the situation at Kirk Aeppel. And then having convinced me of that, he wants me to take decisions which might address the pressing financial concerns. My job is to avoid doing anything very much.

2. He lays out the options – either I can sell one or both of the Matlock properties which currently provide a decent slice of income to the estate. Or I could sell the farm – with Roger as tenant! Or we need to be more creative about making Kirk Aeppel earn its keep. Get the public in – in one way or another. Weddings, people looking around the house and garden, commercialise the cider, dog training weekends etc. All pretty unpalatable stuff and ground we have been over before.

3. I promise to think carefully about what he has presented. He departs – tearing out what little hair he has left.

Friday 16th November - TANUSHI

Travelled down with Tavesh – he'd had to get special permission to miss his lectures! He's very law abiding is Tavesh. Met Amma at Holburn tube station and walked up to LSE. Professor Evans was of course there to meet us with his wife.

For the benefit of the journal I will explain what happened. My Father (a Tamil) worked in the Economics Department at Colombo University. He was a brilliant economist. He had been born in poverty near Mullaitivu in the north east. He won an academic scholarship organised through the Catholic Church and he ended up at boarding school in Colombo at the top Catholic school. Despite the war and the violence towards the Tamils and their human rights being abused, when he entered Colombo University, he rose quickly through the ranks of the economics department. He grew an international reputation in the field of Development Economics and frequently travelled abroad to conferences.

He was in the habit of speaking out against Government human rights abuses. And Tamil Tiger atrocities. Amma says she warned him not to do this. But she says he simply could not, not do it.

On July 9th 1995 the St Peter and St Paul Church in Navaly was bombed by the Sri Lankan air force leading to 125 Tamils losing their lives. He wrote and spoke about the wickedness of this. He had commissioned a painting along the lines of a Sri Lankan Guernica to be placed at the University. It was the final straw.

His passport was confiscated and he was prevented from going to an LSE sponsored conference. On the 29th July he disappeared and Amma could not find out from anyone where he had been taken.

His body was never returned though Amma was informed through unofficial channels about his death in detention. His cross necklace – worth nothing – worth everything – was returned.

She went to the British Embassy. She wrote to Professor Evans at LSE. We were accepted into Britain as refugees fleeing from persecution. We arrived 23rd December 1995.

It had all been arranged by Hugh Evans – that sweet, kind man. And each year on the anniversary of Papa's death (at least when we were told about it) we return to LSE to remember and to lay some flowers at the small memorial. Amnesty are invited.

Someone says something about the importance of the British values of accepting refugees and being an open and tolerant country. We go home.

The Anuradhapura Cross

In truth I hate the day. Being on show. Being the grateful little brown girl. I love Hugh – who continued to play a part in our growing up. But I hate the day. Remembering someone I never really knew and with so few firm memories which seem to be forever shifting. I had insisted (at 6 years old!) that the memorial must have the Anuradhapura Cross on it. Hugh knows it is a difficult day for me but he says it is important for these stories to be told – lest we forget. And Amma of course needs this – to celebrate her brilliant husband who had chosen her – a low caste, clever Tamil girl. He had chosen her! We all need to be chosen.

Sunday 18th November

1. I have come to the conclusion that I am told nothing. Ordinarily I would not mind in the slightest. But I think I do need to know what I need to know.

2. The arrival of Tiff and the accommodation amongst the dogs has been taking up some of my time. All is well. Perhaps I have been less observant than normal – I do not know.

3. Jane, Ted, Jimmy and Samantha were in the kitchen most of the morning. And there was an argument. Definitely – raised voices. Heated debate. Of course, nobody would tell me what's going on. "Is there something I should know?" Equivocation.

Monday 19th November

1. The events of this day are simply beyond belief.

2. Up as usual with the shipping forecast. Beetles. Gathered dogs. Time 7.35 a.m. Just stepped outside. Intake of breath. Dogs heard it first but then the whole of Derbyshire I should imagine.

3. Four sirens blaring, police cars screamed up the drive. Don't pause at the old approach. Don't pause at the avenue. They know where they're going. Up to the farm.

4. I set off at a pace to find out what is going on? Arguments yesterday...now this.

5. Dogs on alert. Carried Tiff. Ribble and Brook take the lead. Tywi by my side. Bright lights illuminated their destination.

6. I arrived. The Police have dogs as well. This was not a good combination. "Get those f****** dogs under control!" Then Roger emerged in all his nightgown splendour and wellington boots, already cuffed. Then to the right, officers exited one of the barns. "In here Sarge. All in here. And there's mushrooms down the far end." I went towards the barn – "Where do you think you're going?" and "Who the f*** do you think you are anyway?" I explained. Pause. "I can see what all the fuss is about can't I?" "So, you own this lot?" I explained patiently. "Roger – the man you seem to have arrested – is the tenant farmer on this land – my land." "You'd best come and have a look then – briefly Mr Havard." I entered. A very distinct smell and rows and rows of extremely healthy cannabis plants. That Roger should have grown something quite so successfully – amazing! I cannot see the mushrooms. (But just to acknowledge that Biggle Hill is a known place for Magic mushrooms at a certain time of year. Roger will have attempted to propagate from them.)

7. It was a long morning. Interviews. Jimmy and Samantha must have been at some party or something. Neither of them present till much later.

8. We had a hastily arranged lunchtime buffet. Jane too upset to cook. Ted standing around looking useless. Then Jimmy and Samantha turned up having spoken to the Police. Tears and hugs all round. Family gathered around the Big Table. And Revd. Dorothy arrived – found out on some social media site, followed shortly after by Charles and Timothy. Cheese, ham, bread, pickle and a frozen apple and blackberry crumble retrieved from freezer. Almost the last of 2011 cider. Water. Wine. I got the medicinal brandy out for Jane.

9. The Revd. Dorothy took the chair. We said Grace and one by one told our stories. I suspect some stories were curtailed as they should be given the circumstances. Yes, they all knew what was going on. Jimmy and Samantha were getting some increasingly poisonous people hanging around. Roger was losing control of the operation. Who tipped the Police off? No-one quite put their hand up. Clearly, as a result of their deliberations yesterday, somebody had screwed their courage to the sticking-place.

10. Jimmy and Samantha's story: Didn't know for a long time. Only very recently became aware. Nothing else. Complete balderdash of course. One suspects they tipped the police off after much family argument, threats to Roger etc. and maybe out of loyalty to Kirk Aeppel? Maybe?

11. Jane clutched the sleeping Tiff on her lap and supped brandy with trembling hands. Dorothy secretly passed cheese to Twyi. Brook nudged Charles for the same. Ribble oversaw all by my side.

12. A plan of action agreed. Charles just needed to find out how long it would take the police to clear the barn and when Samantha and Jimmy could return home. And then he needed to find out about Roger.

13. Then just as the dregs of the custard and crumble were being portioned out, the police turned up. "Sorry to shout at you this morning Mr Havard. I'm sure you understand the situation." I felt I ought to offer him a whisky. My way of saying I understood he had to do his duty. He declined. The barn will be cleared by the end of tomorrow. Jimmy and Samantha can return at 3.00 pm sharp. Roger had declined all legal help. He said he was going to tell the whole truth. That seemed highly unlikely to me though I didn't say so.

14. Exhausted. It has been an utterly traumatic day in many ways. Bloody Roger! Involving me, my land, my estate let alone placing his own son and daughter in such a position.

15. Had a quiet word with Charles – look into tenancy contract. What impact does criminal activity have on Roger's rights?

Tuesday 20th November

1. Jane and Ted don't know what to do with themselves. Village alight with gossip. I instructed they get on with their usual routines. Immerse in the familiar and unchanging.

2. I joined Ted in the orchard as he put the trees to bed for the winter. Spotting damaged branches, clearing encroaching brambles. I worked alongside him for an hour or two. Nothing said. I just grasped him on the shoulder when I downed tools. He said, "Thank you Mr 'Avard."

3. Jane needs Samantha and Revd. D maybe. For all the care she has poured out on me, I find myself unable to comfort her. Call Revd. D. She says she'll be round before the end of the afternoon – and she was. Just turning dark. Kettle on and they talked.

4. Charles called. Roger cooperating fully with police enquiries apparently. And he's looked into the tenancy contract. Criminality clearly committed on estate land is specified as unambiguous grounds for termination. Not that Roger would be aware of that. Ponder.

5. Biggle Hill suddenly a more popular walk today – having, as it does, a clear view down to the farm as the police clear the barn. Disaster tourism they call it apparently.

Thursday 22nd November - TANUSHI

Unbelievable! Wouldn't you just know it – Sara and Josh are going to be there at the Snowball. And she'll be all over him – for my benefit. LOL.

I, on the other hand, will rise above it. I just will practice my "Am I bovered?" face.

Told Tavesh. That was a wasted few words. He just said, "Look, do you want to get back with Josh?" "NO! OF COURSE NOT!" "Then what's the issue? You'll be with me and my friends not with them." Sometimes I think Tavesh really doesn't quite get it – for all he's a Cambridge medic.

Down to Harrow. Final fitting of dress. Amma determined to show a little more of me than I would have expected. She says that now I am in the UK (which I have been pretty much my whole life) I have to accommodate to the rather more revelatory dress expectations. Like fitting in with local customs. She seems to think that this ball is make or break, my last chance of ensnaring someone worthwhile. There is nothing much I can say – except thank her for producing a stunning dress.

On the work front, I have decided I am at a distinct advantage over my peers in studying a module on Judaeo-Christian motifs in Western art because I am a Christian – brought up a Christian even if I'm not a regular at church right now. Tavesh takes me along every so often – to Holy Trinity. He's gravitated away from the Catholic Church. My peers know nothing of Christianity, the Bible, theology. It's all a revelation to them. They're starting from scratch. It's a foreign land. They'd be as well studying Chinese art. They are so completely disconnected from their own history and culture. (That's what Dr Gordon says anyway.)

Thursday 22nd November

1. Revd. D calls. Might we all have a get together after communion on Sunday for a light brunch? Just for an hour or so. She has to get on to the next service. Might be good for us all to chat round the Big Table. She'll bring the croissant / pain-au-chocolate or similar.

2. I make a decision – spontaneously. Yes, let's do that. Good show.

3. Turns out she's already invited Jimmy and Samantha! All I have to do is mention it to Ted and Jane. I do so. Jane doing a lot of holding on to me. This is my role I surmise.

4. A conversation about the tenancy with Charles. I have made another decision to bring about change at Kirk Aeppel. Charles approves. Perhaps there is hope for me after all he says. Practice my lines – Charles has supplied me with some – for Ted and Jane.

5. I go down to the kitchen at 4.00 pm. Ted sitting near to the Aga with brew in hand. Jane pouring her cup. I am suddenly more formal. I realise this is not quite what I intended. I tell them that Roger's tenancy is terminated and that there's going to be a shared tenancy with Samantha and Jimmy at the reins (if that's what they want). They are going to take over at the farm. We need stability and fresh blood and youthful energy and... as I went on somewhat gibberingly, I realised that no protest ushered from Jane or Ted. I stopped mid-sentence. Jane reached out to grip my hand and smiled. All Ted said was, "You're right to do that Mr 'Avard. You have to look after the estate." And suddenly Jane was full of excitement for Jimmy and Samantha. What might they do? What plans they might have...

6. I asked Ted and Jane to broach the subject with them. What needs to happen, needs to happen quickly. Charles has been instructed to draw up the legal papers. Target Wednesday 28th.

Sunday 25th November

1. Communion. One or two more from the village are turning up. Some in-comers. They told me their name. Can't remember it. Retired financial consultant and ex-naval officer of some description. Rather too keen on keep fit and going to the gym I suspect.

2. And so, to Brunch as they call it. Ted had indeed spoken to Samantha and Jimmy. They were fizzing. Like adding dry ice to gin and tonic. "Thank you, Mr Havard, we won't let you down. We'll turn that place around. We've got so many plans and it'll all help Kirk Aeppel.

3. Not sure what Revd. D thought. She could see the smiles on Jane and Ted's faces. The next generation of their family would live on at Kirk Aeppel. She asked them about the state of the place once the police had left. How they had adjusted, sorted things out, what they knew of Roger.

4. In truth, I got the impression that they were not overly concerned about their Father. There was absolutely no spite there – just an indifference really. I was ever so slightly shocked – and then not at all. They were consumed about their future

at the Farm. Good things out of bad things. The cross and resurrection? As a Father, he had not shown a magnificent commitment to them and their welfare. There is a certain reciprocity in these things surely?

5. I felt remarkably energised by making a rapid and bold decision. Unnerving.

6. And in the evening Timothy and Charles came round. I dug out an extremely old bottle of 1962 Glen Moray. Very rare nowadays. Nice combination of sweet and peat. Still got another couple of outings I should imagine. Timothy assured me that all was in hand. Adverts placed. He'd tripled checked everything. And would he like me to speak to his Mother about being the one to raise "the issue" (as it has become known euphemistically). I looked to Charles. He said that he would invite Beatrice next week (with Timothy) and we would all discuss it together. Good plan.

7. The secondary interview is now fixed for Thursday/Friday 10th and 11th January.

Wednesday 28thNovember

1. Charles had already removed the final obstacle. Roger had signed the renunciation of the tenancy on Monday. A little lamb he was, according to Charles. "For the benefit of the estate and my beloved children – you see Mr Parker." Hmmmm – something tells me we haven't heard the last of Roger.

2. And so, gathered around the Big Table, with Charles officiating and Samantha and Jimmy dewy eyed, the documents were signed and witnessed. I told them I had decided to keep the rent the same for the coming year. To help them as they started out. Cue another bout of gratitude and assurances that they wouldn't let me down.

3. Miserable weather as I climbed Biggle this morning. Rain sweeping through. And then just as I reached the top, sunshine. An epiphany of light and beauty. Dogs oblivious of course. Tiff the terrier has very quickly taken his place in the pack. Brook the Spinone is not going to be allowed to take liberties for all her rangy dimensions. Tries to use her height to advantage. Tiff having none of it. It's the little ones you have to watch.

4. I find I am getting behind with the Beetles with all the excess of happenings. Unused to it. Not sure what I think about this.

Thursday 29th November -TANUSHI

It turns out that Sara and Josh were seen having a right ding-dong in the canteen. How dreadful, I say. Tell Tavesh. He then asks whether I want to get back with Josh. NO OF COURSE NOT!!! He then says, "So why do you care?" Honestly, I swear they choose the dumbest people to be medics at Cambridge.

All ready for 7th. Decided to wear sensible shoes because you can't see what shoes I'm wearing under the gown. And I have to walk from The Railyard to Selwyn and back via Christ's. Amma says take a taxi. Maybe. Still I'll be on my feet for 8 or 9 hours anyway even if I take an Uber to Tavesh and then walk up with him.

DECEMBER
2012

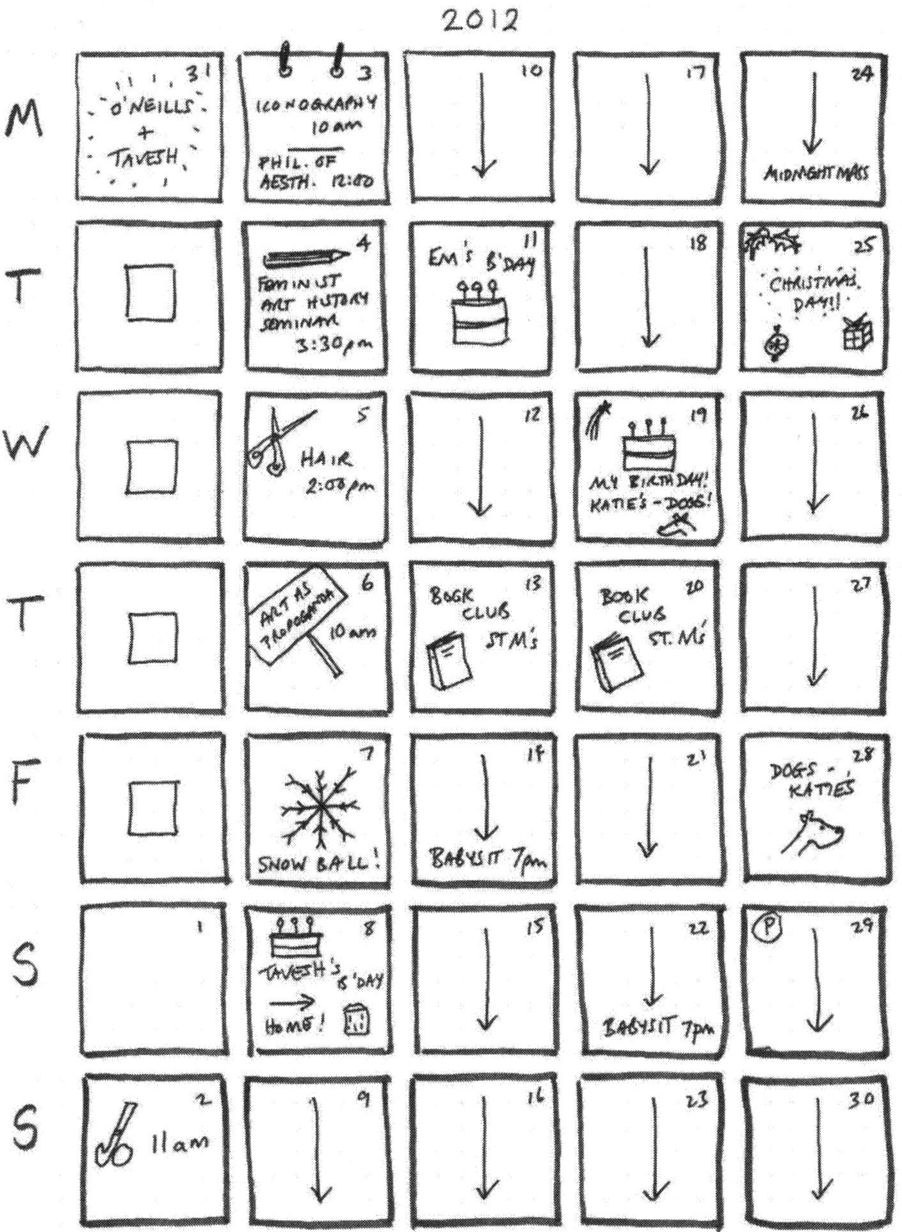

Sunday 2nd December

1. Important meeting to discuss the issue. Just getting glasses and a rather nice Tomintoul.

   Beatrice: "Not yet Henry. Put those away. Now then. Charles has explained your plan. Poor girl. Are you seriously intending to go ahead with this?" All three of us nod guiltily. "Well if you are Henry, it needs to be handled sensitively."

   "That's why we have turned to you Beatrice." (I noticed Charles smother a chuckle.) Not to be flattered she continued. Her points were:

   1. Salary?
   2. Job description?
   3. Accommodation?
   4. Stop calling it "the issue".

   We could answer the first three questions adequately and fully resolved to stop calling the issue, the issue.

   She had planned the schedule for the follow up interview:

Thursday 10th January

1. Arrive c. 12.00 noon. Jimmy to collect from Matlock or Chesterfield.

2. Arrive KA at 12.20 -12.30 pm. Lunch with Ted and Jane round the Big Table. (She is not to meet HH on Thursday)

3. Shown round estate: house / chapel / orchard / gatehouse and farm by Samantha.

4. Meal with Charles and Beatrice and Timothy at the Peacock in the evening.

5. Premier Inn

Friday 11th January

1. 9.00 am collected by Timothy. To KA. Meet HH outside (if possible) with dogs and with Beatrice present. Short walk to woods.

2. Morning tea / coffee with Jane / Jimmy / Samantha. Shown walled garden and Old Oak by Ted.

3. 12.00 noon – light lunch at the Big Table with prosecco on offer (a sparkling white wine apparently). Present = HH + Beatrice.

4. Beatrice explains the full nature of the "offer."

5. Other aspects of role explored / negotiated.

   Repeat this the following week if there is more than one candidate on the shortlist. (I don't think I could survive a second or third round.)

   I looked at the bottle of Tomintoul and Beatrice acceded to my unspoken request.

   This seemed all very satisfactory though I'm not entirely sure why I am not to meet her on day one. Probably for the best. Beatrice is to do the talking. Explaining the problem, explaining the possible solution and the benefits thereof. She is going to ask – although there can be no possible way of ensuring this – that confidentiality is exercised given the embarrassing and personal nature of the situation.

6. She is to be sent on her way with a hamper selection of estate and local produce. Jimmy to return her to station for 4.00 pm

   I am excessively grateful to Beatrice – and not just for the whisky permission. She has come up trumps.

   Timothy says his friend, with whom he is staying, has rooms very near College and therefore he'll be there nice and early on the Saturday to get set up. He will message his Father as the day progresses with updates.

   As Beatrice and Timothy are leaving, I turn to Charles and ask him if he really thinks this will work. He was looking strained. He smiled and said, "What are the chances of life existing at all Henry? Almost nil. But it does. Holdfast!"

   It was the first time for a very long time he had used that – a reference to our undergrad days absorbed in arguments about origins and probabilities and possibilities – life, the universe and everything.

Friday 7th December – TIMOTHY

All well on way down. Using park and ride. Into Christs for 5.30. All rather nervous. Got everything I need – triple-checked. No idea how many will respond to ad. Hoping maybe a dozen or so. Then the filtering and sifting. Awaiting Duncan's return from the labs.

Friday 7th December - TANUSHI

SNOWBALL – 5:30 pm – no, 5:00 pm – start getting ready... Uber to Tavesh at 7:15pm. Arrive 7.30 pm. Time for pre's and walk up to Selwyn. Queue and in by 9.00 pm. THAT'S THE PLAN!!!!!

Saturday 8th December

Survivor's picture 5.30 am and SLEEEEEEEEEEEEEP

Amma collecting us at 4.30 pm – Tavesh coming here with his stuff

WHAT JUST HAPPENED?

I think I might just maybe possibly have landed an interview for a job without even knowing what was going on. Right – think – so great night. Turns out I didn't even see Sara and Josh. Not sure they were even there - probs sold their tickets.

Anyway concentrate. So a great night. Selwyn looked amazing. Brill silent disco. Headline band decent. REINDEER!!!! Free Prosecco ALL NIGHT!!!!! The light show - amazing. It was all amazing.

Didn't drink too much. Water with every drink. So what then happens is not down to drink. Definitely not. Survivor's photo. Brilliant. Then...walked back to Christ's – freezing by this stage. Tavesh actually trying to be vaguely chivalrous – gave me his jacket. Then got to Christs – he said, "I'll just nip up to my room and get a proper jacket so I can walk you home." OK. So, I guess he did – nip up to his room. But I was so cold and so tired, I just went into a room next to the Porter's Lodge just for a bit of warmth. Found a big armchair next to one of those massive cast iron radiators. I remember that. Messaged Tavesh and then phone gave up. I must have draped the jacket over me. Slept.

Saturday 8th December - TIMOTHY

Best laid plans and all that. I had forgotten that Duncan was prone to real ale fuelled nights. We had to go round every pub trying this and that out. Ended up at the Eagle. Don't get me wrong – I was a willing participant. Nice to pretend to be a student again. I suppose my present life is frankly a little dull – maybe. Starting out. Making one's way in the profession. Establishing myself.

I wasn't down to the interview rooms quite as early as I had anticipated. Not that I was late. 8.15am. Due to start at 9.00am. So, no real panic. Entered room – all as expected. Put up the signs outside directing candidates. Established interview room. Checked kitchens had coffee/tea ready for candidates. Set up table with application forms and pens. Then I noticed a candidate had been there the whole time. Asleep. She was definitively pretty. Didn't disturb her. Had a dinner jacket around her – rather odd.

TANUSHI - cont.

Next thing I come to. Vaguely aware of somebody buzzing about talking to himself. I open an eye. Faffing around with pens at a table. I look more closely as his back is turned. Tall, thin, boring jacket. He turned round and caught me looking at him. Argh – why does that always happen?

TIMOTHY – cont.

Looked round and there she was – awake. Those eyes – dear God – recovered myself. Best professional foot forward.

"Hello – I'm Timothy Parker. I'm here to interview you about the position of Preservation and Procurement Officer. Very pleased to meet you. You are here nice and early – we don't officially start till 9.00. But I don't see why we can't kick this off a little early – do you?"

TANUSHI - cont.

He looks at me weirdly which I kind of get. Some random sari-girl asleep. So, he introduces himself – Timothy something. He says something I only half pick up about an interview for a job and why don't we kick off early? I wasn't altogether sure what we were kicking off. He then produces a form and a pen and offers it to me. I remember that.

TIMOTHY – cont.

I offer her the form with clip board and the requisite pen. She just looks at me rather...I don't know, disarmingly. I stutter. "Would you like me to do the honours? Yes?"

So, we start. Name / D.O.B - the usual. Turns out she's from Harrow. She is so pretty. Get a grip. Course – History of Art. Very good. Very appropriate.

"And you are a Cambridge student?"

"Yes."

"At which College?" Her eyes do a quick double take. She asks me to fill in some of the details about the job. I give her the information pack. She reads.

TANUSHI - cont.

Anyway, he fills the form in till we get to the point about which College I'm at. So, I do not lie – or tell the truth. I'm a student in Cambridge. I ask him about the job. He gives me some stuff to read. I read it. At this stage I become interested – I mean really interested. Even in my ever slightly frayed mental state, this looked amazing. And miles from Harrow! I get up and he looks weirdly at me again.

TIMOTHY – cont.

Suddenly she gets up. The jacket slides to the floor. She is wearing the most stunning dress I have ever seen. It's Indian, I guess. Not exactly what one would call the absolutely standard interview wear. I start to say – "Tanushi can I just say – perhaps I ought not to say this in the light of…the interviews, but that is – you look – I mean gosh." Or some similar burbling nonsense. And then she smiled and… and… and… I stoop to pick up the jacket and give it to her. She smiles again. Get a grip man – I don't say that out loud – I don't think.

She asks for a drink of water and a coffee and I leave the room to hurry the kitchens along.

TANUSHI - cont.

He picks my jacket up which has fallen to the floor which is kind of sweet. And he suddenly seems all awkward – in a boyish way. I ask for water just to get my head together and play for a bit of time. He leaves. I look again at the info. This looks very possible. Interrupted – in comes someone else. Smooth and ever so Cambridge. "Hi there gorgeous. My, aren't you looking slightly overdressed? Are you here for the P and P post? My name's Richie btw." I nod. He picks up one of Timothy's clip boards and clicks out his Parker biro – magenta of course and starts filling it in.

TIMOTHY – cont.

I returned – composed – with water and the kitchen waiter with tea / coffee in tow. There is another person who introduces himself as Richie who fills the room with excessive ease like uninvited flatulence. I invite Richie to have a seat and complete the form whilst I invite Tanushi into the interview room. Sitting down with a small table between us, I feel more relaxed and in control. I have the questions. I ask the questions and make a note of the answers. I tell her about the next stage of the interviews and whether that will be a problem. No problem. Are you interested at this stage in what you have read of the job?
"Yes absolutely."

"Obviously there has to be some discretion about the exact place and nature of the post."

"Obviously."

"Are there any questions you would like to ask?"

She says, "I'm really interested. I think I would be able to contribute amazingly to this small northern estate. And I would love to find out more in January if you would put my name forward for the next stage."

She is perfection.

"Then, just one more detail – form filling I'm afraid. Which College did you say you were at?"

TANUSHI – cont.

So, he then invites me in for the interview. I feel OK now. Just getting into my stride. Perhaps an all-nighter is the best possible prep for an interview. He seems nice. I speak like I've wanted no other job. He notes it all down. Just when I think it's all over, he asks me again which College I was at.

I say, "I'm... at Anglia Ruskin."

He just says, "Right, right. Excellent." And doesn't write it down. I can't lie.

Game over?

TIMOTHY – cont.

She says, "Anglia Ruskin." Bloody, bloody hell! I smile. Stand up. Offer my hand and thank her for her time. I say, "We will be in touch."

And then I have to go through the next bit of sword play with Richie. A painful experience. How come these people think they own the world and with such oozing ease and confidence?

Nobody else shows up.

I have one option only – not to tell the strictest truth. If HH finds out she's at the renamed Poly, it is game over. It really is.

TANUSHI - cont.

Went up to Tavesh's room. Banged on door. Got him up eventually. He had come down to see me asleep and draped the jacket over me and left me. I didn't tell him about the interview.

Returned to The Railyard. Packed. Slept. Amma arrived. I have decided to tell no one not even Tavesh. Back to Harrow. Now for sleep.

TIMOTHY– cont.

Messaged Father. May have found somebody. Retrieved car from Park and Ride. Drove back on A14 into dazzling setting sun. And then with the light fading and I turned north onto the M1...it hit me. Why had I not sussed it before? Tanushi was not there for the interview at all. No one dresses like that for an interview! There will have been some do... maybe even a ball...Selwyn used to have a December Ball or something else maybe. Idiot. Why hadn't I realised that? Who knows why she had ended up there? Checked when back – Selwyn Snowball was last night. Despondent.

Sunday 9th December

1. Charles and Timothy came round. Hankering for the Islay now but we will stick with Speyside for two more Sundays. And no need to wait for Beatrice's permission this time. Always had a soft spot for Tomintoul – light and rather too quaffable.

   Charles and I had once spoken of a distillery tour of Scotland – at some mythical future time. But marriage and children for him and my incremental aversion to travel had put to rest that dream.

2. Timothy as keen as ever. Reported back. Disappointing turn out – just 2. One male. But he says much hope for the female. Tanushi – from Sri Lanka originally. "Very exotic" I said or something similar. I noticed Timothy wince when I said that. Clearly, I have crossed some invisible racial linguistic line about which the young know and the old do not. So much of anti-racism these days seems to be to do with playing the Language Game correctly and absolutely nothing to do with intent or motive or fellow feeling. Who gets to write the rules? Identity politics I think they call it. The Torygraph fulminates regularly on this.

3. Anyway, I digress. She came over to UK when little. History of Art. Very presentable. She is young and a Cambridge student and so just might be the right one. All depends upon the visit. Timothy seemed to think she was interested and would, if invited, come up in January.

4. Timothy very committed to the whole venture. He really does think Tanushi might be the one. And a reversal of normal responses for Charles and I. Charles unusually downbeat whilst I remain uncharacteristically optimistic.

5. Timothy to write with invite and details of the two-day visit.

6. Forgot to ask him which College she was at.

Monday 10th December – TIMOTHY

I am feeling uncomfortable – actually probably guilty at not being strictly truthful with HH about where Tanushi is studying. Write and send letter (first class) inviting her to visit Kirk Aeppel with all details. I include a flattering photo of the Georgian frontage and one of the wood and Biggle Hill with old house in foreground.

Decide to speak to Father about the Anglia Ruskin dilemma. Maybe tomorrow. Meanwhile I am in the process of finalising the purchase of my first house. All going to plan. In Wirksworth. Old, stone, run down but with much potential so the estate agent says. Just a small end of terrace two bed. Anxious to move out. Living with parents at 26...no longer acceptable – but has allowed me to build sufficient deposit. Find myself thinking quite a lot about Tanushi. Ridiculous really. As if...

THE HISTORY OF Kirk Aeppel (3) 1700-1800

The one remaining piece of furniture we know about from the time of Gwyn Havard is the Big Table. It is thought the house was constructed around it, such are its bold dimensions. And so, this massive English oak table has provided the setting for all the Havard dramas down the years.

Gwyn Havard's son, David, inherited his Father's business acumen, accumulated lead mines and land and built the family fortune. The family were never quite accepted by the local aristocracy in the early days – incomers and nouveau.

Nevertheless, money eventually talked and David Havard secured a prosperous match with the only child of landowners on the Staffordshire/Derbyshire border. Over the coming century farming practices were revolutionised. Land yields increased and the lead mines continued to produce their bounty. The family fortunes are in large part down to the industry and entrepreneurial spirit of Gwyn and then David Havard. Nor did they squander their wealth.

They were men of good sense and Dissenting spirit. Whilst St Cuthbert's chapel was always of course thoroughly Anglican, David was more at home with the local Baptists and even flirted with the Anabaptists. But that decision came with a social price attached and he was always sure to convince the local Anglican clergy that he was soundly Church of England – even if on the developing evangelical wing.

In his old age David was a committed advocate of education for the labouring classes – male and female. He joined with Hannah More's early educational campaigns and helped to establish the first school in the area, in Matlock. He petitioned, initially unsuccessfully, local industrialist Richard Arkwright to allow his young factory workers time to learn to read and write.

And the estate prospered. Little oak grew. The walled garden flourished enough for the needs of the house. The orchard was tended, though over-zealous cider-making and drinking was frowned upon by David Havard.

David Havard failed to produce offspring and so the estate went to his younger brother John Havard who in the space of just 15 years managed to squander a good measure of the wealth accumulated by his brother David and Father Gwyn. John Havard was not a man of good sense and when he died in 1805 the estate breathed a sigh of relief. It had survived an inebriate and a rascal.

Tuesday 11th December - TANUSHI

OMG – I have been invited for interview. Won't email immediately...sounds too desperate? Reply tomorrow. It looks amazing. All the details about who, when and where...look up train times. Cambridge to Matlock – change at Derby. Can be there for midday no problem. There is next to nothing on-line about Kirk Aeppel. Just some boring stuff about the village, a pub called The Peacock and some distant photos of the house and then a load of recent headlines about a police drugs raid on a farm. Some bloke growing cannabis! Haha!

Wednesday 12th December – TIMOTHY

Tanushi has replied by email. She is coming to KA. Tell HH.

Wednesday 12th December

1. Cold, bleak, miserly weather. Dogs as happy in front of the fire – except Tiff who has all the expected energy of youth. Woken at 3.00 am by noise from walled garden. Peer out; can't see anything. In the morning Ted reports upturned watering cans and much soil disarranged in far corner near the rhubarb – and a dead rat – a littl'un. The marks of the soil-victory all over Tiff's muzzle first thing. Ted said he'd known there were rats about for a month or so but couldn't rightly track them down. Tiff has started to earn his keep. He's a little blighter.

2. Candidate accepted invitation.

Thursday 13th December

1. Revd. Dorothy visit. Discussed the Carol Service. She's decided to sell tickets after last year's little fiasco. Only 30 can be squeezed in to St Cuthbert's. 50 or so turned up. All money to "Womankind Worldwide." I enquired as to what they do. Extraordinary. All a bit of an education for me. There's no electricity in the church so all needs to be lit with candles or oil lamps. Part of the appeal I suppose

– brings in the outsiders. She has of course already spoken to Jimmy about all that. She really is the most proactive of women. She will single-handedly turn the tide on Christendom's retreat – I'm sure of it. Ted and Jane as keen as ever to add the holly and ivy etc.

2. I have summoned the estate for 3.30 pm tea tomorrow. To announce plans.

Friday 14th December

1. Jane had arranged a very pretty tea. She had known for some time that something was afoot. But no amount of fishing had reaped rewards.

2. Timothy arrived. I had expected Charles but he had delegated the task to Timothy...

3. Jimmy and Samantha took the opportunity to announce their re-appraisal of the farm. They had some initial ideas as to the future. They intended to consult widely as to any suggestions and the feasibility thereof. Sounded like a clueless Govt. minister taking over their new portfolio. But I do them a disservice with such a comparison. The place is desperate for a clean sweep. Jimmy then mentioned that there were two remaining pigs. (Afterwards in conversation with Jimmy it became clear that there is no legal documentation attached to pigs. To kill and bury is illegal. To alert the authorities so that they discover the illegality, would scupper their tentative plans (to continue the legal breeding of pigs) and add to family woes. To slaughter and sell on the black market – as has clearly been happening, would obviously be illegal. And nobody would sanction that. Obviously. Solutions were resolved upon. One solution to be 'executed' the following day.)

4. Nobody mentioned Roger.

5. Timothy then read out the statement prepared by his father about the estate and its dire financial situation. No surprises there.

6. I then said we were seeking to appoint a Preservation and Procurement official who might secure the future of the estate. We had advertised and had invited a candidate to be interviewed 10th and 11th January. He or she would live in the gatehouse and become part of our team. And he or she would pioneer the way forward. I said I thought it was time I grasped the nettle of change, that we needed to steer a new course if we are to negotiate the treacherous waters of modernity and just as I was about to launch into a third metaphor, Jane tapped my hand, smiled and said, "How exciting!"

7. I then informed them of their various roles and timings for those days as set out by Beatrice. Timothy just asked for one amendment – that he should be the one to collect the candidate on his or her arrival at the station on the first day – rather than Jimmy. I assented.

8. Many questions.

9. Chat with Jimmy.

10. Somewhat exhausted.

Friday 14th December – TIMOTHY

Father asked me to attend the meeting at KA. Not sure why. Surprised. Anyway, all went well. I read out the document he had prepared. Asked for one small change in the schedule – that I collect Tanushi rather than Jimmy. Think it's best if she sees a familiar face at the start and maybe I can warn her about the potentially tricky issue of HH and his expectation of a Cambridge University student. Maybe we could pass Ruskin off as one of the new colleges? Still feeling decidedly uncomfortable about the whole thing. Must tell Father.

Sunday 16th December

1. Charles phoned to cancel. Touch of the 'flu apparently. Most unusual. I don't like to drink whisky alone. It's the beginning of the end. Cider can be drunk with or without company but whisky needs at least one companion.

2. Splendidly crisp and sunny day and decided to go on prolonged walk with the hounds. It has been so dull these past few days and now the gift of light. Wasn't sure how long Tiff would last. Needn't have worried.

3. Up Biggle, long way round and down to the farm. Sunday and Jimmy and Samantha hard at work, seizing the good weather. Clearing out one of the sheds. Jimmy had one of his mates to help. I joined them for an hour or so. Couldn't keep up with any of them. Still, I showed willing.

4. First proper visit of Tiff to farm (after the drug raid debacle when she was a pup.) She was into everything. Jimmy said maybe he could use her to get rid of the rats. I said, "Are you sure your Father hasn't put down some dreadful poison at any stage?" Jimmy said he wasn't sure. He could ask. Would we trust any response? No.

5. Looked in on pig. Perhaps one final journey down to clear orchard of the final few fallen apples would be in order.

6. Returned, watched Sports Personality and spent the rest of the evening on back editions of Coleopterist Bulletin. Very satisfying. Missed Charles.

Sunday 16th December - TANUSHI

Amma has finally stopped asking questions about the Snow Ball. She now believes her dress was a futile attempt to assist her delinquent daughter find a man. But she likes the pictures Tavesh gave her. Transferred them to her phone to coo and show her friends at church.

So this is what I am thinking about the whole thing. What have I got to lose? It looks a really old, pretty English estate that needs some assistance earning its keep in life. They want someone to work on the interior, the fabric, the paintings and artefacts.

They may want assistance in devising schemes to bring in the public to maximise income. I am pretty sure he mentioned the need for roof repairs. Money is clearly an issue. No mention of salary figure...but I think they want someone young and creative to breathe new life into the place.

I'm gonna write some ideas down on paper. Impress them. A sort of manifesto. Still not going to tell Amma or Tavesh. If I'm actually offered the job, I'll consult. They will be so shocked!!!

The dogs worry me. 4 of them supposedly. Maybe I should go round to Katie to get some lessons? She has 2 large stinky brown dogs. Yes – I'll do that. I need to conquer the dog thing. Message Katie. Also, I need to know what to wear. I'll email Timothy.

Monday 17th December – TIMOTHY

Received email from Tanushi. What clothes? Checked with Mother. Practical country wear – jeans etc. Replied. Thought about putting x at the end – to sign off. Thought better of it. Formality the safer option. Consumed with arrangements for Friday's move. Exchange has happened. Utilities sorted. No work possible on kitchen over Christmas season. I'll have to make the best of it. Got ticket for the KA Carol service from Dorothy.

Wednesday 19th December

1. Cleared small channel at the edge of the pond to secure a spot for the frogs and toads in a couple of months. It is depressingly overgrown and needs a proper mechanical solution. Maybe one day.

2. Continue with beetle batch from Clitheroe Museum. Some monsters in this lot. I hear on the Coleopterist network that there is some concern that global warming is restricting the size of the monsters. Early days re evidence. Another fragment of the eco-system under stress.

3. Ask Jane and Ted at elevenses whether there is anything particular they want for St Cuthbert's. Offered my assistance. They wouldn't hear of it –though they made a big fuss of my helping Jimmy and Samantha the other day. Really.

4. They have heard a date for the trial. February week beginning 11th. Won't take long I don't suppose if he really is pleading guilty.

Wednesday 19th December - TANUSHI

Went round to Katie. She met me outside the house to brief me. So here is the advice:

1. Put treats in jacket pocket.

2. Enter. Calm, upright and confident. Look only at Katie. Ignore dogs completely.

3. Talk with Katie whilst ignoring dogs. Be consumed in that conversation, ignoring dogs.

4. Only when Katie says, can I shift my gaze to the dogs and give them some attention.

5. Tell them to sit whilst getting treat out. They are very food oriented. Chocolate Labradors apparently??

6. Give treat as a reward for sitting. Then pat them.

So, I carry out to the letter all the above. It sort of worked. But then they go crazy for more food and then essentially mug me out of the remaining treats. And I end up screaming and trying to turn away and retreat from them whilst Katie laughs uncontrollably. So that bodes well. Agree to try again before I go back.

Friday 21st December

1. Ted and Jane busy with St C's.

2. Dogs enjoyed the frost first thing. Collected barrowful of kindling from the storms earlier in week. Plenty of wood in store. Feel contented about that.

   Jimmy and Samantha call in and ask me to inspect the shed they'd been clearing. Very impressive say I. And then they say that one of their ideas is to set up a small farm park so that children can come and see the animals. All very tentative. What did I think? I am a past master at delayed decisions and encouraging noises. We'll speak some more after Hen Galan. (Ed: Hen Galan = New Year as celebrated according to the Julian calendar. Traditionally celebrated at Kirk Aeppel since the days of Gwyn Havard who brought this tradition with him.)

Sunday 23rd December

Carol Service

1. Dorothy told the story – one of my favourites from Jane in the nursery – of St Cuthbert and the otters. Got me thinking back. About my yearning to have that sort of connection with nature. For a time, I had become obsessed with a TV programme called "Skippy – the bush kangaroo." I dreamt about being Sonny, the boy with his pet kangaroo. My dogs became Skippy substitutes as I roamed the neglected estate acting out the redemption narratives of each show.

2. Hence the beetles.

3. I have no idea how she linked this to Incarnation. God's affirmation of this physical realm, I think. I should ask her.

4. It was everything the Carol Service should be. Cold, austere but candle-lit and inspiring, with trailing holly and ivy in every conceivable nook and cranny.

5. I prayed a prayer about the future. I have no idea really if God is concerned about this little Eden, this Kirk Aeppel estate. But maybe, just maybe. For all of us.

6. Back to the Big Table for card exchange and drinks. Revd. Dorothy included. Dogs happy to mingle. Jane fishing for details from Timothy. "Male or female – you can tell me that." Samantha and Dorothy talking about the "Zumba" (I think) class starting in the New Year in the village. Ted and Charles being taken

through the intricacies of Jimmy's cider strategy this year. Beatrice alone, sat looking into the fire.

7. "What's up old girl?" She didn't rile as I had wanted. She said she had told them of her intention to go in the summer and as soon as she'd done that, she'd felt the tectonic power plates shifting. And now she's got two terms left to fritter away in a system she no longer understands and has little care for. "The job now is to be complicit with endlessly misguided, over-anxious parental demands not to have their little darlings grow up and accept responsibility for themselves. All is smoothed over. It strips them of their natural resilience; they are left without spine; little under-developed runts incapable of coping with life. And then the problems set in." I paraphrase.

8. It was clear to me that I had little to offer Beatrice. Except I tended to agree from a position of complete ignorance. But nothing of comfort. Ribble came over. Plonked her head on Beatrice's lap. She smiled. She took the drink I proffered and wished me Merry Christmas.

Tuesday 25th December

1. Walk the bounds with the dogs. 3 hours – just over. Not bad. Tiff is such a terrier.

2. Opened my traditional present from the estate – a round of Hartington Stilton. The card – written by Jane and signed by them all.

3. Game pie with instructions as to cooking times etc. I make the roast potatoes. Magnificent. Bottle of claret.

4. Queen also magnificent.

   Christmas has a way of making you remember. Snatches of Christmas past. My Mother made some attempts. That Christmas of my recovery in the Gatehouse was the best. Jane in charge. It was amazing. She bought me the Skippy annual. We watched TV all afternoon. And she put the ointment on my neck scars. They were dry and scratchy and oozy all at the same time. I remember that. It hurt and it soothed. She made a game of it. And she allowed the Springer Spaniel, Molly, to sleep on my bed. It couldn't have been better. Mother called in briefly. Gave me a present. Left. Ted came after I was put to bed for the night. Stayed over. There he was cooking breakfast the next morning. Full of the joys of spring as I would now describe him. Or the cat that got the cream perhaps. I watched him as he fried the eggs. Then Jane came down in her dressing gown opened her arms to hug me. I could feel the warmth of her breast on the side of my face. She started to pull my hair away from under the bandages on my head. I looked up at her and she gave me a kiss on my lips and smiled. "Sit yourself down Hen." That is the first time I had ever been kissed. It was a golden moment. I was happy.

In truth I am still not sure why I was sent to the Gatehouse to recover. I might be because – I speculate – maybe Father had already become too ill and he needed nursing and Mother couldn't cope with the both of us. I was never told at the time what Father died of. Obviously, I worked out it was drink-related. All Jane would say was that it was his not eating his greens and drinking too much gin. I was to let that be a warning. Haven't touched gin as a result.

I didn't see my Father from the time of my accident in October '71 till a few months before his death in November '72. I saw him three times – all from a distance – never to talk to. He never gave me his blessing. No Isaac / Jacob moment. Nothing.

Tuesday 25th December - TANUSHI

Midnight mass – rammed. I think there's even more people than ever. The more indifferent we become towards Christianity the more people turn up drunkenly at Christmas. I must have kissed all of the church families we had grown up with. Lots of comments about the Snowball dress, pictures of which they had all studied. Katie there. Arranged my next visit – clandestinely. Tavesh of course centre stage – the returning Cambridge medic. He towers above Amma now.

The usual on Christmas day. A day of the unspoken absence of my Father – always.

Wednesday 26th December

1. If I could hibernate at this time of year, I would. Decide instead to draw up an action plan for January:

Saturday 5th– cider – weather permitting

Thursday 10th– first day interview

Friday 11th– second day interview

Saturday 12th– Hen Galan's eve

Sunday 13th– Hen Galan

We need:

1. The front door and surrounds to the Georgian wing cleaning and tidying.
2. Check all doors in the Georgian wing actually open.
3. The front and back doors to the Old Hall clearing of debris and cleaning.
4. The walled garden sprucing up. A few pansies perhaps. ALL TED
5. My bedroom needs attention.
6. The Kitchen – clean and paint damp spot near window.
7. Check Gatehouse and paint final room.
8. Heat Gatehouse one week before interview.
9. Put flowers on Nith's grave. ALL ME
10. Spend money on fabrics for Gatehouse (set budget) SAMANTHA
11. Arrange gift box of local produce – given on arrival.
12. First bottling of this year's cider. BOTH JIMMY
13. General clean and tidy of main rooms.
14. Check lamb cowl recipe and source lamb. BOTH JANE
15. Practice party pieces – ALL

Send this round to all.

Thursday 27th December

1. Jane comes round just to check I'm alright. When convinced, she retreats back home.

2. It seems that they have trained a Giant Schnauzer to drive a car in New Zealand. Don't share the news with Ribble. She already thinks she's in charge anyway. It'll only give her ideas.

3. Speak to Jimmy on the phone re cider. Pencilled in Friday 4th if weather amenable.

Friday 28th December - TANUSHI

So – next visit to Katie. I think there is progress – even if it's just getting me used to the company and presence of these bonkers animals. Took them on a walk this time. Quite enjoyed it. Still, shall have to be really calm and controlled on interview. Pencil in one further session. Katie promises more dogs!

Thinking of wearing the Snowball sari for New Year. Amma would like that.

Sunday 30th December

1. A quiet end of year communion. Weather unusually still.

2. Charles came round – glad of the break from Beatrice's endless sisters. All force 10 on the Beaufort scale. Where would I place Revd. Dorothy?

3. Enjoying the Islays – Christmas is Laphroaig. Endlessly rewarding.

4. Charles says he's had to have one or two medical check-ups, tests and the like. Nothing discovered.

5. We discuss the interview, the prospects. What if she walks out offended by our skulduggery, deceit, our patronising assumptions, our audacity at getting her up from Cambridge under false pretences?

6. It could all go horribly wrong.

Monday 31st December

1. Plates bad. Obviously.

2. Nice to see a theoretical physicist – Prof. Higgs – get Companion of Honour.

3. Attempt to ignore New Year. Dogs variously alarmed by bloody fireworks in Matlock. Only thing which upsets Ribble. Stay up for her. Try as usual to avoid the fatuous statements of the great and the good wishing world peace etc. Tiff not bothered by fireworks. I've noticed he tends to sleep alongside Tywi.

Monday 31st December - TANUSHI

Soooo difficult keeping this whole thing quiet. Heading back to Cambridge early so that should help.

So – visited the community celebration early eve – smiled at one and all and moved on with Tavesh to O'Neills. OK. Some had gone in to central – so we came back early – 1.30ish.

My New Year's wish? Kirk Aeppel to be mine!

Monday 31st December – TIMOTHY

No-one around from my school friends to celebrate these days. All in London now. Don't stay up. But have cheery feelings about New Year. House ready for its makeover. New kitchen and bathroom Jan / Feb. Windows sorted for two weeks' time. Happy to be in and in some way newly independent.

And who knows what lies ahead re KA's future… and what the spin-offs might be? No point pretending, I have my hopes.

JANUARY
2013!

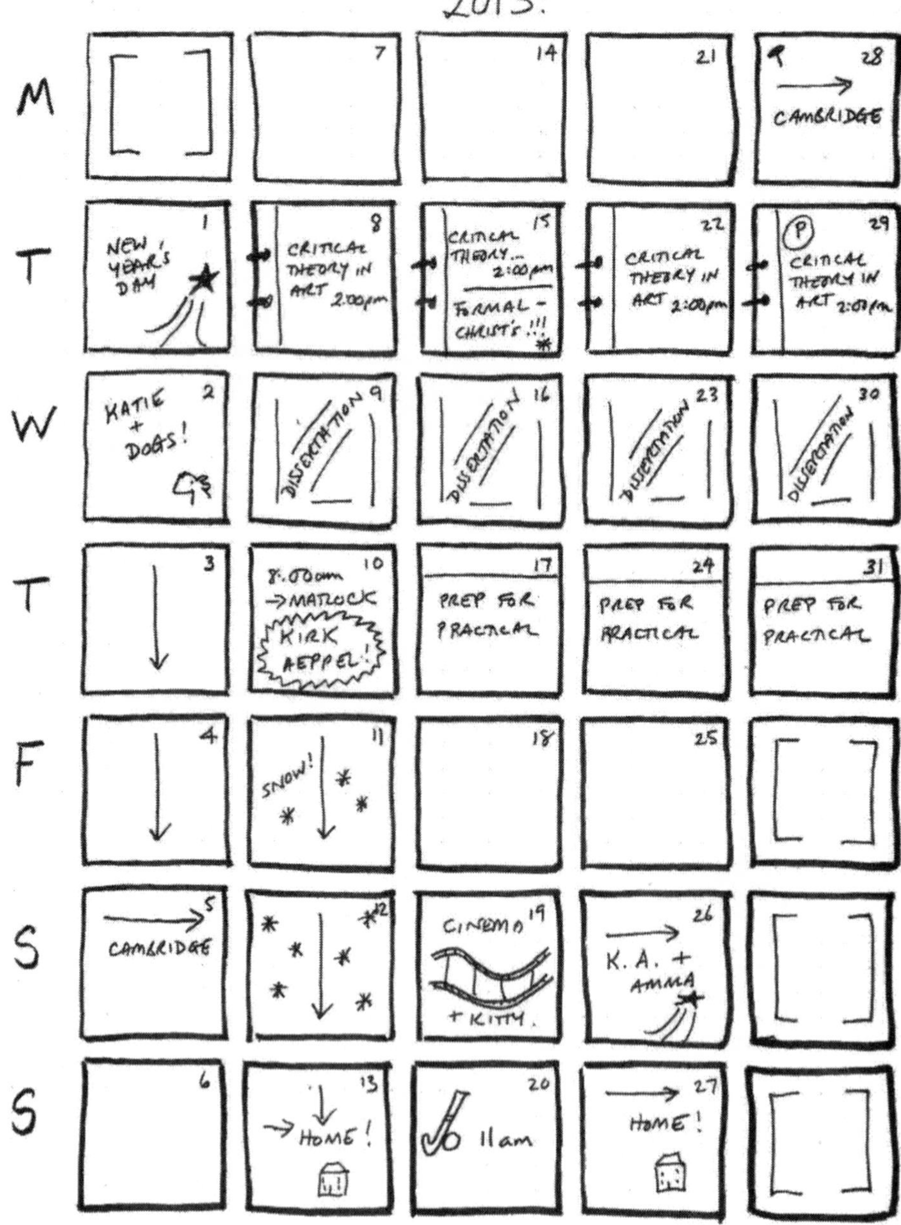

Wednesday 2nd January 2013 - TANUSHI

Amma full of questions about my long walk with Katie. Never been so very keen a friend. And all those pesky dogs! What was I thinking of? Dirty animals!! Total dogs on walk: 2 x chocolate labs, scruffy terrier types x2, a beagle – sweet. Definitely my favourite. And what was called a lurcher – completely bonkers as far as I could judge. General mayhem. OK – I think I am learning. Ignore dogs; let them be dogs; allow them to make their own mind up and engage with you on their own terms. Couldn't resist the beagle though – Squinch they'd called him. Such a sweetie.

Wednesday 2nd January 2013

1. Decide to postpone cider operation. No hurry. Weather looks awful for Saturday. Can wait till after interviews / Hen Galan. Perry still bubbling anyway. As long as the lees are removed which they have been. Jimmy happy with that. Cuckoo some time away.

2. Jimmy and Samantha are consumed by their plans for the farm of course. He has set aside early March for the re-introduction of (legal) pig production. A rare breed he thinks... all organic. Small scale to begin with. Nearest small slaughter house close enough at Holloway. Already been in negotiation. One final execution of clearing the way for renewed pig breeding arranged for Saturday. Then porcine predicament expunged. Dogs have never looked so healthy...very satisfactory.

Friday 4th January

1. Church of England drops its prohibition on gay clergy in civil partnerships becoming bishops – as long as they remain celibate. That'll be a workable solution to the issue. No doubt about it.

Saturday 5th January – TIMOTHY

Very aware that I haven't spoken to Father about Tanushi / College issue. Must do so urgently. Tanushi emails train times.

Saturday 5th January - TANUSHI

Return to Cambridge. Relief. Order train tickets to Matlock. Email Timothy with times. He replies immediately. Very attentive! Get on with final dissertation unimpeded by Amma. Resolved to ask if I can greet every dog I meet along Hills Rd/ Mill Rd/anywhere. Mostly small dogs on offer! Still all good practice.

Decide to spend tomorrow on my Kirk Aeppel proposal. Gonna meet Saskia at Fitzwilliam cafe to ask for her ideas. 12 noon.

Sunday 6th January

1. Why do people keep dogs on a lead – on a walk with no sheep in the middle of nowhere? It's beyond me. At the top of Biggle. A family with a small yappy unidentifiable mongrel – on a lead. Starts having a go at Ribble. Unwise. Owner does nothing. Ribble decides to sit on said dog. That quietens it off. A whimper. Then Ribble gets off. Dog retreats tail between its legs.

2. None of this would have happened if the dog was not on lead. They need to learn how to relate to other dogs without our artificial intervention. The reason that dog feels it can behave so badly is that is permanently on a bloody lead. No lessons ever learnt.

3. Then of course Tiff decides he wants to intervene in the situation and starts growling at the dog. Unnecessarily terrier-ish.

4. Then the owner starts to blame me – of course. I start on an explanation of the above. "Your dog needs to be off that lead and to learn its place in the dog hierarchy. It wouldn't behave so badly..." etc. At which point Tiff bites or attempts to bite the ear of said dog.

5. Not a happy situation. No blood though. They might think twice about climbing Biggle in future.

6. Complete decoration of spare bedroom at Gatehouse. Switch heating on. All tickety-boo. Advise Samantha that we are ready for curtains/cushions etc. She says we need a new small sofa and hold off on the curtains – allow whoever gets the job, some say. Agree. I authorise £350 for two-seater. Got to be in for Thursday.

7. Charles. Settle final arrangements for Thursday / Friday. Weather looking unsettled for the end of the week according to Countryfile forecast. Decide to start a new bottle of Lagavulin. Unsurpassable nectar.

Sunday 6th January - TANUSHI

So good to talk to Saskia. So many ideas for me to put in to my proposal – I don't know where to start. Stress it's confidential. She's keen to talk up Fitzwilliam's services. How they might help etc. Worked all day on proposal.

Saw another Beagle on Trumpington Street just near to Fitzwilliam. Crossed over to say hello! OMG what is happening to me?

Monday 7th January – TIMOTHY

Speak to Father about Tanushi being a student at Anglia Ruskin University. He is not happy. Why wait till now to say something? He decides I must go round to HH and tell him. So, I ring and arrange to visit at 4.30 pm.

HH is initially completely apoplectic. He called me a "blithering idiot." And then immediately and profusely apologised. I explain that there is definitely high intellect in the family. He is a little assuaged. At this stage – as he points out with some force – we have no choice but to continue.

Monday 7th January

1. Timothy comes round to explain that the candidate – the one and only candidate – is not a Cambridge University student at all! I was not impressed. He fully understood that I was not impressed. I then felt I needed to apologise for the force of my initial response. Calmed down and regathered equilibrium. We parted on good terms. A girl from Cambridge Poly.

2. Ted says he has completed all his tasks in preparation for Thursday. He says he thinks the temperature will drop – maybe a bit of snow on the way. Inspect the front door to Georgian wing. He's done a marvellous job and I tell him so. We never use the Georgian part of the house at all these days. Abandoned. No happy memories there. Just storage for past lives.

3. Samantha says DFS can't deliver this week. Unless we have the shop display – reduced by £100. Yes, trust Samantha's judgement. Deliver late Wednesday. Good.

4. Find myself plunging between excitement and foreboding. Not like me. Not a happy place to be. This is the trouble with change or attempted change. You are never sure what will happen.

5. Jane had invited Revd. Dorothy over for supper. I tell them the details of the candidate – female from Sri Lanka – Tanushi. Dorothy full of questions. Far too many and far too probing. I tried to bat them away as best I could. Should have waited to tell just Jane and Ted I reflect. "What's she going to do? What's her precise role? Where's she going to live?" (One I could answer.) Not sure what Jane and Ted thought. I am not sure they will have ever met anybody from the Indian sub-continent. Maybe Ted had on National Service? "The white highlands" some in Derby call this part if Derbyshire apparently. Still Jane is all warmth and welcome. Dorothy leads us in a short prayer.

6. Internal email – we (Timothy, Beatrice, Charles) have decided to keep reiterating the line about the full nature of the post is to be discussed and negotiated Friday lunchtime.

7. Not sleeping well – to be expected. Dread supplanting hope. Is it too late to shelve the whole thing? Dogs do their best to provide solace.

Tuesday 8th January – TIMOTHY

Urgent email from Tanushi. Weather looks bad. What to do? Are the interviews going ahead? Reply immediately. Snow possible overnight Thurs / Fri. We are used to snow here and there's nothing to worry about. The forecasters/news people always make too much of such things. Just bring warm clothes and good boots. We will get you from place to place.

Again, think about signing off with an X just to be friendly and reassuring. Decide against it.

Tuesday 8th January - TANUSHI

SNOW!! For Thursday/Friday in Derbyshire. Email Timothy. All fine. Don't worry.

Tell Tavesh that I am off to Derby as part of my course. To view the Wright of Derby collection. Back Friday night. Don't like the lie.

Wednesday 9th January

1. Snow – calamitous amounts... threat to life and limb – according to nanny weather bulletin. We must wrap up well apparently. Not thought about that.

Thursday / Friday. Probably amount to an inch. Schools will shut of course – health and safety. Dogs will love it – If anything actually materialises. Which I doubt.

2. Immerse myself in Beetles. A useful distraction.

3. Party piece rehearsed. It's the same one every year and it doesn't take much remembering.

4. I don't know why we put the interview so close to Hen Galan. Too much.

5. I have no role tomorrow but still anxious. Will try to observe her at 12.20 pm when she arrives. I have the most profound concerns about all this now and regret ever going down this route. Just let the National Trust have the building if they want it. Or some hotel chain and give the money to Jane, Ted and the Dogs Trust.

6. Perfect weather tomorrow until 4.00 pm

Wednesday 9th January – TIMOTHY

I have decided to be honest with Tanushi when she arrives at Matlock station. When I say honest – obviously not completely honest about everything. But I need to warn her about the Anglia Ruskin thing and about my realisation that she wasn't actually there for the interview. I think that's best.

I am feeling some trepidation and some excitement. 11.26 am – she'll be there. Might offer a quick coffee at Peli Deli before taking her to KA.

Thursday 10th January - TANUSHI

Train from Cambridge at 8.00 am – not too much of a shock to the system seeing as I'm right next to the station anyway. I am feeling pretty nervous. First ever grown up interview. Suddenly it feels like I'm an adult. Looking out of window for Timothy. Can't immediately see him. Panic. Then as I step onto platform, I see him smiling, wanting to carry my case, being urgently attentive. Do I want a coffee before we head off to KA? We have time. Good idea just to allow me to draw breath.

Thursday 10th January – TIMOTHY

Arrive at 11.15 am. Always good to be slightly early. Observe myself in the mirror. Never something I normally do. Text Father to say I'm at the station. Train on time. I see Tanushi immediately. Instantly. So she says "Yes" to the coffee. And we're there in 2 minutes. I sit down opposite her. As in the interview. Conscious that I mustn't stare too much into her eyes. I say that I wanted to raise two things before she starts meeting people at KA. Firstly, I explain the whole Cambridge Uni issue. That the rather eccentric potential employer had wanted a Cambridge University graduate. It has been explained to him that you are at Anglia Ruskin University. Secondly, it dawned on me that she hadn't deliberately come to the interview at all. Then all was revealed about the circumstances. She laughed. I laughed.

TANUSHI – cont.

Timothy being ever so gallant! Bought the drinks. Then explained the whole college stuff – eccentric employer, old fashioned, wanted Cambridge graduate. I knew there was some issue. Will I get fair hearing? It has all been explained to him. Just emphasize that I am from really intellectual family. That won't be too difficult. Conversation then as to why I was really there – not for the interview. Yes, he'd guessed it was the Selwyn Snowball. Much laughter about the whole thing. He seems a boring suit to look at but, really, he's much sweeter than the image. And then we get back to the car and go to KA (as everybody calls it here). He gave me a pack of information with the schedule etc.

TIMOTHY– cont.

Bombarded with lots of questions in car (as well as frequent exclamations about the beauty of the countryside). How is Kirk Aeppel pronounced? What's the owner and his family like? What will the job entail exactly? I spun the, "Well the precise details of the job are to be negotiated with the candidate…depending on their skills and abilities and interests. Broadly the estate needs to pay its way and the job is to secure the future of the estate."

TANUSHI – cont.

This place is so beautiful. If you live knee high in concrete the whole time, with limited horizons and just the occasional tree, the shock of this beautiful space is amazing. I hadn't prepared myself. And we were there soon enough, driving up the extraordinary entrance, tree-lined. And the Georgian façade. Small but impressive. And then we veered to the right and entered the area in front of what Timothy called the Old House. 17th century. Stone – lots of huge windows – like there was some competition to see how much light was possible. It looked stunning in the sunshine – cold and clear and accentuating every fine line.

Thursday 10th January

1. Can do no more now. Dogs enjoyed a good run first thing. Piercing early sun. Crystal clear with a thin haze over the pond. The House could not be set off more to its advantage. Arranged sticks/flowers on Nith's grave.

2. I did manage to see her when she arrived. Seemed to be getting along well with Timothy. He looked up and saw me. She didn't see me.

3. Dogs keen to meet the new arrival. Sent them down. Her first test I suppose.

4. The usual noise especially from Tiff. But all seemed well as far as one could tell.

TIMOTHY – cont.

Arrived at Old House – dropped her bag in the entrance area near to Big Table and introduced her to Ted and Jane. And then the dogs arrived. I attempted to explain what each dog was and their name etc. Ted telling them to stop barking and calm down. Much kerfuffle but Tanushi in the midst of it seemed pretty un-phased. The dogs eventually settled and I said I would pick her up at 6.50 pm to drive her to the Peacock.

TANUSHI - cont.

Entered the Old House. Dark, wood lined walls with a massive table in the centre of the room. Huge fire. Then 4 dogs careered down the far stairs. Remained icily controlled. Ignored the dogs. The dogs settled. Introduced to Ted and Jane. In their 70s probs. Jane just delightful. Ted quieter. Gosh did they have a lot of questions for me. Where was I from and where did I grow up? Did I have brothers / sisters? Was I at university? (Their grandson – Jimmy had studied at both Derby University and Buxton – always studying – latest course on carbon neutral farming! Ever so proud they were.) By this stage we were sat round the kitchen table beside the warmth of the Aga and with carrot and leek soup and with hunks of home-made bread. The kitchen was large with a high ceiling from which all manner of things hung. By the door to the outside a selection of dog bowls, wellington boots, a torch, coats and a cricket bat – for the rats according to Ted. Jane held my hand once I had finished eating. They told me how long they had worked at KA. – a lifetime. Jane had come to help initially when Henry Havard was a baby. And he's now 52 going on 53. Ted had joined 10 or so years later.

They lived just up the road past the house. Their grandchildren – Jimmy and Samantha were joint tenants on the farm a bit further up. And then after a million questions, Samantha – aka Sam – arrived. My age. So like her Grandmother in looks. She was to show me around the whole place. Beginning to relax and enjoy myself. There was a warmth there. They clearly loved their employer even though he clearly was: very odd, better with dogs than people, quite reclusive and shy, could appear rude – I was warned. I am to meet him tomorrow. Finished my tea and left with Sam.

TIMOTHY – cont.

Actually, I returned to work. But totally preoccupied of course. She would be just perfect. Passed on to Father my observations thus far. He was immersed in the tricky property issue that had been brewing for 18 months or more. Ignored me.

TANUSHI - cont.

Before setting off on the grand tour, I went to the loo. OMG nothing has happened to that place in a century. Cold, paint peeling, scrubby floor tiles, just untouched. It was like a sitting on a throne in an abandoned medieval castle. The place must be desperate for cash. Quite shocked.

Made an immediate connection with Sam. Felt I could ask her anything. She lent me an extra fleece layer – even though we started in the house. So:

Back to main downstairs room with enormous table – Big Table. Everything happens there apparently – including Hen Galan this coming Saturday. Explained that – can't remember – New Year? Various random bits and pieces on walls. A large lump of brass on the table which I was told was an Imperial Peck. Lumps of lead shaped as masks. Fossils. Faded photos of dogs. The roaring fire. Stone floor with the occasional emaciated rug.

Then we went round the outside into the Georgian part of the house. Absolutely freezing. Nobody lives here, visits here or even enters, ever I don't think. A selection of light bulbs work. No heating. It has the silent, empty feel of a graveyard. We started downstairs and visited the two main rooms. One the main reception room. Curtains, threadbare, are drawn across 3 large windows. So dark and dusty with empty fireplace. The afternoon sun pierced a gap in the curtains and struck the huge mirror. Clutter everywhere. A hoarder's paradise.

Then what must have been the dining room. TBH if you were filming Great Expectations here, you wouldn't have to change anything except place dear old Miss Havisham at the head of the table. Stuff everywhere on every surface.

Clothes, random stuff, books, glasses, some cutlery and crockery. What happened here? What catastrophe had led to this abandonment?

Sam pointed to the Billiard room at the back of the house adjacent to kitchen.

Sam explained as she led me around the kitchen and back rooms that Mr Havard had shut up this part of the house when his Mother died. He had chosen to live in the Old House. No explanation. There was less clutter in the kitchen. Someone had cleared it and few items were left as debris of former times. Just the odd massive serving plate or jelly mould. It was just extraordinary. Sam has rarely been here before she said. She tried to open the back door and failed!

It was just a remarkable experience. Weird in the extreme. The actual building was amazing. Huge Hall with grand stairs and the two main rooms downstairs and behind the stairs the servants' rooms. Everything drenched with the saddest air of neglect.

The stairs seemed robust and in good condition. The bedrooms however were not. They had become merely repositories of every unwanted item that had once been used over 200 years. Every manner of obsessive collection from stones to fossils to stuffed creatures. Thick with dust and evidence of water penetration in the corner of a one of the rooms. Large ancient lumps of furniture that would on their own fill a modern bedroom scattered across rooms blocking passage to bathrooms and closets. Sam was in no way apologetic or embarrassed. It was the way things were with Mr Havard – and his predecessors. All the windows were large and would have been magnificent at one time. The drawn curtains struggled to bear their own weight.

I didn't know what to say except to express some amazement. Sam smiled and shrugged her shoulders and went on. She said she was helping her brother to sort the farm out. They were the new tenants. Mr Havard had shown great faith in them. And she worked as a TA in the local primary three afternoons a week. She also did Saturday mornings in the village shop and Sundays in the local pub – where we're going tonight.

Gathered my coat and then we set off to the chapel – all part of the estate. Well-worn and polished smooth. We visited the obviously very important orchard. Sam described some celebration she'd helped put on in October just prior to the cider making. She was full of it. And then we walked up to her farm. She told me of their dreams for the place.

I said I'd read that somewhere near here there'd been someone caught growing cannabis. She suddenly went quiet and I regretted the flippancy of my question.

She didn't say anything more. She was clearly upset and I tried to apologise. I felt such an idiot. She just went to find Jimmy – in a barn further up and we went inside for a cup of tea. She apologised about the state of the place. Everything had been let go somewhat. But they had a plan for it all and Mr Havard had been ever so generous.

Jimmy was to drive me back to the Old House, collect my bag and show me the Gatehouse, before taking me to the Premier Inn. Before I left, I again tried to apologise. Sam smiled and hugged me and told me not to worry. She then whispered that she would love to have me here on the Kirk Aeppel team – if it all worked out.

Jimmy – what to say. I would say immediate impressions were – strong, someone who gets on, practical, straightforward maybe. Dark, wavy hair with crinkly eyes. He was happy to make my acquaintance he said. He had helped spruce the Gatehouse up for the new estate worker – whoever that may be. He smiled and raised an eyebrow. Jimmy left a good impression – no doubt about that. A bit gorgeous.

So, the Gatehouse. This is where I will live if I get the post. It is the sweetest of cottages. Limestone with sandstone round the windows and door. The main room had a wood burning stove inset into a massive fireplace. There's a kitchen smelling of paint with a tiny table and a small utility room (with ancient washing machine) leading out to the back garden. And such a delightful square walled patch of land for a back garden. It's all a bit of a wilderness but I could tame that!! Definitely!! Upstairs the 2 bedrooms and bathroom all lovely. "My room" had a view over the back garden up to the Old House. This was just perfect.

I said I thought it was lovely. Jimmy asked various questions about what I did, where I was studying. He said he'd got a degree from Derby University. I told him his grandparents had already mentioned that – "they're so proud of you!" trying to get him to blush a little. He smiled.

I looked once more out of the bedroom window, imagining if I might fit here. And I really did imagine I might. A long way from Colombo.

Arrived at Premier Inn at 4.00 pm and lay on bed shattered trying to take it all in. Timothy and parents were collecting me at 6.50 pm. Fell asleep.

Thursday 10th January – cont.

5. At 4.00 pm went down in search of an afternoon hot drink and something sweet Jane might have rustled up. Of course, I wanted to know what they thought, whether Samantha and Jimmy had been in touch.

6. All very positive. Not a bad word at all. Jane of course could not speak more highly of her. You'd have thought she was the only living Catholic saint. Samantha thinks she's lovely too. So much in common. No word from Jimmy as yet. Even Ted had been won over. "Very presentable Mr 'Avard."

7. Thank them for their efforts and retire to an evening in front of the fire with the dogs and the New Scientist for company. Article on "Quantum Shadows – realty is even stranger than we thought". Ha, who would have thought? Perhaps we don't know everything after all Mr Dawkins. Also interested in the Epigenetics article. Nature and Nurture. Maybe both!

8. Ribble being unusually affectionate – almost as if she intuits that tomorrow is so very, very important.

9. "There are more things in heaven and earth, Horatio, than are dreamt of in your philosophy."

TIMOTHY – cont.

Home for 5.00. Quick turnaround. Jacket or no jacket? Tie or no tie? How formal/informal? I NEVER have to do this stuff. No tie. Jeans with casual jacket. White shirt. Padded ski type jacket or more formal? Dress down I decide. Shower, shave, after-shave. Ready as I will ever be to pick up Tanushi.

TANUSHI - cont.

Hadn't imagined I would sleep so deeply. Woke up with the little cottage in my thoughts. Who gets that straight out of Uni? There is so much to sort out in that house. So much "curating". Such a fascinating place. Pleased with the pitch I've prepared for tomorrow.

We had hardly had holidays as kids. We rarely ventured into countryside. It just wasn't something we ever did. My friends signed up for the D. of E. scheme and went camping. I learnt the flute. The very occasional day trip to the seaside. Never overnight. It had a little to do with money but really, I think Amma didn't know how to explore the country she had fled to and didn't have the confidence to try. The countryside was for uneducated peasants where she had come from. In her community in Harrow, she felt at home. She was content there. And she poured herself into her children so that we would feel bold enough to make this country properly our own.

So, this countryside, this land of crags and caverns (as the tourist leaflets describe it) and wildness – to my eyes – is exciting and beautiful and I want to explore it.

Timothy arrived at 6.50 pm to take me to The Peacock. He'd made a definite attempt to scrub up. He said the weather was threatening to snow but that he was sure we'd be alright.

TIMOTHY – cont.

Collected Tanushi. Still being bombarded with questions. Parents already seated. They rose to greet her. My Mother gave her a big hug – which I thought was unusual and maybe even a bit over the top. Anyway... we sat and small talked.

Mother made it clear from the start that she was not involved in the selection process – so Tanushi should relax – and that she would be there tomorrow when she meets HH – just to mediate and be on her side and ensure all her questions are fully answered. She hinted that not all aspects of the job had been fully explained as yet and perhaps she might prepare herself for a surprise.

Tanushi explained her reactions as she toured the estate. Overall positive. Perceptive. Clearly liked Sam – and Jimmy. She said that she was afraid she had made a terrible mistake by asking Sam about a cannabis raid that she had read about on-line. Father went through the whole thing. No point in trying to cover anything up. Trial next month. Such a shock to everyone.

Then she said she had prepared a document with some suggestions as to what might be done to help the estate survive. Was that OK and should she bring it tomorrow?

We all approved and Mother said that was perfect and that HH needed now to seriously consider what needed to be done to secure the future.

He had been stuck in inertia for too long. Then Tanushi asked about whether HH had ever married, what of children... who would inherit the estate? Suddenly there was a reticence until Father stepped in, explained that HH was not the marrying type, that he wasn't so much interested in romance as dogs, beetles, whisky and cider. He explained that he had known HH from their first day at Cambridge and he had always been his own particular character and not the slightest bit interested in women (or men). And that was where it was left hanging. The inheritance question unanswered.

Father spotted a few snowflakes falling in a disinterested way – not seemingly over-concerned about making it to the ground. That hastened the end of the meal. We'd finished anyway.

And I drove her back. Jimmy to collect at 9.00 am. I said that I might not see her tomorrow and that it had been a real pleasure seeing her again and that I hoped that I might see her in the future and that tomorrow would be OK and she wouldn't be too... and I didn't know how to complete the sentence. I held my hand out. "Too what Timothy?" She reached up and kissed me on the cheek and thanked me and said I had been very sweet and helpful. I blushed – not that she would have noticed and retreated back to the car.

Sweet and helpful – when a woman says that, I am pretty sure it's a damning verdict – romantically at least.

TANUSHI - cont.

Wow – I have so much to say and I am so tired. Really liked Beatrice and Charles. But have I got more questions now than I had before?!! They all liked the idea that I had prepared some ideas for the preservation of KA. Beatrice said she'd be there tomorrow to be on my side??? What's that about??? And then said there'd be a surprise or two. What's that about??? There was a bit of awkwardness when I asked about whether HH had been married ever. I believed Charles' answer but there's something I can't quite put my finger on. Timothy drove me back. Won't see him tomorrow apparently. Thanked him. Pretty sure he blushed when I kissed him. And so, to sleep. Jimmy picks me up – at 9.00 am.

Friday 11th January

1. The thinnest of layers of snow. Almost a thick frost. The forecasters had 4-foot drifts! Dogs enjoyed themselves first thing. Biggle Hill resplendent. Timed arrival back to meet Tanushi. That was the plan. 9.15 am.

2. And at 9.17 am Jimmy drove her to the Old House. They were laughing at something.

3. Dogs swirling about in excitement diffusing awkward social introductions. I bowed slightly – to avoid the inevitable hand shake. But she didn't offer her hand – perhaps someone had said something.

4. I noticed: firstly, she was very presentable, secondly she went out of her way to greet Ribble – by name and thirdly she looked at me and said how wonderful the Old House looked in the snow. I agreed.

5. Jimmy then suggested that I take Tanushi up to the woods, part way up the hill to get a good look at everything. As per the plan.

6. Dogs happy to re-start their walk with a new companion. I find walking and talking much preferable to sitting and talking. I started by saying how strange she must find the estate – somewhat behind the times and then I really didn't have to say very much else. She chattered – about her impressions and how lovely Ted and Jane had been to her and how she got on so well with Sam and Jimmy and how she'd had a lovely time last night with Beatrice, Charles and Timothy. And she asked some pertinent questions about the Georgian wing and why it had been abandoned. I said something about the cost of heating – it just being me who lived here.

7. We stopped at the top of the woods to look back. It provides one of the better views of the estate. She seemed very enthusiastic.

8. I took her to Nith's grave and talked her through all the dogs buried there. She was attentive – to her credit. She straightened the sticks and flowers I had put there.

9. At this point I asked her about her background. Extraordinary story – from Sri Lanka as refugees when she was very young. They are Tamils. Father killed. He was an internationally renowned economist (I have checked this on line.) Has a brother at Christs doing medicine. Mother lives in Harrow – "she must be so proud of you both at Cambridge," I said. She smiled, stopped walking, turned to me and said, "I know you know I'm at Anglia Ruskin Mr Havard. So, I am

a student in Cambridge if not at Cambridge University like my brother. I hope that isn't an issue?" "No of course not. Perish the thought!" "Yes, my Mother is very proud of us both."

10. She is self-possessed.

11. Returned her to the warmth of the kitchen and to Ted and Jane – joined by Sam and Jimmy. The first part is over. Retreated upstairs. Built fire. I do not think that could have gone much better. What a story – about her origins.

12. Then Revd. Dorothy turns up – unannounced at least to me. I suspect Jane had invited her. She came upstairs to wave at me and to stroke Twyi over whom she made an inordinate fuss. Then she said she would say hello to Tanushi in the kitchen – who told her the name? She gets to know everything. Part of vicaring I suppose.

Friday 11th January - TANUSHI

Slept deeply and dreamt weirdly. I had had three kids by three different Fathers and Amma was lecturing me about my lack of moral standards. And there were dogs all over the place – mostly Beagles. And then she said I had to choose and that I was a disgrace to the family. Goodness knows what that was about.

Jimmy collects – pays the Premier Inn – carries bag to car. They're all very chivalrous in Derbyshire. He chatted about this and that on the way to KA. He does have smiley eyes.

And then finally I meet HH. Don't offer hand as instructed by Beatrice and Jane. He is quite small and wiry and angular in the face with slight scarring to the side of his head and neck. Hair is mousey and greying and a bit unkempt. He rarely looks at you when he is speaking to you. But sneaks a sideways glance when you are speaking. Overall, I'd say he is quite youthful in appearance for someone who must be in his 50s. Definitely very shy.

Make a fuss of Ribble. Think that should earn gold stars. And we are off into the woods. He did seem a bit more normal than I had been led to believe. Told him the story of my arrival in the UK aged 5. He seemed interested in my Father's academic prowess and was very shocked by the story and a little solicitous as to my welfare! He raised the Anglia Ruskin thing. And then dropped it when I acknowledged it straight away. They have a dog graveyard! How extraordinary. He had put sticks and some flowers on the grave of a little terrier! Died last summer. Taken to Ted and Jane for a hot drink. Joined by Sam and Jimmy. Honestly the way Sam greeted me, you'd think we were long lost soul mates.

On the schedule was Ted taking me round the walled garden. This was neater and more presentable than anything in the Georgian wing I'd seen yesterday. Still there was not too much to see apart from dormant beds and the huge old Oak. Ted said, "This tree – part of the warp and weft of the Kirk Aeppel story, Miss Tanushi. We're very protective of our special tree." And he caressed the tree like it really meant something to him. I touched it. I was suddenly and unexpectedly very tearful and wanted to hug the tree. Ted had turned towards the house and didn't notice. Strangest, strongest, most intense reaction.

Inside and Jane said, "Your eyes are watering from the cold my dear." And she put me next to the Aga to warm. She scolded Ted for keeping me out and allowing me to freeze. Ted just smiled. I hadn't initially noticed the presence of the local vicar – Dorothy. Keen to make my acquaintance. She walked across the room, eyes fixed on mine, hand held out. Very striking, early 40s. "And what do you think of this very special and ever so slightly bonkers world of Kirk Aeppel, Tanushi?" Everyone laughed and this diffused whatever was happening inside my head.

Then Beatrice arrived and helped Sam and Jane take the lunch things upstairs in preparation for the meeting. Beatrice came down and whispered, "Don't forget, I am on your side. What I'm going to say will come as a bit of a shock but you mustn't be at all anxious. Really you mustn't."

Old Oak

HH – cont.

13. And so the meeting. The much-anticipated meeting. I tried to say little and listen much. Where I deemed it helpful, I grunted approvingly. Beatrice kicked things off.

14. Beatrice: "Tanushi has prepared a document to spell out some of her initial thoughts as to how we might proceed in the preservation of the estate."

15. She had indeed prepared a document. I did my usual nodding as Tanushi spelt it all out. Some familiar ideas. Some entirely new. Mostly distasteful – at least to me...but I know – I do know – that at some stage I am going to have to grasp whatever nettles are graspable. I have come this far.

16. And then to the nub of the meeting. Beatrice now talking and I made a very careful note of what she said. "Tanushi – thank you so much for those excellent ideas. Henry knows things have to change and he himself is determined to ensure that Kirk Aeppel survives for future generations. And so we come to the Procurement part of your role. Now there is no easy way of saying all this but there is an aspect of the role which no one has yet spoken of and which is difficult and perhaps embarrassing to speak about. You see, Henry has no children. He is averse to romantic relationships. He is averse to sex. He cannot thus provide an heir. That is the problem." (At this stage I am fixedly staring into the fire, mouth clenched tightly shut.) She paused. She continued, "You will probably be very shocked by what I am about to suggest and I don't blame you for one minute and I do apologise if this offends you."

17. At which point Tanushi interrupts and says as if humorously, "You want a surrogate. Is that it?" Beatrice continued with only the slightest hesitation. "Well yes, that is pretty much it Tanushi. What would have to happen is that you would agree to artificial insemination with Henry's sperm. There would be no sex, no relationship. You would be guaranteed a life at Kirk Aeppel. To marry whoever – or not. And your son or daughter would be guaranteed to be the heir to the estate in its entirety. You could work on the estate in the ways we have discussed to ensure that what is handed on to your daughter or son is viable and amazing. It is a wonderful place and it is worth keeping."

18. She said, "Shit!" And then seemed embarrassed by her outburst. Then in her shock, she asked a blizzard of questions. Some of which I had not considered. Who knew? Who would know? Who would take parental responsibility? Who would take key decisions? What would my role be apart from providing the genetic sample? Would the child know? When would he/she know? What if she

marries? And she has other children? Is the job dependent upon agreement to this or is there an actual normal, real job? How long are you prepared to wait for her to become pregnant? What if she doesn't or can't get pregnant? She suddenly quietened.

19. No one noticed the snow. It wasn't forecast.

20. Beatrice leant across, smiled and said she hoped that she wasn't too shocked. We could talk further about those questions if she was prepared to even entertain the idea in the first place. We waited.

21. Tanushi got up and walked to the fire. She put her hand on the stone mantel and traced the heraldic Havard dog with her finger. Ribble rose from slumber. Walked over to her and buried her black head into Tanushi's midriff. Beatrice laughed. Tanushi laughed. I laughed. Ribble wagged her tail.
22. And then she said, "I am shocked of course. It is pretty... (and words failed her, hand gestures only) But I need time to think about this." She said this with a seriousness that gave me hope.

23. And then we noticed the snow and the time and we said there was a need to get her to the station. And all was a rush. Jimmy arrived in the Landrover. The hamper given. Farewells. And she was gone. And all was silent again. Beatrice agreed we had done our best and at least she's not fled in disgust and horror. No time was set for her to get back to us.

TANUSHI - cont.

Currently in the Gatehouse having eaten Pizza with Sam and Jimmy. Trains from Matlock had stopped running. Premier Inn full. We thought it best to come back here. Great time with S / J. I am in "my bedroom" under the duvet that Sam had bought that week. Jimmy had lit the fire downstairs and that warmed the whole house. It is cosy except for the lack of curtains. I can see up to the Old House. The upstairs lights flick off. I can see nothing else apart from the falling snow illuminated by the light of my room.
What a crazy day. I can't quite believe what happened. My strongest feeling is not to do with the bizarre offer – to be the Mother of the heir to the estate! It is what happened at Big Oak, which I DO NOT understand, but I sensed I was known, expected, greeted, called and somehow embraced. Like coming home. I cannot begin to make sense of this. Why had I cried? I never cry.

And what of the offer? Is this really happening? It seemed so obvious in retrospect. And what Ribble did? Like it was planned. And Henry Havard – was as warm as he could manage, I guess. Essentially distant but kindly. I could just hear my Mother's outraged voice. She would talk about me being hired as a breeding cow – what an insult to her daughter.

The place is magical and I am in love with it. What on earth am I going to do? But at the same time as looking into an unknown future, I kind of feel weirdly at peace. Like it's meant. Right now, in this room. I know this sounds crazy. It's time for sleep. Still snowing – Jimmy says at least 15 inches now. When will I get back to Cambridge? Message Tavesh to say I'll be back later in weekend.

Saturday 12th January

1. Slept late to 7.45 am. Didn't even hear the shipping forecast. When was the last time that happened? Somewhat discombobulated. Given the circumstances, the fact that my plates weren't giving me gyp was also remarkable.

2. Boots on and straight out only to be met by Jimmy. Tanushi in the Gatehouse. Trains cancelled. A good 18 inches. Will stick around for at least 24 hours. Jimmy off to Gatehouse to deliver some breakfast. What then?

3. If she cannot get back today, she must come to Hen Galan tonight. Tell her to prepare her party piece! I was being flippant. Unlike me.

4. Little traffic on the road save the odd tractor and 4x4. And finally, well past 8.45 am, the snow plough and gritter.

5. Decided I would accompany Jimmy to Gatehouse. He'd brought the Fergie (Ed: Little Grey Fergie – an old tractor) and I perched on the trail bar. Progress slow but it coped more than satisfactorily with conditions. Ribble and Brook follow.

6. Met by the sounds of what I guessed must have been a hairdryer. Tanushi opened the door and welcomed us in. Longest, darkest brown hair loose. Jimmy, who up till then had been Mr Practical and Mr Competent combined, suddenly seemed a bobbing cork on choppy waters. Didn't know what to say or what to do. So, I had to fill in.

7. She did seem to have made herself at home. She had re-lit the fire. Cleared up from their feast the previous evening. Dug out the ancient kettle. Jimmy unpacked the bag. Sam's wellington boots, a load of warm clothes, gloves, scarves and the like and all things necessary for a breakfast.

8. I invited her to Hen Galan. 7.00 pm sharp round the Big Table. And by the morning the snow will be well on its way to disappearing apparently. Trains will be running on Sunday according to local news. She accepted.

9. Jimmy attended to a message from Samantha. Why not sledging in front of Old House? Had she ever sledged before? No. And she definitely wanted to give it a go.

10. I made my excuses to leave. Walked back in the tracks of the Fergie. Not too arduous. Tiff and Twyi keen to get out but wasn't sure how Tiff would cope. But he did in his own way. Had to be rescued a couple of times but very game – of course. A walk round the woods where the snow was lighter and returned to see them sledging on the slope. The dogs had never seen anything like it and were keen to join the party. I am not quite sure that such innocent communal enjoyment had ever been witnessed at Kirk Aeppel in my lifetime.

    I was aware of my Father's parties at the back of the house – by the now derelict swimming pool. Mother always insisted they had little to do with enjoyment and more to do with humiliation (of her) and a sordid pursuit of self-gratification. I was sent away when they happened. I only witnessed the after-effects. That was enough.

11. Went in. Ted had attended to the fires. Jane well on with preparations. Offered help and was given the potatoes to deal with. Good job all delivered the previous day. Busy. Soon after lunch, Samantha / Jimmy / Tanushi came to help set up Big Table. Samantha and Tanushi arranged the drinks – they had brought with them some noxious looking vodka-based bottles. Jimmy had syphoned a couple of flagons – one of dry cider and one of the apple/pear-mix. First tasting tonight – but I could tell he was looking pleased with himself. His swagger had returned. Message from Charles – he's collecting Dorothy and they can all make it now including Hannah who has returned from Uni especially. (Ed: Younger sister of Timothy). Roads passable. So that is a grand total of 11.

12. Let Jane decide the seating order. I gathered mostly familiar details of the party pieces. Popped names in the Welsh Hat. (Ed: Heirloom from Gwyn Havard's time).

13. Retreated to beetles. Feeling remarkably energised given the events of the last few days.

Saturday 12th January - TANUSHI

I slept so well. How inconceivable is that? On my own – first time ever – in an unknown area, estate, cottage – in silence except for wind – with no light outside. The first image upon waking was of that tree. Thick snow outside. Stunning.
Downstairs the fire was still warm and just needed a little encouragement. Found

kettle but no tea/coffee/milk. Still Jimmy had said he'd be round for 8.00. Cleared up and had a shower. I could get used to this.

Today has been another amazing day. Like I have been transported into another dimension of reality – unfamiliar and yet familiar in the weirdest way.

Jimmy arrived with HH in tow. Breakfast. And then the offer to sledge! We had the best time. I have never skied or sledged or had much experience of snow ever. Then towards the end the dogs arrived. Ribble made a beeline for me as I went down and barged me over into the snow! And then she made a great fuss of licking and barking and wagging her tail!

And then they took me back to the farm and I helped Sam with the pudding for tonight. This was "Bara Brith" according to her Mother's recipe as amended by HH. This should be soaked in tea but HH insists there should be a decent measure of whisky in with the tea in which the fruit sits for 24 hours. It was all made and we just had to get the loaves out of the tins and glaze with honey. Sam is just lovely.

Then it was back down the Old House to help set up. A hive of industry. HH doing the veg – I like that. All ready by 4.00 pm and so we retreated back to the farm. And then they insisted I join in with their party piece which was pretty easy really.

HH – cont.

14. Put on the well-worn Gentlemen's Edwardian "White tie" suit complete with silk top hat. They always appreciated this. Went downstairs at 7.00 pm with the battered wooden horse's head. Table ready. All stand. I recite the Latin grace. And then I welcome all to the 339th Kirk Aeppel celebration of Hen Galan. I then charge them to declare their intent to be peaceable and to record their presence honourably. They all affirm, "Our intent is peaceable; we have come to break bread. We will record our names with honour." Jane passes the book around and each person signs their name with the horse's head looking on. I then declare, "Amen!" They repeat. The words were written out for the new comers. A piece of theatre which appealed greatly to Dorothy.

15. The cawl is served by Jane and Samantha brings round the old wooden cawl spoons. None start till all are served. The bread is already on the table.

16. I haven't seen Hannah for some time. She has changed her image. I would now describe it as "alternative". Various piercings and a tattoo visible on her neck. Still full of smiles and appreciation. She had arranged a veggie meal for herself – discreet and no fuss which I appreciated. Good show. She's doing environmental science at Nottingham. Approve.

17. Seating arrangement – Jane is always next to me and Dorothy for her first Hen Galan on the other side. Tanushi next to Sam with Timothy on the other side and Beatrice opposite. Dorothy is simply an excellent guest. She chats away amiably but always intelligently. We discussed in no particular order the homosexual controversies in the C. of E. and the extent of a split in worldwide Anglicanism, the Catholic Church under Benedict and the nature of religious commitment in modern Britain. It has been sometime since I have been so theologically stimulated.

18. Cawl excellent – local mutton. Jane suitably embarrassed by all the praise.

19. And then the party pieces. Pulled the names out of the hat at random. I went first. Donned dog collar and did my "My brother Esau is an hairy man, but I am a smooth man" monologue from Beyond the Fringe. Ted and Jane – crooned Tony Bennet's "Because of You". Hannah joins in with Sam, Jimmy and Tanushi doing some song which was very popular last year called "Gangnam Style." From South Korea apparently. Everyone thought this hilarious and we were all encouraged to join in with the actions. Bizarre. Try to glean some explanation as to what all this meant. No idea. Dorothy then produced a flute and played Debussy's "Syrinx". I hadn't expected that. Absolutely marvellous. Beatrice, Charles, Timothy and Hannah do their usual skit on the shipping forecast – as clever and funny as when Charles first wrote it at Cambridge all those years ago.

20. As we were waiting for the Bara Brith, I noticed Tanushi have a word with Dorothy. And soon enough the Pudding was piped in with Tanushi playing the flute – "Auld Lang Syne." And everyone joined in. Quite, quite wonderful. Extraordinary. What verve! What presence! I am won over.

21. I think I need to say what excellent cider Jimmy had produced. The dry cider was as good as it has ever been. The apple and pear definitely worth the effort. A little sweet for my taste but clearly has integrity and style. I congratulate him and tell him to keep one flagon per week aside for me and he can then sell the rest to the local pubs. He is delighted.

22. So, we toast the New Year in with the cider and all retreat to our beds. Tanushi – I assume helping in the kitchen – the last to leave. Charles to drop her off at the Gatehouse. Contented. What more can one ask for?

TANUSHI - cont.

What an evening! Our Gangnam Style went down well! Performed with Sam and Jimmy and Timothy's sister – Hannah. She's second year at Nottingham. So HH dressed up in some costume from the dark ages! He seemed very jovial. Started with some formal words of welcome and we had to sign a book to record our presence and that we weren't going to do anything wrong!!!! The Vicar played the flute (really well) for her party piece. And then I borrowed it to play "Auld Lang Syne" as the Bara Brith was brought in. Everyone seemed to like that. A weird, wacky, wonderful evening. 12 days late for the New Year the rest of the world celebrates. Somehow entirely appropriate.

At the very end, I slipped out of the kitchen into the garden. It was raining hard and the snow was disappearing rapidly. There were no stars, no moon, no light. I used my mobile to navigate. I went to see the tree, to see if any words of wisdom were forthcoming. I put my arms round the trunk and looked up. I could intuit nothing – only the wind in the branches. Suddenly Beatrice was beside me with an umbrella. "Come to consult the old girl?" Like she had done the same. "Something like that? What should I do? Big decision for anyone my age to sign away their life." She seemed to agree; we will exchange contact details and she said she'd call me to chat things through. She stooped and picked up an acorn and gave it to me. "In the meantime, a little bit of Kirk Aeppel to take with you." She took my arm and led me inside.
Tavesh had sent me a million messages wanting to know if I was alright. He'd contacted the Uni and found out there was no trip to Wright of Derby. What did I think I was playing at? All the usual I-am-your-big-brother (actually little brother) but-really-I-think-I'm-your-Father-and-Protector crap.

So here I am in the Gatehouse – maybe for the final night. I am now utterly disorientated and have no peace. I want Kirk Aeppel so powerfully but the deal is so weird and so out of my expectations and really a bit creepy. Timothy texted the train times for tomorrow. He said it had been great to see me there so obviously in my element. He'd signed it with an x. Just one. I sent one back.

Sunday 13th January

Timothy and Jimmy arrive pretty much at the same time to take me to the station. Timothy won having arrived seconds before Jimmy. All the snow gone. Steady unremitting rain. Could just see HH off walking the dogs as they disappeared into the woods.

Arrived back in Cambridge shortly after lunch with a million unresolved questions. I am going to have to speak to Tavesh and Amma. When?

Sunday 13th January

1. Filthy weather.

2. Charles rang to cancel.

3. Helped put stuff away.

4. Quiet.

Monday 14th January

1. The rain continues.

2. Lots of questions from Jane. Have you offered her the post? When will we hear anything? Etc. I have no idea. She was a hit with everyone.

3. The dogs are restless.

4. Plates bad for the first time for a while.

5. Set date with Jimmy to flagon the cider. He's been in touch with a handful of local pubs. Still pressing me to discuss future plans.

Tuesday 15th January - TANUSHI

Go across to Christs for a formal (Ed: posh dinner in Hall). And finally tell all to Tavesh. He is horrified and cannot believe what has happened. He thinks he has failed in his duties. He thinks I have taken terrible risks and that I should have taken him with me. Of course, accepting is out of the question and he is sure that Amma will forbid it. So that is that according to Tavesh. He says he will tell Amma when we go across in mid-February if I have not already told her.

Completely regret telling Tavesh.
Formulate a plan. Tavesh has all the simple-mindedness of a schoolboy. Reverse psychology would have been more effective than his gilded Indian prince act.

Email Beatrice. Sort dates.

Wednesday 16th January

Take the afternoon off to see Amma. Tell her I have an offer of a most unusual job and that she must come to visit the place and meet the people to assess its suitability. I have arranged the date – Saturday / Sunday 26th/27th Jan. She mustn't tell Tavesh – he has exams and it will only distract. She feels consulted and included and happy. She asks lots of questions which I mostly answer. All is sorted. I extract a promise from her not to speak to Tavesh.

I have decided to tell her the full nature of the job when she is there and can see the whole place. Might I go ahead even with her disapproval?

Email Beatrice to ensure that no one speaks to Amma about the procurement side of the deal.

I carry the acorn everywhere.

Wednesday 16th January

1. Beatrice rings. Tanushi visiting in 10 days with Mother. That's all we need. Beatrice to meet and greet. She is proving invaluable.

2. Walk up to the farm. Jimmy and Samantha have made such a difference in such a short time. Samantha at the school so arrange to speak to them both about possible plans for the future. Friday morning 11.00 am – Big Table. Jimmy asks about Tanushi – of course. Ask him and Samantha to sort the Gatehouse for the visit.

3. Receive a charming Hen Galan thank you letter from Timothy. Offers any further assistance with Tanushi.

4. Let's just say she's made a positive impact on everyone.

5. The news is still dominated by the report into the Jimmy Saville affair. Horrific. People must have known.

Friday 18th January

1. Enjoying the cold snap. Good for killing off those foreign invaders.

2. Meet with Samantha and Jimmy. Jane and Ted join us for elevenses. They have a lot of ideas and somehow, they need to research and prioritise and select the best ones. In no particular order:

   B and B
   Dog related training weekends
   School educational visits
   Expand orchard (and cider production) – longer term
   Free range pig production – small scale
   Rare breed development – sheep / pig?
   Glamping
   Wedding venue with glamping option
   And, rather bizarrely, specialist mushroom producer (non-hallucinogenic)

   My response was to say "NO" to just one idea – educational visits and "YES" to explore the others and the setting up costs and possible revenues. Not convinced rare breeds produce an income. I throw in honey production as another idea – no idea whether money can be made. Most of these are labour intensive...will need some help.

   They seem thoroughly pleased with the outcome to the meeting and we arrange to meet in two weeks – Friday 1st Feb.

3. Brook ate something revolting this morning and has been poorly most of the day. Stupid dog! Jane not amused re kitchen floor. Brook now curled up in front of fire looking sorry for himself.

Saturday 19th January

1. Dorothy popped in – without warning. I have become accustomed to this now. She'd heard that Tanushi was returning with her Mother, would she like me to be around at some stage? Thanked her and said I'd think about it.

2. She does get along with everyone as far as I can see. Even me. And she did share her flute with Tanushi. She can only tip the balance in favour of a positive result, I think. Ring her and leave message saying, "Yes". Will furnish details later.

3. Brook now recovered. Tell him to go and apologise to Jane for his unforgivable behaviour yesterday.

Sunday 20th January

1. Splendid evening with Charles. Lagavulin – the greatest Islay in my humble opinion – possibly along with Laphroaig. Marvellous.
2. Charles interestingly raised the issue of a tour of Islay – just the two of us before it was too late. He was serious. I am conflicted. It was always a dream of youth... and yet travel is so difficult I find. But with Charles maybe it could be possible.

3. He was quite insistent about it.

Tuesday 22nd January – TANUSHI

So looking forward to returning to Derbyshire, to that amazing place – that really is so outside my normal life. I miss Sam! I miss the gatehouse /my house! I miss the tree – that seems to be calling me back. And in truth this is all so confusing that I don't know how I feel. I haven't even thought about the having a baby bit which is weird in itself. How might other men look at me with someone else's baby? And all that clutter to curate and sort. Travelling up with Amma on Saturday to Matlock. Beatrice knows all the details.

Wednesday 23rd January

1. Cameron has promised that there will be an in/out referendum on Europe in the manifesto. Not convinced it is ever a wise idea to ask the public what they think – too audacious an assumption.

2. Beatrice has the arrangements in order for Saturday. Jimmy to collect. Gatehouse prepared. Rather gather that the Gatehouse is quite an attraction for Tanushi – which I rather like given my happy memories of my stay there in 1971/2.

   As I recovered in late 1971 and the early months of 1972 and before Mother employed the tutors, I was free to do as I pleased under Jane's direction. And she was as lenient and soft as could be. And she let me think I could get round her. The only thing I remember troubling me was my loss of memory about quite what had happened. Jane was always reassuring me. "What happened, happened. You're here now with me to get better and look to the future." And she would put "Sibby" sandwiches into a paper bag so that we could walk to the pond to feed to the ducks and occasional geese that were there. (Ed. Sibby apparently means golden syrup).

   I couldn't even remember the names of any teachers at Prep – or any friends I might have had. It is possible that I had friends...

I remember I spent my time reading the journals of Victorian / Edwardian naturalists which Jane sourced from the Georgian wing. Hence my love for beetles.

Friday 25th January – TIMOTHY

I so regret that I will not be seeing Tanushi this weekend. I have messaged her to wish her well. She just replied with smiley emoji. I am giving some legal tutorials down in London. First time. Lucrative… but if I had known about the visit…

Mother has made the arrangements. I am worried about her re retirement – what will she do? Why is she going so early? The Tanushi project has definitely given her a mission for the time being. It has preoccupied her. Absorbed her. Kirk Aeppel has a habit if doing that to people I have noticed and I am a willing victim.

Saturday 26th January

1. All was prepared. The weather variable but with flashes of sun throughout the day. A little rain early on. It was with some foreboding that I readied myself for the meeting and what would be the judgement days.

2. As before they arrived just after midday. I was outside pretending to do something with Old Oak. Beatrice had advised that. No idea why. Only Ribble allowed out. Tanushi was at ease and full of chat to her Mother as she made her way up to the walled garden. Gesticulating towards the house and the wood. She and Ribble had a splendid reunion.

3. Introductions. I made the utmost effort and shook Mrs Dias' hand. Tanushi very warm in her greeting. And then quickly she wanted to show her Mother – whom she calls Amma – the tree. Curious.

Saturday 26th January – TANUSHI

We had the best time on the way up on the train. I chatted to Amma like I used to when I was a child and we were cooking together. I told her all about my first visit – the snow, the gatehouse, Hen Galan and all the various people.

Anyway – Jimmy drove us to KA. Amma said how pretty everything was. We dropped off the luggage at the Gatehouse. No time for any inspection. And straight up to the old house. HH outside near to my tree. Ribble rushed down and as I embraced her I noticed Amma's initial fear and then amazement. Took Amma straight over. Introductions – I noticed that HH actually shook Amma's hand. I had forgotten to warn her. And then I showed her the tree. Amma looked up and smiled and said, "Why have you shown me this tree Nushi? It is like you are introducing us!" I didn't know what to say. I burbled, "It's just so wonderful and..." "You don't remember do you?" And then I could have sworn I saw a little moistening in her eyes. "I'll tell you later my dear."

And then we went in through the kitchen door meeting Jane and Ted both of whom greeted me in the warmest way possible. The other dogs swarmed inoffensively. And then it was to the Big Table which had been set out with a light lunch.

We were introduced to Derbyshire pikelets which Jane had made that morning. Everybody making the utmost fuss with Amma. She was loving the attention! She insisted everyone called her Kia and not Mrs Dias. If she was nervous, no one would have noticed.

HH – cont.

4. The first part was negotiated without hitch. Jane of course welcomed everyone and took charge of the meal. And just as more tea was offered all round, Dorothy arrived. More introductions and re-telling the flute story for Mrs Dias' benefit.

5. Then I took the two of them upstairs and talked a little about Beetles and Science. I asked about her engineering degree and her work in Sri Lanka. And we both agreed as to the vital importance of Science education. She said that Tanushi's artistic flair had surprised her (by which I suspect she meant disappointed). She spoke with evident pride about her son at Cambridge doing medicine. Quite right too I say.

6. Then she asked what Tanushi's job was to be. I said that it might be best if that were explained as they toured the house a little further. Samantha was to lead them around as before. Much kissing and hugging between Tanushi and Samantha. Why do young people these days do that? So much unnecessary bodily contact.

7. Dorothy bade them goodbye till tomorrow after communion – "to which they would be most welcome if they wanted to come."

TANUSHI - cont.

Sam arrived. Sooo good to see her. And she unlocked the doors as before. Amma could not quite believe her eyes – of course. I explained that my job would be to clear and sort and curate and sell and display etc. everything here. The estate needed to pay its way and we must start by clearing and then setting the house to profitable use. Then set about finding a way to make the place earn some money.

Didn't visit farm. Pointed towards Chapel and orchard. Sam walked down with us to the Gatehouse and then left us. Jimmy had lit the fire and there were supplies in for drinks and snacks. Still no curtains – I can choose them. Amma gob-smacked with everything.

And then, heart in mouth, I took her into my bedroom – as planned. We walked to the window and looked up towards the Old House. HH taking the dogs out for a brief late afternoon walk. The setting sun, askance from left to right, lit up the estate. "Wouldn't it be wonderful if my child could live in such a place? If my child could own such a place? If my child might take over from Henry one day?"

Amma seemed not to hear. "That tree. Do you know where you have met her before? In the garden in Colombo. There, it was an ancient tree, a Bodhi tree – taken it was rumoured from the seeds of the sacred fig tree at Anuradhapura. Each evening when he returned from work, Papa would spend the end of the day, until dinner, with you on a little platform he'd built in the tree. And you would chatter to him as he showed you how to draw and to write. Even when you were very little you could draw the Anuradhapura cross. Do you remember? Even in that last summer, in the monsoon, he would sit under a ramshackle tarpaulin with you at the end of the day." This time she allowed some small tears to trickle.

In truth, we had not spoken of Papa for many years. And I held her.

And then she broke free and said, "Your child inheriting this? Are we all enchanted by Mohini?" (Ed: In Hindu mythology Mohini is the enchantress, the femme fatale, the only female avatar of the god Vishnu.) And she turned to go downstairs to make the tea. And I replied, as I trailed after her, that maybe we were. And I explained the full nature of the post. And she said nothing...until we were sat down in front of the fire. She fretted with her wedding ring, widow-worn for all these years.

She said, "You to be a surrogate? No relationship with Henry whatsoever. Your son..." "Or daughter." "Your child, your first-born to be the master or mistress of all this?" And then she looked at me and said nothing. She drank her tea gazing into the fire. Silent. Communing with Papa no doubt. And then she appeared to sleep or rest her eyes as she would always say.

When she woke, she went upstairs, prepared to leave for the meal (wearing yet another stunning osariya), came back downstairs and then she turned to me, held my hands:

"Of course, you must do this. I came to this country with nothing so that you two could inherit Britain and all it has to offer. If the money and estate are sound (I imagine Papa's voice clear and rational), this is what you must do. In two generations, from poverty in Kilakku Makanam, to this? Of course. How will this be legally agreed? How will it be arranged?"

This was so unexpected. I gasped and cried and hugged her. I told her that at the meal tonight with Henry, Charles and Beatrice, all of whom "knew", she could ask her questions. Much talk of Henry and his eccentricity, that he was very definitely not wanting sex or a relationship of any sort. Amma seemed reassured and taking the arrangement in her stride.

Of course, now I think – she would have a thoroughly pragmatic approach to such things.

"It still allows me to fall in love and marry." To which she said nothing. She was away with her own thoughts.

At 6.00 pm we walked up with torchlight to help to the Old House. Almost immediately Charles and Beatrice passed us on the way and offered a lift for the final 200 metres.

HH – cont.

The evening meal – an excellent fisherman's pie followed by bought Bakewell Pudding.

8. Mrs Dias clearly not at home with the dogs, so I sent them upstairs. Mrs Dias largely took control of the conversation. Tanushi had now told her of the plan for an heir. She was now here to ask all the legal questions, financial questions and practical questions. It was left to Charles and Beatrice to respond in the main. I was quiet.

9. I looked across at Tanushi, part way through the first course, as Charles was speaking of the contract. She seemed content and happy and unconcerned and breathtakingly beautiful. She caught me looking at her and she smiled.

10. I suppose the very fact that the conversation happened, was in itself good news. The deal was actively being considered.

11. It is time now for sleep. Early communion tomorrow.

TANUSHI - cont.

I spoke little during the meal as Amma quizzed Charles and Beatrice. I remembered Hen Galan and smiled. I caught HH looking at me. I knew then with a certainty, I wanted to be a part of this community and this land and this house and this world. Charles and Beatrice dropped us back at the Gatehouse. Beatrice whispered as she hugged me goodnight, "Keep in touch. Have you consulted Old Oak again? Pretty sure I know what she thinks."

So here I am again snuggled in my bed, in my house, with my patch of land to be tamed and cultivated. The curtains – will be something bright and cheerful with a Sri Lankan motif! I am already planning, home-making.

Sunday 27th January

1. I was weary first thing. Communion passed me by somewhat. No sign of Tanushi and Mother. Catholics.

2. Breakfast with all including Dorothy. We were able to praise Jane for her excellent Fisherman's pie. Dorothy took the reins of the conversation and talked of her 3 months in Sri Lanka during her Gap Year. And then talked of life in Derbyshire and how she'd found the move. What a wonderful and welcoming place etc. etc. And then she cleared off for her next service. I thanked her profusely.

3. And then, when the dust had settled after whirlwind Dorothy, Mrs Dias said, "I think Nushi has something to say." And Tanushi clearly had not expected that. And then Mrs D said, "I think a decision has been made." She smiled and looked at her daughter. "And it comes with my blessing." Then Tanushi smiled and said, "I want to be at Kirk Aeppel (pronounced incorrectly) and I will make it work and I will be the Preservation and the Procurement Officer and I will start in August."

4. And that was more or less that. We are to send the contract and accounts for Mrs D to peruse and it will be returned forthwith.

5. Jane is ecstatic. Ted somewhat bemused in his inscrutable way.

6. We sent them on their way with another Derbyshire hamper for good measure.

7. I spent the rest of the day in shock. Told Charles when he arrived. He will get Timothy to do the honours with the paperwork.

8. Charles had brought with him a 12 year-old Coal Ila he'd managed to acquire couple of years ago. Suitably spicy in the circumstances. I'd forgotten quite how much I enjoyed it.

9. He mentioned once more his plan to tour Islay with me. This summer. Quite insistent. Will think on.

10. This might just happen. (Not the tour of Islay with Charles – that seems very out of my reach.) Dear Lord! An heir for Kirk Aeppel! Just maybe.

11. Ribble picked up on my strange mood and stuck closer than a sister in the evening. She sensed something. Brook sat at Charles' feet sucking on one of his shoelaces – a bad habit Charles has always tolerated with affection.

Sunday 27th January - TANUSHI

Well that's it. Job sorted. Life sorted. And with Amma's approval and she even prompted it. She knew that this is what I wanted. Perhaps she saw how everyone had welcomed me and embraced me. She saw me happy and independent. It will be difficult for her to have me so far from Harrow. I will never forget her saying, "I think Nushi has something to say!" Then of course – along with all that – came the doubts. Can I walk away if it all goes wrong? Of course.
Jimmy gave me his and Sam's numbers when he dropped us at the station. They'd be completing the Gatehouse with curtains and functioning washing machine etc. They would need to be in touch. He even suggested that they could visit me in Cambridge after my exams!

Amma did say – and this surprised me – "It is very white. Isn't it? That area of Derbyshire. I saw no other Tamils! (She was smiling when she said this.) I hope that is alright. That everyone accepts you as the new face of Kirk Aeppel." But that was her only caution and she was thrilled for me and I was thrilled that she was thrilled. And for her generosity of spirit and allowing me to venture out. I guess that's what parenting is all about. I felt a surge of love for her that I not felt for many years. Not since I was little and we were newly arrived. Just us in a strange world. Perhaps we have reached a new adult stage of our relationship.

I now have to plug back into my dissertation.

Monday 28th January

1. The news spread fast. Everyone was intrigued... wanting more details... what's the plan? Timothy clearly delighted. Sorry not to have been there – to "help". Dorothy even called in to offer congratulations. I thanked her once again. She said she had done nothing – she was pretty sure that Tanushi had already made her mind up some time ago. How do women know this sort of thing? It is that gift of divination that led to the witch trials. It unnerves me.

2. There is a letter that has been on the Beetle table for several weeks. Opened but unattended to. Roger is going to plead guilty. The trial will be short. The judge therefore hopefully lenient. And as part of his "defence," his solicitor wants me to write a letter essentially saying what a splendid chap he has always been. What a hard worker. How reliable and trustworthy. And how out of character this has been. The trial is in one week and I cannot put this off any longer.

3. Clearly the reason I have not done this is that I am somewhat conflicted. I generally see myself as basically an honest man who supports the forces of law and justice. Of course. By and large I am law-abiding. In which case I should be telling them the truth that Roger is one of life's feckless chancers with few redeeming qualities. But Jane and Ted are downstairs worried as to what this time in prison has done to him and will do to him. And then there's Samantha and Jimmy.

4. This is what I send to the court:

TESTIMONIAL for Roger Baxter 28/1/13

I have known Roger for most of my life. He is the only son of the faithful couple who have tended to the Kirk Aeppel estate – the House and the Land – for more than half a century. I offered him the tenancy of the Kirk Aeppel farm in 1988 when the previous tenant died. In the 24 years he has been the principal tenant, he has ensured that there remains significant unrealised potential in the farm. This has now been handed on to his two children to develop.

It is true that there was a certain wildness in his adolescent years in the late 1970s and early 1980s. But in his defence, those were wild years for many.

But he then met a rather splendid young woman by the name of Sophie whom he courted and eventually married in 1987. Sophie was able to bring out the very best in Roger and his life settled and the farm began to prosper once again after some years of neglect. Jimmy, his son, was born in 1988 and Samantha, his daughter, in 1990.

And then tragedy struck, from which, I would say, Roger has never really recovered. Sophie died in a car accident in the spring of 1994. Utterly awful – drunk driver. If that had not happened, Roger would not now be in his present predicament. But we are where we are and it is to his credit that Roger has cooperated fully with these legal proceedings.

One thing that cannot be denied is that Roger, with the help and love of his parents, has brought up two fine and upstanding young people. Whether through good luck or good management – and we never really fully understand the inner workings of family life – Roger has produced the hard-working, committed, initiative-taking and responsible Jimmy and Samantha who are the new tenants of the farm and more thoroughly excellent, community-minded young people it would be difficult to find. This remains Roger's greatest achievement.

5. The testimonial does not lie.

6. I won't go to the trial. Charles or Timothy will go to support Ted and Jane. I don't know about Jimmy and Samantha. I think they feel some ambivalence maybe at what has happened to their Father and as a result to them. Totally unnecessary of course. Should be all over relatively quickly according to Charles.

7. Samantha and Jimmy are now rightly focussed on developing what has been handed on – the farm. Timings for Friday's meeting confirmed.

Monday 28th January – TIMOTHY

Really tired. Returned late on Sunday to the news of Tanushi's appointment.

Lecturing all good. Lucrative to pursue this in the future. Just four weekends pays for kitchen / utility / downstairs loo!

Sense of achievement in the part I played in Tanushi's appt. And perhaps some excitement but... I just feel rather detached and gloomy about that right now. I don't know why.

I email her my congrats. House so cold on return. Need the log burner to be installed asap.

Will send all pertinent documents to Tanushi and her Mother as requested.

Monday 28th January – TANUSHI

Exhausted and feeling pretty flat right now and the inevitable sense of doubt. Spent night with Amma and returned to Cambridge first thing. Emailed by Timothy – sweet. Just need to get my mind focussed on the next few months and not start living the life I will lead in Derbyshire!

Went round to tell Tavesh. He is full of injured pride and resentment. Not one ounce of him could be pleased for me. He is the by-passed man of the household. I have zero sympathy and told him just what a miserable git he is being. Long walk back to The Railyard – freezing fenland easterlies.

Tuesday 29th January – TANUSHI

Amma has spoken to Tavesh. He messaged to apologise and it sounded genuine. No, he cannot assume to have Papa's position. I reminded him that he is junior to me in age and has no right to attempt to regulate my choices. He said all the right things. I will need to hear him say it in order to be sure.

Documents received from Timothy.

Wednesday 30th January

1. Back to Beetles after much distraction.

2. Somewhat becalmed at the moment. Windless day of mist and murk.

3. Much eager anticipation from Jane – "Won't it be nice to have a young woman to help sort us all out? A friendly face around the place?"

4. Tiff starting to settle and find his place in the order of things.

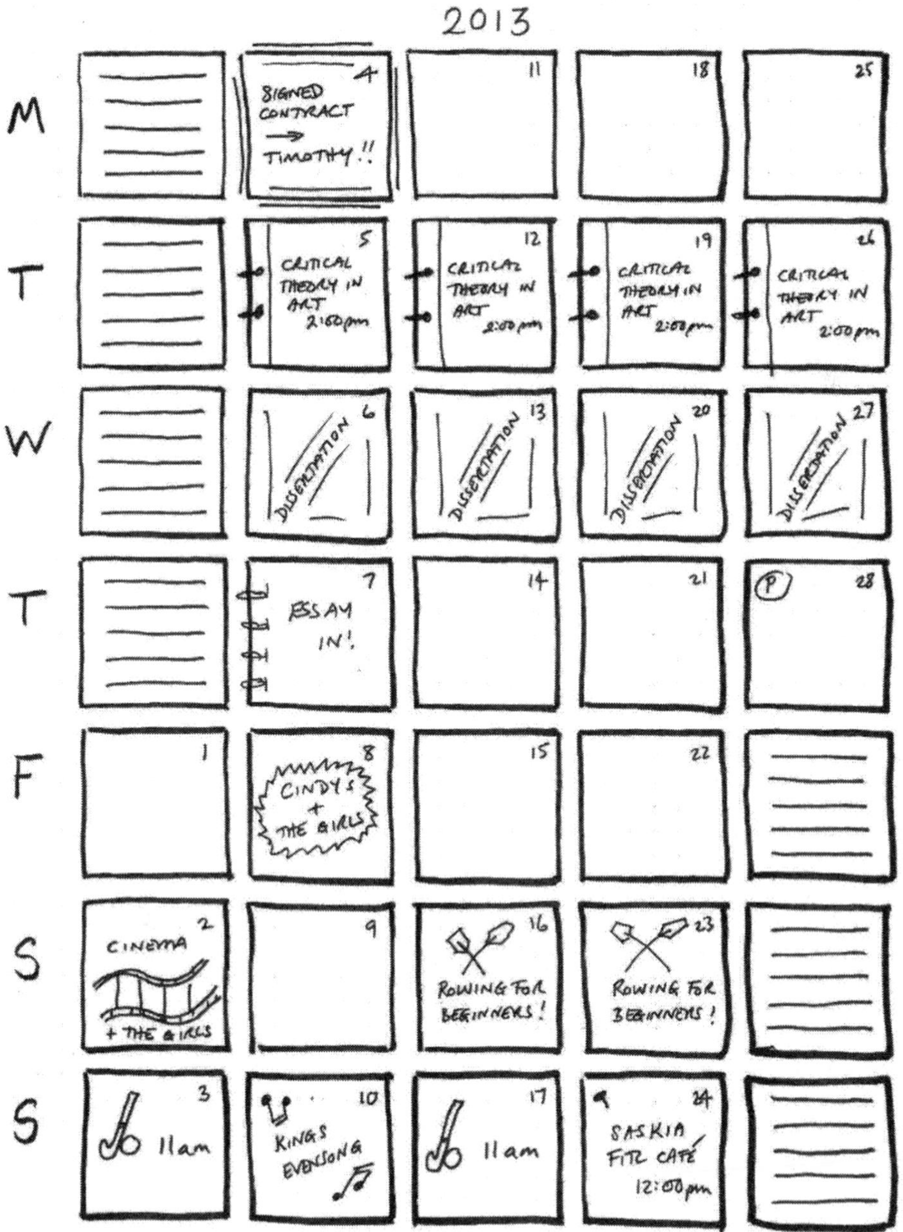
FEBRUARY
2013
M
T
W
T
F
S
S
4
SIGNED CONTRACT → TIMOTHY !!
11
18
25
5
CRITICAL THEORY IN ART 2:00pm
12
CRITICAL THEORY IN ART 2:00pm
19
CRITICAL THEORY IN ART 2:00pm
26
CRITICAL THEORY IN ART 2:00pm
6
DISSERTATION
13
DISSERTATION
20
DISSERTATION
27
DISSERTATION
7
ESSAY IN!
14
21
P
28
1
8
CINDY'S + THE GIRLS
15
22
2
CINEMA + THE GIRLS
9
16
ROWING FOR BEGINNERS!
23
ROWING FOR BEGINNERS!
3
11am
10
KINGS EVENSONG
17
11am
24
SASKIA FITZ CAFÉ 12:00pm

Friday 1st February

1. Important meeting with Samantha and Jimmy. To cut a long story short we agreed that they would start the following projects:

2. Glamping just up from the orchard to the west of Biggle Hill. Initially three units with washing / toilet facilities. Costed. Permission sought. Sourcing and installing. Estimated start date – maybe summer holidays. Jimmy + Samantha. I am to look into local authority permission.

3. Expand orchard. Start immediately. Prepare ground. Source west country cider apple varieties to lend bite to what we currently produce. Graft from current stock also. Jimmy.

4. Re-start pig production. Discuss breed. Something distinctive. Narrow choice down to: Gloucester Old Spot – the orchard pig – gentle nature and easy to handle. Tamworth – good in woodland locations. Berkshire – good maternal instincts. Oxford Sandy and Black – tender and good flavoured meat. We'll see what he decides upon. Jimmy. Start spring.

5. Explore dog training weekends. TV celeb? Samantha.

6. Develop 3 holiday cottages. 2 x couple and 1 family sized accommodation. Longer term. Seeking to restore and kit out next autumn / winter / spring. Jimmy + Samantha.

7. It seems to me they have bitten off a lot but such is the enthusiasm of youth. Jimmy mentioned some antipodean scheme for getting a young lad to labour for 4 months for the price of air fares, food and accommodation and pocket money. To be looked into.

8. Said I would help in whatever way. But they are confident that they can pay their way. No monetary assistance needed.

Sunday 3rd February

1. A particularly refreshing sunlit walk to early communion. Such a change from the previous week's gloom. And Dorothy on top form. It is now the custom for her to return for a brief breakfast. The least we can do.

2. Sarah (financial consultant) and Andrew (ex-navy) are regulars now. Positivity and health oozing from every suntanned pore. Despite that they seem relatively benign and friendly. Might invite them to breakfast next month – Dorothy says I should. (If they are not off on some gym-fuelled, healthy-eating Artic survival cruise or similar.)

3. Charles came round in a strange mood. Almost fell out with him.

4. I dug out a long forgotten 1971 Port Ellen. Seaweedy. They send some spirit off to Langavulin apparently. Excellent. Another three outings.

5. Charles starts by saying that it is now all booked for May. Our Islay adventure – as he keeps referring to it. All is sorted – it is a done deal and he doesn't want any argument whatsoever. He'll drive. Ferry booked. Hotel booked. Port Ellen.

6. I said little. I had rarely seen Charles so determined. I only asked about what was to become of the dogs. He said he was sure Ted and Jane could manage them.

Monday 4th February

1. E-mail local council about Glamping permission. Received by return the longest and most obtuse form to fill in. It asked me to choose between 26 different gender assignations 24 of which I did not understand. Chose: OTHER – obviously. Groaned so grievously that Brook leapt up to see what was the matter with me. Start researching composting toilets – seemed appropriate and satisfying in the circumstances.

2. Discombobulated by Charles last night.

Tuesday 5th February

1. Same-sex marriage voted through in the commons – 400 – 175. Extraordinary. Cameron, "Because we're Conservatives!"

2. Ted and Jane seek permission to go to the trial on Monday. Of course! Timothy is going to pick them up and look after them. I did attempt to warn Ted and Jane that the likely outcome is prison. Not sure they appreciate this.

Wednesday 6th February

1. Timothy has now received the returned and signed contract from Tanushi. Finances agreed. All seems to be in place. Arrive Saturday 3rd August. Tell Ted and Jane, Jimmy and Samantha. You'd have thought they had won the lottery.

2. Also raise with Jane the possibility that I might go away with Charles in May – she seemed surprised and pleased. "So good for the two of you to get away together."

3. She assured me that the dogs would be looked after and that I should have no worries about them. Had Charles prepared the way? I did stress it was just a possibility.

Thursday 7th February

1. A golden day. Cambridge have been in touch. It is an entirely new species and a name needs to be considered. And the entomologists are out searching as they write. Very pleased they are. A real feather and all that. Something about cementing relationships?

2. They invited me (again) to their annual bash in June.

3. Not quite sure what to do to celebrate. Phone Dorothy. She was thrilled. And then, quite out of the blue, she invited me to come to the concert at Elton church followed by some light supper afterwards. Couple of young professionally trained local musicians – one singer and one violinist. Felt I couldn't say no really given the enthusiasm of her response to the beetles. Tomorrow night at 7.00 pm.

4. Regretted affirmative answer as soon as phone put down. Too much going on – Islay, the concert, Cambridge. All invitations to venture out.

5. Gather dogs around and watched Question Time. Scottish Lib Dem, SNP chap, Conservative MP, Labour legal chum of Blair and a business man who has given large amounts of money to SNP. All ruminating about the Referendum.

6. Spirits not entirely lifted.

Friday 8th February

1. Avoided showers. Dogs on good form on walk. Tiff a treat to behold. Has a lion spirit. Twyi his key sparring partner.

2. Spoke to Jane about the concert. Light tea at 4.30 pm. Jimmy is going to do the carrying and fetching. Most kind. He says he was going to Bakewell anyway taking some cider to the Castle Inn.

3. Arrived in good time at the village hall, as per orders. And then extraordinarily Dorothy grabs my arm and navigates, with me in tow, from group to group welcoming them, saying how good it was to see them, how we are in for a treat etc. Very little required of me. For the majority who didn't know me, I dare say they thought I was a long lost decrepit, tweeded uncle.

4. Concert was splendid and definitely worth the effort.

5. And then to supper at the vicarage. One of the few Victorian C of E piles not sold off. A flat had been carved out and rented to someone. Otherwise big draughty kitchen. Lovely cosy sitting room with real fire. And on offer cheese and biscuits, olives and grapes and a choice of drinks – port/wine. I chose the former. Immediately regretted choice. Cheap.

6. I felt conspicuous. I had not been in this situation for some considerable time – alone with a woman – probably since Cambridge. I was nervous. Unsure of expectations. And when in that state, I say even less. Don't initiate.

7. I had assumed – wrongly – that she was a lesbian. Why on earth would someone that attractive not now be married to some successful go-getting man? She had had one or two serious liaisons. But they had not ended well.

8. And then she asked me about why I was not married. And I gave my usual answer that I wasn't the marrying sort and I was far more interested in Beetles than the opposite sex. She allowed me off the hook. And we talked Beetles.

9. And then we talked of Tanushi's arrival and the future of the estate. She didn't say anything but I now think she knows about Tanushi's full role – I don't know how.

10. Jimmy arrived at the agreed hour and tooted his horn.

11. As I retreated to the door, I apologised to her – saying I was not very well practised in this sort of thing and I felt I had been very quiet. She smiled, grabbed my arm again and said words to the effect, well we'd better be doing some more practising hadn't we. She then kissed her hand and put it boldly on my arm with a "God bless."

12. Very confused.

Tiff – Glen of Imaal Terrier

Sunday 10th February

1. Charles – Bunnahabhain – a wonderful evening of contentment.

Monday 11th February

1. Pope Benedict resigns. Pretty sure that isn't allowed. There will be some story behind this... some skulduggery.

2. TRIAL: Over before it started by all accounts. Roger pleaded guilty. Judge sentenced him to 3 years – already done 3 months so he could be out by May next year. Ted and Jane full of sorrow. It was all their fault supposedly. The logic escaped me somewhat. And I started down the path of: well he's a grown man and therefore fully responsible for himself. The law recognises this and thus... But I was cut off at the pass by Timothy – who had delivered them back – he gave Jane a hug and asked if the kettle might be put on. She busied herself with that and Ted retreated to the walled garden.

3. The more I think about Friday, the more baffled I am. And yet much as I dislike bafflement, I seem unable to cease thinking about it. Which is why bafflement is so profoundly irritating.

4. I can appreciate Tanushi's concerns about who knows what. The issue of what these days is called transparency, needs to be dealt with. Currently 4 people know (Beatrice, Charles, Timothy and me) in addition to Tanushi and her Mother. The key people who don't know are Jane and Ted and Jimmy and Sam – nor the wider world whose prurient interest I fear greatly. Dorothy is in her own category of witch-like divination.

   Who knows what she knows and how she might know it. She is a veritable epistemic mystery. Personally, I favour utter secrecy.

Monday 11th February TIMOTHY

Roger did well enough to escape with 3 years. Jane and Ted inevitably in tears. That was always going to happen whatever. TLC (me) and "routine" (HH) is what has been advised to them. Jimmy and Sam not at the trial but came down to the Old House when we arrived back. Much talk of the future.

Update on house: All electrical / plumbing / baths / showers / loos – all done. Wood burner in but cannot be used for one week to allow sealants to properly dry and fix. Lots of decorating now needed. Find myself googling Sri Lankan colours – Saffron, Maroon, Gold, Green...I might settle for various shades of magnolia.

Wednesday 13th February - TANUSHI

Well – I don't know how – but it has gradually crept out that I have an amazing job next year in a major country house as chief preservation curator and business opportunities entrepreneur. I may have told some people. And some photos were shared – of the gatehouse and the view up to the Old House.

And guess what – Josh messages me out of the blue – "So pleased for you blah blah..." and then "maybe we could have coffee? Sorry about the way things ended blah blah." Don't reply... immediately. Then say I think it's wise if we don't have a coffee. New life to lead and all that. Wish him well in his career in Ophthalmic Dispensing – he has a placement in Slough. Smiley face waving goodbye. Crack open a bottle of Prosecco.

Friday 15th February

Sam messaging to get me to visit KA – under the pretext of discussing curtains / colours and any other fixtures and fittings needed. She is just the best.

Tell her it'll have to wait till later in March. Exciting!!

Starting beginners rowing tomorrow!!

Saturday 16th February

1. Only Jane is allowed to mark the day. Lovely card with an arrangement of daffs.

Sunday 17th February

1. Barrington rang. So predictable.

   (For the benefit of the published work / journal / diary, which I assume next to no one will read, I have been asked to explain a little further about Barrington. Barrington fell into our group at Jesus, really for want of falling into any other group. He was training to be a vet – generally accepted to be conspicuously bright. He looked at 18 about 12 years old and little – not much over 5 foot 5 inches. And had the most grotesque and unacceptable way of "approaching" girls which frequently got him into trouble. Sang in the Chapel choir and it fell to the Chaplain to try to explain to him that his behaviour was completely inappropriate. "Barrington Brodie of that ilk" had been brought up in a small Scottish castle which we had all visited one Hogmanay. A memorable evening mostly for positive reasons. He had had perpetually frustrated designs on Helen – a fellow Vet from Girton – part of our group. She was a strongly built rower – rowed for Blondie – and she broke his nose in the skirmishes. That dampened even his ardour. Of course, we were all delighted. Barrington's life ambition has been to become the President of the Royal College of Veterinary Surgeons. And he travels down to the Easter Conference every year to further his cause and present his research etc. etc. He has become something of an expert on Lyme's disease in dogs.)

2. He is dropping by on his way back on Friday 5th April and staying until Sunday 7th April. Usual thing each year. He'll bring decent bottle of whisky and drink two of mine in return. I exaggerate only slightly.

3. Tell Charles about Barrington's visit. He is somewhat indifferent and keener to talk of his plans for Islay. It really is all set-in-stone now. Not at all sure how I feel about this.

4. Still, firmly book Beatrice and Charles in for the Saturday evening meal. Essential support needed when Barrington comes to stay.

Monday 18th February

1. Try to press on with glamping licence. Enlist Timothy's aid in the face of the syrup of town hall bureaucracy. Think we are making progress. The local planning chap couldn't be more helpful and seems to think there will be no problems. Hearing mid-April. It will be a struggle to get them up and going for the summer. Jimmy thinks we will and is delighted. Tell him of compost loo research – a key pre-requisite for obtaining planning permission.

2. I don't know where Jimmy and Samantha get their energy from. They are working on all fronts simultaneously. They have decided to write to Roger together. They are going to tell him of their plans. They are going to tell him they will not be visiting him in prison. They make clear his future will not include the farm. Tough love. So, he needs to make alternative arrangements.

3. Jimmy has drawn up the organic spray schedule for the orchard.

4. Dorothy called in – unannounced of course. Seems she had things to discuss with Jane. Then came up with cup of tea in hand. She thanked me for accompanying her on Friday. She hoped I had enjoyed it all. She faced the fire warming herself whilst looking at me in the mirror above the fireplace. And before I could reply beyond a few burbling sounds, she asked me if she could invite me to other cultural events. Turning to face me, "So difficult going to things on your own... never quite got used to it." She smiled and then giggled – "Henry – what a face you are pulling!" She moved towards me, stopped and turned in her tracks. "That's a Yes then is it?" And she was gone. Yes.

Wednesday 20th February

1. Jimmy dropped in late afternoon – full of enthusiasm. Said he'd met a farmer at Bakewell livestock market on Monday. Wants me to accompany him tomorrow to a farm the other side of Kirk Ireton. He promised me a pint of cider on the return journey at the (most wonderful) Barley Mow. The purpose of this to look at and possibly buy some Sandy and Blacks. Whole litter just been born.

2. I am beginning to think that everyone is conspiring to get me out of the confines of the estate – Dorothy to "cultural events", Charles to Islay and now Jimmy to Kirk Ireton. It's unsettling.

3. I had known this farmer's father many years ago and liked him. And a visit to the Barley Mow is always a treat. So, I agreed!

Thursday 21st February

1. I have enjoyed myself today.

2. Managed the journey without music / blindfold props – not that it's far but nevertheless...

3. I have learnt that Oxford Sandy and Blacks are sometimes referred to as Plum Pudding Pigs. And they were as docile and winsome as you could ever imagine piglets to be. Good outdoors in all weathers. Jimmy spoke pigs for some considerable time whilst I attended to the couple of very handsome German Wirehaired Pointers. Fine dogs. Terrific on the moors and in water apparently. Joe was all for selling me a puppy from a litter nearby! What a salesman!

4. The deal was being done when I interjected with, "The last time I was here was in 1977 – helped with the geese for the Christmas rush for your Father." At which point the poor man became quite nostalgic – overcome almost – and he shook my hand suddenly and thanked me. And then he turned to Jimmy and said, "I tell you what. I'll throw in for next to nothing a couple of Magalistas. I need to shift them. They take too long to produce 'owt for me." Woolly pigs apparently – Hungary – late maturing – wonderfully flavoured, fat veined meat. Jimmy did some deal or other.

5. And then to the Barley Mow. Has not changed one bit. Why can't everywhere be like this? Why does there have to be "progress" at all? It is normally regress disguised as progress. You could not wish for a more comfortable boozer with a real fire, real beer and real cider and the odd dog. That's it. And then I became nostalgic for those goose plucking times when I'd sneak a pint at the Barley Mow in the early evening. And I felt grown up and worthwhile – like I'd done something.

6. Jimmy said he'd enjoyed himself too. Pigs delivered mid-March.

Friday 22nd February

1. Dorothy rang to say she'd invited Sarah and Andrew to breakfast after early communion on Sunday. Knew I wouldn't mind.

2. She also mentioned a play at the Lyceum (Ed: In Sheffield) – got two tickets. Called "The Full Monty" – been a successful film apparently. Never heard of it. She'll collect me on Tuesday next at 5.00 pm. She can't wait.

3. I think I am going to have to say something to Dorothy. I am not sure what quite I need to say – but something.

Sunday 24th February

1. Dorothy, Sarah, Andrew all back to Big Table. Actually, rather civilised. Despite their outward glow of health and happiness, Sarah and Andrew are thoroughly ordinary and decent folk and with a story which is not uniform perfection. Essentially, they had not been able to have children of their own, had adopted a brother and sister and it had all gone badly wrong.

2. They were very appreciative of the invitation which Dorothy had clearly said was most unusual! Really? They are busy doing up their retirement property on the edge of the KA estate as you enter the village. Almost there re the interior. Invited me across.

3. Dorothy told them of our outing to The Full Monty. They all loved the film and had heard good things about the play – although what this play is about, I have no idea. Decline in post-industrial Sheffield is what Dorothy has told me.

4. Charles dropped in briefly not looking at all well. Heavy cold. So, told him to go home forthwith. Brook appreciated his brief visit.

Sunday 24th February - TANUSHI

Had lunch with Saskia. She'd been at the Fitzwilliam for 18 months now and was loving it. Jobs there are as rare as hen's teeth. She must be good. Of course, I told her all about Kirk Aeppel. She was fascinated and even said she was jealous! Can you believe that? What did I think might be there, hidden in all the clutter? Anything to be unearthed? Nothing I had seen apart from impressive lumps of dark wood furniture. But there could be almost anything. I was unable to see so much – especially upstairs. She did say she'd love to come across when I was established. Just to look around.

And I thought why not? I will have a little cottage all of my own and I can invite whoever I want.

Making progress with dissertation. Finally.

Tuesday 26th February

1. Just returned from the Lyceum. Somewhat shocked by the subject matter of the play. I do not see myself as a prudish man really but I was nevertheless surprised to have been taken there by a vicar who seemed to be loving every minute of it. It was about men taking their clothes off for the entertainment of women – stripping naked. And these men were inclined to do this because of their socio-economic decline – their poverty – which was portrayed touchingly. Can't help feeling that it would have all been very different if it were women forced into that position at the hands of powerful men.

2. I suppose the evening had not overall been a roaring success. Even before the play. I had worked out what I wanted to say to her. And at the meal I said that I was worried that she might be thinking that there was a possibility of a relationship of some sort which went beyond the normal bounds of friendship. I wanted to assure her that that was not going to happen and I was concerned that she shouldn't be misled somehow into thinking that was "on the table". Which it wasn't.

3. And we had a "discussion" on the way home over the moors about the play in which I said that I thought that nakedness was not something to be flaunted and was for the privacy of the marital bed – which to be fair now legally included homosexual people. Revd. Dorothy very quiet which was unusual. We parted at the entrance at my insistence and I walked up the drive.

4. I really should know better than to venture down paths long since sequestered. It's my fault naturally.

Wednesday 27th February

1. Wrote note to Revd. Dorothy – first class – "Dear Dorothy, I apologise for spoiling your evening. I should not have spoken as I did. It was unforgiveable. I think we should abandon the 'cultural companions' idea. I am sure you can do much better. Yours sincerely, Henry Havard."

Thursday 28th February

1. Glorious day of warmth and sunshine. First hints of spring. Daffs out near the pond looking resplendent.

2. And responded to the invitation from Sarah and Andrew. Walked down via gatehouse. Had a look in. One or two things need doing still. Reminisced as always in that place.

   Evening round the fire with Jane on my birthday in Feb '72. Ted popped in with some pellets from an owl's nest – for me to investigate. He'd become a regular but there was some fuss about him staying over. Mother didn't approve. Jane and Ted just laughed about it. Not quite out of my hearing. My scars were completely better by then. Still Jane put on the cream to help soothe. Bandages were still over the plates mainly to protect them. I was in my dressing gown holding on to Jane as she applied the cream.

   Mother breezed in, as she was accustomed, announcing the need to get tutors in. "Stop that now Jane! No need for that anymore, thank goodness! The scars are all healed." She had asked the vicar for recommendations. He had volunteered himself for Latin, Greek, Classical Civilisation and Scripture. He'd enquire as to the other subjects.

   "Time to get busy with your studies Henry. See how much you have forgotten! Just on your way home Ted?"

   "Yes Mrs Havard – just popped in with a birthday gift for Henry here..."

   Mother then clocked the date and turned, "Yes I see. You're doing a fine job Jane, just don't mollycoddle him too much that's all." And she left.

3. Visit to Sarah and Andrew. Fine home they have made of it. Showed me around the ground floor. Gym area would you believe with various fitness machines. Extraordinary. And upstairs one bedroom was a study for Sarah and her financial consulting which she still does a little of. The double garage has become Andrew's boat yard! He sails at both Ogston and Carsington. Very keen. Tried to tempt me into a boat! Bugger off!

4. All beautiful I said but the one thing missing here is a dog – a proper dog. Now I happen to know where I might be able to get hold of one. Never crossed their minds. Always been city people. I was left with the impression they would consider the possibility.

5. Sarah has a tautness to her. Yes, a honed and trained physique but something brittle, fragile, stretched about her face. A dog is my solution to most issues. Andrew is an amiable old cove. I could share a whisky with him I dare say. But they would benefit from a German Wirehaired Pointer. Without a shadow of a doubt.

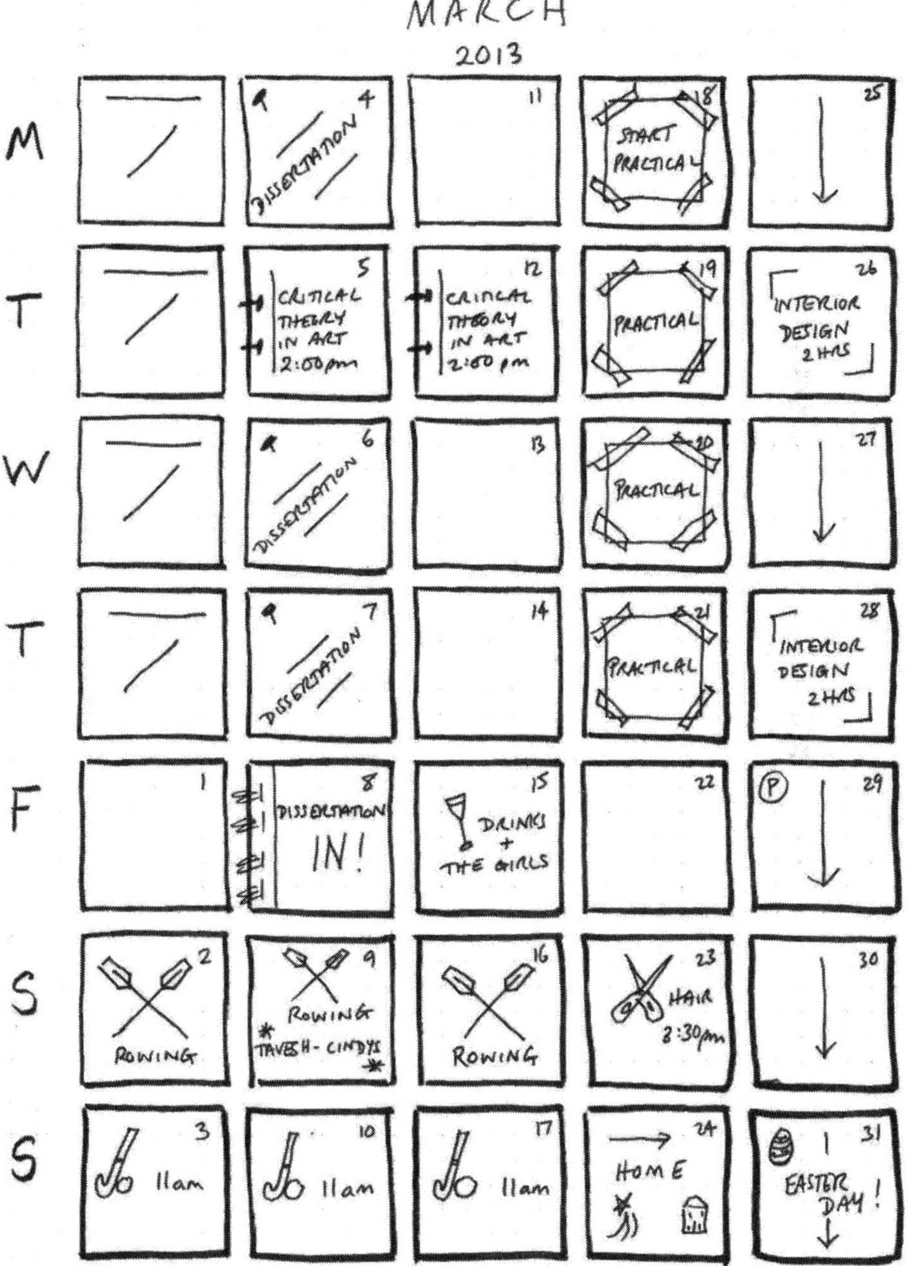
MARCH
2013
M
T
W
T
F
S
S
4
DISSERTATION
11
18
START PRACTICAL
25
5
CRITICAL THEORY IN ART 2:00pm
12
CRITICAL THEORY IN ART 2:00pm
19
PRACTICAL
26
INTERIOR DESIGN 2HRS
6
DISSERTATION
13
20
PRACTICAL
27
7
DISSERTATION
14
21
PRACTICAL
28
INTERIOR DESIGN 2HRS
1
8
DISSERTATION IN!
15
DRINKS + THE GIRLS
22
P
29
2
ROWING
9
ROWING
TAVESH - CINDYS
16
ROWING
23
HAIR 3:30pm
30
3
11am
10
11am
17
11am
24
HOME
31
EASTER DAY!

Saturday 2nd March

1. Rent day. Subsidised Samantha / Jimmy rent by 25% to chip in for new developments. Seems only right to co-invest with them.

Sunday 3rd March

1. Lay reader standing in for Revd. D. at communion.

2. Charles much recovered. A quiet evening. Said Timothy's house coming along a treat. He spoke quite a lot about Timothy and Hannah and Beatrice. Polished off a long opened 15 year-old Bruichladdich. Such a long, gentle, warming, enduring finish.

Sunday 3rd March - TANUSHI

Does it matter if I get a 2:1 or a first? Does the job at KA depend upon either outcome? No. Will one result or the other improve my fertility? No. Will Sam or Jimmy care? No. Will anybody here remember for more than 10 seconds what I got in finals? No. I pretty much know it's gonna be a 2:1 anyway given the marks already banked for coursework. Assuming a decent outcome for the dissertation, it'll be a 2:1. But Amma hasn't been told any of this of course – she thinks life without a first will not be worth living. She got a first. Papa got a first. I must keep up the family tradition. Achieve something academically, finally after all these years.

But there is somewhere else I need to be. I've arranged with Sam to visit just after Easter – Thursday / Friday / Saturday probs.

THE HISTORY OF Kirk Aeppel (4) 1800-1900

John Havard's brief but miserable profligacy came to an end with his death in 1805. And so at the age of 43 Peter Havard came to the estate of Kirk Aeppel. He was a man of great vision and little common sense, of profound aesthetic awareness and no financial acumen and of fine sensitivity but with a vapid appetite for hard work.

Peter managed through his life to marry no fewer than 4 wives. All died young in childbirth having produced 2 or 3 offspring each. They were innocent creatures no doubt, in an age when innocence was not rewarded.

Peter sold the lands around the Roaches; he sold all the remaining lead mines. He was on a mission to make Kirk Aeppel a fine Derbyshire estate once more – fit for none other than himself. It needed modernising. The new Kirk Aeppel was built, the avenue altered with the grand entrance now north-west facing. A more grandiose, pillared, Palladian entrance could not be wished for. A mini-Kedleston Hall if you will.

But whilst Peter was running out of money, he was not running out of children that needed to be housed and to be fed. And hence the Old House was not demolished but remarkably survived the structural revolutions. The Old House, with its Big Table and walled garden, was neglected and overlooked. But they survived largely untouched. Once the splurge of architectural creativity (and money) came to an end, Peter spent much of his time ensuring that his children were either married off to (6 daughters) or became (4 sons) Anglican clergymen. The history of the impact of the Havard offspring on rural Anglican ministry around the country in the 19th century is yet to be written.

His eldest son, Gwyn, spent time in the army before returning one day rather unexpectedly with an Andalusian bride, Carilla, who brought with her 6 Andalusian horses and 6 casks of sherry (the dowry apparently). They had met in Cadiz where she had been born some 22 years previously in 1793. It took a week from Cadiz (via Lisbon) to Liverpool (a ship returning with its sugar and rum) and 3 days to journey from Liverpool to Matlock. From the moment she entered Kirk Aeppel, there was no doubt who was in charge. Peter and Gwyn were whipped into shape. The estate and its farm were transformed and the horses well cared for. A stable of eccentric proportions was built for the 6 noble creatures and their offspring. She also attended to the parlous estate finances. Kirk Aeppel became over the next 15 years a chief source of imported sherry and claret to the burgeoning midlands and north of the country. The horses also more than earned their keep and were much prized.

Peter died of exhaustion in 1826. Gwyn now took the reins (under the guidance of his wife of course). The orchard was tended and extended. The walled garden restored. Much was learnt from the widely publicised work of Joseph Paxton at nearby Chatsworth. Experiments with glass allowed the growing of the more exotic Spanish fruits.

Carilla became something of a local celebrity even earning a place at the Cavendish table (at Chatsworth) on several occasions. She was a big character as noble and well-formed as the pure-bred horses she brought to Derbyshire.

She ensured her son and daughter were properly tutored both academically and practically into civil and rural life of the county. There is a fine portrait of Carilla which still hangs at Kirk Aeppel acquired on an exploratory claret buying trip to Bordeaux in 1825 – painted, so the family story recounts, by her Father. It shows her resplendent besides a fine Andalusian horse.

Gwyn Havard died in 1871 and Carilla 14 years later. They left the estate in fine fettle. Camilla, the eldest child, was deeply religious and somewhat caught between the Protestantism of her birth place and the exotic Catholicism of her Mother's Andalusia. So it was that the emergence of the Oxford Movement in the 1830s spoke to her not just theologically but also in a profoundly personal way. In 1848 at the age of 30 she entered the newly formed Community of St Mary the Virgin at Wantage. She eventually rose to be Mother Superior and as the movement grew, she was actively involved in several educational initiatives.

George Havard assumed command of Kirk Aeppel in 1871. His 28 years as master of the estate was unremarkable in every way.

This is in contrast to the 6 years he spent as a "Commissioned Gentleman" in the Hudson Bay Company in the 1840s. A whaling voyage and his horror at what he witnessed ended his time in Canada. His words are worth repeating. "Anyone who has looked into the dying eyes of a great whale, as it is butchered, will know who it is that is sentient, who noble and who savage, who soulish and who brutish." These words are inscribed upon his grave.

When he returned, he insisted on the prohibition of all hunting at Kirk Aeppel and he threw himself into the work of the RSPCA. He even entered the annual RSPCA essay competition from which those words are taken.

The wine business turned a steadily diminishing profit. George continued breeding horses to good effect and treating them with inordinate care

When he died in 1899, he did so peaceably one summer's day in a chair besides his Mother's beloved horses.

Monday 4th March - TIMOTHY

A renewal of lecturing contract in London and now in Cambridge. Lucrative too. All weekends. The dates in Cambridge May and September. Tanushi definitely there in May. Signed up.

Tuesday 5th March

1. Went up to the farm. What a transformation Jimmy and Samantha have already made. He's going to house the pigs in the old stable when needed – in winter mainly. All cleaned up already. Otherwise they'll be out and about. Went to discuss this "out and about" bit. Where exactly? He reckons he's got 30 acres to play with including some woodland that does need some clearing. Electric fencing. The pigs will be regularly moved on. Other side of Biggle Hill. What's there that needs not to be destroyed by the pigs? Trees? Walls? What of pig huts - £250 - £600 a go? Recycled plastic / galvanised steel? Water trough? And there needs to be sufficient distance between them and the glamping yurts...

2. I am nervous. Jimmy is assured and calm.

3. We then visited and pegged out the glamping area. Privacy required. Further trees to be planted. Showers + proper loos available in farmyard – accessed from far side nearest to yurts. Still a trek of 150-200 yards. But compost loos one per yurt at a distance of max 10 yards. It is a mystery to me why people choose to do this. Jimmy says city/town dwellers are desperate for nature. Should we go for 3 yurts with good levels of privacy or 4? I think we can push 4 in without too much compromise. Apply for 4 on the licence. Then we can decide. And there's getting the clean water to each Yurt + electricity. Jimmy had thought of it all.

4. Finally visited the orchard extension. Here, he had already made a start. Land cleared of scrub and levelled to some extent. He reckons there's room for another 175 or so productive trees. According to size of apple/pear cultivar.

5. I leave it to Jimmy. He's done his research. The trees are on order. He's marked the trees from our collection he wishes to graft.

6. Overwhelmed by the sense of drive and commitment. I say this to Jimmy. And then later to Ted and Jane.

Friday 8th March - TANUSHI

Dissertation in – hooray! That was so painful at the end. But it's done. Plan night out tomorrow – and even invite Tavesh. Haven't seen him since end of Jan. We'll see.

Not much to do now work-wise. Lectures are tailing off. The odd seminar. Term ends in two weeks. Decide to enrol on line in a course on 18th and 19th century interior design recommended by Saskia.

Friday 8th March

1. Call from Sarah. They are actively considering a dog and would like some advice. Readily assented. Dogs are one of the few things I do know something about.

2. They came up at 3.00 pm as arranged. Jane had a little tea ready. We had a splendid conversation. They had been on line – a mine of utterly useless and sage advice, gold and fool's gold. How to sift? Started with their life – how much exercise did they think they can give to the dog? Any allergies? How house proud? Function of dog in household? This inevitably led on to the tricky ground of the absence of children. Steered away from that.

3. They suggested all the usual designer mongrels their friends had bought and immediately I spoke about Wally Conran and his regrets at having bred the first Labradoodles and spawning the "Frankenstein" (his word) dog trend. He had opened the doggy Pandora's box. I mentioned genetic health disorders which unscrupulous breeders had ignored and which had multiplied in designer dogs. Dogs with conflicting behaviour types and instincts etc. Andrew reckoned he wanted to run with a dog. Sarah spoke about her desire for comfort and protection.

4. I then suggested that they take for 24 hours – first Tiff as an example of a smaller, terrier type dog. Then Twyi as a medium sized but energetic dog. And then either Brook or Ribble as a bigger, more robust dog. Both delighted with this option. Meanwhile don't look at puppy ads. I advised. Start with Tiff tomorrow.

5. Very pleased with this process.

Saturday 9th March TIMOTHY

Lecturing weekend in the Premier Inn, Putney Bridge. Hard work after a week in the office – I won't lie. But it is money for old rope. Spend too long in evening constructing an email to Tanushi which sounded really casual just mentioning my lecturing weekend in Cambridge in May. Be great to meet up????

Saturday 9th March -TANUSHI

Tavesh turned up for pre's at The Mill. He greeted me warmly with long hug and said he'd missed me. I took that as a proper apology. Said he was really pleased I'd found a job that I was going to love but couldn't help having concerns about the surrogacy bit. I said I have concerns too but life's a risk – coming to this country was a risk – Mother risked everything. He gave me another hug and said that he'd like to go back to being my "little" brother once more! "Little" I repeated and we laughed. He then bailed as expected. Not one for Cindies (Ed. a Cambridge nightclub). But I felt happy and we had the best night concluding at the Van of Life – cheesy chips never tasted better.

Sunday 10th March

1. Conclave due to start tomorrow. Much analysis of the Papabili. (ED: something to do with election of the new Pope).

2. Tiff returned. Twyi handed over.

3. Jimmy out in the orchard despite the north easterly.

4. Brook on particularly fine form on our walk today. Loves playing in water.

5. Charles back to good form. 1 more Islay after this one. And that is traditionally Lagavulin. So, we chose the Laphroaig of course.

Monday 11th March

1. Black smoke.

2. Twyi returned. Brook handed over.

Tuesday 12th March

1. Black smoke.

2. Brook returned.

Wednesday 13th March

1. White smoke. Argentinian. Bergoglio. Calling himself Francis. Interesting. It occurs to me that Revd. Dorothy might approve. Tempted to but don't go any further with that particular thought.

Saturday 16th March

1. THE ARRIVAL OF THE PIGS - very exciting. Jimmy more than happy for me to be there. Jimmy has gone for the whole batch of Plum Puddings. He'll select one of the boars if appropriate to sire the next generations. He'll raise and send to slaughter all the rest in 3 or 4 months depending on growth etc. See how it goes.

2. And the unexpected surprise – 2 x 6-month old Magalistas. They really are remarkably woolly. But docile enough. He'll see how the goes but will send for slaughter in all likelihood just before Christmas.

3. Wonderful animals already looking at home. Jimmy as pleased as punch. A farm is not a farm without animals.

4. Wales crush England in the decider 30 – 3 and take the championship.

Sunday 17th March

1. The hungry months these were once called before anything could really grow properly – to be eaten. Winter stocks consumed. Biting easterly again today and meagre amount of sun breaking through. Landscape stripped bare by winter needs some TLC in the form of sunshine and increased temperatures.

2. Charles and the Lagavulin – the last of the Islays until December. We have a little annual review on the Sunday before the Spring Equinox. Just evolved that way. A recap. And it has for me been disorientating in the degree of change and with more to come in August. Charles was happy with progress with regards to the Estate. He thinks Sam and Jimmy are just what is needed and out of the ashes of Roger's cannabis joint has risen something rather positive. Timothy is more contented; more centrally involved at work; working hard both on his career and house. Nothing attracts a suitable partner better than a well turned out house. It's as old as nature. Hannah is fine at Nottingham – he worries she is a bit radical in her commitments to vegetarianism and eco-sustainability and all things green. I think she is delightful and say so. "We need more like her – you've done well!" Charles pleased with that.

I mourn Nith's departure and celebrate Tiff's arrival. I am amazed we have travelled so far to procure an heir to Kirk Aeppel. Who could possibly have imagined that 12 months ago?

And one new beetle discovered. Another year older for the two of us and both surviving just about! And we drink to that. Charles has a slight eye moistening I notice.

And we look forward – him with great anticipation of Islay in just a couple of months and me, with some trepidation, to the arrival of Tanushi in August.

Brook content lying under Charles' feet – a symbol of fidelity. Tiff and Tywi sprawled by the fire. Ribble curled up beside me.

Monday 18th March

1. Couldn't help myself having a peek at how the pigs are getting along. All well it seems. Rooting and snuffling around contentedly. Which is the best we can all do in life really.

2. Walked down to the village to see Sarah and Andrew. They were most grateful for the loan of the dogs! And they had made a decision. They had heeded my advice on celeb. dogs (as they referred to them) and had done some research which confirmed those thoughts. They wanted to support one of the more unusual British (and fairly local) breeds and so had decided to investigate purchasing a Clumber spaniel. They are off to a breeder in Shropshire to meet her Clumbers and we shall see what we shall see. I am delighted and thrilled for them.

3. And then who should arrive but Revd. Dorothy. Innocently planned no doubt. Sarah got the door. Andrew busied getting tea and scones out. Clearly, she knew nothing of this meeting. I suppose we did our professional best. I enthused about the dog experiment and the outcome thereof. She talked about visiting her Mother in Camden. Parents are never straightforward – cf. Larkin.

4. Then Andrew asked about the play. To which I said, "Not sure it was quite my sort of thing all in all." And she said she had enjoyed the film much more. And we moved on swiftly. Left as soon as decently possible.

Wednesday 20th March – TIMOTHY

Received an email back from Tanushi: Hi there – sorry missed this. Yeah, that would be great. Send us a message nearer the time. T x

I guess she didn't have to spend quite so long getting the right note of casual indifference as I had.

First fire in the wood burner – some solace.

Wednesday 20th March

Spring Equinox. Speyside.

Friday 22nd March

1. Formal invitation and details have come through re event Friday June 7th for Cambridge University Zoology Dept. Their summer "do" always in early June – special invitation to celebrate my many years of "dedicated" research and my most recent discovery. They do hope I will come this year. Anybody who is anybody in the world of Coleoptera in the UK has been invited. At Jesus College – in my honour. Gosh. I am tempted – and repulsed and I recognise those familiar impulses.

Saturday 23rd March

1. Plates bad for the first time for some time. Feeling perturbed. Pulled and pushed. Agitated. I am reminded of the story from John's Gospel. The healing of the infirm man at the pool of Bethesda: "For an angel went down at a certain season into the pool, and troubled the water: whosoever then first after the troubling of the water stepped in was made whole of whatsoever disease he had." To jump or not to jump?

2. Of course, Jane immediately noticed my plates were giving me gyp. Explained the dilemma. She was so pleased that the university had decided to honour me thus. Which was a nice response but not hugely helpful. She suggested I walk the dogs.

3. Temperatures reluctantly creeping up. Bracing wind. Approached top of Biggle. Saw hunched figure seated in the mouth of the cave (old lead workings). 3 yards away. Dorothy stands up. No pleasantries. She launches in, "Great note Henry. Thanks. Situation dealt with satisfactorily no doubt." Pause. "Do I get a say as to whether we should abandon the 'cultural companions' idea? Do I get to judge whether I can do better than you?"

4. I am not good in these situations which is why I avoid them like the plague. I splutter. She continues, shouting, "Too bloody right it was unforgiveable – what you said. And why all this body hatred anyway?" (Whatever that is.) "Why do you get to write the rules about our relationship or friendship or whatever it is?" She's approaching me walking pole in hand. Ribble observant and close.

   Tywi intercepts her with wagging tail. She pauses and cradles Twyi's head. "Hello sweetie. Why is your master such a..." She probably completes the sentence. (Not sure I hear all of it.) She turns into the wind, tears streaking her face. And, she realises she will get no sense out of me. It must be like shouting at a rag doll I imagine. Eventually you run out of energy.

   "I will be there tomorrow doing what I am meant to do. Giving out the bread and wine. Ministering. And then I will walk with you, to your table, to be fed breakfast, by you. And you will be bloody civil to me and enjoy my company. Do you understand?" She waited not for an answer.

   Stumbled back down the hill in something of a daze.

Sunday 24th March

1. I went to communion. As it was an unusual timing (not the last Sunday in month – next week is Easter Sunday and no communion at St Cuthbert's so switched to this week) – there were less people – no Jane and Ted or Sarah and Andrew. Think they had been intending their Shropshire jaunt today. Not many places to look except downwards and upwards.

2. Then it came to the Peace. People know to greet me with a smile and a nod of the head. Dorothy headed my way, paused, stepped closer, held both hands as if to hug. Which she then most certainly did and held me squished somewhat in her vestments and she whispered, "I am sorry for..." Released, I gasped out of surprise. And I nodded my head.

3. As we walked down to breakfast little was said. Over breakfast we talked of the new Pope and the theological and political machinations that must be going on in the Vatican – a non-European Pope... a reformer... despite all Benedict's conservative cardinal nominations. How do such things happen?

4. As she gathered herself to leave, she said, "You don't have to enjoy my company Henry. Really you don't. I'll stay away if you'd prefer." She stood close. I stuttered and stammered. The gist of what I said was: I like your company. I like you. I am different and I don't understand why I am different and I am sorry that I am the way I am. But I have always been this way. She smiled. "Right" in that matronly efficient sort of tone, "Well said Henry. I like you too. I am now going to hug you both on arrival and departure – I'm setting new rules." And so, she did. I will have get used to it no doubt.

5. Charles came for the first of the new season of Speyside whisky samplings. We tend to start with Glenlivet and Charles dug out an old favourite – a 21 year-old bottling – such a sherryish contrast to the Islays. Utterly delightful. Distilleries seem to be producing more and more different bottlings – often variations of cask character or length of time matured. It all gets very confusing. You think you know a distillery and its one or perhaps two products (12 or 15 year-old perhaps) and then suddenly there's 5 more variations. Double Wood – Caribbean Cask – Triple Cask – The Estate – Port Wood – Flora and Fauna – Founder's Reserve etc. etc. This a classic case of progress meaning regress.

   I was perfectly happy before they brought out the plethora of new offerings. We both completely agree on this.

Sunday 24th March - TANUSHI

Home for Easter. Brought loads home to save massive clear out at end of next term. Feeling like the end of Uni now. 5 "teaching" weeks, 3 exams and it's over. It's gone so quickly. And I am one of the few who knows for sure what's happening next. Amma is positively beaming – still full of questions. Our shared experience. There is no one in Harrow that does not know what is happening next for me. How she will handle the next part of this journey – if it should happen – I have no idea. Tavesh is in full-on revision mode as usual. Can't wait for next week to see my new world once more.

Wednesday 27th March

1. Delivery of apple trees. Jimmy has a job on his hands. He has a set a target of 30 trees a day – so a good 6 day's work. Sam has taken on the pigs. No school so she has some more time. I offer my help. They say they'll ring if needed.

2. Pigs visited – all well.

Thursday 28th March – Maundy Thursday

1. Dorothy has encouraged me to a church meeting at All Saints. Some creative Passover / Last Supper sort of re-enactment. Not my thing. I send my apologies.

Friday 29th March – Good Friday

1. St Cuthbert's opened as usual for private prayer and reflection.

2. Weather starting to be more promising – temperatures into double figures in the main. Ted beginning to start work in the walled garden.

3. I am informed that Tanushi will be staying in Gatehouse – her house now I suppose, for a couple of nights – Thursday / Friday next week. All arranged via Samantha. Good. It's a start.

4. Jimmy hard at it still. Ahead of target he says. He wants me to drive the tractor tomorrow.

Saturday 30th March

1. Worked hard. Some simple earth digging / moving. Lots achieved. It'll make Jimmy's job much easier. All ready now for the final 70 or so. Jimmy reckons all done by midday Monday.

2. Jane has the weekend off including Monday. Have to look after myself which is fine because she has it all ready and instructions displayed. I offer to serve lunch for Dorothy on Monday. She accepts. Decide on a roast. Walk before if weather suitable.

3. Sarah and Andrew run up and view the work in progress. They have decided on a Clumber and are registered for the next litter whenever that might be. They are hoping June / July maybe. Off they trot looking full of the joys of spring.

Sunday 31st March – Easter Sunday – * clocks forward

1. Can't help looking "ahead" to the arrival of Barrington on Friday – not looking "forward" as such. He's always been so unapologetically tiggerish which is most wearing. Still I will survive I dare say.

2. Prepare the potatoes and veg. Meat out of fridge and in larder. Fully confident re meal. The rest – not so much.

3. Tend not to tackle beetles on Sundays. My nod to Sabbath precept. So, decide to thoroughly sort the whiskies – all a bit disordered. Put them all back to their rightful places – alphabetised so we know where we are re Speysides et al. Look resplendent on the shelves opposite Big Table. 117 in total.

4. Charles caught up with big family meal.

Sunday 31st March - TANUSHI

Easter service. Nigerian priest – great. Lots of questions and comments about where the place is and what it's going to entail and how far from Amma. "You have to let them go. That is what parenting means. And if you have done a good job, they will share their life with you," were Amma's words of wisdom. Tavesh forced to enthuse to folk about it all – which I enjoyed.

Sam collecting me from Matlock at 12.36 on Thursday.

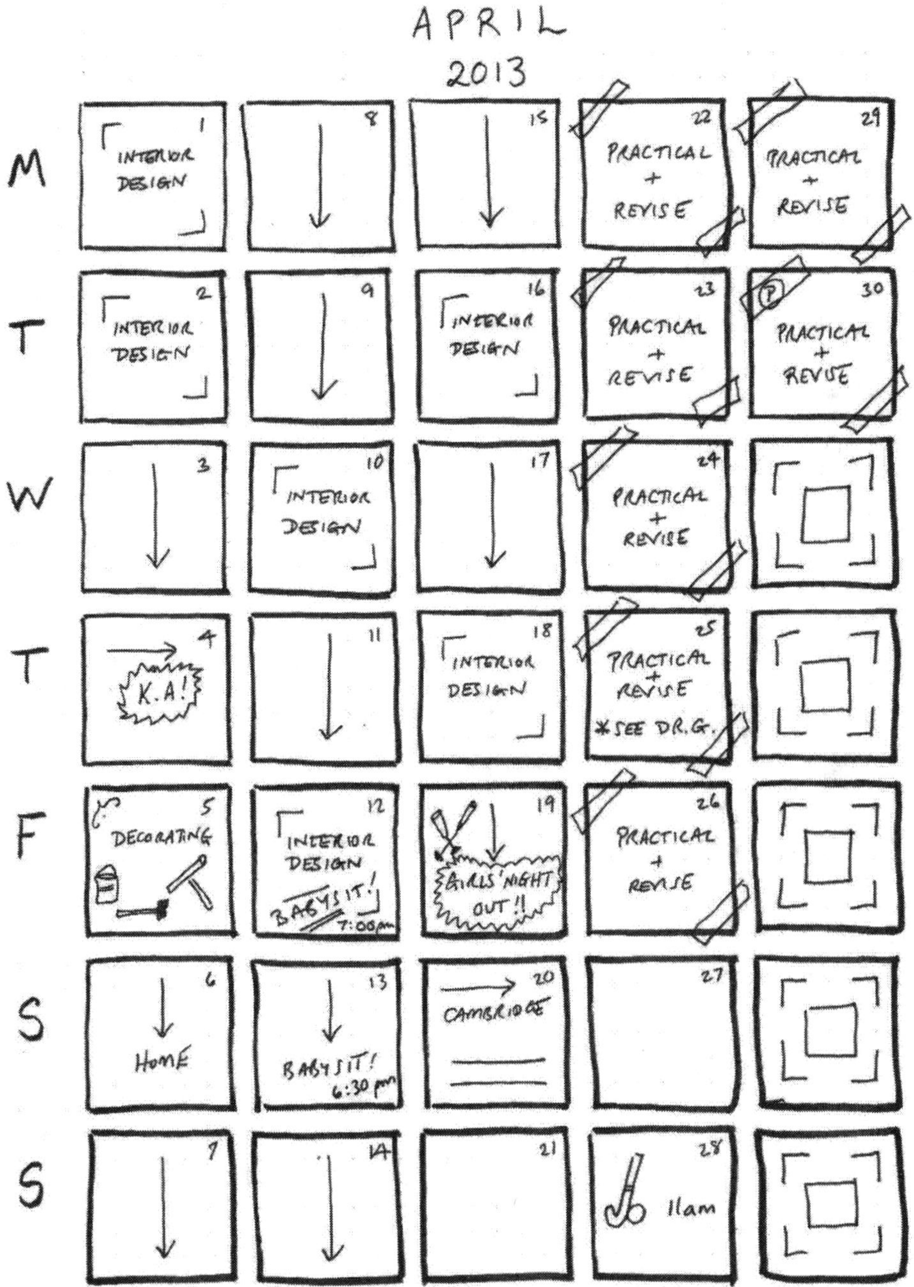
APRIL
2013
M
T
W
T
F
S
S
1
INTERIOR DESIGN
2
INTERIOR DESIGN
3
4
K.A!
5
DECORATING
6
HOME
7
8
9
10
INTERIOR DESIGN
11
12
INTERIOR DESIGN
BABYSIT!
7:00pm
13
BABYSIT!
6:30pm
14
15
16
INTERIOR DESIGN
17
18
INTERIOR DESIGN
19
GIRLS' NIGHT OUT!!
20
CAMBRIDGE
21
22
PRACTICAL + REVISE
23
PRACTICAL + REVISE
24
PRACTICAL + REVISE
25
PRACTICAL + REVISE
*SEE DR.G.
26
PRACTICAL + REVISE
27
28
11am
29
PRACTICAL + REVISE
30
P
PRACTICAL + REVISE

Monday 1st April – Bank Holiday

1. A splendid day. Dorothy arrived 10.30 am and we walked up to farm to inspect progress. Weather held. Dogs unusually frisky to have another companion. Jimmy was just finishing. He invited Dorothy to place the final couple of trees. A pair of pears. Simple. She was very touched it seemed. He's such a fine young man.

2. Up Biggle. Slight tension approaching the cave opening – diffused by Dorothy who re-enacted her outburst – "You will enjoy my company!" And we laughed.

3. Meal very decent. Top Rioja someone had given me several years ago. Meat and potatoes spot on. Dorothy helped with veg.

4. And there were times it all felt... normal.

Tuesday 2nd April

1. New batch of beetles arrived.

2. Discuss with Jane, Barrington's imminent arrival. She cannot stand the man. He'd tried it on with her – inevitably – when visiting in the 80's. She'd used a wooden spoon to good effect. He then apologised as he always did. Jane has not forgotten. He is banned from the kitchen. He has reformed a little over the years – having married the long-suffering Caitlan. Testosterone levels must have diminished surely. As a dog he'd have been castrated long since.

Thursday 4th April - TANUSHI

Here at KA once more and in kinder weather. So much to say!! No pressure this time. No: will they / won't they, will I / won't I. Just able to enjoy everything. Sam's just left for the farm and we're going to do some decorating tomorrow and choosing of curtains and enjoying our few days together. She's introduced me to the new pigs. Jimmy working like a Trojan. I can't tell you how good it is to be here.

Friday 5th April

Thought I'd call in on HH. Caught him preparing for the arrival of some old college buddy. Got the impression that he wasn't so very pleased to have this chap coming. He was, to me, courtesy itself. Asked about uni. and of course about my Mother. And sent his best wishes. Said he'd been advising a couple about choice of dog. Said he was looking forward to August and that I must ask if there is anything he can assist with.

Then it was decorating with Sam all day. Music blaring, doors open, to dilute the smell. Suddenly in comes this tiny chap in a kilt. Acts like he owns the place. "Stayed here a time or two, if you know what I mean." Sam knew it was Barrington – visits each year. Just arrived, heard the music, thought he'd find out what was going on. So he took great delight in finding out all about me... Sam kept her paintbrush fully primed, out in front of her, as she ushered him out. "Busy, busy here Barrington. We can't stop I'm afraid. Have a nice time with Henry!" Barrington retreated having viewed what he wanted to view. Told why it was best to be firm with Barrington. Creep!

Pizzas in the evening. We've chosen curtains for the bedroom and blinds for the kitchen. And the washer will be replaced. I pointed out the back door needed fixing – she'll get Jimmy on it. Not a lot it seems that Jimmy can't do. Fished with Sam about his status. Single – for once – she added.

Friday 5th April

1. Preparation for Barrington involves getting the lilo out and pumping it up, taking away key malts from the rack, anything expensive (now have 73 bottles), getting Jane to set up for evening meal and then ensuring she disappears.

2. He arrives at 3.00 pm in his ancient 1964 Rover P5 3.0 litre – one of 5000 – Betty as he refers to it. "Still going strong Henry." Not sure whether that was about me or Betty. And from that point on he talked animatedly at me. He'd clearly called in at the Gatehouse and met Tanushi. So full of questions of course most with sniggering reference to having consulted some online Philippine bride site. Do such things really exist? Sri Lanka, I say. Not that that assuages his innuendo.

3. We toured the estate and farm. Barrington impressed with plans and progress and said so to Jimmy. And on our return, Barrington sets up his vet stuff to inspect the dogs. He does this each year. I think he feels this is part payment for hospitality received. In truth I have always felt that there has been a diffidence towards Barrington from whatever dog he has in front of him. Maybe that is to

be expected – like going to the dentist. Anyway, all well. Barrington asked about ticks. Slightly more common. Deer – need culling – do I have someone who does that? No. Get on to that. All landowners need to be doing this. Derbyshire experiencing significant growth in Cervidae numbers.

4. I ask about Helen – vet from Girton. They keep in touch professionally more regularly. Husband died of Pancreatic Cancer – 8 weeks from diagnosis to death. February. Bloody awful. Leave Barrington to get / write card. Of course, he said – outrageously – that he remembered I'd had a bit of a thing for Helen at one time. "As did you – I do remember that famous Hogmanay..." Barrington involuntarily touched his nose and looked away.

5. Walked into village, posted card, pint at the Peacock (it goes without saying that he tried to ingratiate himself to barmaid. Embarrassing). Returned. Ate. Drank. Endured evening with one extra bottle of 14 year-old Oban – better then might have been.

Saturday 6th April - TANUSHI

Decorating all done and ready for August. The remaining stuff will be completed by Jimmy and Sam. Can't wait. Called to say goodbye to HH but he was off with Barrington. Sam took me into Matlock. Looked in nice furniture shop. Amazing huge beds. Coffee at Peli Deli. Caught train back.

Saturday 6th April

1. Walk up Biggle after lunch. Had pre-arranged to "bump into" Dororthy at the top – she was keen to battle the old lech (her term). Twyi raced up to her. Barrington noticed this of course. Introductions. Barrington already leafing around in his smutty vicar joke book.

2. Dorothy having none of it. Utterly ruthless with him as she deconstructed his witticisms. He simpered in submission. I enjoyed the spectacle – though a bit one sided. Barrington talked of her as a "fine mare" on the way down. "You could do worse Henry, if she's not taken or even if she is!"

3. Charles and Beatrice do their best to jolly things along at the meal. Charles always had a way of pointedly ignoring Barrington's humour and hence the conversation finally moved to matters less puerile. Beatrice talked of her last term with acceptance. Appointed replacement.

Sunday 7th April

1. I have survived another year. Barrington off before communion. Not one for religion is Barrington – a strict reductionist materialist – which he uses to justify his behaviour. "Men are as men are. We are evolutionarily hard wired." He would say. A pleasant post communion breakfast at which Jane retold the story of the wooden spoon. She is convinced she broke his little finger – somehow symbolically appropriate as Dorothy pointed out.

2. Replace the whiskies.

3. In the evening Charles fished out a 14-year old Craigellachie. Not to my taste especially. I'm not a fan of the "orangey-ness" in chocolate, with duck or in whisky. Charles appreciates it.

Monday 8th April

1. Thatcher dies. Much discussion of her legacy (although not in this household).

Friday 12th April

1. Dorothy came round with film from new "network" called Netflix – I think. All through WiFi. Old film apparently – Truman Show. Remarkably clever. Thoroughly (and surprisingly) liked it. A version of Plato's cave asking questions about reality and how we know what we think we know about reality. And Dorothy of course a wonderful companion to chew over the ideas.

Wednesday 17th April

1. Glamping licence gained as expected. Jimmy had already pre-reserved 4 units, 4 compost loos, water / shower / sink paraphernalia. He tells me he has a small business loan with the bank – instinctively revolted with the thought of bankers getting their teeth into KA. He just smiles and asks me to research fire pit / wood burners. Something that could be outside all summer but be moved with relative ease indoors during the cooler Spring / Autumn months. Smoke dispersal issues... or just separate systems altogether might be easier.

2. Samantha is going to place ads for summer holiday start. Amazing.

Saturday 20th April - TANUSHI

Back to Cambridge for the final time. Amma drove me up. It's about the maximum distance she can manage (on the return) – just over an hour. Maybe she's going to have to learn to drive all the way to Derbyshire...

5 weeks in which I complete practical exam and revise – 3 exams – done.

Saturday 20th April

1. Visited Dorothy for second time for return meal. She is a bit more cosmopolitan and, I would say, experimental in her food choices. All sorts of foodstuffs new to me. Who knew chickpeas were so delicious? Spot on flavours without a doubt.

2. I have done nothing about the invitation to Cambridge in June. I have discussed this with Dorothy. She has come up with a plan which she proposed to me. Extraordinary. She has researched "Emotional Support Animals" – a new thing apparently. Would I be happier going into the "do" with Ribble by my side? Well, obviously, that would be fine. The focus would be entirely on Ribble and not me. So, if she worked out how to get Ribble certified as an ESD (Emotional Support Dog), it would be all OK.

3. She has a way of not being defeated...

Sunday 21st April

1. Write acceptance letter – mentioning (by name) the ESD I will bring. Let's see what they think of that. Buy special harness on Amazon – just £14.00 with EMOTIONAL SUPPORT written on it. Great.

2. Charles keen to explore a Macallan 18 year old he seen on offer. Absolutely luxuriously warming, intense, strong, robust – amongst the best ever. Congratulate him.

3. Charles details the week away – actually 8 days. Travel up on Friday to Carlisle to break journey. Booked into B and B – twin room one night. Then ferry Saturday and one week in the Islay Hotel – platinum single bedrooms – shown room pictures. All very plush. He has pre-booked all distillery tours. Back down for late Saturday.

4. He's done some work. He's even given me a list of what must be packed. Can't fault him! Can't help but feel Charles has invested greatly in this. Less than four weeks away.

Wednesday 24th April

1. Apparently, I need a mental health professional letter if I am to receive authorisation for Ribble to be my ESD. Cannot believe this. I have already replied saying I'd be there with dog. Now I have to jump through some trick-cyclist-shyster hoop – for the payment of silly money no doubt. Just to extract a letter from her (probably). And there'll be questions, lots of questions. I did not want this. Dorothy not happy with my response. She tried to talk me through it. Won't be complex. She'll take me there – some trendy therapy centre in Wirksworth – a nice little town that has become a little bloody offshoot of some left wing, arty, psycho-babble, veganised, Notting Hill type of place. Used to be an honest toiling town. Now you can't move without a fairly traded diploma in something.

2. This opens cans of worms.

3. I have to bring Ribble to the meeting. All set up of course – for next week.

Sunday 28th April

1. Report on walled garden from Ted: All's well Mr 'Avard. Tiff has sorted the rats. Early rhubarb now ripe for picking. Cloches all ready. I say to Ted – and I have no idea whence this thought came – that he should think of hiring an apprentice to teach him or her all the accumulated wisdom of his gardening mind and experience. He then said, "You're not trying to get rid of me, are you?" No!!!

2. Jimmy tells me that all necessary excavation work is completed for Yurts and toilets. Concrete in. Decking next. He gathers no moss. Pigs happy.

3. Charles insistent on continuing with Macallan. Didn't argue. Charles then started a discussion about Dorothy and the nature of my liaison with her. He does sometimes have a way of preventing obfuscation and evasion. It's the lawyer in him. So eventually I pleaded agnosticism as to the precise nature of the liaison. He said agnosticism was the retreat of cowards and cads. And we laughed.

4. Told Charles of the visit to the mental health worker to get Ribble assigned as an ESD. He found this tremendously funny and asked if he could be there. Unhelpful.

Tuesday 30th April

1. The visit. Dorothy said she'd pick me up at 1.30 pm and was 7 minutes late. Ribble on back seat unaccustomed to such. I sat next to her. First instruction is to come in without the dog. Dorothy will look after Ribble.

2. It was a woman – Janine – naturally.

3. Questions. Why was I wanting an ESD reference letter? What were the particular reasons I thought I needed an ESD? Then: When did these issues become apparent? Why did these issues arise? What were the causative events in my life?

4. Answers. I had prepared a line of argument. I had to say I was anxious in order to get the letter. So, I put it all down to introversion and increasingly isolated work regime related to Beetles. And my extreme introversion nurtured by my solitary life surrounded by dogs. She was going to find no chink in my psychological armour. She didn't have the brains or intellectual agility of a Charles or Dorothy.

5. She made an attempt to dig and delve. Unforthcoming.

6. Went to get Ribble. She fawned over her in the way that lap dogs are fawned over. Ribble largely indifferent. But patient and gentle.

7. She spoke of her fees – no surprise there – she was minded to write such a letter of authorisation. It would be with me before the end of the week. Paid. Left.

8. You have to say if you can make a living that way – why not? Comfortable chairs and ready supply of coffee.

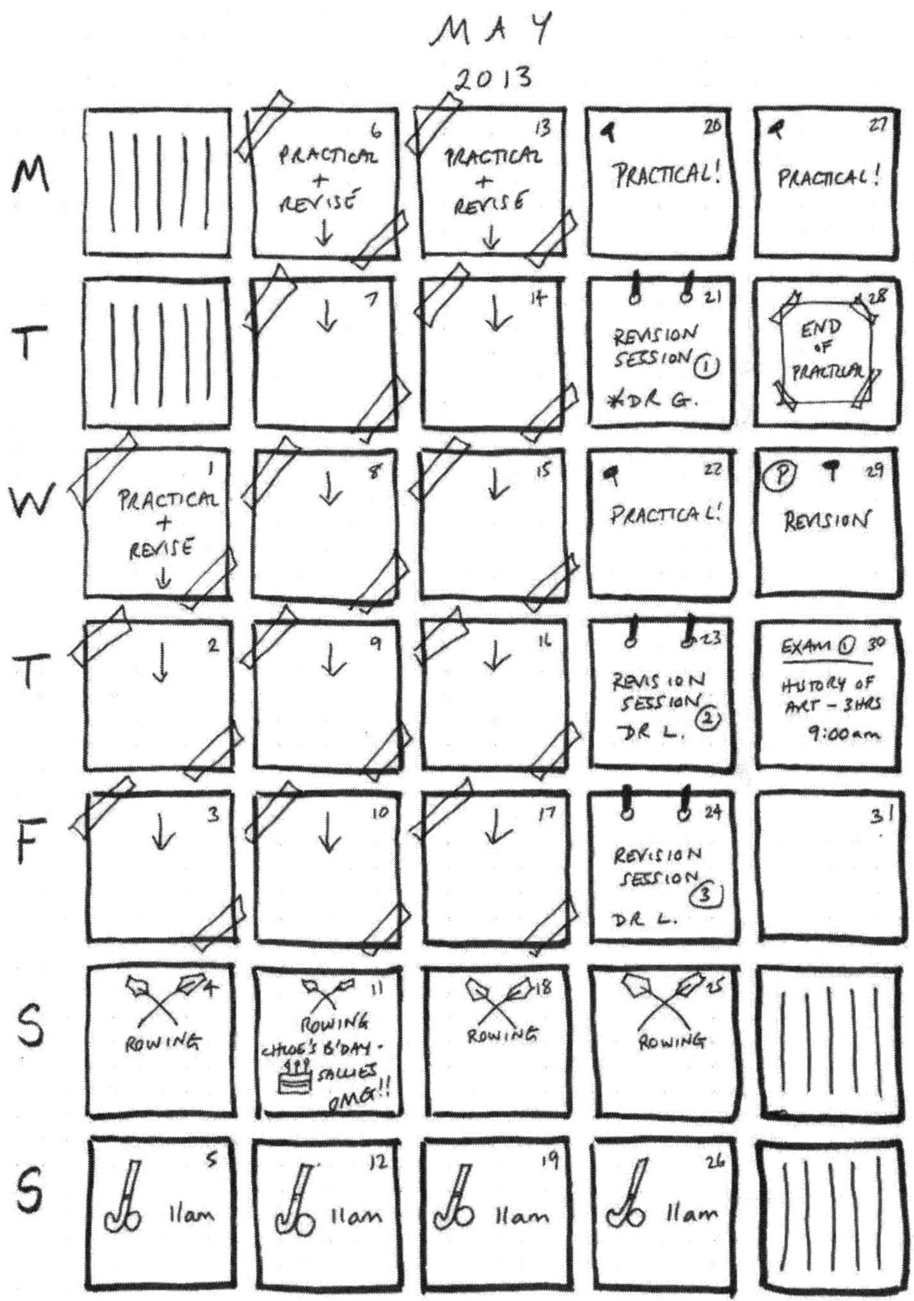
MAY
2013
M
T
W
T
F
S
S
6 PRACTICAL + REVISE
13 PRACTICAL + REVISE
20 PRACTICAL!
27 PRACTICAL!
7
14
21 REVISION SESSION 1 *DR G.
28 END OF PRACTICAL
1 PRACTICAL + REVISE
8
15
22 PRACTICAL!
29 P REVISION
2
9
16
23 REVISION SESSION 2 DR L.
EXAM 1 30
HISTORY OF ART – 3HRS
9:00am
3
10
17
24 REVISION SESSION 3 DR L.
31
4 ROWING
11 ROWING
CHLOE'S B'DAY - SALLIES
OMG!!
18 ROWING
25 ROWING
5 11am
12 11am
19 11am
26 11am

Friday 3rd May - TANUSHI

Working my way through practical. I have chosen 18th and 19th century wallpaper design. Creating 3 separate designs to show evolution from one century to the next. Colours and motifs etc. all researched. I am enjoying myself. No particular time-pressure. Just have to ensure all is documented and evidenced properly. I'd taken a few photographs at KA in the Georgian bit. I wonder if this is going to prove useful?!! That's why I had negotiated this theme after all.

Friday 3rd May

1. Letter and harness arrive on the same day. Ribble is now officially my Emotional Support Dog. Try harness out. Ribble is unperturbed.

2. Allow Ribble to greet Dorothy in harness. She is delighted that her scheme has worked out. I am grateful and it has undoubtedly eased some of the trepidation at going to Cambridge. And I say so. She hugs me. Am getting used to this.

3. Try out another Netflix film. There is such a choice! "Remains of the Day." Interesting discussions afterwards about repression and openness – which is why she "arranged" for that film to be chosen – obviously. "Transparent!" I scolded her.

4. Begin discussions about getting to Cambridge and accommodation with dog. Tricky.

5. I sometimes think I am like a project for Dorothy, that I am something she is determined to change and redeem.

6. I have no idea what I am providing for her in this deal. I do not say this to Dorothy. I fear such conversations – like Mr Stevens perhaps.

Sunday 5th May

1. Early communion. Sarah and Andrew have confirmation of Clumber litter – ready around end of June. Excellent. Want some advice re dog or bitch upon which I am so knowledgeable – in the dog world.

2. Charles attended communion. Unusual and on his own. He stayed for breakfast but said little. Said he'd give tonight a miss. Cited work issues. He said he had to go to a conference to do with changes in property law. Setting off tonight.

Monday 6th May – Bank Holiday

1. Helped Jimmy in orchard in morning and Ted in walled garden in the afternoon.

2. Tiny Toads and Frogs emerging now from the pond. Hence the night time visits of the badgers that Brook has scented. No idea what Brook would actually do to a badger if confronted. Probably want to play with it... or chase it if it retreated. Somewhat exhausted. Be glad to get back to the beetles tomorrow.

Tuesday 7th May – TIMOTHY

Drop Tanushi an email reminding her I'd be in Cambridge this weekend – Saturday evening for a meet up? Maybe – if she was free – and had nothing else to do...could manage the Bath House for a meal? Only if she wasn't washing her hair etc.

No reply as yet. A bit soon probably.

Tuesday 7th May - TANUSHI

Email from Timothy about meeting up. Suppose I ought to make the effort.

Wednesday 8th May – TIMOTHY

No reply

Thursday 9th May – TIMOTHY

Reply: "Great – yes definitely meet up. Maybe lunch on Sat?" NO!! Lecturing – no can do.

Thursday 9th May - TANUSHI

Suggest we meet on Sat lunch. But he cannot do that. Lecturing. So going to have to give that a miss.

Thursday 9TH May – TIMOTHY

NOT going to meet. Another great weekend at the Ibis to look forward to.

Friday 10th May – TIMOTHY

Scoot down to Cambridge. Meal in hotel. Never quite get used to eating in public on my own. Research where to go Sat evening. Salisbury Arms – not too far. Text James in Christs if he wants to join me – free meal and drink. Turns out he's attending a conference in Berlin. Eating alone again.

Saturday 11th May

Lectured – a piece of cake. Very earnest foreign students from all over the world. Keen and compliant. Just reproducing first year stuff. Company produce all the notes.

Hotel and showered. Had booked table at 7.30 pm. Only 5 minutes away.

Saturday 11th May - TANUSHI

Going out with the usual. Pre's with Chloe down corridor. Sallies at 8.00 and then we'll see – was the plan. We all pile in just past 8.00. Shots ordered. Find a place to perch. A little riotous.

TIMOTHY – cont.

Busy but table reserved. Pint and fish and chips ordered. Have a Sudoku to keep me going whilst waiting for food to arrive. Students pile in. Exceedingly noisy. Food arrives. Decent tartare sauce – always a mark of good fish meal well made.

TANUSHI - cont.

So, Chloe has a habit of starting "odds on" – followed by dare. I fall at first fence and have to go over to the suit at the far table and declare my love. He has his back to us. Go across, kneel on ground beside him, look up as he is eating chips and IT'S TIMOTHY. Aaargh! So embarrassing.

TIMOTHY – cont.

Even more commotion from bar behind me – suddenly just beside me is kneeling female student – looks up – IT'S TANUSHI. My mouth filled with food. So embarrassing. She ends up giving me huge hug and apologising again and again. She's certainly very, very, merry. Drags me up and across to her friends. Introduces me. They all look so young – is my first thought – except Tanushi who just looks so good whatever. Try to smile. Or is it that I feel so old?

TANUSHI - cont.

Give him hug and apologise and drag him across. And he doesn't know what to do with himself – half way through a quiet meal and screaming girls are suddenly devouring him. Poor guy. He is very gracious and accepting and good-humoured. Escort him back and sit down with him. Explain it's Chloe's birthday and we'd arranged an evening out. What a coincidence. Turns out he's at Ibis which can't be more than 100 metres from me. He talks about his lecturing stuff. All money being ploughed into his house. I ask after his parents – he's a little non-committal. Mother is retiring – and Timothy's not really sure why. Too soon to sit in an arm chair. Father has been at a conference all week so not seen him.

And then he says, "I'm having a brandy – a double. Can I get you something?"

TIMOTHY – cont.

So, she then comes across and we talk as I finish meal. She seems to be really looking forward to coming to Derbyshire. She tells me all about her final practical – wallpaper in stately homes. The department have been very obliging in allowing her to pursue something which might have actual relevance to her future work.

I then offer to buy her a drink.

TANUSHI - cont.

I look across at the girls. Don't relish nursing Chloe home in a state of total inebriation. Clearing up the sick, getting her in to bed. Staying with her.

Done that too often. That's the past.

I say, "Thanks. I'll have a brandy too." Go to loo. Tell the girls that I am going to bail. No regrets.

TIMOTHY – cont.

This is not turning out how I had expected. Two brandies. And then two more. In the end we leave just after 9.15 pm. We exit into deliciously cool evening and rather than turn towards the station, we turn towards the centre (it just happened) and we cross Parker's Piece, along St Andrew's and we pass the Porter's Lodge at Christ's – and we look in and laugh and we keep walking to nowhere in particular.

And we keep talking. She tells her story of Sri Lanka, her Father and her family. Of her feeling the academic also-ran to her brother. How she loves art and that never really counted next to Chemistry which she hated. And that meant she turned her back on Medicine – the only respectable career. Or Physics which she hated and that meant saying goodbye to Engineering – the only other respectable career.

And we ended up at "Six" on the roof top cuddled under the blankets with two more brandies. Stars out. It was a moment of perfection I shall never forget.

TANUSHI – cont.

I don't quite know how this happened. We just talked and talked and he listened to me like few have ever listened to me and I thought we could have talked for ever. We ended up at "Six" on the roof terrace. And we cuddled the blankets to keep warm. And he spoke of his visits as a kid to Kirk Aeppel each Sunday evening in the summer. He'd play with his sister, climb Old Oak, and explore everywhere including the forbidden, abandoned swimming pool. He spoke of KA as a place he felt free and unencumbered; the place he belonged. And now he feels he is doing his dutiful best to build a career in the family firm. But it's hard starting out and, I sense, he is a bit lonely.

It was an enchanted evening. Something unexpected. He was the perfect gent. We walked back. He said really slowly and deliberately, "Thank you Tanushi – that was a totally, unexpectedly perfect evening which I will never forget. It was a gift." And I didn't know what to say except, "Yes it was." And then he turned to go back to his hotel.

Me and the suit? Not quite so boring after all.

TIMOTHY – cont.

And we walked back and I thanked her for the most perfect time and she nodded her head and we parted. And that was that.

Sunday 12th May

But what was that? Preoccupied all day including drive back. Happy if confused. How did that happen?

Sunday 12th May TANUSHI

Woke and struggled to believe what had happened had happened and what it meant – if anything. He is gentle and thoughtful and sensitive and listened to me and had a quiet, quick humour. And... and I am going to live near to him soon and so that's all for the future. I guess.

Sunday 12th May

1. Arranged to chat to Jimmy and Samantha. Met in orchard. All looking well – early days. And then to see the glamping area. Not my idea of fun. We've developed modern sanitation infrastructure for a reason. Sufficient space – showers all ready for installation. Likewise, loos. I advise separate fire/burner inside to outside. He had come to that conclusion. I will buy "fire pits" as they are called for outside areas.

2. Plum puddings growing. Just some concern re water. Considerable hassle at the moment. Solutions may be tied in to provision of glamping water. As happy as pigs should be. Jimmy has identified the lucky boar and arranged to purchase breeding sow.

3. Charles cancelled – too much catch up work to get through from week away. Reminded of timings for Friday. Now it's almost here I confess I am looking forward to the adventure – because Charles is in charge and I trust him. Unusually optimistic.

Monday 13th May - TANUSHI

Email from Timothy. "Thank you once again for those happy memories. I shall never forget them! A toast to creating some more in Derbyshire perhaps?"

Reply: "Cheers to that! August 3rd" xxx

Left it at that.

Monday 13th May – TIMOTHY

Can't concentrate. Send email to T. Responds quickly. Happy.

DIARY OF ISLAY 17/5/13 – 25/5/13

Friday 17th May

1. Dogs walked and handed over to Ted and Jane. Not sure how dogs will respond to my absence. Packed and ready to go for 10.00 am. Charles appropriately early. Set off.

2. I know nothing about cars. Not slightest bit interested. This car strikes me as being a superior car. Comfortable. Music on and only had to use blind fold on motorways. We go the scenic route up via Peak Forest to Stockport and then it was motorways all the way. Arrive at planned pub (White Bull) off M6 in good time for soup and bread. Ham and leek. Not at all bad.

3. Little village called Ribchester. Had time, so went to inspect Roman Baths and museum. Interesting.

4. Arrived in Carlisle for 6.15 pm. Had brought reading material. Decided to try a novel – it being a holiday. Dorothy has lent me a book called "The Name of the Rose" by Umberto Eco, an Italian academic. She says she thinks I will enjoy it. Cannot remember the last time I read a novel – disgraceful really.

5. Charles spent an inordinate time in the bathroom prior to going out to dinner. Meal was a dismal offering of stringy steak and damp chips.

Saturday 18th May

1. Plenty of time before the ferry. So, we travelled gently. Stopped here and there at a promising looking antique shop or church. Charles' planning meticulous.

2. Ferry and arrival at Port Ellen all went smoothly enough. Some choppiness and rain. Nothing of note except views were obscured. Tomorrow's weather set fair.

3. Arrived at the splendidly newly rebuilt Islay Hotel. Rooms magnificent. It turns out you can bring dogs here! Met a rather imperious Weimaraner and a skittish Dalmatian. Ribble would have been a good addition perhaps. Charles said not – we have distilleries to visit and they are no place for a dog. Lagavulin tomorrow afternoon. Start at the top!

4. Receiving dog updates from Jane as arranged. All well.

Sunday 19th May

1. I have to set this down carefully. This has been amongst the most troubling days of my life. Even now trying to understand everything. I can hardly set it down in writing.

2. We were taking a walk in the morning – along the sea front. Charles told me to sit down next to him. Said he had something to say. He confessed that he had been less than honest with me over the previous few months. The fact is he was ill – very ill. He said he was going to die. "We're all going to die old chap." "I am going to die quite soon. A matter of months or maybe a year or slightly more. They don't know exactly."

3. He then spelt out all the grim details about his illness. He'd had an op a couple of weeks ago to allow the liver to function for a little longer. Buy him time. It had gone well. He's going to have chemo after our return again to try to delay that which will happen. He hadn't told his children. Of course, Beatrice knows – part of the reason she is retiring. To be with him for the last period of time. However long. Or short.

4. I have nothing to say. It seems futile to try to argue him out of his resignation. I ask a question or two. Why hadn't he told me before? When had he found out?

5. It is stage 4 bowel cancer and it has spread.

6. He urged me to enjoy this last holiday with him. It was why he wanted me to come now whilst he was well enough. So that together we could enjoy the place, its whisky and each other's company.

7. Devastated. Understand the reasoning that there will be a time to mourn and it is not now.

8. Visit Lagavulin.

Monday 20th May

1. Inevitably you begin to live the time when he won't be there. But he doesn't want this. He wants to live this day right now without any reference to the future. That sounds like the Gospel message. "Take therefore no thought for the morrow: for the morrow shall take thought for the things of itself. Sufficient unto the day is the evil thereof." Like all dogs – of course. As always. Live the day. Try to implement this.

2. Visit Laphroaig.

Tuesday 21st May

1. Stunning weather. Stunning vistas. Charles says he is glad he was alive to experience this.

2. Visit Bowmore.

3. Decent evening meal. Retreat to guest sitting room to avoid live music.

Wednesday 22nd May

1. Lots of discussion of what exactly we shall take back with us in terms of whisky. The hotel has the most expansive collection to sample – for money. So, we are trying to make informed choices.

2. Visit Bruichladdich.

3. Eating far too much but enjoying myself. Such a huge choice for breakfast.

4. Sleeping well and no problem with plates. This is striking.

Thursday 23rd May

1. Charles thanks me several times for allowing him to enjoy everything. For living without the shadow for a few days.

2. Each night I pray before getting into bed. How do I pray? For a miracle? For a good death? For each day lived? For all of this? Can God reverse this inevitability? Or is he constrained by the intractable nature of nature and thus not really God at all. Need Dorothy.

3. Visit Bunnahabhain and Caol Ila.

4. Dogs well.

Friday 24th May

1. Finalise and execute purchases. Reminded that my Sunday evenings will be changing...

2. Visit Ardbeg.

3. Final meal – at the hotel. Had something of an end of term feel – thoughts of home, returning to Kirk Aeppel and fond memories of a week well spent with my friend.

Saturday 25th May

1. Slept badly. Plates. It is over. This 30-year planned jaunt.

2. Travel back – arrive back 8.00pm

3. Dogs in splendid form. Good to be back.

Sunday 26th May

1. Communion. Jaded but it was good to see Dorothy.

2. Write to Charles – settling up the finances and thanking him for absolutely everything and promising whatever help he is going to need. Chemo starts tomorrow. I say, "I stand by you." I don't know what that means but it is the only thing I can think to say that expresses my fellow feeling and hope to support him.

3. He is going to tell Timothy today and Hannah after her exams on Friday.

4. Apart from the gloom that descends, I am quite proud of myself. I have managed to cope with a whole week away from everything here.

5. Arrange proper "catch-up" (as people say) with Dorothy. Dorothy already knows about Charles apparently. Of course, she does.

6. Seems there was some dreadful atrocity whilst we were away. A young soldier murdered in London. Islamic terrorists. I can't think how dreadful it must be for ordinary, law abiding Muslims each time something like this happens in the name of their religion.

Tuesday 28th May - TANUSHI

Practical done. Really pleased with the results and what I have learnt. That's what education should be like. Just as I'm leaving education, I feel like I'm ready to start real education properly. Ten days, three exams and that's it. Haven't heard from Timothy. Sam has emailed to ask if she can come down after exams are over. Last bit of her half term. Yes! Yes! She's going to travel down with HH who has some do on re beetles!

Wednesday 29th May

1. Have lunch with Dorothy. The compulsory hug seemed to be unusually long and intense today – and I didn't mind overmuch.

2. I told her all about Islay.

3. She said she'd been round to walk the dogs with Jane and Ted on a couple of occasions.

4. Then she said what she'd done about "our" visit to Cambridge. Since when "our"? And she laughed – "Oh I'm sure you invited me to help with Ribble. Didn't you?" She had reserved two single rooms in a pub outside of Cambridge. Happy to take a dog. She will drive me down and come for the "do" of course. And Sam would like a lift down because she's going to meet up with Tanushi. And she can't wait! Can she confirm the rooms?

5. As is often the case, I am somewhat breath-taken by Dorothy.

6. Also, she's got a "Good Luck" card for Tanushi for us all to sign.

7. And then we discussed Charles. Well in truth we didn't discuss Charles just the minutiae of his treatment and what might be expected. And we discussed ourselves and our responses. And I asked her how to pray for him... and she said that she too was at a loss but asking for God's good will to be done in him and through him and with the family. I tried to pin her down on whether she believed God might save him? She said she believed that God can do anything. To pray for him to be well is an expression of our love for him and therefore good in itself. And she quoted someone or other: suffering colours our lives – but we get to choose the colours. In the Christian tradition, suffering is always seen as something potentially redemptive. Difficult. No one understands of course – but that's not the end purpose of faith. Any relationship ultimately was not about being intellectually understood but about being known and held.

8. We end up walking to the chapel and lighting a candle and she said a prayer and we parted. And I walked up to the orchard to take some comfort in the trees – in full blossom – looking resplendent.

JUNE
2013

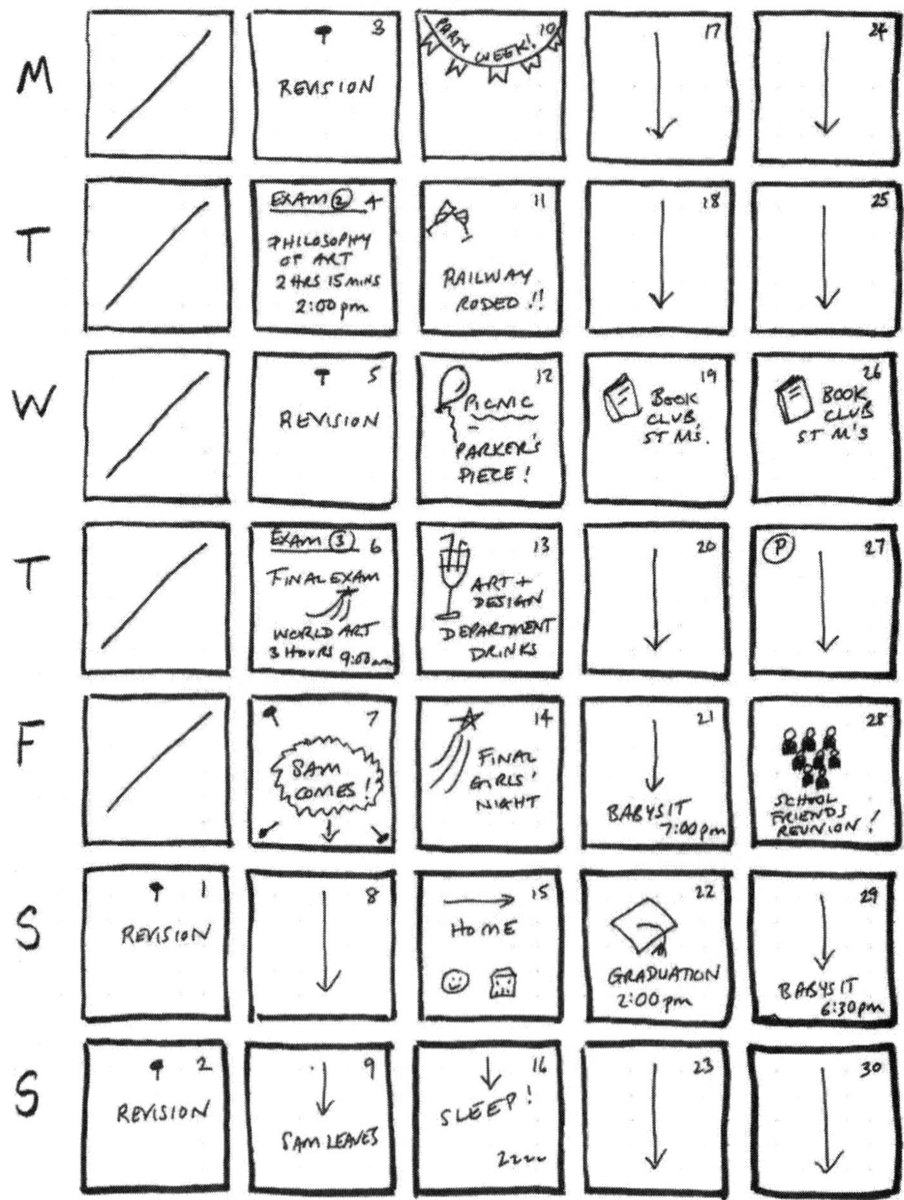
M
T
W
T
F
S
S
1
REVISION
2
REVISION
3
REVISION
EXAM 2 4
PHILOSOPHY OF ART
2 HRS 15 MINS
2:00 pm
5
REVISION
EXAM 3 6
FINAL EXAM
WORLD ART
3 HOURS 9:00 am
7
SAM COMES!
8
9
SAM LEAVES
PARTY WEEK! 10
11
RAILWAY RODEO!!
12
PICNIC
PARKER'S PIECE!
13
ART + DESIGN
DEPARTMENT DRINKS
14
FINAL GIRLS' NIGHT
15
HOME
16
SLEEP!
Zzzz
17
18
19
BOOK CLUB, ST M'S.
20
21
BABYSIT
7:00 pm
22
GRADUATION
2:00 pm
23
24
25
26
BOOK CLUB
ST M'S
P
27
28
SCHOOL FRIENDS REUNION!
29
BABYSIT
6:30 pm
30

Saturday 1st June - TANUSHI

Got a card signed by everyone at KA. So nice. Even included a tiny cartoon of each dog – that's done by Sam! Henry signed himself "Henry Havard." Very formal!

Sunday 2nd June

1. Communion. Dorothy working her way through some Iona liturgy – Celtic inspired spirituality. Interesting.

2. Charles arrived in perfect form. No effects thus far. He says it normally takes time. Each person is different. And that's all he intends to say on the matter. We talk mainly about Islay and the distilleries – all very different and fascinating in their own way.

3. Decide on a Dalwhinnie. A real favourite of both. (We allow it to count as a Speyside based on water source – though maybe a Highland?)

4. Then Charles spoke of telling Timothy a week ago and Hannah just two days ago. Hannah in a fair old state; wanted to return immediately but has to wait for the end of term. He will collect her with Timothy on Wednesday. Timothy quiet. Tearful. Resentful at not being told earlier. Wanted to know the details.

5. How hard it has been for Charles – having to deal with his own concerns and anxieties and juggle the anxieties and fears of others. I resolve not to add my own concerns to his burdens. Play everything with a straight bat – which is good advice in most situations I find.

6. Discuss Cambridge visit with Charles. He is most interested in the accommodation in the pub of all things. I assure him it is two single rooms. "According to Dorothy," he whispers with a smile. An inappropriate comment I suggest and he smiles some more. I say, "She's a woman of the cloth!" "Exactly."

Thursday 6th June - TANUSHI

It is finished!! All done – the last exam I will ever take. They were OK – I feel I did my best. Constant reassurance required for Amma – daily updates. Now I am going to have a Gin and tidy the room for Sam's arrival tomorrow. So glad to have finished. Receive message from Timothy saying well done and enjoy the celebrations.

Thursday 6th June

1. The order of proceedings is that I am being shown around the Dept. of Zoology at 4.00 pm and then after a brief break it's on to Jesus College at 6.00 pm – canapes (whatever they are – food Dorothy tells me) and drinks in the Fellows' Garden. Just have to get to Downing Street and they will take care of the rest. Nervous.

Friday 7th June.

1. Dorothy on time. 10.00 am. Ribble packed in. This is a less superior car to Charles'. A smooth enough journey.

2. Eat a light lunch in our pub. Too anxious to eat very much. Regret that later.

3. Downing Street at 3.30 pm. Met by Richard Cawthorne – who has sent me the trays of beetles through the years, whom I have emailed often enough and exchanged regular pleasantries. Delightful to meet him once again after so many years. 30? This is all his idea. Meant well. Such an entomologist through and through. As am I. Splendid.

4. Escorted throughout by Dorothy and Ribble. Both help in equal measure.

5. Shown around. Academia at its most avaricious. A real emphasis on recording and addressing climate change, habitat destruction etc. Quite right too – impressive. Met several of the current PhD students keen to explain their area of interest. And several showed high respect to my work too which was unexpected.

6. And then on to Jesus. It is profoundly strange to go back to somewhere you once utterly belonged and to find oneself a stranger amongst such familiar stones. At the entrance to our 'first year' stairs I suddenly missed Charles greatly. Turned to Dorothy. "This is where Charles and I..." and she steadied me.

7. Already by this stage grateful for the focus to be on Ribble who took all in her stride - naturally. And equally irritated by introducing Dorothy as my friend and having her then re-introduced variously as my girlfriend, partner and even wife on one occasion. Dorothy not at all phased and enjoyed the confusion greatly. "Wife!" she declared, "Promotion at last!"

8. To call canapes food is somewhat of an exaggeration. I was hungry and drinking only fizzy white wine which was (I have to say) surprisingly drinkable.

9. Speech. The Master welcomed all and sundry from the world of entomology, old friends and younger colleagues. Here to "honour" Henry Havard etc. Tirelessly toiling to extend beetle classification, to document their range, their size and set a benchmark by which the changing world might be measured.

10. And then he said something which I had not expected. He turned directly to me. "Henry – you represent an old and noble tradition of the amateur gentleman scientist. The roots of Science in this country very much rest upon this tradition. There are not many left. On behalf of the Zoology Department, Jesus College and Cambridge University we would be delighted if you would accept an honorary doctorate as a mark of our esteem for your dedicated work in the field of Coleopterology." Everyone in rapturous applause including Dorothy. Ribble barked. Laughter. I had no idea what to say except, "Yes – what an honour indeed." I am told by Dorothy that my eyes moistened a little.

11. And then it was over. I spluttered my thanks to the Master, to Richard of course and to the various Zoology fellows. More drinks. We returned to the pub by 9.00 pm.

12. No food available. Too late. But Dorothy had some pizzas delivered to her room unbeknown, she said, to the landlord. Ribble in my room. I perch on the bed and Dorothy in the chair. A celebratory pizza she said and she had even brought some whisky in a hip flask. Astonished at her perspicacity.

13. She said how pleased she is for me that some recognition had come my way for all the work I have done and she wants to know how to address me once the doctorate is conferred. I knew she was teasing me. I smiled and said, in faltering words, how much I had appreciated her being there but not as my wife. She smiled and reached across to clutch my hand and proposed a toast.

14. Then she said, "Henry, it is time for bed." Once again, she extended her hand to help me off her bed. She led me to the door, gave me the signal for a hug – arms outstretched; she hugged me and said how precious it had been to be with me today. She spun me round and smacked my backside to send me off – and the last thing I heard is her laughter. She used the word "precious" – definitely.

    What irony that Cambridge should bestow a doctorate upon me. Mother had forbidden me from continuing at Cambridge after my Nat Sci degree. I was needed back at the estate and under no circumstances was I to contemplate further time wasted in academia. A PhD was offered. Might things have been different? Helen still had a couple of years of veterinary left to do. She had encouraged me to stay. We even looked at a house share.

Friday 7th June - TANUSHI

Meet Sam outside Fitzbillies at 3.00ish. We wander through the centre and out towards Mill Rd. Sam just wants to hang out – not to do anything in particular. So, we peek in at various Colleges along the way. First, we stop for coffee at Benets. Weave in and out of the stalls in the market. We go into Christs so that I can introduce her to Tavesh. Tavesh curiously rather awkward. Tell her the story of the interview with Timothy. Show her the room and the chair where I slept! Eyes wide open – she can't believe it. Show her a picture of my dress! Sam is like a sister I never had – honestly. I think I can tell Sam anything.

And we end up back at the Railyard. Crash and then we make dinner together. And in the general merriment of my 4th glass of wine and without having pre-meditated this – I say, "Can I tell you a secret? A really secret secret? You mustn't tell anyone." And she nods her head and I tell her about becoming a surrogate for Henry and that my child will be the heir. And she is totally disgusted by the thought – and I say it's not sex – and she says even so – and I say no it'll be fine – it's just a donated sample from Henry – not sex – and she says I don't know how you can even think of doing that – and I say you mustn't tell anyone – not Jimmy – not anybody – and she says she won't – and then we're quiet. And then she says, "Henry Havard!" And she laughs hysterically and I laugh too. And then we're OK again.

Saturday 8th June

1. Woke with Ribble's nose in my face asking to go out. Take her out hastily. Shower – modern showers are a revelation to me after KA. One of the best things about the Islay hotel. Sit on bed and try to reconstruct the previous day. What a day. And left with strange and unidentifiable thoughts.

2. A feeble breakfast – Dorothy keen to set off and I comply. We are quiet though amiable in the car. Just as she has delivered me home, I say thank you one more time and she says, "Henry – stop saying thank you! I know it's nice to say thank you, but when I do something for you, it's not a favour; it's because I (and then she hesitated) I like you." And then she was off before I had time to work out what to say in return.

3. Dogs happy with our reunion.

Kibble - Giant Schnauzer

Saturday 8th June - TANUSHI

We had the best time today. Lazy rise. Brunch at 11ish. And we wandered into town and she asked about punting. So that's what we did with a group of Chinese tourists. Started at Silver Street. We didn't listen too carefully to the punter chap in his striped blazer. But we did admire his physical skill with the pole. And we traded innuendo in between his learned commentary and giggled.

And then we just sauntered and shopped, enjoying the sunshine, eating Portuguese pasteis de nata from the market just because we could. And we ended up on Parker's Piece with a Wagamama's takeaway and a bottle of wine. And then the day was over.

Sunday 9th June

Sam left early by train. Less than two months to go now!

Sunday 9th June

1. Still feeling somewhat shell-shocked by the whole thing. A little proud I suppose, overwhelmed maybe. Happy memories. To be honoured in such a way.

2. Charles determined to finish the Macallan – and I now understand why. A passing reference to how he is feeling and then on to other things. Timothy brings and collects him.

3. Of course, he is keen to hear all about Cambridge. He too enjoys the story and congratulates me.

4. And again, he presses about the precise nature of what is going on between Dorothy and me. He said he worries that she will want something – a physical relationship – which I am unprepared to offer. Again, I do not know how to answer except to acknowledge his concern. Then he said something which made me think. "Be wary of classifying yourself fixedly. It's not like beetle classification – once done, it's done and can't be altered." (About to interrupt to say it's not quite as easy as that but don't get the chance.) "People change. People can change if they want to change. People change when they're not looking to change. Even you have changed over the years. Even you Henry."

5. I protested vehemently and he smiled and said, "There was a time you didn't like Talisker (Ed: a whisky) and you do now. Too peppery you used to say." He had, with one swift and unanswerable example, skewered me. "People can change in all manner of fundamental ways. Remember Archie? Chap who did ASNAC? (Ed: Anglo-Saxon, Norse and Celtic course at Cambridge) Married for 25 years, had kids, did the whole heterosexual thing – went off with Nigel from work. In a civil partnership now." I do remember Archie. Nice chap with an odd dress sense – but then he did do ASNAC.

6. Redemption – change – is part of the Christian narrative.

7. He concluded by saying something eminently reasonable and completely impossible. "Why don't you talk to her?"

Monday 10th June

1. I have been so taken up with Cambridge that I have neglected to do some planning for the next couple of months before Tanushi arrives.

2. A welcome return to regular and steady habits. No more gallivanting. So, unlike me. I shall content myself with pigs, dogs and the orchard; with Charles of course; with the farm inasmuch as I can help Samantha and Jimmy; with the usual routines and rituals which are part of the countryside; with Dorothy.

3. Ted and Jane have told me their dates for their Scarborough two weeks – Saturday 20th July – Saturday 3rd August.

4. Saturday 3rd August – Tanushi.

Monday 10th June - TANUSHI

Party week and then Amma collects both of us. Graduation in the Corn Exchange October 14-17. They will confirm when. For now, I am in a liminal space (thank you Luce Irigaray!) betwixt two worlds, two realities. Best not get lost.

Friday 14th June

1. Jimmy has arranged for the pigs to be slaughtered over the period of a week. He'll take them there two at a time – very small slaughter house at the back of the butchers in Holloway. First pair go today, then Monday, then Wednesday. He's already bought in the breeding sow for the new litter. They've done well now he's sorted the water supply. Compliant. Put my order in for half a pig with usual bacon / sausages / joints etc. Jane happy with that. So, Jimmy will have the Sandy and Black boar and sow and the two Magalistas. They do chew up the land but Jimmy assures me it will be rotated and have chance to recuperate.

2. Dorothy is to be away next week and so she popped round for an evening meal. She is taking her Mother on holiday to their traditional haunt in Dorset near to Swanage. She does not find her Mother an easy woman. She has to gird her loins. Which strikes me as a shame because it is her holiday which she should enjoy. She said she will retreat into her reading. And she asked me how I had got along with

"The Name of the Rose" which she had lent me. Had to confess I hadn't opened it. But promised to do so when she is away. She laughed.

3. Then Dorothy did that most dreaded thing – suggested we have a conversation about "US".

   "Can't be avoided Henry. You know that in your heart." (I had always doubted I had a heart except for strictly circulatory reasons. Think but do not say that. A cheap reductionist joke.) She said that she did want what I had said was impossible – a more romantic/physical relationship.

   I said, having thought about what Charles had had to say, "I think people might be able to change and that maybe I am in a place to possibly want to change – perhaps."

   She said gently, "Could you put more qualifiers in that sentence Henry?" "The qualifiers are in because," at this point and for the first time I looked at her directly, "I am afraid and I am unsure and I am feeling like a little boy who has no control over anything and I have been there before and I didn't like it."

   There was a long silence.

   And then I noticed a tear fall from her face. It made a little mark on her red dress where it landed.

   She said, "Henry, the truth is that we're all in that place a little bit. I am too. Maybe it doesn't seem like that to you and maybe it's not to the extent that you feel this. But I am too. I don't want to get hurt. I don't want NOT to be in control. But..."

   The sentence was not finished. She got up and wiped her face. "Thank you, Henry. For being honest with me. That took some courage. I will take you at your word – that you will read that book whilst I am away – to demonstrate that change is possible in all of us." With that she smiled, hugged me and said she'd email me through the week.

   Exhausted.

Monday 17th June

1. Invited down to Sarah and Andrew who wanted to talk dogs. They are to visit litter and choose a puppy this week. They wanted advice: a) gender b) how to select from amongst 7 adorable puppies. So, I talked through the dog / bitch issue. I think they will request a bitch. Difficult to advise re which pup. Be

guided by the breeder. Say you are first time owners. Watch for dominant dog, runt if there is one, who is wilful, who is calm and responsive etc. They were decidedly pleasant. Sarah had made an elderflower cordial. Good show. They had heard about the honorary doctorate and were very impressed. They asked after Dorothy. (Folk are starting to ask me how she is...)

2. Already heard twice from Dorothy. She is bearing up and balancing one cream tea a day with one swim in the sea. They are in some shared property scheme her Mother owns and it all sounds acceptable. She asks me how the book is going.

3. I am allocating one hour a day to the book – after walk and breakfast and finding it rather fascinating. What a scholar! Remarkable detail about medieval life and religion. A whodunit in a monastery.

Friday 21st June

1. I have enjoyed Dorothy's emails which have become more and more amusing as her Mother has become more and more unreasonable in her demands – to be waited on hand and foot. Insufferable I sense. We spoke this evening and she invited herself round for Sunday lunch. Whilst this will not be said, I have been missing Dorothy more than I expected. Or perhaps I should say it...

2. Jimmy is employing me to assist in the orchard which I am happy to do. Follow instructions. He has handed on the pork to Jane. Looking forward to Sunday lunch.

3. Summer Solstice 6.04 – Highland and Lowland.

Sunday 23rd June - TANUSHI

Bored with Harrow and with waiting and with stepping on toes.

Sunday 23rd June

1. Pork was magnificent and enough for sandwiches through much of the week even after Dorothy agreed to take a slice or two.

2. I was able to say how marvellous "The Name of the Rose" was. Enthralling plot, theologically gripping, beautifully painted scenes, bizarre characters and stupendous eye for detail. "So Henry, change is possible. Here you are reading and enjoying a novel."

3. She then filled me in on the details not communicated by email. Her Mother is one of those most bizarre women – she is a strong character who has organised and run all sorts of things and yet insists that men are the real leaders who should be followed. She does not approve of women vicars which has been and is a little problematic in their relationship. And she insists that things are done, food is done, the car is driven according to the ways she has always expected. "Your Father would never have accepted that!"

4. Charles arrived looking wobbly. Timothy stayed. We resumed a bottle of rather rare Jura. Just for a drams-worth. Again, he refused to discuss illness. So, I chatted away until he'd had enough.

Monday 24th June

1. Pup to arrive on Friday. Bitch – to be called Imogen – after the WW2 minesweeper Andrew's Father served on briefly. Invited me for late afternoon Friday. Delighted.

2. Cold nights still and bright days. Should discourage some of the bugs in the orchard.

Friday 28th June

1. Samantha has taken the first booking for the Yurts! School Holidays for one week. It's a start and a real testament to their hard work. However still some work to do to be fully ready.

2. The new apple / pear trees are alive thus far. A couple look a bit reluctant. Otherwise healthy.

3. Eager to see new puppy. Left dogs behind of course – only first set of jabs as yet. Delightfully oversized paws. Both wide eyed and sleepy when I was there. Keen to leave quickly therefore. Discussion on food. So much different advice on line about these matters. You get the raw food fundamentalists yapping on. The breeder has sent them home with a couple of bags of kibble. I advise a particular website which grades all the foods. I have now switched to "Cold-pressed food." Discussion on toilet training. They seem to have their heads screwed on. I don't think they will treat Imogen as if she is a human being like so many seem to do with their dogs. Treat them as sentient obviously but not as having human sentience – far more advanced I suspect.

Sunday 30th June

1. The summer is shaping up nicely. Communion and breakfast. Joined by Dorothy and by Andrew. Sarah minding Imogen. Warm enough to venture into walled garden. Andrew in raptures. Particularly struck by Old Oak.

2. Dorothy mentions on leaving that she's coming round on Wednesday – her day off – with all ingredients for the evening meal. Excellent.

3. Pop into the farm on the way back from walk. Samantha asks advice about the "goodie" package for guests (now two families for first week and more beyond that). Some cider and selection of local goods not exceeding £15.00 is my advice. Start with good reviews. Would she like me to get some dry wood and stack near to fire pits? Affirmative. What about local tourist advice / recommendations? All taken care of already.

4. Beatrice calls. Charles not coming. Not up to it – but she will call round.

5. Beatrice just wanted to talk to me about Charles and his prognosis. It's all pretty grim. If he can complete this chemo round, it might buy him a year or so. She looked a bit sad and sorry – of course. Couldn't wait to finish school in two weeks. Lots of farewell do's for her. Governors, Staff, Parents etc. She's been there 17 years. But needs to be at home now for Charles.

6. What can one say? It turns out she didn't really want me to say anything. Just to listen – which is something I can do pretty well.

7. Egypt in chaos.

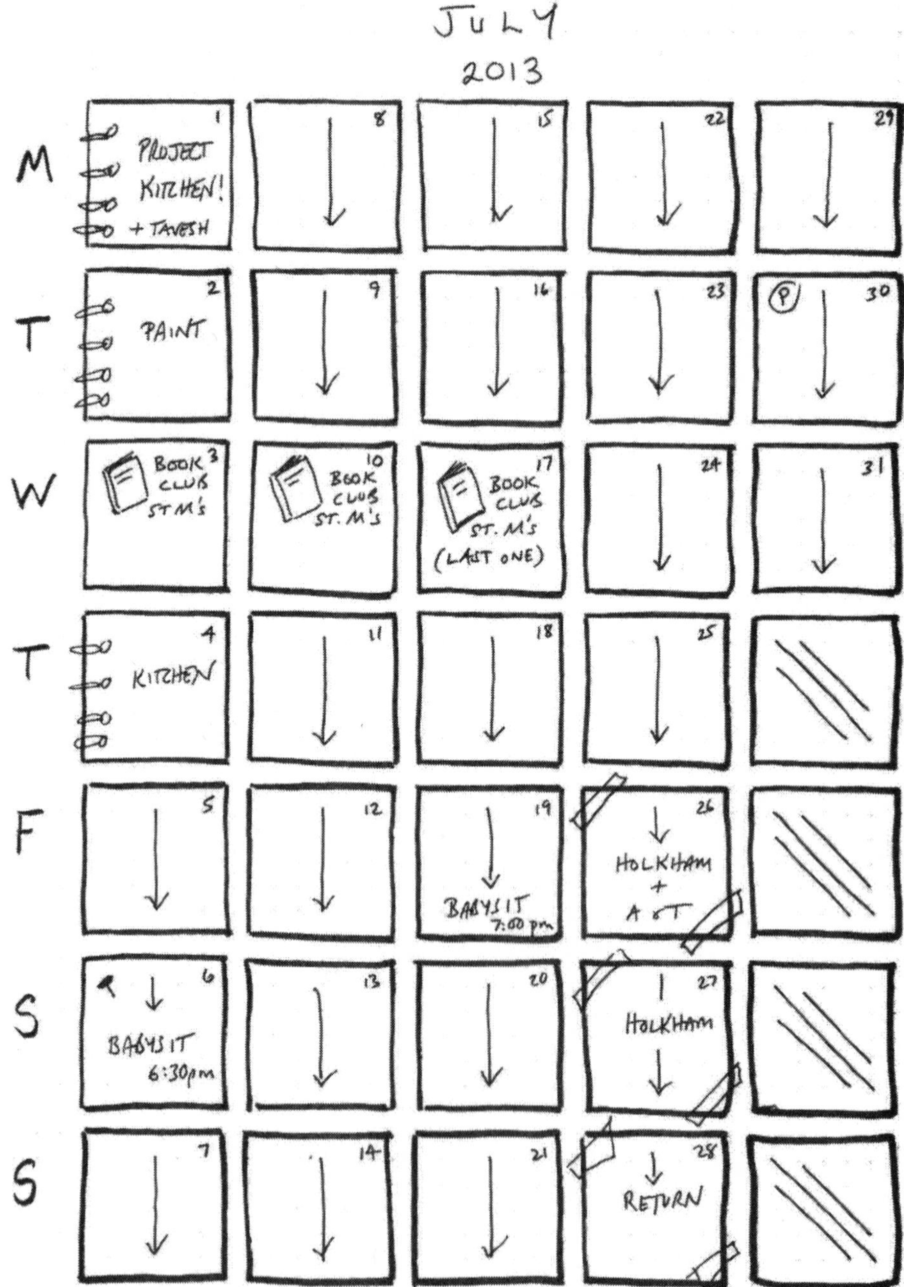
JULY
2013
M
T
W
T
F
S
S
1
PROJECT
KITCHEN!
+ TAVESH
8
15
22
29
2
PAINT
9
16
23
P
30
3
BOOK
CLUB
ST M's
10
BOOK
CLUB
ST. M's
17
BOOK
CLUB
ST. M's
(LAST ONE)
24
31
4
KITCHEN
11
18
25
5
12
19
BABYSIT
7:00 pm
26
HOLKHAM
+
A & T
6
BABYSIT
6:30pm
13
20
27
HOLKHAM
7
14
21
28
RETURN

Wednesday 3rd July

1. When working on the beetles today, I had a vivid recollection of returning home from school one Easter.

   It was just before O' Levels – 1976. So, I would have been 16. Mother had sent Ted down to collect me from school. When I returned, she was off on one of her Horse weekends – dressed up for some competition or other. Staying in the horse van. Getting tiddly until late in the evening. The only place she ever drank. She never drank at Kirk Aeppel. She hated the association of alcoholic dissipation that had characterised the first 20 or so years of her time there with Father. I had dinner with her once that holiday and then bumped into her at the farm as she was grooming her horse in the stables. And Ted then returned me to school. That was a new nadir in our relationship. She couldn't abide me, my company, my interests (in science and nature) which she thought weird and unhealthy – "like your f***** father" – not that anyone could describe him as having intellectual interests but he had studied Science at University. After his death, she always referred to him with the "F" word before saying his name. It was eventually something Kafka-esque that I should nurse her in her final year and she should soften towards me...

2. What an evening! Dorothy had gone to town on the ingredients. Duck breasts with a Chinese sauce called hoisin, dauphinoise pots, various veg. And a cracking pudding – ginger and banana something or other. I supplied Stilton + biscuits, sherry / wine / port. What a splendid spread. We ate the two main courses in the walled garden and the cheese course we took upstairs and ate on our laps on the settee. With port. Marvellous. I am afraid Dorothy is not for enjoying whisky – actually that maybe for the best.

3. Then, when the debris was cleared, she held out her upturned hand and beckoned me to put mine there... which I did. And she said she wanted to tell me the story of her second major and final broken relationship four years previously and she wanted me to hold her hand as she told this story. She told her story. And she said there was every temptation for her to a hold a deep grudge at the behaviour of the cad (and there was), nevertheless, she had decided – not to do that – and in trepidation – to start again – with me – maybe. And then she transferred my hand to her face and as she did that and I cradled her cheek, I burst into tears.

4. I have absolutely no idea why I did that. Deeply embarrassing. Blubbing quite so pathetically. I apologised profusely. And she just laughed, leant across and planted her lips on mine in what you might describe as a big smacker. (The second time I have been kissed.) And she laughed some more. She said, wiping the tears of laughter away, "You old sausage!" And then she declared, "Henry, we are now

at Stage 2: "hand holding in private". I trust you are happy with that." It wasn't quite a question. I asked what Stage 1 had been. She said it had been hugging on greeting and farewell. She did not clarify: firstly, how many stages there were and secondly what Stage 3 might be. But grateful for a little structure nevertheless.

5. It was clear that Dorothy had had far too much to drink to drive home. So, a dilemma was presented. Taxi – v. expensive. Plus, not convinced we'd get one to come this far out at this time. Jimmy?

6. Meanwhile she had worked out the plan. She would curl up on the settee with Twyi and a blanket and she ushered me off to bed. Most irregular – Quite an evening.

Thursday 4th July

1. Dorothy had gone before I woke.

2. Can't help feeling embarrassed and stupid about my behaviour last night. This mood coloured the rather grey and dismal walk up Biggle.

3. Collected and deposited wood for Yurts. Something useful achieved.

4. Dorothy sent me an indecipherable message. I have a pay-as-you-go non internet simple phone / text type of mobile – which is totally sufficient. Everybody else seems to be getting internet phones. So, when Dorothy sends me a message with lots of pictures or cartoon characters or whatever they're called, it just becomes gobbledygook. Which is irritating. I then send back, "This makes no sense." And I don't hear anything back.

Friday 5th July

1. Andy Murray through to the final. My goodness me – that would be something if he could win Wimbledon. The whole nation going bonkers.

Sunday 7th July

1. Suggest by text that we should pray for Andy Murray at the early communion. Dorothy makes a quip about this. At breakfast Andrew invites Dorothy and I to come down to watch the final with them. All agreed. Good time to see Imogen too.

2. A simply splendid win – three sets – the last game agonising. How marvellous for Andy. Deserves everything. Learn something about Dorothy – she likes her tennis.

3. Imogen does not quite know what is going on. Growing rapidly. Putting on muscle. Developing that classic Clumber soft as butter dopey look.

4. There aren't many significant sporting achievements now that Brits haven't now achieved in my lifetime. Amazing.

5. No show from Charles. It's all a bit grim according to Beatrice. Can I call round sometime? Yes absolutely. She will liaise with Dorothy. Timing is everything.

Monday 8th July

1. Something of a heatwave at the moment. I suggest watering the orchard but Jimmy insists we hold off for another week or so. All is ready for the first glamping guests. The Sandy and Blacks are particularly good in sunshine – don't get sunburnt as a rule. But there are places they can retreat to out of the direct sun. The Magalistas carry around a permanent mud pack enmeshed in their wool – so they cope too. Funny creatures.

2. Dorothy suggests she books a tennis court in Matlock Park and we go play doubles with Andrew and Sarah. This seems a fantastically bad idea. Firstly, I cannot play tennis. Secondly Dorothy, I suspect, can and clearly likes to win. And Andrew and Sarah will be nothing if not fit and athletic. I am not going to come out well in any scenario.

3. The court is now booked for Wednesday...

Wednesday 10th July

1. Well tennis was played – mainly by Dorothy. Andrew and Sarah fit though they undoubtedly are, were no more coordinated than me when it comes to hitting a tennis ball in a vaguely appropriate direction.

2. Must have been 30 degrees C. Frequent drinks required. We only got through one set in the hour.

3. Back to Kirk Aeppel – Jane had prepared a little spread and she and Ted joined us for a late tea / early evening drinks in the walled garden. Jane asking after Tanushi. And have we heard anything recently. Only heard from Samantha after her weekend in Cambridge. But will be in touch to finalise arrival details. Just over 3 weeks.

Friday 12th July

1. Shoulder still aching.

2. Call from Dorothy. We are to visit Charles today. So downed tools and made ready.

3. One cannot be made ready… to see a dear friend of 33 years looking quite so poorly. And the agonising spectacle of him trying to put a brave face on everything – which is what a gentleman should do – but it was unconvincing. What if the cure is worse than the disease?

4. He tired quickly. Dorothy had brought bread and wine and we had the shortest of communions. We left him to sleep.

5. This is Beatrice's final teaching day. And she is coming home to her man in such a state. It is sad beyond all telling.

6. Dorothy dropped me back. Got out of the car and hugged me tightly. "We must seize life, Henry."

Monday 15th July

1. Jimmy agrees to watering orchard.

2. I receive updates of first glampers – all well so far. A little more traffic but nothing untoward. They were very interested to visit the pigs. Molly – plum pudding sow – is well into the 3 month, 3 week and 3 day gestation period. That raised interesting questions for parents. Keen to meet the dogs too. So, all that arranged. Family of 4. Children about 6 - 8 I would guess. Little girl fell in love with Tiff. Wanted him to stay with her in the Yurt. Or to take him home with her perhaps. Little boy fixed on Brook. I suppose these urban types often don't

experience interaction with and the healing of animals in their lives. Too busy. Too preoccupied. Too unimportant to them. Too difficult. Screens matter more.

3. So grateful to live here. Once again, I am reminded of that.

Wednesday 17th July

1. Preparations for Ted and Jane's holiday in full swing. I have instructions for Ted re walled garden and from Jane re meals prepared etc. They have been to the same B ad B in Scarborough for 25 years or more. "Tall Storeys". I write the cheque. It's part of their overall remuneration package. They consider themselves part of the family there now.

2. Dorothy visits in the afternoon to help water the orchard. And clearly, she had evil intent from the start. Suffice to say a change of clothes required. Less easy for her. I lent her an old and battered shirt in which she looked remarkably fetching. And I say so, in a ham-fisted sort of way, which she mocks. "Oh, you fancy the peasant girl in her rough clothes. Well don't be getting ideas Mr Lord of the manor – Mr High and Mighty. Us peasant girls know our rights these days."

3. I do find her – at times like these – remarkably beguiling.

Saturday 20th July

1. Have now finalised arrangements re Tanushi's arrival. She is bringing as much as possible by train to Derby. Jimmy to meet her there. Mother might supplement at some stage.

2. Ted and Jane set off to Scarborough. Ted can't bear to leave the walled garden and Old Oak – his constant companion.

3. I have the house to myself now – all day and every day. Still I have to keep on top of things otherwise I will be in trouble! And there's still the dogs and the beetles and the orchard. Beetles take a back seat in the summer.

4. Hot weather continues. First reviews of glampers are encouraging. Samantha says something about Trip Advancer – a website. Tremendously important apparently. Anyway, they are both happy and getting ready for the next guests. I suppose if you don't enjoy a glamping experience in this weather, there's no hope for you. You chose wrong.

5. No wood used. Perhaps they've never lit a fire before – bless'em. Maybe we should leave instructions? Imagine never to have looked into a real fire and seen eternity at play.

6. Dorothy popped by on her way back from a wedding. She will come round on Wednesday for her lunchtime meal – I'm cooking.

Monday 22nd July

1. Succession assured. Prince George born.

Tuesday 23rd July - TANUSHI

All arrangements made now for Saturday 3rd. Amma knows how desperate I am to get going. And she understands. I guess it might break her heart a little to see her daughter fly the nest. She coped when I left for uni. though – I think. She never said anything. But Tavesh was still around then. And he never said otherwise.

Decide to teach her how to use Skype and we practice. And I say on our first call from bedroom to living room: Thank you Amma for everything. For setting me free and allowing me to follow this dream. I love you. And she said: I'll be coming to see you Nushi. This mustn't be seen as an end – and I'll be sending you eligible Tamil boys as and when I come across them. I think she was joking. Also decide to buy some robust walking boots which will be my work boots. Research extensively.

Wednesday 24th July – TIMOTHY

I have not written for a while. Life seems suddenly very busy and very bleak. And I don't know what to do with all that except to keep working very hard. There seems no immediate relief. I hate seeing Dad in that state. It makes me angry. And I don't know what to do with that either. I don't know whether he'll ever be better enough to come back to work. The other partner is carving up the load amongst us. Keep plodding on. Glad I bought the house to be away from it all – sounds horrible to say that. Hannah has been great.

Wednesday 24th July

1. Find myself consulting on-line recipes. Not often that happens – actually never. Decide on a veggie meal – Dorothy thinks we eat too much meat in the West. The meal involves chickpeas with various spices. Called Falafels. The recipe said 16 minutes prep time – took me a while longer. Leave out the celery – an abominable foodstuff. Anyway, all contained in flatbread with a tomato and onion salad and a green salad and various nuts and dates on the table; it was a feast of sorts.

2. Dorothy was mightily impressed – I think more with the effort made than the actual result. At the end of the meal she held out her hand for me to hold – stage 2 – and said thank you. And then we walked hand in hand round the walled garden until we got to Old Oak. And she, like so many, put her hands on its trunk – almost in an attitude of worship – or maybe connection might be a better term. We talked about the journals from the early days of the building of Kirk Aeppel and the planting of this tree. And she said that perhaps it would be good to get all this together into a book which told the story of the place – get it published – make some money for the roof.

3. There was no one else there and at no stage did I feel awkward. It was friendly and sort of OK.

4. She mentioned that there was an outdoor concert coming up in late August at Chatsworth – did I want her to buy tickets? Indeed.

Friday 26th July

1. Another visit to Charles with Dorothy. He is definitely looking better. Treatment over. Able to hold a rational conversation. Grateful for the support. Back to Sunday evenings before too long he said.

Sunday 28th July

1. At breakfast after communion, Andrew and Sarah decide it is time for Imogen to meet the dogs. They will walk her up in the afternoon.

2. Imogen meeting 4 dogs requires a little careful handling. Quite overwhelming. So, we do this one at a time. Starting with Tiff and working upwards to Ribble. All fine of course. She is a perky wee thing. Not so 'wee' actually. I like what I have seen thus far.

3. Keeping up with the various tasks. Jane texts to check I am surviving. They are having a wonderful time in the glorious weather. Replenish wood at one of Yurts. Help Jimmy organically spray the orchard. Walled garden watered every evening in the way Ted requires. Tomatoes harvested and eaten. Mentioned to Jane that I had cooked for Dorothy from a recipe found on-line and she was amazed. Now left with an excess of all sorts of spices – will have to repeat that meal at some stage.

4. Quiet evening. Takes me to thinking about the future. Without Charles. What then?

Monday 29th July

1. Get Samantha to contact Tanushi to ask whether she would like a welcome meal here on Saturday or Sunday – or whether she doesn't.

2. There's a crying baby in the night problem in one of the Yurts apparently. Jimmy and Samantha handling that one.

3. Walk down with Samantha to inspect the gatehouse. What a change a lick of paint makes. And Samantha has lavished some care with the curtains and blinds. All seems lovely. Garden is a mess... but Samantha insists that Tanushi will be wanting to sort it out herself.

Wednesday 31st July

1. Tanushi says yes to meal. So, on a little excursion with Dorothy to a pub at Monsal Head for lunch, she plans the welcome. Suggests I make falafels for everyone on Sunday evening. Give Ted and Jane time to unpack and sort themselves out. Likewise, Tanushi. Invite everybody. Dorothy will come up with a pudding. Stock fridge / larder. Flowers. Dorothy will liaise with Samantha.

2. Stop by to collect the necessary ingredients for Sunday.

3. Who would have thought I would be cooking a non-meat meal for the estate, to welcome the new Officer for Preservation and Procurement? What strange changes are being wrought? With what to come?

AUGUST

2013

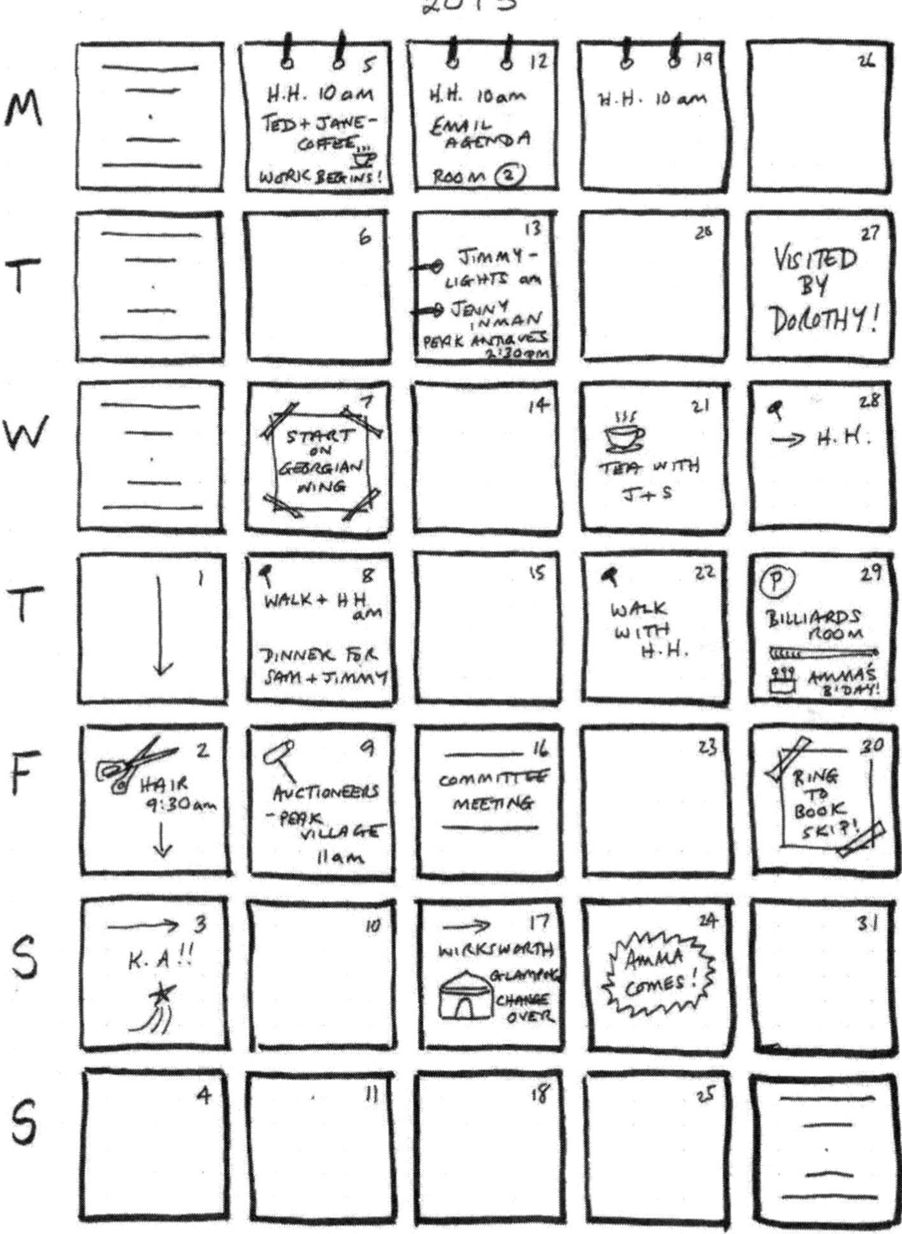
M
T
W
T
F
S
S
5
H.H. 10am
TED + JANE - COFFEE
WORK BEGINS!
12
H.H. 10am
EMAIL AGENDA
ROOM 2
19
H.H. 10am
26
6
13
JIMMY - LIGHTS am
JENNY INMAN
PEAK ANTIQUES 2:30pm
20
27
VISITED BY DOROTHY!
7
START ON GEORGIAN WING
14
21
TEA WITH J + S
28
→ H.H.
1
8
WALK + H.H. am
DINNER FOR SAM + JIMMY
15
22
WALK WITH H.H.
29
P
BILLIARDS ROOM
AMMA'S B'DAY!
2
HAIR 9:30am
9
AUCTIONEERS - PEAK VILLAGE 11am
16
COMMITTEE MEETING
23
30
RING TO BOOK SKIP!
3
K.A!!
10
17
WIRKSWORTH GLAMPING CHANGE OVER
24
AMMA COMES!
31
4
11
18
25

Saturday 3rd August

1. The day we have all been waiting for. Jimmy and Samantha at full stretch with change-over day in two Yurts, collecting Tanushi from Derby and helping her to get settled. Ted and Jane return. And me ensuring all is perfect in the walled garden and with the right food in the kitchen and that the dogs are happy.

2. In the midst of this I receive a letter informing me of the date for conferring doctorate – October.

3. I decide to see if I can help in any way with the Yurts. No, they have a well-oiled system in place (already).

4. In the afternoon I walk down with Ribble to say hello to Tanushi. She and Samantha are sitting in the garden at the back having a break. Ribble keen to appraise the situation. I accept offer of tea. I waffle a little and then invite her to the official Kirk Aeppel welcome meal Sunday evening. I am even hoping that Charles may be there. Speak a little about his illness which has so upset us all. And add that I will be cooking the main course which I sense did surprise them.

Saturday 3rd August - TANUSHI

I was so glad Jimmy was there at Derby to haul my bags in his particularly manly fashion. Not much conversation on the way – it is clear he has much on his plate right now. Such a beautiful day to arrive at a new job which might just be for the rest of my life!! Sam at the gatehouse to greet me. So nice. She stayed to help me unpack. Flowers in a vase in my bedroom and in sitting room. Plus food in larder. Curtains and blinds look great. HH called round in the afternoon to formally greet me. I wonder if he ever relaxes. Nice to see Ribble again. The garden is a mess. Wonder about tools etc to help sort this. Sam says she will ask Jimmy.

So here I am – in my room now with curtains – overlooking my garden and my estate. Was this all planned by some deity – arranging for the offspring of a single migrant Mother to end up here? Trepidation mixed with excitement.

Sunday 4th August

1. Communion – one of those unusual moments when one is transported unexpectedly to new worlds. Unbidden and transitory and utterly beyond words. I can imagine some sad little reductionist – Barrington maybe – explaining how this was just the product of the pressure the plates placed on my temporal lobes. Irritated by such a thought.

2. Beatrice rang to say she and Charles would stay for one hour tonight and no more. He is looking forward to it. Can Hannah come too? Of course.

3. Dorothy and I take on the bulk of the prep though Samantha comes down, after her shift at the pub, to help out.

4. And so, to the meal – the last time we met as a Kirk Aeppel community was Hen Galan. Timothy particularly warm in his greeting of Tanushi – vying to sit next to her. But she sits next to me tonight with Samantha on the other side. Next to me also sits Dorothy. Charles arrives as the meal is served as promised at 6.30. Well you would think I had served something of surpassing brilliance such were the comments. Ted said, "Very tasty Mr 'Avard" and I think, but could not swear, he winked at Dorothy. Able to speak to Hannah briefly. Her course is to involve some practical hands-on conservation next year. She has to choose where in the world. What an opportunity! She is torn because of her Father's illness. Essentially, she doesn't want to be caught in the Belize rainforest and hear her Father is to die imminently. Or have to miss his funeral. Death when it comes, obeys its own agenda.

5. And then it fell to me to propose the toast in between courses. To welcome Tanushi to the Kirk Aeppel team. And all cheered and hollered and clapped. And she looked radiant and stood and tried to teach us to say a Tamil blessing which translated something akin to: may the Lord bless this place and all who live here. And she thanked everyone for making her so welcome. And then she added – "and business starts tomorrow at my first meeting with Henry at 10.00 am."

6. Charles and Beatrice left at 7.30 p.m. Pleased to have come – Charles said. By 8.00 pm all had drifted off. Dorothy and I cleared and stacked the dishwasher. (She seems to have this idea that I don't stack the dishwasher efficiently. Preposterous idea.) And we chatted about the evening. I admitted I was tempted to thank her but remembered she didn't want that. She smiled and made our arrangements for Wednesday.

Monday 5th August

1. 10.00 am meeting with Tanushi to discuss her work plans. This seems all very business-like – as it should be, I suppose. This is her proposal:

- In the short term try to make an inventory of the ground floor of the Georgian wing. Identify that which is worth nothing and needs disposing of. Make an educated guess (with the help of professionals if deemed necessary) regarding other items. Any money raised in the short-term through this process will go into a protected account for roof repairs.

- There is to be a Kirk Aeppel committee development team. She will chair the meeting. It will decide upon the action and projects needed to secure the future of the estate. These projects will be divided into short-term, medium-term and long-term. We need to agree on who should serve on this committee. She says she will ask everyone if they want to be considered and then we – between us – will decide a small number who will serve. Maybe two nominees each.

- She needs to identify a person who will be her support and confidante and champion in the team. If there are difficulties, it is to this person she will go. Independent of me. A sort of personnel manager.

- She will set up a KA WhatsApp group. Then frustrated to learn my phone doesn't do internet. Have to be email for the time being.

- She suggests that minutes and decisions are recorded and agreed.

I say very little. Nod and mumble occasionally. How can someone that young be so assured. It's as if she has been planning all this for some time. And getting advice maybe. There's the distinct and uneasy impression that I am being stitched up like a kipper.

Additionally, she needs WiFi at the gatehouse. Something we have not attended to. She will arrange.

She closes her Apple iPad and slots it into a cover. She says that she thinks it would be beneficial for us to meet each Monday at this time – for the next few weeks or months. As we see fit. And then she pauses, "I know there is the other matter. I think it best if that is dealt with entirely and exclusively by the two of us at a separate time and apart from anything else going on." I entirely agree on this point. She is to join me on a walk this week to discuss this.

Monday 5th August - TANUSHI

Meeting with HH this morning. He said little. I felt sorry for him in the end. Possibly I went in a bit OTT. Too much of a steam roller maybe. Anyway, need to set up various things. And he needs to know I mean business. First WiFi to sort. Email all KA team. Invite all to put their name forward for the development committee if they wish.

Have coffee with Jane and Ted. She is so thrilled that her Sam gets along so well with me. Get keys off Ted to the Georgian wing. Speak to them about the development committee (they do not do email etc.). Neither think they wish to serve on the committee – but Ted forcibly says that if there are plans to muck around with the walled garden or other parts of the estate grounds, he is to be consulted! He hasn't worked for 50 years to see his walled garden turned into a farm park for little brats like at Chatsworth. Jane calms him down.

And so to the inventory. I enter up the grandiose steps. Door opens willingly. Decide to go anti-clockwise. Room 1 – this is going to take some time! OMG. Start taking notes on the "Big Items" – the relegated lumps of furniture that crowd the room. Photo of each plus my description and rough dimensions. Need some light bulbs attending to. Plus the whole of the electrics I shouldn't wonder. Still whilst it's light, I can see the big stuff fine. Draw back curtains – one of which collapses in rags. Have to retreat outside for air whilst dust settles.

Decide to meet the local antique auctioneers. Arrange for Friday. Peak shopping village – wherever that is. Also phone several other auctioneers and have a conversation about their offering.

Tuesday 6th August

Email HH > T

Dear Tanushi,

Thank you for meeting yesterday to discuss your hopes and plans for the future of the house and estate. I am entirely in favour of the formation of a committee to talk of such things. However, I do feel it is right to point out at this stage that I own the estate and therefore I have to agree to whatever is planned. I am the decision maker. The committee cannot outvote me – no matter how many may be on that committee. I do hope you do not feel that this puts any sort of damper on your enthusiasm to get started.

Yours sincerely, Henry Havard – Kirk Aeppel.

1. Slept badly. Plates irritating. Sent above email. Best to make things clear from the start.

2. Receive no reply.

Tuesday 6th August - TANUSHI

Receive email from HH asserting his dominion. Ignore. It's precisely what Beatrice predicted. Will chat when I next see him – tomorrow.

On with Room 1. All furniture catalogued. Not much of any great worth given the undesirability of brown furniture in the present market. And they are all of the stately home kind of size. One nice piece which I might have valued. Wonder whether American market might be more sympathetic. Otherwise a couple of thousand – tops. So, we shall have to decide what to keep and what to sell. Haven't checked drawers or anything else. All the clutter visible or invisible, I am ignoring for the time being. I am enjoying myself. Morning coffee in the kitchen with Jane.

Wednesday 7th August

Call in on Henry bright and cheerily. Say how much I am enjoying myself and thank him so much for the welcome meal. Do not refer to email. He then says, "I sent you an email. I hope..." "I don't really do emails Henry. Much better to talk, I think. I have the list of names of those who are happy to be on the committee."

Jimmy, Charles, Beatrice, Timothy, Dorothy and of course me and you. "Anyway, have a think and let me know who you'd like. Your two picks! And how about that walk tomorrow?"

I leave before he has much time to reply. Beatrice was right. Always deal with him face to face and never via email.

Dinner with Jimmy and Sam (or tea as they call it!)

Wednesday 7th August

1. Tanushi called in unannounced. Just as I am starting a new tray. She admitted ignoring my email. Then she tells me of the replies to her email about the committee! Said she'd meet me to walk tomorrow.

Dear Tanushi,

In my previous email I attempted to say that, effectively, all decisions are my decisions. That is all decisions regarding Kirk Aeppel and its future. With regards to the people on the committee, I think we cannot ask Charles to serve. So, I choose Jimmy and Dorothy and that means you will have Beatrice and Timothy – good luck tracking Timothy down – he's very busy from what I hear. Yours sincerely, Henry Havard – Kirk Aeppel.

2. No reply.

3. Dorothy calls round very briefly. Something's come up – even though it's her day off. Seems grossly unfair. Some parishioner in need no doubt. Anyway, we don't have long together. Just a tea and a slice of cake.

   I inform her of Tanushi's disappointing behaviour and she just smiles. "You do understand, old sausage, that she is doing precisely what you appointed her to do?" We arrange to meet on Friday.

4. Receive an email to all committee

Dear all,

Thank you for your willingness to serve on the Kirk Aeppel development committee. Henry has said he is completely in favour of the forming of such a committee to steer the estate into the future. I would be grateful if you could tell me when would be the best time for you to meet on a regular basis – of once every two months.

So far, I have started on the first of the rooms in the Georgian wing. Quite a task ahead but very exciting! I am meeting with someone from the local auctioneers tomorrow to discuss what they might offer to us and under what arrangements.

I look forward to hearing from you,

Tanushi xxx

5. She put three kisses after her name. She said I was completely in favour...

Thursday 8th August

1. Meet Tanushi for walk. Dogs greet her very nicely. She doesn't want to talk committee matters – just producing an heir. She has been in touch with medical friends of her brother and knows (of course) exactly what to do and how to do it. All that needs to be arranged are the precise details and timings. She has the requisite paraphernalia. We both agree to talk to no one else about this and that this should not infringe upon anything else re the future of the estate. Two separate, utterly compartmentalised matters. A good solution to a delicate issue.

2. She then talks a little of her story at school. She says she has never really been on the receiving end of significant racism. The only thing people picked on her at school was for being in the Christian Union. And she asks if I think she will come across racism in Derbyshire – "It seems very white?" I bluster and say it had not crossed my mind. I don't think so. I'd be horrified... obviously you are already loved by all at Kirk Aeppel.

3. She then asked about my schooling. And I went through the story of being sent away at 8 and then the accident and then eventually on to Public school. She looked at the plates (she did ask) and at my neck. "Poor you Henry!" She was careful not to touch.

Thursday 8th August - TANUSHI

A nice time with Henry today (must walk with him + dogs in future –he's much more relaxed) in which we sorted all issues with regard to procurement in a mutually satisfactory way.

If only it might be so easy with regard to the estate.

He spoke of his childhood and the accident. He's still no memory of what happened. How did he come to fall down the stairs? Surely someone must have known a fuller story. School – parents. I shall ask Jane – she was around at that time.

Cooked dinner for Jimmy and Sam. Starting to feel like home now. Wi-Fi in tomorrow.

Friday 9th August

The great thing about being young, female and pretty is that it does confer advantage when dealing with older men. (I am talking about meeting the chap from the auction house.) Firstly, they assume you know nothing, that you're naïve, that they can take advantage of you. This means you can play around with that for as long as you want and then tell them that you have much superior offers from X, Y and Z. Is he really serious about wanting my custom? Or is he a patronising git like so many men of his age? Secondly of course a good number of them just want to have sex with you. And reckon they offer an attractive proposition – which they really don't. Again, you can play this to your advantage in the short term. Found out what I needed to. There's a female furniture expert I might contact. Jenny Inman works for an antique shop in Bakewell.

Called in to see Jane. Talked about my conversation with Henry. What was the story? Didn't anyone know anything more of the accident? She said she was told that it was a fall down the stairs – hard stone stairs. No details of how that happened. It was in the evening – somewhere about 8.00 – 9.00 pm she thought. His parents were phoned and his Mother set straight off to the hospital in Manchester. And it was touch and go to begin with. After about three weeks he was brought back to the gatehouse for Jane to nurse him back to full health. That's all she knows.

Friday 9th August

1. Life is suddenly rather more complicated.

2. Weather changes. First proper downpour for several weeks. And the temperature plummets. Suddenly it feels like autumn.

3. Check on orchard. All well. Check on pigs. Next litter due start of September. Another sow added for alternate breeding.

4. Glampers have had a fine time as far as I could see. Keen to meet the dogs. They were off to Alton Towers today. Ghastly.

5. Just need to watch how the glamping site responds to rain in quantity...speak to Jimmy.

6. Dorothy collects and takes me across to her place in the evening. She has a sweet cottage garden with a fine Chilean pine at the far corner planted some considerable time ago – maybe when they first became popular in this country in the late C19th.

7. We discuss Tanushi. She reassures me that everything is as it should be. Dorothy remains very impressed with her professionalism. It's early days and nobody is trying to take Kirk Aeppel away from me. And she will serve on the committee and be a friend and support for me.

8. After the meal Dorothy produces a whisky from new distillery – Arran – one of her friends had invested in a bond when it first set up in the 90s. He had given her a bottle years ago for marrying them.

9. "Founder's Reserve". What a treat. Ask her if she really wants to open this – probably worth a bit. She insists. "It's a bribe to ensure you come back to visit me." Inevitably I miss the humour and say earnestly, "I don't need a bribe I assure you." And then I realise she is laughing and holding out her hand and I grasp it and we hug for a good length of time. Then Dorothy opens the Arran.

10. On the way back in the car, Dorothy asks if I am happy. A strange question I am very rarely asked. In fact, I can never remember being asked that – ever. I think so. I have no right to be unhappy. I am above all people most privileged I would say. I am happy. I think, but don't of course say, I am happy when I am with her or when I am looking forward to being with her. I ask her the same question. And she says that she is happy. And that she feels settled for the first time for a long time. And she's driving and she places a hand on my leg and squeezes and says, "And I'm happy when I'm with you!" It was dark and she could not possibly know of the lump in my throat. Except she says, "Are you alright Henry?" The idea that someone might be happy when or because they are with me... that a small measure of their happiness is somehow contingent upon proximity to me! Extraordinary. I manage a grunt of some sort.

Saturday 10th August - TIMOTHY

Just coming up for air. Been so busy. Booked the next week for a break – now that Dad is back to work on a part time basis. He's looking OK and can clearly function. Not quite the same stamina. Was it kind not to tell us immediately?

Taking Hannah out for a meal tonight – before she sets off to Belize. I think we need to talk about the future. Seems strange to be the ones now having to think about such things. The two kids becoming the two adults. Mum is hugely capable of course.

Been emailed by Tanushi – re the committee she wants to form for KA estate development – clever idea. Say yes of course. Hardly seen her since she started. I know she's been in touch with Mum lots. Perhaps this week we could meet up?

Decorating this week. House is going to look great.

Sunday 11th August

1. Timothy brought Charles across and stayed. Charles wanted a Lowland... and he's always had a soft spot for Glenkinchie. Very satisfying. There is something right about a Lowland in the summer.

2. Charles wanted to put in place the requisite legal arrangements for Kirk Aeppel – for when he dies. Essentially Timothy is to take over in all relevant ways. All very far-sighted I say. I hope. I have every confidence in Timothy.

3. I appreciate the way Charles abhors sentimentality. Quite against the spirit of the age I sense.

4. Again, we talk of our adventures in Islay and which was our favourite distillery visit.

Monday 12th August

1. Tanushi emails details of first committee meeting. She has asked Dorothy to do the minutes just for the first meeting only. She has produced an agenda. Very unspecific. She has requested we meet around the Big Table with afternoon tea on Friday – 4.30 pm. She will help Jane with the tea. Reply saying, I will be there. Try to strike a suitably resolute note.

Monday 12th August - TANUSHI

Crack on with second room. Trying to ignore the clutter but cannot help getting diverted by this and that. There's a relic of an old piano. Might that bring in some money? I have no idea but photograph and note the maker.

Send emails setting up meeting on Friday. Go and look in on Sam and Jimmy. Glamping going really well. Weather a bit dreary but lots of enthusiasm. Sam showed me these weird pigs they are breeding. Got Jimmy to promise to come down to replace some light bulbs – need v. large ladders. And he'll bring some tools for my garden.

Just liking the freedom and being my own boss and just getting on and dropping in on people. Jane now expects me at 11.15 each day. Ask her about tea on Friday. Sorted!

Tuesday 13th August

Jimmy down first thing with step ladders. Asks me to hold them steady as he changes the 6 downstairs bulbs. A novel and enjoyable perspective afforded.

Head off into Bakewell to see Jenny Inman at Peak Antiques. She's great and very keen to be involved. Raise the issue of the US market (or elsewhere – China is where the money is) for the size of furniture involved. She said she would look into it. The cost of transport may be prohibitive.

And at the end of the day Timothy drops in – just passing – in full decorating gear! Not working this week. Looked quite different. We greet kind of awkwardly but warmly. He just says he'll be there on Friday and if he can be of any help, to just call.

Tuesday 13th August - TIMOTHY

Decorating entrance / stairs / landing. Decide to call in on Tanushi on way back from collecting supplies from Wilco's. No idea if I should greet with kiss / handshake / no contact at all. Aaargh. She's thriving as I expected. Said I'd be there on Friday to support her. Admire her place and say she must come over to mine once it's all done. She said she would.

MINUTES – KIRK AEPPEL DEVELOPMENT COMMITTEE

Friday 16th August 2013 4.30 pm

Present: Henry, Tanushi, Jimmy, Beatrice, Timothy, Dorothy

1. Venue, timing, minutes of meeting. Dates were arranged for the rest of the calendar year. Friday 4.30 pm Big Table – October 11th and December 13th. Dorothy happy to continue doing minutes. Agenda items to be submitted by 4.30 pm on the Monday preceding the Friday.

2. Tanushi's present work. Itemising major furniture in Drawing room and Sitting room. Plans to work through the house. Contact with Peak Antiques. Then to start on smaller miscellanea. All spoke warmly about the start she has made.

3. Roof repairs. Tanushi said she wanted an up to date quotation on replacing the roof on both buildings – Old House and Georgian House. She needs a monetary target to work towards. Jimmy offered to acquire two quotes. Tanushi thanked him for his help in this. The question was posed re heritage grants. Timothy will investigate. Tanushi thanked him for his help in this.

4. Future income generating. Tanushi proposed that she and Beatrice speak to all members of the estate team to research income generating initiatives. And they will visit local stately homes large and small to see what they are offering and to see what the gaps in the market might be, what we might offer that is different. They will submit proposals by the October meeting. All in favour.

5. Estate car. Tanushi has coped by borrowing Sam's car thus far but will need her own. A cheap run-around. Beatrice says she can use Hannah's car when she's away. Problem solved for the time being.

6. AOB. A vote of thanks to Jane for the excellent refreshments unanimously agreed.

7. Meeting closed at 5.30 pm

Revd. Dorothy Richardson

Friday 16th August

1. Committee meeting. What to say? Tanushi has it all sewn up it would seem. I said almost nothing. I couldn't disagree with anything thus far. The battles lie ahead.

2. Dorothy stayed on. A very pleasant evening after a rather dismal and blustery week. We sat with drinks in the walled garden. I find her an increasingly calming and reassuring presence. She rustled up some poached eggs on a muffin with

smoked salmon. Enjoyed with a crisp Muscadet. Splendid. We held hands as we circumvented the garden and caught the dying rays by Old Oak. I couldn't help blurting out that I was happy – and happy because I was here – with her. She smiled and kissed my hand and held it to her face. She has very smooth skin.

3. I have noticed, whenever some physical contact happens, that Ribble or one of the other dogs tries to intervene to prevent this. Is that a protection thing?

Friday 16th August - TANUSHI

Really pleased with committee meeting. Avoided HH having a strop – important at this stage. All on board with the way forward I have proposed. Intrigued by what Dorothy thinks of me. Not sure. She is happy to do minutes. Jimmy and Timothy falling over themselves to be helpful. Long call to Amma in the evening. She's thrilled for me and we make plans for her to come up before term restarts.

Going to help Sam with the Glamping changeover tomorrow.

Saturday 17th August

Glamping changeovers take a couple of hours for Sam – and only one hour if I help. Plus Jimmy does all the heavy stuff. I have a great time with Sam so it doesn't seem like work.

In the afternoon Sam and I head over to Wirksworth to have a mooch round and maybe call in on Timothy if he's there. He is there, busy with paint brush.

Gorgeous old cottage (like mine – limestone with sandstone lintels) in the centre with tiny but private back yard and two bedrooms. It looks onto a sort of crescent graveyard around the ancient church. He has painted it magnolia – throughout. I'm not joking. He says it's just to get it habitable and that he will take advice from more experienced interior designers (indicating us) when necessary. We stay for a drink. It really is the sweetest little house. And the new kitchen/utility/bathroom etc has all been done tastefully. He is most proud of the wood burner! What is it with men and fires?

And the story of our Cambridge meeting was retold for Sam's benefit. She was amazed of course. And on the way back she was full of questions about "Me-and-Timothy" which I didn't answer because there is no "Me-and-Timothy." And then she said she reckoned Jimmy fancied me which I said I thought was rubbish. Had he said anything? No. And I asked about her and romance. And we giggled like teenage girls!

Sunday 18th August

1. Timothy brought Charles round in the evening. He said he'd enjoyed his week at work... back to some sort of normality. Another Lowland. We drained the very last of an ancient bottle of St Magdalene 1979. Distillery now long closed. Rather sad. Keep the bottle for old time's sake.

2. Timothy started talking about how he'd always loved coming round on summer Sunday evenings with Hannah. How he'd fallen in love with the estate then. And he asked about the swimming pool and how come that came to be there. So, I told the story of my Father – after returning from the war – determined to enjoy life after 3 years as a Japanese prisoner of war. He spent money hiring some modernist architect to create – on the north facing side of the house – a swimming pool and party area. Vast amounts spent... used for a dozen or so years of decadence. Probably 6 parties per summer season. My Mother had significant cause to despise him.

   It is said that he did not wear shoes for six months after his return from war and would crouch over his food while shovelling it into his mouth with knife poised in his other hand for a further three months and that he never slept in a bed ever again – until the last few months of his life. That is what is said – by my Mother – latterly.

   The swimming pool and pergolas and seating area had no planning permission and the council, when it found out about it (after a tip off it is rumoured), ordered their removal. And after much lengthy legal entanglement costing more money no doubt, he admitted his "crime" and promised to take it all down. At that point the council lost interest in the issue and he continued – in the summer – to use the pool. Until he became too ill. And it fell into neglect and disrepair. A fitting tribute, my Mother said, to his life. Abandonment.

   And then I tell the story of the one good thing he did – to buy the new thread for the cider press.

Monday 19th August

1. Meet with Tanushi. We can expect Mrs Dias at the weekend apparently.

2. Tanushi seems to have settled well – confidently. Getting on in the way hoped for. I do fear for the changes that might be demanded – but I know – I do know – that things must change. This I reflect on my walk with the dogs. Imogen joined us because Sarah and Andrew are off somewhere or other all day. She's

an unfussy character happy to muck in with the troops. Has a nice sparring relationship with Brook. Tiff rapidly being outgrown by the Clumber. But they play nicely too. Young'uns together.

Wednesday 21st August

1. Dorothy's day off and we decide on an outing to a cinema. It is a long time since I have been to the cinema. Probably in my 20s. Chesterfield have one of these multiple screens – so lots of choice – and Dorothy chooses, "The artist and the model."

2. What a dreary and depressing place a modern cinema is. All chewing gum and plastic. But the film held my attention. There was some nudity which I suppose was not a surprise given the title. But maybe one would call it tasteful nudity essential to the plot. Dorothy cried towards the end. She says she loves a good cry at a film. These are words I do not understand.

3. This all represents change – going to the cinema – and I recognise this is good for me.

4. Dorothy then asks if I want a "Macdonalds" takeaway meal. I suspected she was joking. But decided to respond robustly just in case not. She says, "You can't beat a Big Mac, Henry," and I realise she is indeed being "humorous". Instead we find a pub on the way back. Whitebait and a pint of my own cider – Jimmy supplies to The Old Poets Corner – something of a real cider centre of excellence. Very pleasant.

5. Assad doing unspeakable things in Syria – and him an ophthalmologist working hard to save the eyesight of those in England and blinding his compatriots with poison in Syria. Achebe's Vultures. (Ed: Nigerian poet.)

Thursday 22nd August

1. Walked with Tanushi. I asked her whether her Mother would enjoy a meal round Big Table. Tanushi said she thought that would be appreciated. Saturday.

2. All arrangements in place for attempt 1 – somewhere around September 10th.

3. Tanushi mentioned that she might like to get a dog. What would I recommend? I

asked her various questions – she had met a Beagle and seemed impressed. I have my reservations about single Beagles... better in pairs in general. I said I would mull over the issue but am thoroughly in favour. "What about a rescue?" She asked.

4. She then changed tack and asked me if I was lonely as an only child on this big estate. It hadn't crossed my mind of course because we accept the normality of our life no matter how that might appear to others. I suppose I was the only person of my age. But I was allowed time to pursue my interests without interruption and what a place to be interested in nature and animals and bugs. And there was Jane and Ted.

5. Tanushi is very direct. She means no harm.

6. I then asked about her Christian faith. (It was my turn to be direct.) I sensed she was uncomfortable with this question initially. She had mentioned she had gone to the Christian Union at school. At University she had somewhat lost the habit. She was uncertain what she believed except she was definitely a Catholic! I asked her how she intended to bring up her potential child. To pray each night? To believe? To go to church? She said she had not thought about it. She turned to me, paused and thanked me for asking and getting her to think about this. It was important she said.

7. As soon as I had told Dorothy about Saturday, she had contacted Tanushi for contact details for her Mother. Dorothy wanted her to teach her how to cook a traditional Sri Lankan curry? On Saturday. She had enjoyed them so much on her year abroad and had never really been able to replicate them here. A shopping list resulted and Mrs Dias said she would bring some special spices to assist.

Thursday 22nd August - TANUSHI

We have arranged 10/9/13.

HH asked me about my faith today on our walk and how I might bring up my child. I was a bit flummoxed to begin with. I just hadn't thought. I defaulted to how I was brought up... but then Amma was and is a committed Catholic. And that's not true of me – right now.

Dorothy rang about whether Amma would mind showing her how to cook a Sri Lankan curry on Saturday – a great idea. And whilst she was on, I asked her if she would mind calling round next week to chat about faith issues. I left it at that.

Saturday 24th August

I had told Amma to bring some shoes to walk around the estate in. But I don't think she has any. We did our best to walk around the farm. Amma wide eyed at the glamping area. She struggled to believe that people could pay to have a reduced lifestyle – to live like a peasant she said. She admired the pigs from a safe distance. And we met Andrew and Sarah on our way back with Immie. I said that I was thinking of getting a dog. "Dirty animals! What are you thinking of Nushi? You'll be knee deep in dog dirt in no time! You have become so English!" And she laughed as she said it.

We set off early for the dinner and I left Amma putting her apron on talking to Dorothy in the kitchen. It was nice enough to have drinks in the walled garden.

HH came down with a sherry. He poured me a drink. I asked him about the Old Oak and we walked down to it.

"You asked me about friends when I was young – here is one of them. I used to be able to shin up this when I was 10. Not after the accident. Wasn't allowed. I have spent many an hour here." He put his hand on the bark and smiled. "People say Old Oak has special powers. Carilla (my Great-Great Grandmother) first wrote that. 150 years old by then. She would bring her horses to this tree to calm them, to shelter them, to water them in the stream. Some people talk to her." He looked at me and smiled. "The first Gwyn Havard planted a Pembrokeshire acorn from the Gwaun valley when he came here. I plant one of her acorns annually here and there on the estate. Half a dozen have taken and survived the deer."

I resolved to plant the one that Beatrice had given me – in my garden.

The meal was quite ordinary for me; but for everyone else it was a delight. HH in raptures. Sam and Jimmy had joined us. Dorothy seemed unusually subdued and excused herself early. Amma glowed with the praise. She liked the grandeur of the setting, the silver cutlery and fine glasses and the thought of course that her grandchild might one day be at the head of the table. This she told me as we walked back. It was clear and cold and quiet.

Saturday 24th August

1. Splendid evening all round. Wonderful meal cooked by Mrs Dias and Dorothy. A very convivial atmosphere in which Tanushi could show off her new acquaintances and friends. And all spoke well of her and how she had settled so well and was just what the estate needed. Dorothy left early saying she was not feeling well. She had been a bit quiet during the meal.

Sunday 25th August

1. Early communion. Dorothy clearly not recovered.

2. Charles drove himself and stayed briefly. Glenlochy chosen – starts well but peters out with something of a whimper. Another long-since closed distillery.

Tuesday 27th August - TANUSHI

OMG – that did not go well. Dorothy came round supposedly to talk faith matters. We'd sort of started and she said suddenly, "You'll be thinking about how to bring the child up then. That'll be it. Catholic... Protestant... or let them make their own mind up. Bit of both. Pick and mix? It'll be a shame if it can't go to the wee chapel now won't it?"

I didn't know what to say. I was thrown.

"Still there's a Catholic church in Matlock, Bakewell and Hassop – that might be the nearest maybe?"

I said that whatever she had heard...

"From your Mother whilst cooking curry."

...was meant to be confidential and she shouldn't have said anything. And I'm sorry you disapprove but I'm not sure it's any of your business to come here to be spiteful to me about this. And she said, "No – maybe you're right. What possible business could it be of mine?" And with that she left.

Shit – should I warn HH? She definitely leaves on to main road and not up to the house.

Wednesday 28th August

See HH first thing and tell him. He is properly shaken. Poor lamb.

Two rooms complete. Now for the Billiards room except I find I cannot enter as the door is stuck. Message Jimmy. Move on to kitchen. Not much there – I suspect Jane had properly sorted it when they moved to Old House. One or two bits of pewter, jelly moulds, ancient utensils and the like. Can be sold into vintage shops of which I've seen a few in Matlock. Photos taken and catalogued.

Join Jane for coffee and Jimmy turns up. Jane says that door to the Billiards room was always a problem. Henry's Father had fitted a lock on it for some reason. Jimmy confident he could solve the problem with his crowbar.

Jane said, "Don't you go wrecking that beautiful old door. Henry would not be pleased. And he's not in the best of moods. I've just taken him his tea. Did you call in earlier Nushi dear? D'you know what's bothering him?" I said I had and he'd been fine. I don't like lying to Jane.

Wednesday 28th August

1. This has not been a good day. Dorothy knows. Back to square one. Tanushi warned me of the coming tsunami. Went to the higher ground – Biggle Hill. The weather was properly autumnal. Knew I had to return at some stage. Hovered in the opening to the lead workings sheltering from a squall and contemplated my defence.

2. If rationality has any part to play in the judgement, then the Scottish "not proven" might result – dependent on the charge –

- "wilful deceit" surely not proven or

- "being an incompetent and insensitive friend" – I plead guilty.

   The punishment for both is termination I assume and I have resigned myself to this.

3. Rationality will have little part to play I suspect.

4. I hear nothing from Dorothy all day. Even though it's a Wednesday. A suspended sentence as yet. Maybe a little distance in time will assuage the oncoming storm?

Thursday 29th August

1. No contact with / from D – does not bode well. Resolved to make contact tomorrow. Running away from danger has always been my way of avoidance of all things unpleasant. And by and large it has been a successful strategy. But something tells me this might be a time to lance the boil – to mix metaphors somewhat.

2. Had a letter from Roger of all people. It would appear that he has caught religion whilst in prison. He is truly sorry for his crime, for putting Kirk Aeppel at risk, for not being good and loving to his children, his parents and me and for assisting the pernicious spread of drugs in the area. He says he has started going to a Bible study and has given his life to the Lord Jesus Christ and wants to start a new life of service to his fellow man. He asks for my forgiveness. He knows I am a Christian man and if I have any suggestions of how he can best engage in charitable service, he would be pleased to hear from me. He has decided to go for counselling concerning the death of his dear wife. He thinks unresolved grief may have caused deep trauma.

3. What am I to do with all that? Normally I would consult Dorothy for assistance. But that option is no longer open to me. I put off writing back.

4. Take solace in the orchard brimming with fruit.

Thursday 29th August - TANUSHI

Ring Amma to wish her a Happy Birthday.

Jimmy manages to open door to Billiards room this morning. There is a Yale lock on door which is odd in this old house. But it wouldn't open because so much stuff is crammed the other side and something had fallen across the door. Jimmy enters with me.

The room stinks. It stinks of rats and urine and mould and every other noxious smell you can think of. There's an open hole next to the fireplace where the rats have come and gone. There are rows of bottles unmarked with who knows what in them. Over the Billiards table itself, there is a large cloth which drapes unevenly and in threads down to the floor. Under the table there are the remains of two small double mattresses eaten to bits by the rats. Eventually it would seem even they thought this place was beneath them as a living space and they left. There is the usual mismatch of furniture. The table itself is rescuable probably. On the table there are a load of cues and balls. And a whole lot more detritus. An ancient electric shaver, talcum powder, washbag etc. And in the corner a rather imposing chest of drawers with clothes spilling out – men's clothes. And very (!) distinctively – on the walls – a collection of pictures from the early 20th century (at a guess) of titillating male nudes (ie gay porn!) from various corners of the world.

It would appear that this room was used as a bedroom and more.

Friday 30th August

1. I leave a message with Dorothy first thing – saying that I think I need to apologise to her and that perhaps we could meet up to enable me to do that properly and for me to attempt to explain.

2. No reply. This is what it must be like being on death row.

Friday 30th August - TANUSHI

Speak to HH in the morning. We need to clear and fumigate that place asap. He is distracted – still no sign of Dorothy. He's happy for what is clearly rubbish to be binned and what is salvageable to be kept.

He explained that the Billiards room is where his Father always slept. I asked him whether he had ever been in there. He said not. Would he like to go in now to see what's there? He said not. He trusts my judgement. I start to say about the pictures... but think better of it.

Get in touch with skip people. Jimmy – the ever obliging – gives me a number. They deliver immediately and I set about the task. Sam lends a hand after returning from school. We wear masks and gloves and goggles and dungarees. We make a start only. It is properly disgusting.

THE HISTORY OF KIRK AEPPEL 1900 - 1972

George (2) took over Kirk Aeppel in 1899 upon his Father, George (1)'s death. He faced the enormous challenges endured by all country estates of that era with an ostrich like equanimity. Life would go on. As normal. Staff may have to be shed as and when, corners cut here and there, a slice of land sold if really necessary. But appearances would be maintained. He inherited his Father's love for animals of all sorts and in particular dogs. He became one of several honorary vice-presidents of the Kennel Club. Regular dog shows for setters of all sorts (his chosen breed) were held at Kirk Aeppel. The dog cemetery (started by George) is a testament to his love for Gordon Setters in particular – Pinch, Puggle and Parsnip. The warmth of his relationship with his beloved setters stood in marked contrast to that with his son – Desmond – with whom there was little of mutual interest or affection.

Desmond was just 18 when his Father died in 1936. His Mother had died in his infancy of the Spanish Flu. Desmond's life was shaped by the trio of his Mother's demise, his intense dislike of his Father and above all, the war.

Desmond hated the Public school his Father sent him to and to which he duly sent his son Henry in time. Desmond then went to University College, London where he studied Physics, the first Havard to have a formal tertiary education. In reality he immersed himself in an alternative musical scene and spent his time in bars such as Billie's club and The Caravan club. He scraped a third, entered the army and found himself on the tiny island city of Singapore in 1942.

The war years were grim for the neglected Kirk Aeppel estate. With no one to direct affairs, light its fires, tend to its walled garden, it fell into an abandonment which looked for a time like it might be permanent. The farm, with the assistance of the land army, continued to function. The orchard spluttered on unloved. Old Oak observed the decay.

Upon Desmond's return in 1946 and after his physical recovery, he set about restoring the estate to some health. He upgraded the estate cottages – putting in central heating and indoor toilets and bathrooms. This in turn attracted returning soldiers willing to toil on the estate for a few years before leaving to pursue their lives elsewhere. This provided a therapeutic bridge between life in the army and civilian life. The orchard was tended once again, the rooms swept, patched and decorated where necessary, the roof received a little attention, the woods cleared of invasive brambles and ferns.

During this time Kirk Aeppel developed a reputation for the outrageous and extravagant parties which Desmond threw. He seemed determined to bury his ghosts in a display of flagrant hedonism. Carpe Diem and all that. The Derbyshire constabulary were called out on several occasions in 1954, 1955 and 1956.

In 1955 at great expense he built, without planning permission, the swimming pool, bar and outdoor eating complex at the back of the house. This he used, despite the Council's best efforts, until 30th July 1966. In 1957 Desmond was married to Harriet whom he had met on a visit to a small estate in the Trough of Bowland. She had had a sheltered rural upbringing and was significantly younger than Desmond.

In 1960 Henry was born thus ensuring the future of Kirk Aeppel estate. Outwardly things seemed to be settling down towards a more stable and orthodox country life. This was not to be.

Desmond was in possession of a certain entrepreneurial charisma and was somehow able to generate the cash needed to keep the estate afloat and to finance his parties which soon resumed in the swinging 60s. He had maintained his London contacts from his time at University. However, his dependence upon alcohol was becoming increasingly obvious and debilitating. By 1966 his health was beginning to fail. At the final party, around that pool, with the drink flowing, with England's finest playing Germany at Wembley, he fell from a table upon which he had been dancing. He broke his hip and was taken to hospital. There he was told in no uncertain terms that he had to stop drinking or he would kill himself. He spent time recuperating (and drinking) in Whitworth hospital. He limped around the estate for a further 6 years as if looking for something he could do – apart from drink. He never found what he was looking for. He died unloved and unregretted by his family and by the estate. Few beyond the vicar attended his funeral which was held in St Cuthbert's Chapel.

The 12 year-old Henry was now in charge – under his Mother's guidance of course.

Saturday 31st August

1. Message from Dorothy. "I am coming round at 3.30 pm."

2. A fine day – a break from the cycle of westerly fronts trundling across the Atlantic. The dogs enjoy a splash in the stream as I try to wash off the fox poo Brook has managed to roll in. A diversion.

3. Dorothy arrived. We sat at Big Table. I apologised that she learnt about Tanushi's role in the way she did. I apologised that I hadn't told her. I apologised if it seemed that I was betraying her, not trusting her, being deceitful. I said it was not just my confidence but also Tanushi's confidence I had to keep and we had agreed to be very discreet. I started to say that obviously no sexual intercourse – but she waved me silent as if to say she knew that. I said I understood that she must be upset but she should be upset with me and not with Tanushi who has done nothing wrong in all this. (I am exhausted at his point.)

4. Dorothy then interjected to say yes, she acknowledged she behaved badly to Tanushi and she will apologise to her.

5. I then rose and said I was sorry it has had to end this way. I thanked her for at least attempting to have a friendship with me. Very few have managed that. I walked over to the door to hold it open for her. But she didn't move. So we paused – me by the door looking at her – she, back turned and facing the fireplace. It seemed like a whole minute of silence.

6. She then said, "Don't I get a chance to speak? Before you dismiss me?" I walked back and sat down. "Why can't you have a baby with me? Why can't I have a baby? Why can't our baby be heir to Kirk Aeppel?"

7. I couldn't think of anything to say. I can now. But I had rehearsed the first bit – the apology – I knew where I was going. But I hadn't anticipated this and was, not for the first time in my life, tongue-tied. "It's a question Henry. It demands a response."

   I say, "I don't know" – I can't think of anything.

   She then gets up. "No-one it appears would want to have a child with me. Unfit for motherhood. All those bloody eggs secreted month by month and for what?" She looked at me, realised she was not going to get any further meaningful response and then she departed the house.

8. As stated previously, I had already resigned myself to this outcome. I wonder if I will have a companion when my doctorate is conferred. A selfish thought in the circumstances.

9. I cancel Charles for tomorrow citing a virus – and in his immuno-suppressed state, it would be wise not to come.

SEPTEMBER

2013

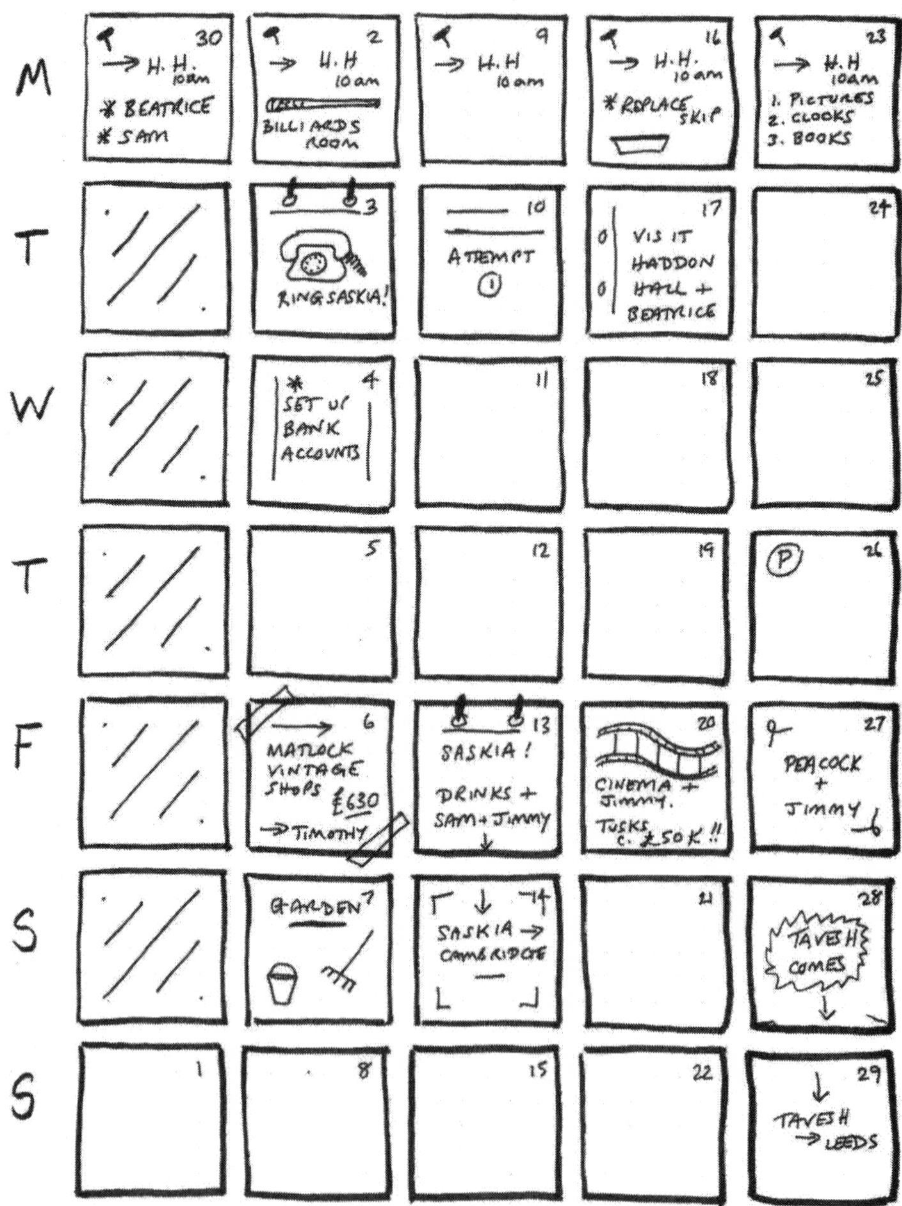

Monday 2nd September - TANUSHI

Received hand delivered note from Dorothy waiting on the mat first thing:

Dear Tanushi,

I write to apologise for my outburst last Tuesday. As Henry pointed out, I should not have been angry or upset with you. You have done no wrong in this matter to me or anyone else. And what's more, at the moment you were seeking some spiritual counsel, I was entirely preoccupied with my own hurt. I am so sorry.

I hope you can forgive me.

I also write to say that in the circumstances, I will not be part of the ongoing life of KA and its development committee. I am not sure I had too much to offer anyway. But I wish you all well in your endeavour to build a new future for the estate.

Yours sincerely,
Dorothy

I go straight up to HH and show him the letter. He reads it and hands it back and says nothing. I start to say I am so sorry but before I can go any further, he ushers me away from the beetle table and down the stairs and out. He says he is slightly behind in his work and needs to get on and that I must forgive him.

Get togged up in protective gear and throw myself into clearing the Billiards room. Jimmy joins me unannounced. He looked wide eyed at the pictures and says, "Bloody hell" and starts laughing. And we discuss what on earth this room was used as. Tell him that Henry said his Father slept here. We get to the point of removing all drapes, remnants of mattress, curtains and scraps of rugs – all soft materials basically and then give up.

Jimmy invites me up to the farm for lunch and we pass Ted and Jane on the way up. I feel I have to tell them that Dorothy and Henry are no longer an item – or whatever it was they were. Jane very upset. Do I know why? No. Sam starts speculating over lunch as to what's happened. Jimmy thinks it's because Henry is gay but 'in the closet' and no relationship can prosper whilst he's in denial.

I say I'd rather not think about it... but Dorothy will be a loss to the estate. She's got some get-up-and-go. And then Jimmy says, "What'll happen when Henry dies? Whatever, it won't affect us because we're legal tenants and have certain rights in the event of the sale of the estate. Who'd buy it? Might they want to sell off the farm and then we'd have first refusal?" So clearly Jimmy had thought it all through. Sam betrays nothing.

They offer to help in the Billiards room some more in the afternoon, but I put them off. I want no further speculation. I return to my labour. All the paper, magazines and newspapers need sorting – mostly for the skip. Interesting selection of mags. Loads of bills for this and that I keep just in case. Anything to do with the estate – put all that in a folder. Then attack the wardrobe and chest of drawers. Some stuff here is vintage and worth taking to Matlock – including some ostentatious jackets and gorgeous patterned shirts. Other stuff gets chucked.

Just as I am leaving, I turn to examine my progress, I look at the billiard table with most stuff cleared away. It has balls and cues and not much else left.

What to do with that table? It will need totally refurbishing before it can be used. Is there a market for such a table? Research needed.

In the evening phone Amma to chat. She's all ready for the new term. There's a new Head of Science who has laid down new regulations about how the technicians are to operate. As she is talking, the Billiards table comes to mind with its balls and cues and also the long thin cue box. And something irritates me about that long slender wooden box.

Tuesday 3rd September

OMG – first real discovery of note!! So, I return to Billiards room first thing. I look at the long slender box on the table which I had assumed contained a cue. It's got markings and decoration which are clearly not British. It's wrapped/tied in ribbons in three places. These fall away easily. Then there's a little beautiful wooden mechanism which operates as a latch. This still works. I open it. What is this? There are two long cream coloured sticks. The wood spirals the full length to a small round point. At the wider end they both have similar "carvings" for the first 6 or so inches (before the spiralling starts) – which I recognise. These are stencilled into the wood – maybe burnt into the wood. The pictures are of the famous abolitionist image, reproduced by Wedgewood on his pottery, from the designs by the Clapham Sect, of the supplicant, a manacled slave, with the phrase, "Am I not a man and a brother?" So that dates it to c.1800. Phone research so useful!

Ever so carefully I lift out one of the sticks. And immediately I don't think it's made of wood. I'm not sure. It feels different and on closer inspection of the grain, it just looks different.

Breathe and think. The decoration on the box is of "primitive" eagles and bears. I have an idea what this might be. But I need to be sure. I take a picture of everything and send to Saskia – asking her to say what she thinks they might be. I put everything back really carefully.

Saskia phones within the hour. She asks questions. I send a few more close up pictures and she says what I think. These could be matching narwhal scrimshaw tusks. And if they are what we think they are, they are worth a fortune. She cannot find any example of abolitionist scrimshaw of this quality and on narwhal tusks. UNBELIEVABLE!! She immediately suggests that she comes up and takes them into the Fitzwilliam for authentication and valuing. I said I would have to check with my employer but that I thought that would be a great idea. AARGH!!

Immediately start trawling for scrimshaw prices... lots of noughts! For the best stuff.

Go straight round with them to Henry. He is having a tea with Jane and she is holding his hand as I walk in. I lay out the box on Big Table. Say nothing. "Now what is in here? This box was on the billiards table. I thought it was for a cue. (Ribbons off. Wooden latch opened.) But what is it?"

In a flash Henry said, "Those are narwhal tusks – well I'll be damned!"

"And with scrimshaw markings, Henry. If they check out... they are worth a lot of money!" And Henry poured over them and I explained the drawing – of course he knew about the Clapham Sect and that famous image.

Then he said, "Ah! It's George Havard – of course. He went out to Canada in the middle of the 19th Century to work for the Hudson Bay Company. That's how they come to be here. Must be. Nice old bean was George. Loved his horses. I wonder how the old bugger got hold of these."

Checked Henry was happy for Saskia to authenticate them. And he was also happy for me to take stuff to the vintage shops in Matlock.

Tuesday 3rd September

1. Tanushi proves her worth – already. A fine discovery of two narwhal scrimshaw tusks. Her hard work. I have no idea what these might raise but she seems to think a lot. Awaiting roof estimates. Delighted.

2. Reply to Roger:

Dear Roger,

Thank you for your letter. I am so pleased (and a little surprised) that you have found comfort and sense of renewed purpose in the Christian faith. The choices you made in the past are in the past. I thank you for your apology. I can say from my personal perspective, that I hold no grudge against you and that I forgive you.

I do hope you have been in touch with Samantha and Jimmy. I think it important that you have a similar conversation with them.

You will be pleased to know that they are thriving and that the farm is blossoming.

With regards to engaging in charitable enterprises upon your release, I think perhaps it would be best for you to communicate with Revd. Dorothy at the vicarage in Elton. I think it is likely she will have far more ideas and contacts than I do.

All I can do now is to wish you well.

Henry Havard. Kirk Aeppel.

(I couldn't think of a better word than blossoming.)

3. Start of the new academic year. I decide the throw myself into the beetles with renewed vigour after the summer break.

Wednesday 4th September – TANUSHI

Busy today. Set up bank account specifically for roof repairs (on Beatrice's advice) because I do not want whatever money comes in to be spent on anything else. Henry and I are co-signatories.

Visit a range of the vintage shops in Matlock and show them a selection of stuff. Work out who I can do business with – and who to avoid.

Visit Jenny at Peak Antiques with some initial photos. Reluctant to get her in at this stage before I have had a chance to see everything. Don't tell her about narwhal tusks. Anyway, she is really enthusiastic about the quality of furniture. She is exploring avenues in USA and China.

Interview Ted and Jane separately re the development of KA and getting the public in.

Ted not enamoured of the idea!

Arrange with Saskia to come up.

Beatrice and Charles come round to deliver Hannah's car. She is leaving for Belize on Friday. Send card to her to wish her luck.

Still buzzing from narwhal tusks! Ring Amma. She's amazed and so pleased for me. I do say that she shouldn't have said anything to Dorothy. She apologises. Of course, she won't say anything to anyone. All confidential. Didn't mention the fall out.

Timothy messages – he's heard about my find – and sends his congratulations. Arrange to meet up at his for a pizza on Friday.

Feel so sorry for HH.

I love my house, my home, my estate!

Friday 6th September

So, £630 now deposited in the new account. All from Vintage shops on Dale Rd. A start has been made.

Round to Timothy in the evening. It was just really relaxed. There didn't seem to be an agenda. Just comfortable. He is really pleased with his house. Work had settled down a bit; he was now just doing London lecturing 4 times a year ("now that there's no chance of bumping into you in Cambridge!!" is what he said.)

We spent time talking about the Henry-Dorothy thing. I tell him as much of the story as I know. And we talk about whether I should go and see Dorothy. What for... to plead H's cause? To clear the air? To put everything back together again? Dorothy is pretty headstrong and she does like things the way she likes things. Little chance of achieving much. Not sure what to do. If anything.

It was good to see Timothy – as he walked me back to my car, we both said it was nice to chat again.

Friday 6th September – TIMOTHY

The treat at the end of the week – the something to look forward to – pizza with Tanushi. She is a delight and I am so grateful we are at ease with each other – after that wonderful evening in Cambridge. There seems nothing to have to prove. I think she just wants a friend – outside of KA itself – to get her out of the bubble. Although we do spend a lot of time talking about Henry and his upset with Dorothy. Who knows what was going on there or indeed what really brought it to an end. We don't have all the information and judgements therefore difficult to make. Tanushi says that HH now spends all his time on beetles, dog walks and checking the new pigs.

Friday 6th September

1. Receive PCC minutes. These I usually turn immediately into fire-lighters. But alerted by a highlighted section:

- Alterations to rotas in the light of personnel changes: The services at St Cuthbert's will continue on the first and last Sunday of the month. There will be a rota for the Readers to cover this. Mr B. Bradshaw, Miss G. D. Simpkin and Mrs T Manifold will officiate. Arrangements will be made regarding the consecrated bread and wine. New arrangements effective immediately.

2. The second batch of piglets arrive over-night. The runt is touch and go. I wonder what the evolutionary purpose of such is. I try to persuade Jimmy to let me look after it. "Too early – he might make it with the rest and that would be far more preferable" – which I completely accept.

3. Letter from Calow hospital re annual check-up. Friday 20th Sept.

4. Dig out George Havard's journals to see if I can find anything more about tusks.

Saturday 7th September

1. I now have the runt to feed and raise. It really is wee and just clinging on. Pretty full-time occupation. I wonder if my sense of engagement with any possible human offspring will be as fascinating and all-consuming as this. I doubt it.

2. Check with Charles he is able to come round tomorrow.

3. Sam and Jimmy pay the rent – of course on time and in full. Arrange to review glamping on Monday.

Sunday 8th September

1. Bad news re the wee piglet.

2. Charles fit and able to drive himself. Get out an old favourite – Highland Park. I've always thought that it's a whisky that is difficult to categorise neatly. Complex and powerful and wonderfully long-lasting.

3. Charles wants to know what is going on between Dorothy and me. Of course, he does! Had anticipated he would. Well nothing is going on. I tell him the story. He is incredulous that such a thing would end what might have been or might have become an actual relationship. I have nothing to say and no skills of analysis to offer. It came and went. Charles clearly irritated by my saying this.

4. We move on to the tusks. Charles fascinated. The size of them – and how they are essentially an extended tooth. Remarkable. I say that Tanushi has earned her keep already. Need to be verified and valued. Tell him that she says it could be lots of money in the roof repair account.

5. Good to have Charles back and on form.

Monday 9th September - TANUSHI

Saskia coming up on Friday and will stay overnight.

Met with HH as usual for a quick chat. He's is in a sorry state really. Not the slightest bit interested in what's going on, what I'm doing, what's next. Just wanted to return to the beetles. I could tell him anything and he'd pretty much ignore what I've said. Mumbled about how pleased he is with the tusks. Told him about Saskia coming from Fitzwilliam.

On way out met Jimmy and Sam going in to review summer glamping with HH. Can't imagine they will get much sense out of him.

Returned to cataloguing and clearing. Nearly finished downstairs in terms of anything major. Utility room / pantry has one or two nice things. But like the kitchen that has been pretty much cleared already. The door to the back from the kitchen was unshiftable. Tempted to get Jimmy to flex his muscles. Instead I explored round the back from the outside. It was just brambles and I could not make much headway. I couldn't even see where the swimming pool started or stopped. Just the outline of broken-down wooden structures and what must have been a bar. It has a sense of lostness, of not being in the right place, of being out of kilter with the Georgian dressed stone. A place the sun does not shine.

Unsure whether to move on upstairs or to clear the two main rooms and look for smaller valuable items. There's still space in the skip. Pleased with the cleared Billiards room so decided to set about the first room again.

Met Sam later. She said HH was distant and disinterested which given how much he had encouraged them and invested time and money in the yurts... and it's all good news. They made money – enough to pay off nearly all of the debt and there's still quite a few weekends booked up before they shut down for the winter. All glowing reviews on line.

Monday 9th September

1. Met Tanushi.

2. Met Jimmy and Samantha.

3. Annoyed I lost the pig. Don't know what more I could have done.

Tuesday 10th September

Attempt 1

Tuesday 10th September - TANUSHI

Attempt 1

Wednesday 11th September

1. Dogs in a funny mood today. Argumentative. Suspect it's Tiff.

Friday 13th September

1. I dislike people remarking "Unlucky for some! Ho ho." It riles me. Heard it on the radio. Bloody nonsense.

2. At 3.30 pm Tanushi turns up out of the blue with someone from the Fitzwilliam Museum supposedly. Come to take the tusks away. Bloody cheek. "Can we trust her?" Says she's going to authenticate them, date them and value them and suggest a way forward. I say, "They're narwhal tusks dated to around the turn of the 19th century. And I am going to sell them for as much money as I can." And she smiles and looks at Tanushi who says, "I told you Saskia was coming here today and there's no need to be so rude. We agreed that she would do this. Authentication by the Fitz will hugely help their saleability. And she will advise on the best place to sell them."

3. I don't remember her saying anything of the sort. Allow her to get on.

Friday 13th September - TANUSHI

Collect Saskia from the station. It is so nice to see her again. Go straight to see the tusks and encounter HH at his worst. Couldn't remember me having told him about Saskia supposedly. Just being a miserable old git. Anyway, Saskia took it all in her stride. (So grateful again to Beatrice for her forewarning and advice on dealing with HH.)

I'd invited Sam and Jimmy down for drinks before all heading off to Matlock for the night. Jimmy promised to show us the sights of Matlock! I thought Saskia would think it very provincial but she had a good time, I think. Ate at Herd and ended up via Monk at Moca. Jimmy in his element surrounded by the 3 of us. Quite the cockerel as Amma would say.

When we got back and Jimmy and Sam had left, Saskia immediately asked about Jimmy because she said she thought he fancied me big time!! And did I like him? I said I didn't believe her at all. He hasn't said anything. She said he just needs a bit of encouragement!!

Saturday 14th September

Having signed all the forms and done all the legal stuff and double wrapped the box, I drove Saskia to the station. She will let me know within the week. Exciting.

Messaged by Tavesh. He wants to come up to see what all the fuss is about, before term starts.

Sunday 15th September

1. Charles came round with a Talisker – a whisky he has always admired and I very gradually have come to appreciate. Peppery.

2. He said it had been hard to say goodbye to Hannah but he was sure she was doing the right thing. And if he should decline suddenly, which was unlikely, she could come back very quickly. Been in regular contact. She is well, spending the first weeks on a manatee sanctuary and having a ball.

3. Young people have such opportunities these days. What might I have done – if allowed the option? If given choice? Or if I had had the courage to force the choice?

4. For Charles – he says he would have changed little. He has had a splendid life and has no regrets. He just feels so regretful now to be leaving them all. Financially there are no issues. But both children are without partners. Timothy settled professionally but who knows for Hannah. Beatrice has left teaching.

5. All death is inopportune I suppose.

Monday 16th September - TANUSHI

Went round to see HH first thing. More to check on him than anything else. He did not refer to his behaviour with Saskia – it was as if it hadn't happened. Now he's looking forward to the authentication and valuation! Almost acting as if it was all his idea. Getting a top museum to look into it!

Continuing doing a preliminary clear out of disintegrated soft furnishings. The variety of clutter from the past is amazing – stuff from mid 1930s side by side with clutter from 200 years previously. Some quality Bakelite and I did come across half a canteen of silver – mid Victorian. Black – a struggle to know it was silver. That's got to be worth something. If it were complete... wonder if Jane knows more. Was it with kitchen stuff? No, but she thinks it might be in Harriet's bedroom. For some reason. We shall see! Set about de-tarnishing cutlery. It's going to take time. Set out to do 4 items in front of each Corrie.

Get the skip people to collect and replace.

I've decided to invite Jimmy out. Will speak to Sam to say when, where, what.

Tuesday 17th September

Go to visit a local rival (not that they would recognise us as that – yet!) with Beatrice – Haddon Hall – to suss out the competition. What are they up to? What a place! Just beautiful and old and romantic. I guess Gwyn Havard must have been trying to match the extraordinary long gallery when he constructed his original house. Take all the literature. Informative guide. Loads of events to bring people in – local and from further afield. Clearly, we are not on anything like that scale but food for thought.

Spoke to Sam re Jimmy... what would he like to do? Why not a film followed by meal?

Friday 20th September

1. Hospital for plate check-up. Usual palaver – finding the place. Tests. No change. Intermittent headaches. Fit for one more year. The doctor who deals with me is surely not yet trained – the most junior of junior doctors. I'm sure of it. They wheel me in annually as some sort of training guinea pig. Same questions as usual. "What do you remember?"

2. Tanushi calls in. Saskia says they are narwhal tusks with scrimshaw drawings. Dated turn of the nineteenth century. Estimate at the right auction house – £50,000 – £70,000. What do we want to do now? I'll be damned! That'll buy some lead.

Friday 20th September - TANUSHI

So Jimmy and I go to see "Prisoners" – "How far would you go to protect your child?" Not bad. Jimmy liked it. Then go to Frankie and Benny's... so busy. Can hardly hear myself speak. Not exactly the best place for a quiet romantic conversation. He talks about his plans for the farm and I talk about the estate and what we might have to do to survive and get enough money to re-roof. He asked me about boyfriends before and during Uni. He's had – it seems – quite a lot of girlfriends – why doesn't that surprise me? Anyway, we had a nice time.

I say on the way back in the car, "So I have a rule: no kissing on a first date."

He says, "So you are kind of saying that if it was a second date, you'd definitely be kissing me. So, I have a rule: no second date without a first date kiss."

"OK – seems we have an impasse Jimmy. What do you suggest?"

"A kiss that doesn't count as a kiss?"

"Right – so you kiss me on the cheek and then I kiss you on the cheek?"

"OK, I'll settle for that...for now!"

He smiled the sweetest smile and looked at me.

All rules kept – we arrange to meet up next Friday.

Sunday 22nd September

1. One of those very unusual times when the Autumn Equinox falls mid-meeting with Charles. Uniquely therefore we can have a Highland and Lowland followed – after 21.44 – by a Speyside.

2. Charles can't keep going to that late in the evening. So, we have a very small Talisker followed by a very small Cragganmore to compare. What a treat.

3. Charles says he is going to visit Revd. Dorothy this week to discuss matters to do with his funeral arrangements. Charles always the most practical and well prepared of men. Every "t" crossed and "i" dotted. Typical solicitor. Do I wish to send a message? What a ridiculous question. The last conversation with Dorothy had ended on multiple unanswerable questions. Whence progress? Wish him well.

Tuzi – Wire-haired Vizsler

Monday 23rd September - TANUSHI

Visit HH to update him. Not much better than last week.

Sam keeps bugging me for details of Friday. Jimmy won't tell her anything. Just got a cat-that-got-the-cream look. So, she comes down at lunch for some soup before going into school. Tell her the details... she is suitably encouraging. She thinks he's keen. I say I am going to proceed really cautiously... workplace romance is a dangerous game. She agrees with me.

Decide to deal with downstairs pictures, clocks and books. All pictures are draped. So, the ones that are small enough I skip the covers and take down from the wall. Two nice sentimental pieces by Thorne Waite – pastoral – blackberry picking and cows coming home. Classic stately home pictures. Not sure they're worth a great deal. Better off in situ here. Likewise, 4 country scenes by George Turner – of nearby locations including one of Kirk Aeppel itself dated 1883. Can't imagine we'll be selling any of this lot. Otherwise no Wright of Derby unfortunately. Still everything catalogued and more rubbish skipped. Lots of old leather bound books of little distinction as far as I can tell.

Tavesh arriving on Saturday.

Monday 23rd September

1.. Strong to gale force winds overnight. Dangerous with trees in full leaf still.

2. Meet Tanushi.

3. Pick up kindling for winter.

4. Ted has coaxed the walled garden into copious quantities of produce again this year – tell him so. And out of the blue he says, "Bin thinking about your apprentice idea...may not be such a bad'un. Our Sam says yer can get funding to help with the costs. And I have got some... experience to pass on." I reply cautiously and say I will look into it. Phone Timothy to ask him to check out apprenticeship schemes.

5. It seems to make sense. But I hate change. I can't help feeling it heralds the end. Something Ted might sense too.

Thursday 26th September - TANUSHI

Period.

Thursday 26th September

1. I have been trying to piece together George Havard's adventures in his early days. They are a trial to decipher but a delight to read. He is particularly eloquent upon the issues of the native Indians and upon whale hunting which he clearly abhorred. I like the pen drawings – simple and expressive. There is no specific mention of the tusks – he says merely that he is returning with various treasures some of which were given to him in lieu of debts owed. I think I would have liked dear old George number 1.

Friday 27th September

1. Manmade global warming 95% likely. Listen to the beetles you denying dullards.

Friday 27th September - TANUSHI

Jimmy chooses where and when and with all his originality, he decides upon the local – the Peacock – an apt name in the circumstances. I thought beforehand, "I bet he just wants to show me off to his pals" and that is indeed what happened. I try to needle him by asking who he'd been out with each time a girl comes in. Anyway, I get to try some of the cider which I can't say is my thing but I'm not rude about it. Clearly the deal is that Jimmy is allowed the occasional pint for free. We end up playing a game called Bar Billiards which is great as it happens.

Anyway, at the end of the evening as we were walking back, I say, "No coffee on a second date. That's the rule." And he says, all sincere now he's away from his mates, "There's lots of rules Tanushi; it's just that I quite like you and I wouldn't want to be infringing the rules accidentally." So, I turn round and return his smile and laugh. And he caresses my hair and I kiss him and feel his arms strong around me. He is definitely all man. Quite different to the boys I have kissed. Not that there have been many.

It takes me a while to settle.

Saturday 28th September

Tavesh drives up in Amma's car and stays the night. He is clearly impressed by my cottage and by the estate and by everything. Take him to meet HH. He is terrified by the dogs which amuses me of course and I say I am thinking of getting one to join the pack. I say this to him, his hands in the air, as Brook and Ribble are circling around sniffing him intimately! So funny. HH asks him about Cambridge and medicine and whether there's still a chap lecturing in whatever. He then invited Tavesh to his Higher Doctorate ceremony in a couple of weeks. Tavesh properly pleased! And then I show him around the whole place including the farm. He meets Sam and Jimmy. Sam invites us in. She has done so much to get that place in some sort of order – in just a few months. She keeps badgering Jimmy to dig out their tiny front garden so she can plant something. He just says, "Priorities!"

Tavesh leaves Sunday after breakfast to visit a friend in Leeds (male/female?). Not sure Amma knows this. I ask and do not get an answer – so assume not.

Sunday 29th September

1. Communion.

2. Andrew and Sarah come round for breakfast. They probe politely as to Dorothy's whereabouts. I say little. PCC minutes – we're on a rota now.

3. Charles and I continue with the Cragganmore.

4. He reports on his meeting with Dorothy. She has been given some additional role by the diocese. She misses Twyi. Charles suggests there would be no objection to taking her for a walk occasionally. I know the game Charles is playing – the arch mediator – and I tell him it is not required. He presses the question about Twyi. I have no objection.

5. Charles has taken to talking about some memory from our Cambridge days when he visits. This time we reminisced about a chapel choir tour to Cologne and Bonn. And I realise that my life was for moments slightly broader in its scope than it is now.

   Charles asked what I wanted for any child that may be forthcoming... so I set about seriously thinking about such a question after he left and came up with these four qualities:

   - Intellectually interested and engaged.
   - Socially confident.
   - Compassionate.
   - Spiritually alive.

   And as Charles had pointed out – children learn through example. And I needed to model whatever it was I wanted to see in my child. I resolve to talk to Tanushi about this. All very difficult.

Monday 30th September

1. Jane asked about the Harvest service. I said I had heard nothing and I assumed it is not happening. She was not happy. There has always been a harvest thanksgiving. Later in the day she said she has spoken to the Revd. Dorothy and she has said that the following Sunday would be the best time. She said she would inform whichever Reader was on the rota. Jane and Ted will do the necessary in the chapel. Fair enough.

2. Tanushi calls in. She invites me to inspect the progress to date. I think I cannot resist this invitation any more. And the next committee meeting is under two weeks away. Arrange to do this tomorrow.

Monday 30th September - TANUSHI

Call in to see HH. I invite him yet again to see the progress I am making and he finally agrees – tomorrow.

Working with Beatrice on the submission to committee meeting on 11th October. Crucial meeting. Quotes in. Grant info from Timothy expected soon. So glad I have the success of narwhal tusks in the bag and so glad Beatrice is my mentor and confidante and guide to dealing with HH! We need to think carefully about pitching the ideas. How we say it may be as important as what we say.

HH is slightly more animated today. He tells me he would like me to attend the Harvest service next Sunday. Happy to do that I say.

If anything marks the Havard household out as unusual (apart from the present chaos it has been left in), it is the clocks. Just downstairs I have counted 14 clocks of all types. Some are definitely worth something – beautiful mantle clocks, grandfather clocks, early electric clocks, travel clocks. They represent many genres of design – classical, rococo, art nouveau (including a delightful pewter Liberty and Co. mantle clock), art deco etc.

One clock I think might be a "Banjo" clock. I am no expert. But everything is logged and photographed and I am meeting up with Jenny on Friday to see what she thinks.

The Havards loved their time keeping.

Message from Sam – needs to talk! Meet up on her return from school. She needs a blow by blow account. Jimmy not saying anything as expected. I say, I like him and yes, we kissed! She punches the air and squeals!!!

OCTOBER
2013

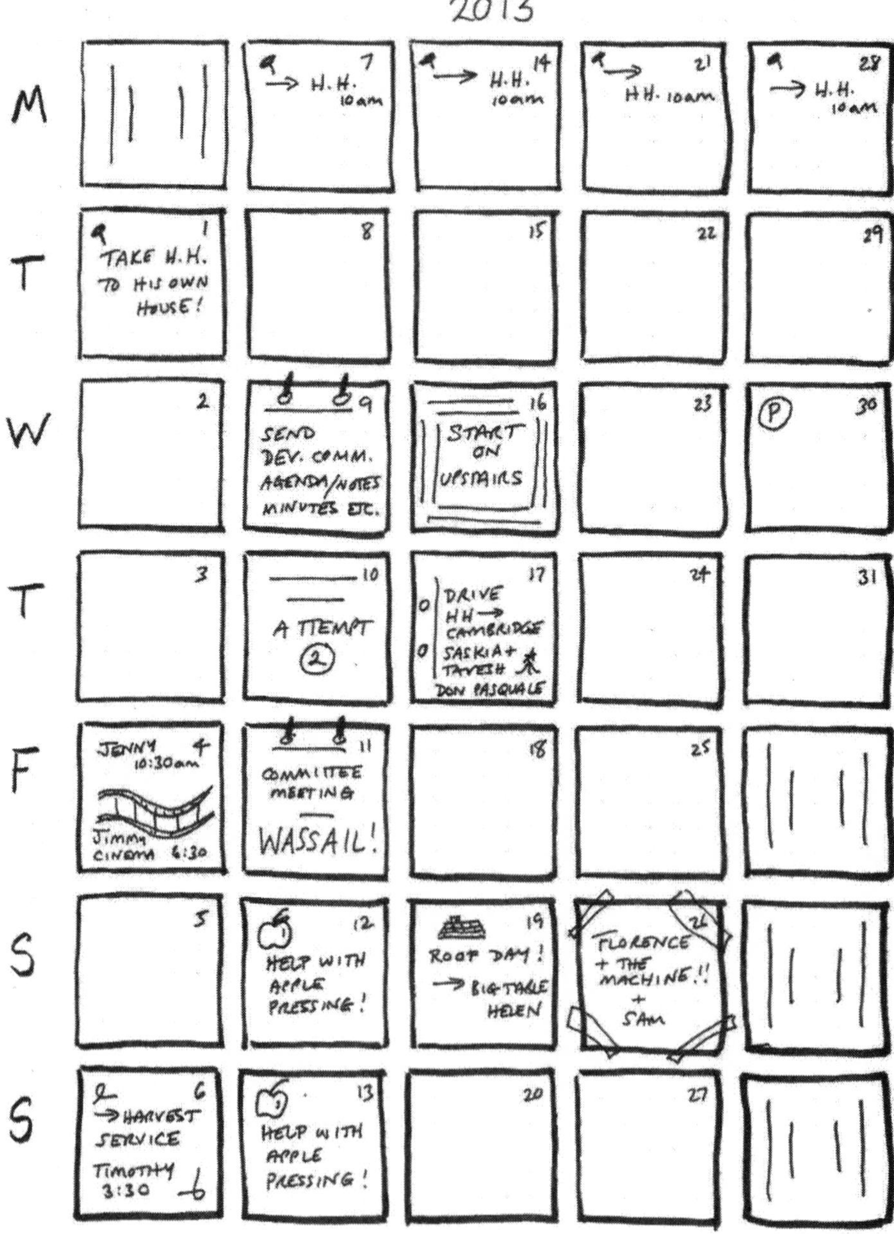

Tuesday 1st October

That was an education – as they say. 10.30 am on the dot I present myself to HH. There then followed a series of increasingly bizarre diversionary tactics. Fancy a walk with the dogs? Just need to complete this classification... Jane has made some delicious courting cake... can we discuss the wassailing (which I know Sam has in hand)? Etc. He did not want to go to see what he had committed to inspect.

Anyway... finally we are at the grand entrance. And he's turning this way and that. So I ask him when he was last in the house. And he replies three weeks after his Mother's death in 1999 – December. One or two things had to be sorted supposedly (you wouldn't know it) and he hadn't ventured into the place in 14 years. "Are you reluctant to go in Henry?" Long pause. "I am...but I am going to go in. That is the thing you need to know. This place does not hold happy memories for me." He looked at me plaintively. "Silly really – as if haunting is real. As if the matter – the stuff of the fabric of this building – can retain its toxic memories and harm me still." He laughed unconvincingly and stepped up.

I showed him the rooms that had been cleared. He said he had never been in the Billiards room in his life but wanted to see where I had discovered the tusks. The room still stinks. I pointed to where his Father had made his bed – seemingly. He shuddered. He looked at the collection of pictures on the Billiard table – expressionless. He stood at the entrance to the room and held the side of his face with his hand.

He passed comments on what a thorough job he thought I had done – "in very trying circumstances." And I pointed to the clocks collected and catalogued. He too admired the pewter art nouveau clock – desperate for a bit of attention.

He commented on the picture of Kirk Aeppel. "This could do with a good cleaning." He was right – but not spending any money on anything other than the roof. "Quite right," he nodded. "Of course, you are right. No doubt about it.

You're doing a marvellous job Tanushi. Such a wonderful start. We have to work out what to sell and what to keep." Indeed. And he left. And as he left there was a sense of renewed desolation. It was marked... in the air... in the silence... in the negative space.

Tuesday 1st October

1. Inspected the progress that Tanushi has made. I went into the Billiards room. For the first time.

   I recalled the time when I was sent on an errand by my Mother to fetch my Father for a reason which now escapes me. I was 9 years old. Fresh home from school. Excited for the 8-week summer holidays. I knocked on his door. There was some noise. I knocked again. My Father appeared. He smelt. His appearance frightened me. He shouted, "Why have you the temerity to disturb me boy? Who the **** do you think you are?" And then he struck me with such force – with his open hand – that I was knocked across the hallway floor. Then I saw a shadow of a man and a male voice attempting to remonstrate with my Father. And the door slammed shut. I looked up the stairs to my Mother on the landing and she screamed at me to run up the stairs to her.

   She said that my Father was drunk again and that he had no care or control over what he did. She told me to stay in her room. She went downstairs with a raised poker. Banged on the door and there was lots of shouting and slamming of doors. She returned and she hugged me and the poker fell to the floor – a hug was the rarest of events. She told me to steer clear of him at all times. He wasn't well.

   I wasn't much hurt.

   My Mother did not send me on any more errands of that nature again. I went to Jane in the kitchen who sat me down with much fuss and with squash and tiffin.

   I have long mused on the nature of exorcism. Do these events – or the memory of these events – require forcible extraction from me? So that I might walk into that place without qualm or fear? Is it the place or is it me that needs spiritual purging? I wonder briefly what Revd. Dorothy would say?

2. Saw Sam later to discuss the Wassail. She is so like her Grandmother. It is uncanny. She has it all in hand of course.

3. Met Jimmy in the evening in the orchard. He is all set up for the harvest. Some modest loss of apples in the storm.

4. In the evening I review October. Always an important and busy month. Tanushi has agreed to drive me down to the ScD ceremony and back in the day. She wants to see Saskia and collect tusks. Tavesh will be my one supporter in the Senate House.

Thursday 3rd October

1. Utterly dreadful scenes in the Mediterranean. Large numbers killed fleeing to Europe. Shocking.

2. Meanwhile I enjoy another day of security and stability at Kirk Aeppel.

3. For which I will give thanks on Sunday. Jane in charge of the chapel. Mrs Manifold rings regarding the service. She is the designated Reader. I have no idea why she wanted to talk to me.

Thursday 3rd October - TANUSHI

Awkward – Timothy rings to ask me round for a catch up tomorrow. Already planned to go out with Jimmy. Say I'll pop round Sunday afternoon.

Friday 4th October

Met with Jenny. She is really excited by some of the clocks and is desperate to come round to see the place. I delay, saying that it all has to go to the committee to authorise that. I tell her they decide what is and what is not to be sold. Meeting in 7 days' time.

She thinks China is a possibility for very specific items that we can photograph in situ in an "English Stately Home." Otherwise for the run of the mill stuff that is oversized, it's still America that represents the best bet. She will research the Banjo clock.

I take Jimmy to the cinema again. I choose Sunshine on Leith which I LOVE!! He says he'd have rather seen Captain Philips – next time maybe? "Is there going to be a next time if you don't say you loved Sunshine on Leith?" He laughed at that. "Defo loved it then."

We go to an Italian on Chatsworth Rd. Newly opened – trying hard. He's a bit of a gourmet is Jimmy. He must be watching all the cooking shows in the evenings. He can talk about food. Suddenly articulate. Knows all the lingo. I enjoy myself. I prattle on about my week and he listens – which is something of a novelty with my boyfriends. And he talked about the week coming up – Wassail and harvesting – and the committee meeting I remind him. "It's important Jimmy." And he pretends to have forgotten and arranged something else in its place and laughs at me as I start to wind myself up.

I have a good evening.

Sunday 6th October

1. Harvest. The positives – St Cuthbert's looked wonderful, bedecked in the flowers and greenery and produce of the estate. Dorothy's amazing harvest loaf centre stage. And Tanushi was there looking a little conspicuous. The negatives – one would have thought that a scintilla of charisma, some ability to project one's voice, to modulate intonation, to engage with theme and congregation would be necessary in order to be a Reader. Not so apparently.

2. I thank Mrs Manifold of course at the end.

3. After breakfast Andrew, Sarah and of course Imogen join us in our walk up Biggle Hill. It is a bracing and clear day. See all the way to the Roaches. I like their company. They share my impressions of the Reader. Imogen very much part of the pack now. She is quite scent orientated and has to be watched in case she wanders off.

4. They ask whether I would mind looking after Imogen if they went on a holiday sometime – without her. Of course.

5. Charles chooses a Singleton – the very first whisky I can remember tasting. They say it's the smoothest of all whiskies. A good choice.

6. Charles says that Dorothy will call round for Twyi on Wednesday at 1.30 pm – there is no need for me to feel obligated to accompany her on the walk. I feel no such obligation. Charles speaks most positively about her and about how she has been very helpful in planning the funeral and talking though hospice/home issue. "She's a wonderful woman – without a shadow of a doubt." I know the game he's playing and say so. He smiles in that boyish way.

7. He asks me two things. Firstly, whether he can be buried at St Cuthbert's. That is an easy question to answer – of course. The second question is whether I would mind speaking at his funeral – alongside the family. That is more problematic. I delay answering.

8. Charles has decided to cut down on his hours at work. Spend what time he has left doing retirement things that he and Beatrice had long planned for their future. Whilst he can. It is unutterably sad. Not that I or he express any trace of sadness – only that this is a jolly positive step which he should embrace. Whilst he can.

Monday 7th October - TANUSHI

Call round to see HH. Tell him that agenda and accompanying notes and report will be distributed on Wednesday. I bring round a little black tie with his name tag which I had found upstairs on the floor. He said it was from his days at Prep School.

HH thanks me for attending the harvest and apologises for the poverty of the service – so much better when Dorothy led it. He says it is to be a busy week and weekend with the harvesting and pressing.

Spend the rest of the day getting the development plan into shape. Beatrice joins me in the afternoon.

Monday 7th October

1. Tanushi brought round my Prep School tie with my name tag sewn on.

The uniform was black leather tie-up outdoor shoes. Knee length grey woollen socks. Grey elastic garters. Grey flannel shorts. White Y-front underpants. Grey Clydella shirt. Black tie. Grey long-sleeved woollen jumper. And for Sunday a heavy grey Harris Tweed herringbone jacket and matching shorts. All with name tags sewn on – Jane had been busy after our visit to Kendals in Manchester to get the uniform. (Not forgetting the games uniform.)

And on that first day my Father decided he would drive us there. Before getting in the car, he looked at me. "Those shoes need the soles scuffing properly otherwise you'll be slipping and sliding on the wooden floors." I didn't know what to do in response to this. Something was expected. "Scuff the bottom of the shoes Henry." Still it was unclear to me what I was required to do. "Bloody hell boy. Like this." And he stamped and dragged his feet along the gravel vigorously. I imitated him.

Of course, he had forgotten that the outdoor lace ups were never worn inside anyway. That would be the black leather slip-ons.

Jane kissed me goodbye and was shooed away by Mother.

When I arrived, after my parents left, I stood on those wooden floors for the first time next to my trunk amidst the chaos of arrival day. I looked around the room, with its throng of unknown boys and adults, and I understood then that I was absolutely alone and always would be.

Wednesday 9th October

1. Ensure I am busy in Orchard at 1.30pm. I have told Jane about Dorothy collecting Twyi. She is most disapproving of my not handing over Twyi myself.

2. As it happens, she calls by the orchard on her way back down. She talks to Jimmy and nods towards me – I am at some distance – and I nod back.

3. Receive by email the agenda and plans and quotes. I bridle at just about every suggestion. But I cannot fault the thoroughness and professionalism of her approach. Just have to remember that this is not personal.

Thursday 10th October

1. Attempt 2

2. Busy with apples.

Thursday 10th October - TANUSHI

Attempt 2

Friday 11th October

The Meeting:

4.30 pm – present Timothy, Jimmy, Beatrice (who agrees to take the minutes in the absence of Dorothy), HH and me.

I divide the meeting into two parts. Firstly, round the Big Table we discuss strategy, possible ventures and finance. Then we move into the Georgian wing to discuss progress and agree on what can and cannot be sold.

Proposals which survive the cull:

1. Writing a journal of the estate including its history and the recent developments based upon the diary entries of HH and me – principally (Ed: Timothy's contribution gets added later). Beatrice happy to edit.

2. Explore the possibility of dog training weekends based at the farm but with grand meals around the Big Table. Hosted by both Tanushi, Sam and HH.

3. Accommodation. Jimmy and Sam are looking to convert the old stables and associated buildings into self-catering accommodation. This together with the glamping option could be used for all manner of themed weekend breaks. At the moment we couldn't do cooking. But we could explore alternatives.

4. Longer term. Weddings. Chapel on site. Though very small. Possibility of marquee etc. Need to invest in infrastructure – kitchens and loos.

5. Arts events – external in the summer. Parking an issue. Internal small venue events in winter.

6. Christmas invited events. Decking the place out in its Christmas glory.

7. Selling KA themed produce – what / where / how?

8. Develop cider interest – at harvest / pressing and other times of the year.

9. Charity events e.g. run up and down Biggle Hill.

HH was variously gloomy and insisting everything was provisional. Nothing decided.

Then it was finances.

1. Essentially each roof costs £350K each and if done together you save about £50K.

2. Grants for the various lottery / heritage funds might be £75K IF we do it right and to the satisfaction of the heritage fundamentalists.

3. Already "in the bank" a possible £50-70K thanks to the tusk find. It still seems a long way to go which is why we won't sell our way to the total – we have to earn our way there. There is more to be sold but barring another major find that will only bring the total up to a possible £100K.

4. So, we have a possible total of £175K at which point HH says, "If we sell the tusks!" And everyone looks at him as if he's mad. And he justifies himself by saying, "I have a soft spot for dear old George who brought them back from Canada. I think it would be honouring to him if we mounted them somewhere prominent." At which point Beatrice said it was time to look at the amazing work that Tanushi has been doing and decide on the first few things that definitely need to go.

So we move on to the Georgian wing. Jane accompanies HH for this and she holds his arm as they mount the stairs. Everyone is universally in raptures about what I have achieved and Jimmy puts his hand on my back – discreetly when he says how hard I have worked.

Some furniture is beautiful and fitting for one of the rooms. This gets a red never-sell label. Some furniture is clearly out of place and will not conceivably fit anywhere. That receives a green sell-now label – including Billiard table. And there's amber spots on the rest.

Decide to hold fire on the clocks until research / estimates are in. That gives me enough to work on for the time being. Pictures and the mirror stay. Told to go to "Scarthin Books" in Cromford with the remnant of the library. HH had removed all books he thought worthy.

And then it is back to soup and bread and cheese round the Big Table. Sam, Charles and Timothy join us in preparation for the wassailing at 7.30pm.

I just love this place. Sam was amazing with the torches and the dancing of the little ones from the school and their parents there. Dorothy is there saying some prayers about the Lord of the Harvest and the need for generosity – as the Lord is generous to us – in these difficult times. I conclude we must not to be so shut away. More part of the community.

And I notice HH slip away back to the house well before the end.

Friday 11th October

1. Today was brightened by a letter from Helen in reply to my sympathy card. She sent a picture of her and the children. Nice. She and they are coping. She had seen that glamping was offered now at the farm. Was it too late to book for the first weekend of half term? Contact Samantha and email back to confirm that would be fine.

2. The committee meeting was as grim as I expected. Everyone massed against me. I rightly said that I did not want to sell the tusks and it was awful. It's my bloody estate.

3. Charles managed to join us for a little wassail. Sam had invited Revd. Dorothy. Managed to avoid her. Watching the little children dance around, I realised perhaps that it is incumbent upon me to share this place and its traditions with others... we do need, after all, to pay our way – for such privilege. This is all very uncomfortable.

4. Walk Charles back to his car. A decent excuse in the circumstances.

Saturday 12th October

1. The day consumed with final harvest and first pressings.

Sunday 13th October

1. Second and third pressings.

2. Pigs brought down and watched carefully as they clear the orchard.

Monday 14th October

1. Utterly exhausted. Jimmy still hard at it.

2. Tanushi calls in all bright eyed. She is going to get properly started on the upstairs. She gives me a list of tasks to do connected with development priorities. Ghastly.

3. I tell her about roof repair Saturday coming up. Not convinced that she thinks that patching the roof is part of her remit. Which it isn't.

4. She said how wonderful the Wassail was and that we should be aiming to be more part of the community, drawing them in to our world. I tell her that the same thought had occurred to me. Don't think she believed me.

5. We confirm arrangements for Thursday's Cambridge jaunt. I will not take Ribble this time.

Wednesday 16th October

1. I decided to take the day off completely. I am tired from the exertions of the weekend and wearied by the committee meeting and its outcomes.

2. Decided to sort the whisky; it's amazing how they become ill sorted so quickly. The labels have to be showing. So, choices can be easily made. Then disaster struck – knock at the door. The whisky racks are immediately to the right of the door. There is no chance of not answering this. Jane was at the hairdressers. I

opened the door and Dorothy was there. She was surprised. I was surprised. She said she has come to collect Twyi.

3. I do not remember being told about this. As if this has become a regular thing. Jane had not said anything. I have no objection of course. The lead hangs by the front door. Twyi delighted naturally.

4. Upon her return, she wished me all the best for the ceremony tomorrow. I was at my inarticulate and mumbling worst.

5. She had remembered about the Sc.D which is surprising.

6. Later I asked Jane whether she knew Revd. Dororthy would be calling. She dissembled unconvincingly.

Wednesday 16th October - TANUSHI

Familiar with the routines now. There's even more crap upstairs than down and even more furniture crammed into each room. But the water coming into the northern two rooms is terrible. Wallpaper hanging off, floor boards crumbling and the smell of rot and decay. I am going to leave his Mother's room till the end. Skip is newly supplied. Mask and gloves and camera and clip board at the ready.

All the way up the stairs are boring pictures of long dead ancestors all the way back to Gwyn. I look out for George – who brought back the tusks. He is kindly looking and podgy. They (the pictures!) all need professional cleaning. I don't think I could do that even though I know the basic techniques.

Thursday 17th October

I drove HH to Cambridge. He was plugged into his music with blindfold on and therefore no conversation. Dropped him off outside Jesus.

Parked by arrangement behind Fitzwilliam and Saskia was there. She introduced me to her line manager – Martin. He said he had agreed that she could do this valuation report at a cost-neutral price. Very reasonable. Mates rates if you will. I was suitably grâteful which is what he wanted. I smiled prettily at him. "But don't hesitate to put whatever business you have our way. You may not know that we are one of the foremost museums in the country, Tanushi."

We wandered through the museum with Saskia and she showed me what she was working on. I said that there were a lot of paintings that would need cleaning eventually. "Just the sort of business Martin had in mind Nushi!"

Left her to meet up with Tavesh for a coffee. He's fine. He then went to watch HH get his degree. I bought one or two treats from the market. Came across the Brazilian stall and remembered the day spent with Sam in the summer.

Eventually HH with Sc.D certificate (he is now officially a Doctor of Science) and Tavesh and Saskia met at Don Pasquale for a late lunch. I had bought Henry a button hole to say well done which I pinned on him. A red rose. (I think he was a little touched by that.) We had a really nice time and HH even apologised to Saskia for his "curt manner" the last time they met. Tavesh described the ceremony – having never been to one. Lots of Latin. He was very impressed and had a long conversation with Henry about beetle classification in which the word penis was mentioned with great regularity.

And Saskia (via the Fitz) pays for the drinks as a "gesture of goodwill and future cordiality" (as Martin had instructed). And then we collect the tusks and leave. The tusks fit in from the passenger foot well upwards diagonally to the back. All fine which was a relief!

It has been good to get away from the KA bubble for the first time. I think HH had a good time. He said little on the way back. He clutched his certificate like a little boy with a swimming badge!

Thursday 17th October

1. A good day. Journey to Cambridge uneventful. Very grateful. Slow on the final stretch past Huntingdon.

2. Jesus had all the requisite robes at the ready. I was escorted to the Senate House by Richard Cawthorne and the Nat.Sci. (they say "nat-ski" these days!) Director of Studies – Helena Fraser. All rather pleasant. And the ceremony was splendid. After that drinks. And I managed – without Ribble or Revd. Dorothy.

3. And then on to a celebratory meal at Don Pasquale with Saskia and Tavesh and Tanushi. My Mother came to Cambridge once only in three years of my time there – for graduation – and we ate at Don Pasquale – just the two of us. By which stage I had turned down my chance of a PhD. Tanushi gave me a rose which was unexpected and much appreciated.

4. I notice that the family call Tanushi – "Nushi." Long conversation with Tavesh. Splendid chap. Mention that to Tanushi.

5. Collected tusks. Saskia (to whom I had apologised) did say that they were worth a lot of money at one of the top auction houses, that they were of "museum grade" significance and they really ought to be seen and the full story told. It could be part of the story of whale exploitation which George Havard had railed against. A lone voice in his lifetime. Food for thought.

6. Returned to Kirk Aeppel successfully.

Friday 18th October

1. Slow to rise. Dogs eventually pestered me to action.

2. Walked up to farm to inspect the new cider. Jimmy as pleased as ever with the bubbling promise of life's elixir! Pigs happy. Two Yurts left for the two families arriving tonight. I said I would pay for Helen's weekend away with her daughters – I explained the situation.

3. Jane is happy to arrange a meal for Saturday evening. Fisherman's Pie.

4. Helen and daughters arrived from Burnley at 7.15 pm and I was there to greet her. She threw her arms around me with a warmth and vigour I had not expected.

5. 2 daughters and one dog. Yasmin aged 12 and Millie aged 15. The dog – a rescue – was a massive Newfoundland. 4 years old. A gentle giant. Sam had arranged some treats (food/drink) and I left them to it.

6. They will do their own thing tomorrow and join us round the Big Table in the evening. Sam and Tanushi will be there too.

7. Dreading roof day.

Saturday 19th October – Roof Day

1. It happened; it's over for another year. We are battened down for one more winter. Jimmy supplied the muscle with several local youths with the promise of £40.00 and copious cider at the Peacock in the evening. (Not with the promise of weed as last year I suspect.)

2. Nothing is going to improve the far roof much except professional attention. Don't venture there.

3. Helen arrived with girls and dog. What a treat for my hounds to meet such a beast. All as good as gold. A good deal of sniffing. Sam and Tanushi looked after the girls which was the plan. And Helen and I fell into a conversation long interrupted. I spoke of beetles and the Cambridge visit and Tanushi's appointment. She spoke of Mike's death – all so sudden and the girls and how they had coped so well really and her vet practice. And then we moved on to Barrington with much laughter. Memories of Hogmanay will never be quite the same – nor will his nose. He is in touch with her on vet matters. Ticks and deer in the main.

4. We went out between courses to greet Old Oak which she had remembered from her visits 30 odd years ago. She had her phone torch on and we stepped down the slope gingerly. She held my arm and then – as all do – she placed her hands on the old tree. The wind dropped and there was a moment of serenity. And I said after a bit, "I regret not doing my PhD all that time ago." And she said, "Yes, I'm sure." And she paused before adding, "But it's all water under the bridge now. And they have honoured you, Henry. Rightly so. Well done!" And we re-joined the party.

5. The girls were clearly highly intelligent. Millie wanted to be introduced to the whisky display. So I am glad it was looking at its very smartest.

6. A truly convivial evening. Sam walked them back to their yurt.

Sunday 20th October - TANUSHI

Jimmy had invited me to the post-roof piss-up at the Peacock. Sam had warned me not to go and as it happened, I was able to say I was helping HH host his friend and her daughters.

Timothy came round in the afternoon and we had a short walk to Old Oak and back again.

HH reported how the old roof will last the winter – he's confident. But the Georgian roof is knackered. Something I know already.

Helen is so delightful and impressive. Her husband dies quite suddenly and she just gets on and runs the vet practice, raises her two girls. And remains so positive. And so "friendly" with Henry. Quite a surprise!

Sunday 20th October - TIMOTHY

A depressingly routine visit to Tanushi. It seems clear where her interests lie.

Sunday 20th October

1. A day of recovery from the exertions of the week.

2. Charles, over a Singleton, tells me of his excursions with Beatrice during the week. Where they've been. What they've done. It's like a newly born love. Each experience is savoured with an intensity that only an acute awareness of finiteness can bring about.

3. I tell him that if he wants me to speak at his funeral, then I will do so.

4. Helen then joins us as arranged. She greeted Charles warmly. And we talked inevitably about long-lost worlds. And about children and the hopes and fears for the future. Helen is, it would be fair to say, quite a progressive thinker. She is condemning of the present devotion to capitalism and consumption and the environmental headlock these twins have us in. I share the analysis entirely but cannot come up with any easy solutions. Charles tells her of his prognosis. Helen tells her story in a little more detail and speaks very highly of Pendleside Hospice. We rejoiced together and we wept together.

Monday 21st October

1. Tanushi arrives just as Helen is bidding goodbye with much gratitude. She has insisted on paying. And then a prolonged discussion starts about what dog Tanushi should get. Girls waiting in car and the Newfoundland is goaded into play by Tiff. A beginner dog is needed – but not a toy dog – such a waste living on an estate like this – and she starts suggesting all sorts of monster dogs (clearly her preference) and Tanushi is busily writing down her (highly inappropriate) thoughts. Helen gives Tanushi her contact details – anything you want to ask...

2. Helen and her daughters and the Newfoundland leave.

3. Tanushi reminds me of my tasks and says that Beatrice will be round at some stage this week to collect my diary for photocopying. I reiterate the rules re any proposed publication. She smiles. I say, "Tanushi, I have noticed how some

people including family call you Nushi. Would you like me to call you that?" She replies, "It is entirely up to you Henry." And as she says this, she reaches out her hand to touch my hand. And then she says, "Oh I'm sorry Henry – I forgot you..." I attempt to reassure her.

4. I wonder whether Revd. Dorothy's touch desensitization therapy has helped? It was only ever therapy. I realise that now.

5. First Christmas tree spotted in the village. Bloody ridiculous.

Monday 21st October - TANUSHI

Good discussion with Helen as she was leaving about dogs. Got her contact details. She is so nice. I touched Henry today on his hand. I just forgot and he did not react quite as dramatically as I expected. He was OK. Remind him of the tasks he has to get on with.

Clearing out stuff from the far bedrooms to the right of the stairs where water ingress the worst. Need to expose the extent of the damage. It is hard and unpleasant work. Getting along well with the skip man now!

Contemplate dogs until Jimmy comes in surprising me. The general dirt and smell doesn't do too much to dampen his ardour. He lends a hand for half an hour or so.

Tuesday 22nd October

1. I ask Jane a simple question. "Am I to expect Revd. Dorothy tomorrow to collect Twyi?" She says she has no idea. "Didn't you ask her last week?" Clearly, I didn't ask last week or I wouldn't be asking now. "You can always ring her. Have you got her number?" "I don't want to ring her." "Then you will struggle to find out whether she sees the Wednesday Twyi walk as a regular weekly fixture in her diary." A most unsatisfactory conversation.

2. Time spent putting orchard to bed for the winter.

Wednesday 23rd October

1. Working on beetles. I am not able to settle with this uncertainty. Go up to farm to see if I can help put the yurts away for the winter. Jimmy says he has done it all. Troop back down track only to see her car turn into and up the drive. There's no possibility of turning on my toes. Too obvious. So, I arrive at the front about 60 seconds after she does.

2. "Hello Henry. Is Twyi around for a walk? You could come too if you like?" I say, "Are you going to do this every week? I just need to know that's all." "Well if you have no objection? I'd like to. It's a fine walk up Biggle Hill. I am grateful to you for allowing me access via the wood." I say, "I have no objection. I will fetch Twyi. I am sure she'll enjoy your company."

3. I do just find all this profoundly unsettling.

Friday 25th October - TANUSHI

It has taken the full week to clear debris away from waterlogged area in one of the two rooms. All the furniture is shifted back as far as possible (with Jimmy's assistance of course). All soft furnishings skipped – mattress, curtains, drapes, carpets and rugs. Danger tape preventing access put up. This room specialises in random taxidermy and a collection of propelling pencils and has a rather nice unspoilt revolving circular bookcase in yew and mahogany. Quick look at books reveals nothing earth-shattering. Nothing else of any great worth, I wouldn't have thought. Maybe a little money in the two clocks – one wall mounted and one mantel. All pictures taken down and made safe. Next room next week.

Knocked off early and went to see Florence and the Machine at the Sheffield arena with Sam. Just brilliant. Love that woman (well both of them really!) Best night out. Get back – get the Baileys out and we fall asleep on the sofa in front of the fire. Ha! Getting old!

Sunday 27th October

1. Communion. Nothing to add.

2. Charles stays but briefly. Tired out from today's visit to Mr Straw's House, Worksop. National Trust. Fascinating apparently.

Monday 28th October

1. In winter setting now. 4 months of fire lighting and keeping winter hours. Ted has the walled garden in order. Orchard shut down. Jimmy has applied for planning permission to convert stables and adjacent buildings and is getting on with all preliminary works for that. His plumber and electrician mates in the village are helping. He doesn't let the grass grow under his feet. The pigs are beginning to turn a steady profit and earning a decent reputation at the butchers.

2. Tanushi calls in to report progress. She has seen the damage wrought by water ingress into two rooms in particular. Of the 10 identified "green dot" items of furniture – 2 are off to America, 5 are in the local auction house on Thursday and 3 have gone to Peak Antiques in Bakewell. She hopes for a total of c. £7,500 from all this. Not at all bad. And she's exploring how to get rid of the Billiard table. Impressive in one so young.

3. I am ready for hibernation.

Wednesday 30th October

1. Ensure I am completely unavailable all day. To any visitors. Jane is clear on this.

Thursday 31st October

1. Furniture at auction makes a modest amount. They rob you of course on the commission. 12.5% Decided not to go. Filthy weather.

NOVEMBER
2013

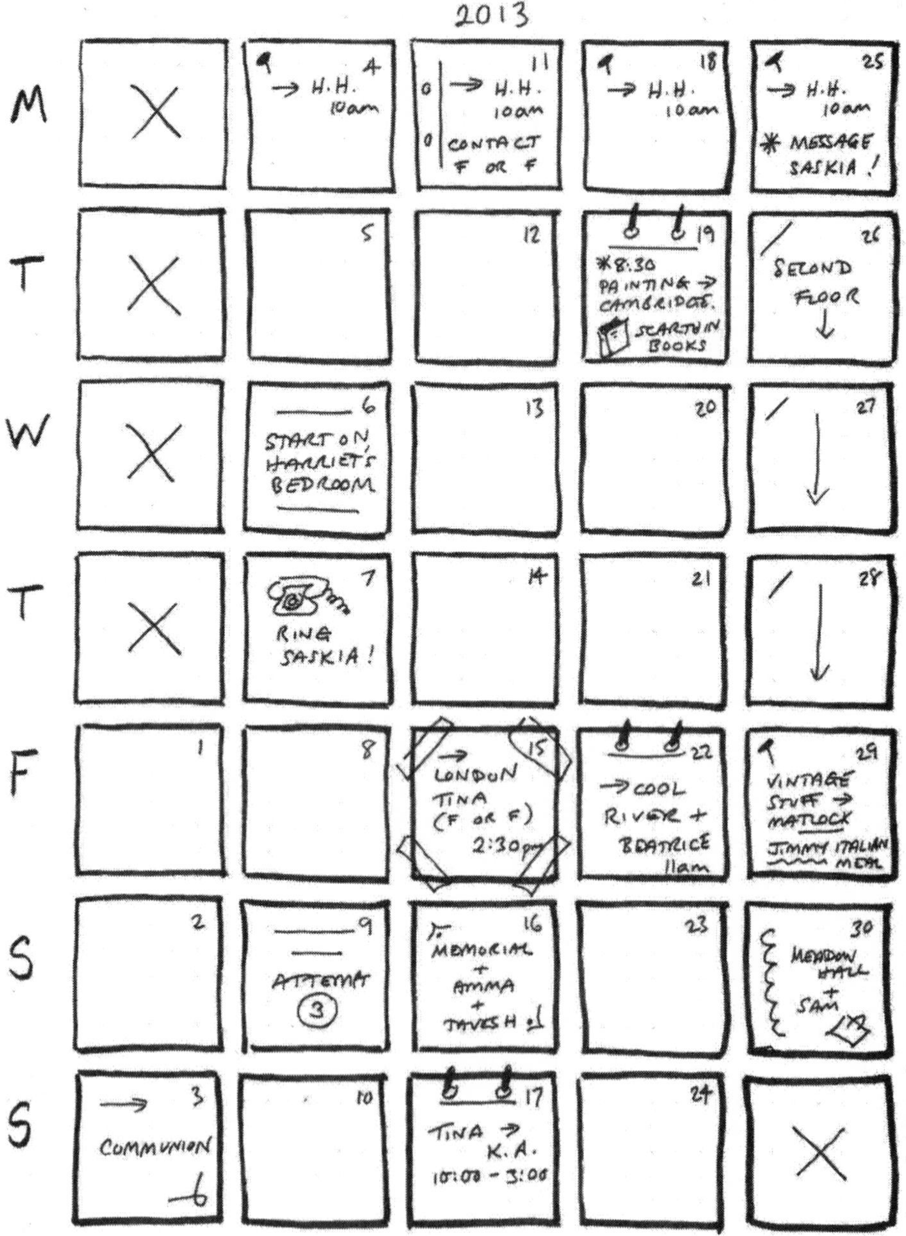

Friday 1st November - TANUSHI

Now completed second enormous bedroom. Same as before. Two sweet old rocking cradles. All furniture shifted and protected as best can be from the elements. Such a lot of crap to shift. No need to go to gym for muscle gain.

I might start on HH's Mother's room next week. Go round to farmhouse to be cooked for by Jimmy. Sam out with some friends. Jimmy is amazing in the kitchen. Goes against his macho image I suggest. He likes me teasing him I can tell.

We talk about his Mum and her death. He resents that there is no memorial to her on the estate. We can change that I think. He rarely sees his maternal grandmother – she lives in Tarleton near Southport. He says they were really brought up by Ted and Jane rather than his Father – Roger fell to bits after her death. But he is without rancour. He showed me a picture of his Mum – Sophie – with the two of them. So beautiful.

Sunday 3rd November

1. Communion. Tanushi there. Jane and Ted there. Andrew and Sarah there AND Revd. Dorothy. I don't believe in coincidences. (When I return, I find I cannot locate the rota for readers but I could have sworn she was not on for St Cuthbert's – ever.) Tanushi said she had enjoyed Harvest and thought she'd come again. Needless to say, it was a beautifully and intelligently led service. Now what do you do about breakfast? As it happens, she had to rush off to welcome a baptismal party to All Saints. So, difficulty sidestepped. As she left, she said or asked – not sure – "See you Wednesday."

2. Charles cancelled. Feeling tired. As am I.

Monday 4th November

1. Tanushi calls in. Tells me Beatrice is going to call later for the diaries. She does seem to be in touch with Beatrice an awful lot. She also says that she intends to start on Mother's room this week. I tell her that I tried not to touch or move very much. Just covered everything in drapes. She mentioned that Jane had said there might be the remains of a silver cutlery service there – something I could confirm. No idea where.

Mother lived in that room entirely in her later years. As soon as the last of her horses died, she never went outside again. She wrote copious letters, watched TV, read cheap romance and pined for her horses. Jane was up and down the stairs looking after her. In the last few months, when her needs became more pressing, nurses were in attendance some of the time and – for some reason – I started to spend more time with her. Reading to her, talking about her childhood in Lancashire, the gymkhanas she had won, the boys she had flirted with and she told the story of her whirlwind but ill-fated romance with Father. She also spoke of him – in a way I had not heard before – what happened at his Public School and what happened in the war. I suppose she was trying to adjudicate whether there were any grounds for clemency.

In the end she said she was sorry for how she had treated me. She too was a lost and lonely soul whose only solace was her horses. She was repulsed by me because I reminded her of what my Father had done to her. She asked for the local vicar to be brought in right at the end – "to make her peace with God and Man." She had never shown the slightest interest in religion beforehand.

My Father I feared and hated. He was a bully. What reason is there – now I have more information – to change that judgement? He is dead. My attitude towards him is in historical formaldehyde.

My Mother – I felt sorry for. She was not equipped to cope with an abusive, unfaithful and largely absent husband. Who could possibly cope with that? She too was absent to me – until the very end.

And so, I am as I am. A combination of genetic and environmental accident. We none of us choose our combinations but we can learn to play the cards that are given with skill and creativity. Otherwise we are just the creatures of deterministic fate. I think I have believed the former too little and lived the latter too much.

Tuesday 5th November

1. Bloody fireworks. Imogen in bits apparently. Tiff barks at each noise. I have no short-term advice really. Apparently, desensitization therapy can be helpful over time.

Wednesday 6th November

1. Not at home. Twyi has a second walk apparently.

Wednesday 6th November - TANUSHI

I am not telling ANYBODY about this... until something is confirmed – one way or another.

Much easier task in Harriet's bedroom. This is the room – when you are going round a stately home – when you get to the room and they say, "This is where King/Queen so and so stayed when they visited in whenever." All the really quality furniture and decorative items are in this room. A fabulous four poster with tired but rescuable (I think) tapestry drapes. And a bedspread which looks at the very least "special" – not sure. Little trinkets and dressing set and of course massive and ornate mantel clock set with candlesticks to match. Harriet had managed to cram all the wonderful heirlooms into her room – and why not?

BUT all that is as nothing...maybe. Coming towards the end of cataloguing. And the pictures. I pull down the sheet covering the huge central painting over the fireplace. And there she is – Carilla Havard standing beside an utterly monumental horse. She is portrayed as a great beauty, vivacious and noble but not haughty. And there is something very different about this painting. It oozes character, quality in composition, in technique, in refinement and delicacy of touch. It oozes love for Carilla. There is no visible signature just a date aside the name "Carilla Havard 1825". And this is not on the actual painting but on the frame itself. The trees and landscape in the background are not Derbyshire. Carilla is a Spanish name. But I am not convinced it looks like Spain either. In the foreground, strategically arranged are two barrels with Bordeaux inscribed on the tops. The red contents have stained the sides in places.

So I go round to HH and ask what he knows of Carilla Havard and he points to some journals. He is in a non-communicative mood at this stage engrossed as ever in beetles. I establish that she was the mistress of KA in the nineteenth century. That she was Spanish, from Cadiz, born 1793, and that she funded the estate with a wine and sherry business based upon visits to Bordeaux and her native Cadiz.

So this was painted by someone maybe in Bordeaux in 1825. Look up regional French artists. Then national French artists. Interesting.

Get Jimmy down to see if he thinks we can get this down from the wall between us – safely. Jimmy jumps to it! He thinks we need some help and I don't want to disturb HH further. It is hanging on two chains from the picture rail. He calls a mate for the village to help. I go up the ladder to release the two hooks whilst Jimmy and Neil hold either corner. And it is brought down in a controlled way successfully. Phew!

We prop it against the bureau bookcase. I feign indifference. They leave. I explore the picture in more detail with torch and magnifying glass. I am no expert but when viewed up closely the brushstrokes seem to be broken and separated. I am not convinced that it was painted entirely with brush. The central figures are framed in a grey blue background. From a distance there is an impressionistic air to the piece (which I realise is anachronistic nonsense.)

On the back...there is an inscription. "A mi hija, Carilla Havard. Pintado por su padre. 1825." ("To my daughter, Carilla Havard. Painted by her Father. 1825.") And then three, somewhat obscured, short, utterly electrifying words.

Shit. Research. Research. Shit.

I need a gin and tonic.

Ring Saskia at the end of the day. Swear her to total secrecy. She must not consult with anyone at all. Tell her what I know. Send her a few pictures.

Within an hour she's on Skype with G and T in hand saying OMG a thousand times!!!

What now? She's going to think how we go about this.

Thursday 7th November

Long call to Saskia. I don't want anyone here to have any idea of what this might just be. She says that I must not get ahead of myself. Proving a picture is actually painted by someone 200 years ago is very, very difficult. We have all seen that TV programme. You need a level of proof beyond "reasonable."

If I ask for the painting to be removed and sent to London or Cambridge for verification, then everybody knows it might be something. Can the tests be done here? Some tests can, some cannot. For full authentication it needs to leave Kirk Aeppel and I cannot sanction that...

She then starts to talk about provenance. How good is the documentary evidence? Don't know really. There's something to go on.

She then suggests that I consider contacting local TV and Fake or Fortune to see if they would be interested. Money can be made even if it turns out to be a fake. They might help with the financial costs of authentication if they deem it a sufficiently good potential story. And none of that can be done without HH's consent either.

Then she raises the issue of security at KA. There is none. Is the roof going to be secure enough to protect the painting? Hopefully in that room.

She hasn't spoken to anybody her end. They have an expert who might be able to help. I have to decide what to do with all this.

Friday 8th November

1. Cambridge have been in touch re naming my "discovery" – not quite as impressive as the Higgs boson – for which Peter Higgs was awarded the Nobel Prize for Physics last month! Good show.

2. Very exciting to name a new species. Can't be a rude name I am advised! And not to worry about the Latin.

Kingdom: Animalia

Phylum: Arthropoda

Class: Insecta

Order: Coleoptera

Family: Cerambycidae

Subfamily: Laniinae

Tribe: Mesosini

Genus: Coptops XXXXXXXX

And I get to choose the XXXXXXX.

I am interrupted mid-deliberation by Tanushi – just dropping round to check if it was OK if she got some painting checked out by that lovely Saskia at the Fitzwilliam Museum and get in touch with the media to generate interest in Kirk Aeppel – and that's when I knew it had to be Coptops Kirk Aeppel. Sounds good. Has a ring to it.

Signed her bits of paper and said as long as no camera comes anywhere near me, she could do what she wanted.

Essentially, it's a rather pretty longhorn beetle with the typical oversized antennae – as long as the beetle's body. Would it not be rather wonderful if they discovered this in the wild?

Friday 8th November - TANUSHI

Phone Saskia. Got permission. HH caught up in beetle world. Just brilliant. Getting in touch with Fake or Fortune. See if they are interested. Will insist it goes firstly to the expert at the Fitz. Got his name. Don't say anything yet!

Go to sleep imagining Philip Mould eating my banoffee pie downstairs in the candle light. He says, "I think Tanushi that I can authenticate that as the best banoffee pie ever made." And I collect a drip of toffee sauce from the spout of the jug and lick my finger.

Saturday 9th November

Attempt 3

Saturday 9th November

Attempt 3

Sunday 10th November

1. No Charles – having a procedure tomorrow – a colostomy bag. Things are suddenly sounding grim.

2. Decide to use the time to start on the speech for the funeral. There is too much to say. This is not normally an issue for me. To say too little is unthinkable. I give up within 10 minutes. Retreat to Coleopterist Bulletin.

Monday 11th November

1. Tanushi calls in – nothing much to say. Mother's room pretty much sorted and catalogued. Lots of nice stuff apparently. She is off to London at the end of the week to her Father's memorial day at LSE.

Monday 11th November - TANUSHI

Contact BBC – Fake or Fortune. Request urgent call back. Impress upon Roberta the urgency and secrecy of situation and seriousness of potential coup. She advises against contact with local news sources. When can someone get up here? To film discretely? This painting needs to be moved down to Cambridge asap.

Later a longer conversation with principle researcher (Tina). Appraise her of the situation here and the sensitivities. I still don't mention any specifics about what I suspect. She is reluctant to send anyone without a name. That would be to commit money to something without knowing the potential reward. I get the issue. I tell her in the strictest confidence. Gasp. She will get back to me.

Wednesday 13th November

1. Jane speaks to me sternly. She will no longer be a party to the games. Allowing me to hide away. Her having to come up to get Twyi and hand her over to Dorothy. Not acceptable. I need to sort it out – whatever "it" is – with Dorothy and not run away from the issue.

2. Hand over Twyi at 1.30 pm with as minimal fuss as possible. She has chosen the best time in a miserable and damp day. I realise I ought to offer some hot drink when she returns Twyi. She says she has to be off and that lets me off the hook.

3. There's no doubt that Twyi has developed a very special bond with her that would be a shame to bring to an end.

Friday 15th November - TANUSHI

Travel down to London. And meet up with Tina. She says that she can be there this Sunday with one camera and one light. She wants the provenance documentation ready. She wants to film from 10.00 am and will be finished by 3.00 pm. All the commentary can be added afterwards if it actually ever makes it to TV.

Then if she is sufficiently interested, she will sanction the removal to the Fitzwilliam to the expert there – who she knows of. She assures me she has told no one.

Stay with Amma.

Saturday 16th November

Go into London for the memorial. All as usual except that Hugh Evans suddenly announces he is retiring this year. He does not know if the University will want to continue this act of memorial. At this point Amma (I assume she had been prepared for this announcement) stands up and takes the mic. She speaks incredibly calmly but beautifully and movingly about what Hugh had done for this refugee family seeking asylum in Britain. She speaks of what Tavesh and I are doing and how this is only possible with the courage and compassion of Hugh. It wasn't his problem but he made it his problem. There wasn't a dry eye in the house.

Sunday 17th November

Tina arrived (with camera guy) very discretely at gatehouse and I drove her up to the Georgian entrance. The plan is to do this entirely unobserved.

I had everything ready. No pictures were taken outside – that can wait. Everything filmed in the bedroom. We just about manoeuvred the panting around for a proper look at the back. Her eyes widened. The journal was photographed and each relevant page. True to her word, everything was completed by 3.00 pm. She is sure they will pursue this but needs to authorisation of someone senior. They are used to total secrecy on the programme, so there should be no trouble. She will want me to be the representative of the estate at all times and be ready to come down to be interviewed as and when. I show her my authorisation from HH.

She warned me that more often than not people are disappointed with the outcome and that I will not find out until the very end of the process. And then I signed the various documents. Yes, they will pay for investigations etc. But if the painting proves to be genuine, they will want a percentage of that money back.

She will contact me tomorrow afternoon to confirm.

Monday 18th November

See HH as usual first thing. He is in full "hibernation" as he calls it. Missing Charles. I say nothing much is going on – just working upstairs on the remaining rooms. He asks me about London. I think he is strangely proud in a weird way of my story. Told him what Amma said.

I say that it would be nice to have some memorial at KA for Jimmy and Sam's Mum – Sophie. He is surprised but very open to that; he was very fond of her and asks if I would liaise with them as to what they might want – tree, bench, something else.

Tina rings up – it's a yes. It will be collected and taken to the Fitz and she has been in touch with the expert there to contract him in the process. He is a top specialist she assures me. The people will arrive tomorrow at 8.30 am. She has wasted no time. I ask her what she thinks. She says her job is to assess whether there is a story worth telling and if there is a decent chance of a definitive outcome one way or another. She has no expertise in paintings and so cannot judge at all. Bit downcast by that.

Tuesday 19th November

The deed is done and I now feel incredibly nervous – both that KA has lost its wonderful painting – and essentially only I know that – and of course for the outcome. Desperate to talk to someone!! Should I say something to Beatrice?

Continue in the remaining bedrooms and bathrooms.

So far the roofing bank balance is c. £8,500 with a few more bits and pieces to go to the vintage shops in Matlock, plus the Tusks at say c. £60,000, quite a lot more furniture to go I would imagine. We cannot possibly keep all those clocks and one or two of those will fetch a bit. And Ted mentioned there are the sheds at the back of the swimming pool area which might be worth investigating. Gardening stuff in the main. Take a selection of books to Scarthin Books. OMG what a place! Such a paradise for getting lost in old books. A whole room on Art – so I browsed there for ages! And settled on two "strategic" books. They were keen to buy the books. Apparently leather-bound books bought by some to "improve the look of their bookshelves" – can you believe that! What sad people.

Need another red, amber green spot meeting.

Wednesday 20th November

1. I did invite her in after her Tywi walk – merely out of Christian charity. But sensibly she said she must get on. But she thanked me kindly. I think that is exactly the stability of interaction now needed and tacitly agreed upon. Civility established.

2. Charles is picking up and will come round on Sunday.

Wednesday 20th November – TIMOTHY

Father is not well but insists on putting an infuriatingly positive face on everything. He is dropping one or two stiches at work...and needs to cut down some more, I think. He is reluctant. I suppose he thinks, maybe rightly, that that is the beginning of the end and that he'll never get back to the practice again.

So, I am once again shouldering at least some of the burden.

Fed up with lack of social life. Fed up I never see Tanushi and that that bus has seemingly gone – or whatever the phrase is. Going to go on dating website. No idea which one to choose.

Friday 22nd November - TANUSHI

Go to Cool River with Beatrice and tell her everything. She pours over the contracts with "F or F". She does say one or two fierce things like, "If you were a junior member of staff and you had gone out on a limb in such a way, I would be furious."

But she's happy that everything is legally kosher. And she understands my feeling that I should keep everything as secret as possible. So glad I have told her. Feel so much better now. I have heard nothing. Even Saskia has gone a bit quiet. She just messaged on Wednesday: "Package received safely and undergoing inspection."

Sunday 24th November

1. Communion. Nothing to add.

2. Andrew and Sarah tell me of the measures they are going to, to desensitize Imogen re fireworks.

3. Charles – a bit wobbly but spirited. Enjoyed our evening with a 15 year-old Strathisla.

Monday 25th November - TANUSHI

Messaged Saskia. Went to see HH. Reminded him to get his tasks completed by 13th December...

Worked on completing second floor. Mind totally wrapped up in awaiting Saskia's call back.

Saskia called back in her lunchbreak. She can't say too much. All the tests are being conducted and she has been kept out of it all. But it has created a lot of interest. They are filming next week sometime. That is the actual item – without the presenters. But she doesn't expect to hear anything one way or another for ages. Any little rumour – one way or another – she will pass on. Eventually the decision will be made by the experts in Spain. Expect not to hear anything about the picture until well into the New Year.

I had naively thought that it would be done and dusted by now! Or soon enough anyway. I need to get on with things here without constant anxiety about Carilla.

Wednesday 27th November

1. Made the usual offer re Revd. D. Politely declined. Perfect.

2. Beatrice returns diaries. Photocopies made. I reiterate to her – nothing gets published without my say so. She agrees.

3. We talk of Charles. How brave. How he's asked me to speak at the funeral. Beatrice happy with that. She doesn't think she will be able to do that. Maybe Hannah and Timothy can do that between them. Maybe. She hopes he'll make another summer.

4. The one thing I will say for Beatrice (amongst many things) is that she's never begrudged or been jealous of Charles' friendship with me.

Friday 29th November - TANUSHI

I think I am finished upstairs. There's a load of stuff in Harriet's room which I haven't yet sifted through. But all the major stuff is done.

Take down a second load of vintage stuff to Matlock to hawk around. First lot went really well, so lots of interest. £500+ banked.

Went out with Jimmy to an Italian in Bakewell. Just had the best time. The further he is away from his mates in the village the better.

Saturday 30th November

Shopping with Sam at Meadowhall. It was rammed.

DECEMBER

2013

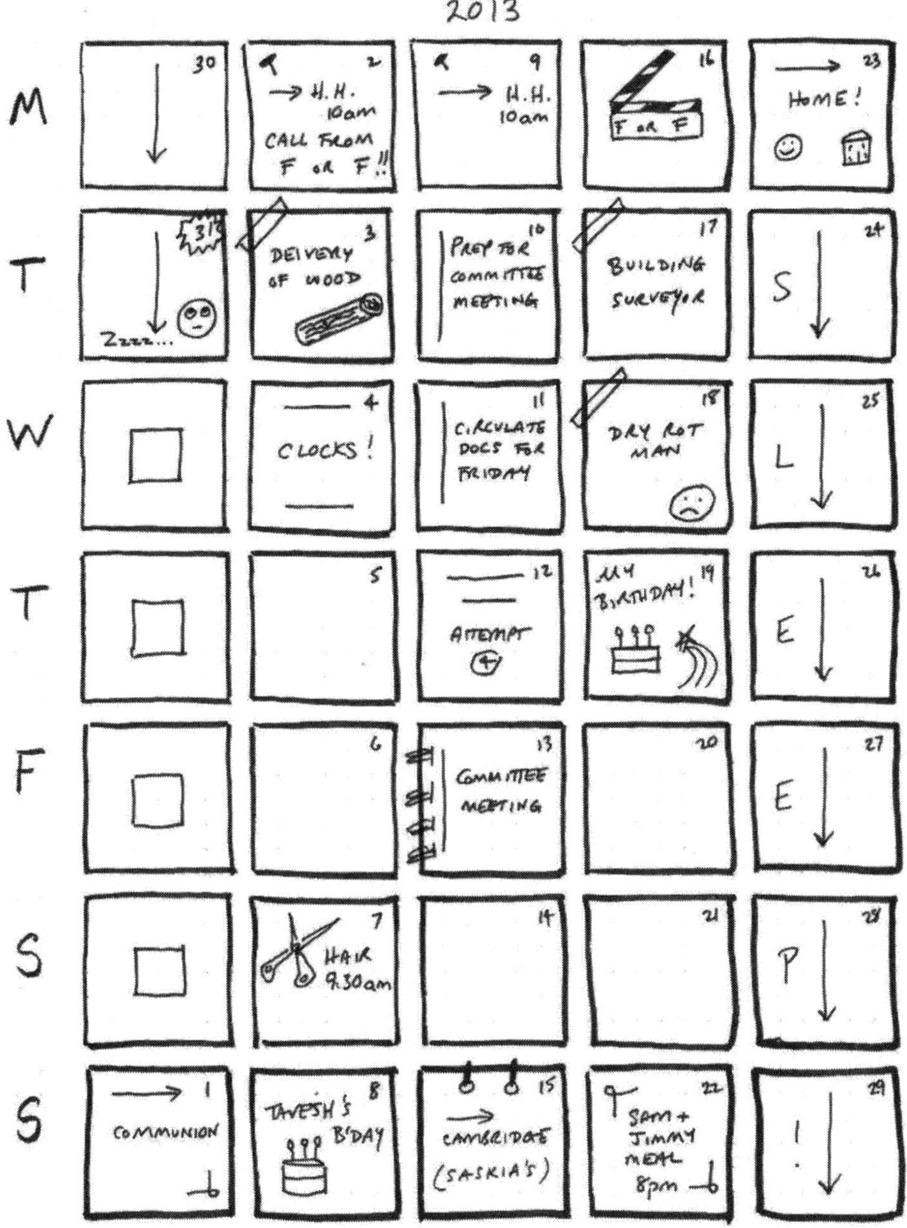

Sunday 1st December

1. First Sunday in Advent. Communion. Mrs Manifold presiding.

2. Splendid walk with the dogs. Fast moving clouds speckle the sky. Weather looks poor for the end of the week.

3. Charles comes round with Beatrice. She allows him a little whisky – more of the Strathisla. Pleasant evening.

Monday 2nd December

1. Tanushi calls round to ask what we do for Christmas. Apart from the Carol Service – nothing. No decorations. She thinks this is appalling. Money is tight. And I have no need to celebrate for myself. Jimmy and Sam and Ted and Jane of course decorate in the traditional way in their homes, I am sure. "And you must too!" She leaves unimpressed.

Monday 2nd December - TANUSHI

I get a call – they want to film me before Christmas in Cambridge with one of the presenters and the picture. I can make any day except 13th. They will get back to me.

Tuesday 3rd December

1. They have discovered that there are anatomical differences between men and women's brain structures. Well who would have thought that?

Wednesday 4th December

1. Same offer made to Revd. Dorothy at the end of her walk. Do come in for a cup of tea – and she accepted. That was not part of the rules. Twyi wet and dirty. So, I busied myself towelling her down whilst she went through to Jane in the kitchen. Jane sat in chaperone-like during the excruciating pleasantries. She wanted to talk about the Carol Service. She planned to sell tickets as last year. What did I think? Fine by me. Over finally. Retreated to my fire. Jane says on leaving, "See, that wasn't too awful was it now?"

Thursday 5th December

1. Mandela dies.

2. Tremendous storms across the country. East coast inundated. I fear for the roof. Ask Tanushi to have a look in the other place and see if it has destroyed even more. Just as bad as ever. Great.

Friday 6th December - TANUSHI

Get the call up to go to Cambridge – they pay – on Monday 16th. Start really early morning. Ask what I should wear. "Smart casual" which is absolutely no help at all. I ask which presenter but Roberta does not know. Phone Saskia to see if I can stay over Sunday night. Fine. She is so excited. She doesn't know which presenter either. Say I'd rather like it to be Philip and she giggles!

Meet up with Sam – Jimmy off with his mates.

Sunday 8th December

1. Beatrice phones. Charles not venturing out. Filthy weather. He's fine. But she feels she needs to protect him, wrap him up. I understand. They have taken to playing Backgammon once again. A game they played endlessly in their younger days.

Monday 9th December - TANUSHI

It is wild weather. Checking the two worst leaking rooms each day now. Not sure what more we can do. Jimmy has no suggestions.

Check in on HH. Meeting on Friday.

Get a whole load of bumph from F or F through the post about what's going to happen next week and the process and how long it will take. I need to consider how I am to be introduced and referred to. It is likely that there will be two or three further filmed meetings in the New Year. I might be invited to go to Spain ultimately for the verdict. I now have a rough idea of what's going to happen. They are expecting it taking 6 months!

Wednesday 11th December

1. Revd. Dorothy stops for a tea and cake provided by Jane. I am suitably quiet. Tanushi then suddenly pops in to report on the roof in the other place. I find this excruciatingly awkward. They seem to smile and greet and converse as if all is well with the world. I find this quite remarkable. Something really which I do not understand. And Tanushi drops off the documents for the meeting on Friday.

Thursday 12th December

Attempt 4

Friday 13th December - TANUSHI

Again, the meeting was divided into two parts.

1. Dog idea. Sam has taken the "lead" on this. Some options:

- A regional one or two breed competition run by Kennel Club
- Local dog show – with a dozen stalls and fun competitions.
- Taking a small number of dogs for a training weekend.

Parking was an issue for any bigger event. She advised we start with the latter two ideas. When the accommodation is ready. Book a date in the summer / autumn for local fun dog event. Portable loos?

2. Update from Jimmy on accommodation development. He thanked Tanushi for her input into the design. Planning approval now granted after slight delay. He was well on with all foundational work. The stable feel will be preserved. In total there will be separate self-catering accommodation for 4 couples with some additional bed space for children. He was confident this can be ready by May / June. Glamping – 4 yurts – accommodating up to 6 in each – has been very successful.

3. Arts events. Tanushi has been in contact with various local arts groups to see how they might be able to use the indoor / outdoor space at KA. Lots of interest but all very dependent on developments at KA in the next 12 months. Car parking and loos again raised as an issue.

4. Christmas. Nothing happens – but it must in the future. Tanushi. Must be an opportunity for markets – everybody mentioned Matlock/Chatsworth/Haddon already hold such events. More thought needed. Chapel? Christmas round Big Table – hire in caterers?

5. Development of KA produce – HH. No progress.

6. Cider – Jimmy happy to run weekends during the summer and autumn on cider making. Happy for locals to bring apples in for pressing. HH offered to approach Camra (Ed: real ale campaign group) which takes on real cider under its wing.

7. Dorothy (completing the task set last time) sent a report with some suggestions for local charities she has contacted – who might be able to use KA. Helen's Trust, Church on the Bus for local homeless people, Aquabox. Given the appropriate infrastructure at KA – parking, loos, catering facilities, they would love to use KA.

8. Roof finances. As last time. Banked approaching £10,000 + tusks + furniture and clocks + grants. HH made his pitch about the tusks once more. (175-200K)

Then we visited the Georgian wing. Cold and damp. People amazed by progress. Jimmy promised to block up the fireplace in the Billiard Room. We did the red/amber/green spot for the remaining rooms upstairs. I managed to steer people away from Harriet's room altogether saying that has not been completed. I am authorised to get quotes on all the clocks and then we can make a decision.

They are shocked by the state of the two northern facing bedrooms now that all the clutter is cleared away. Beatrice said that this needs someone professional in immediately to assess its structural viability and safety. We agree for Jimmy to arrange that as a matter of urgency.

Then we retired to Big Table to enjoy Jane's homemade soup, bread, cheese.

Irritated with HH that he should have done so little to look into the produce side of things.

Pleased no one ventured in to see the tell-tale staining on the chimney breast in Harriet's room revealing a missing picture. Beatrice helped usher everyone on their way out. All wanted to get out of the cold and enjoy Jane's soup which they had been smelling in preparation during the meeting

Next meeting Friday 14th February – Jimmy then said he thought he'd got something on that evening. Couldn't remember what or with whom. Very funny.

Friday 13th December

1. I hate these meetings. No one there on my side. They all go on about this scheme or that scheme. How much progress is being made and each time the need to build infrastructure here – that means loos, kitchens, car parks. On this precious site. Commercialise, rip up the land and tarmac it. Next, they'll be suggesting we chop old oak down.

2. I hadn't done my homework so detention for me.

3. We trooped round to see what Tanushi has done in the other place. Isn't she wonderful? Look what she's achieved. And the assumption still is we are going to flog off the tusks.

4. How is a man to achieve peace?

5. Tanushi said she'll be away on a marketing course on Monday.

Sunday 15th December

1. Jimmy drove me to see Charles. He was well enough. Took round the 18 year-old Glenlivet. Beatrice indicated only a small amount. Seems to me if you are dying, why not glug it down? Live for the moment? You've not got many of them left. I didn't say that.

Sunday 15th December - TANUSHI

Slow train journey down to Cambridge and taxi to Saskia's flat. She is so excited for tomorrow. We have to be in and ready at the Fitz v. early.

Monday 16th December

Arrived at 7.00 am. There was no need to arrive at 7.00 am! It was 2 hours before I was called upon. Makeup told me it was going to be Philip!! All shots to begin with are of me looking intensely at picture, holding the picture, studying the picture. The shots of the expert (Richard Bowler) speaking to me in front of picture, pointing to picture and explaining stuff to me. I asked, obviously, what he thought and he was professional caution epitomised. Well this is encouraging but we have to run this test and that test and it all depended on x, y and z. It was a pity there was nothing on the painting itself – just the title of the piece on the frame but this wasn't too damning. Then there was the strange assignation on the back etc.

Enter Philip. Greeted me charmingly – kissed on both cheeks. (He smells nice!) "So delighted to meet you. Isn't this so exciting Tanushi? Well what a splendid painting – whoever it's by. Let's hope we find out! How should we describe you?"

I have decided upon the Preservation officer at Kirk Aeppel. He then asked how to pronounce KA. So out of deference to HH, I said "EYEPUL."

"And I understand that things are in something of a parlous state there. Would that be fair to say?"

"Yes absolutely. Everything depends on this."

"Splendid – just make sure you say that to camera!" And then we talked briefly about my degree and my role at KA. He was as utterly charming as I had imagined.

He then scooted off to makeup and we were on. I have forgotten how many times I have to tell the story of its "discovery". Then there were shots of me looking through Carilla's journal and the story of her arrival at KA. Then Richard talking about the problematic provenance. It took all day

Philip said he looked forward to seeing me in the New Year and wished me Happy Christmas. "You have been an utter delight and most professional Tanushi. Thank you so much." Kiss kiss.

I arrived back at Matlock late.

Tuesday 17th December

Meet with Jimmy and building surveyor. It has not stopped raining for weeks. He does his stuff. He says it's a mess, then laughs, but it's not going to fall down any time soon. You do need a new roof entirely. (Really?) And I reckon you have both dry and wet rot. Wet rot is sortable by stopping the water coming in and replacing the damage. Dry rot is much more serious and unless this is treated soon, you could lose the whole house. We need another expert in to suggest solutions. No idea how far this dry rot has already spread.

Send round an email to everyone on the committee with this news.

HH emails back immediately: Perhaps we should surrender the Georgian house to the elements. Just save the Old House.

Timothy replies immediately: "Both parts of Kirk Aeppel are listed and there is a legal duty on the owner of the building to maintain the fabric of the building in good order. I know of a reliable damp and wet/dry rot specialist and I will send him round to get his assessment. I have used him before. I hope this is acceptable to everyone."

I reply: That would be so helpful Timothy. Let me know when and I'll be there.

Timothy: Booked him for tomorrow at 1.00 pm. See you there.

HH's negativity is so unhelpful.

Wednesday 18th December

1. Terrible storms overnight. The stream is a torrent. Dread to think what's happening to the roof. Then Jimmy says there's a problem with the chapel. Go round. Indeed, a large damp patch appearing above entrance and some damage to rendering/stone work evident. Next to downspout. That is all we need. The chapel is estate responsibility.

2. Phone Revd. Dorothy to cancel Carol Service.

3. Ask Jimmy – who as always remains optimistic – to get someone round to have a look. He thinks it'll be difficult this side of Christmas but he'll do his best.

4. Email estate to that effect.

Wednesday 18th December - TANUSHI

Meet Timothy at 1.00 pm. He is reassuringly prompt and comes with his chap in tow. "Now then duck, we can sort this out with a bit of luck and I'm feeling lucky today. You don't mind if I loosen this plaster. It'll all need re-doing anyway." After all his patter, the verdict is: yes, there is dry rot. In one not two rooms as far as he can tell. He cannot guarantee that but that is his professional best bet. Its spread is relatively limited he thinks. We may have caught it in time. He could do this before Christmas for £500 in cash and a mistletoe kiss.

Timothy says £450 which he accepts.

I don't consult – tell him to do it and that Timothy will supply the kiss. He is about to complain, when I say that he didn't specify who gave the kiss. Schoolboy error.

"Tanushi, it breaks my heart but it's a deal. You'll get our 10-year guarantee. I'll do it tomorrow and Friday and no one must come in to the house after midday Thursday until Saturday. Pleasure doing business for you Mr Parker." And he leaves.

I thank Timothy profusely. He smiles. We drive back down to the gatehouse and I offer him a cup of tea/coffee.

He thinks for a while and says he'd like to but he better not. He's meeting someone tonight and has much to do before that. I am about to ask, when he says he's joined an online dating site. First date tonight.

"Hope it goes well," I say and wonder who the lucky lady is.

The weather is terrible still. Go round to HH to update him. Jimmy there. The chapel looks worse than it is according to Jimmy. Someone he knows can do a temporary patch now and come back in the spring to do it properly. All that is sanctioned.

Sunday 22nd December

Dry rot dealt with we hope. The whole place stinks. Chapel sorted for the time being. Tusks safe with HH. I am off to Harrow tomorrow and wanted to have some assurance about the house. The weather has been incredible. No one can remember such an inundation of rain. Go to see Ted and Jane to give them a card and small present each. They are all ready for Christmas. Can't thank me enough for the help I've been and the hope that there might be a future for the estate.

Jimmy and Sam come round in the evening and we cook together in my tiny kitchen! And I give Sam, Jimmy's present and I give Jimmy, Sam's present. And we say Happy Christmas like we've been friends for our whole lives.

Sunday 22nd December

1. No question of Charles coming out. Tanushi off tomorrow. We have averted a cataclysm with the help of Tanushi, Jimmy, Timothy. Perhaps we will live another year, if the weather gods permit.

Monday 23rd December - TANUSHI

Back to Harrow.

Wednesday 25th December

1. No question of walking the bounds. The most dreadful storms continue. I have plenty of wood and coal and Game pie and Brussel sprouts and potatoes and red wine and cider. I am content.

Sunday 29th December

1. Jane looks in to check I am surviving. I am. She does worry about me. She is the only person who has ever worried about me.

   I phone to check on Charles. He has had a decent Christmas. So pleased to see Hannah again back from her travels. Looking forward to Hen Galan.

JANUARY

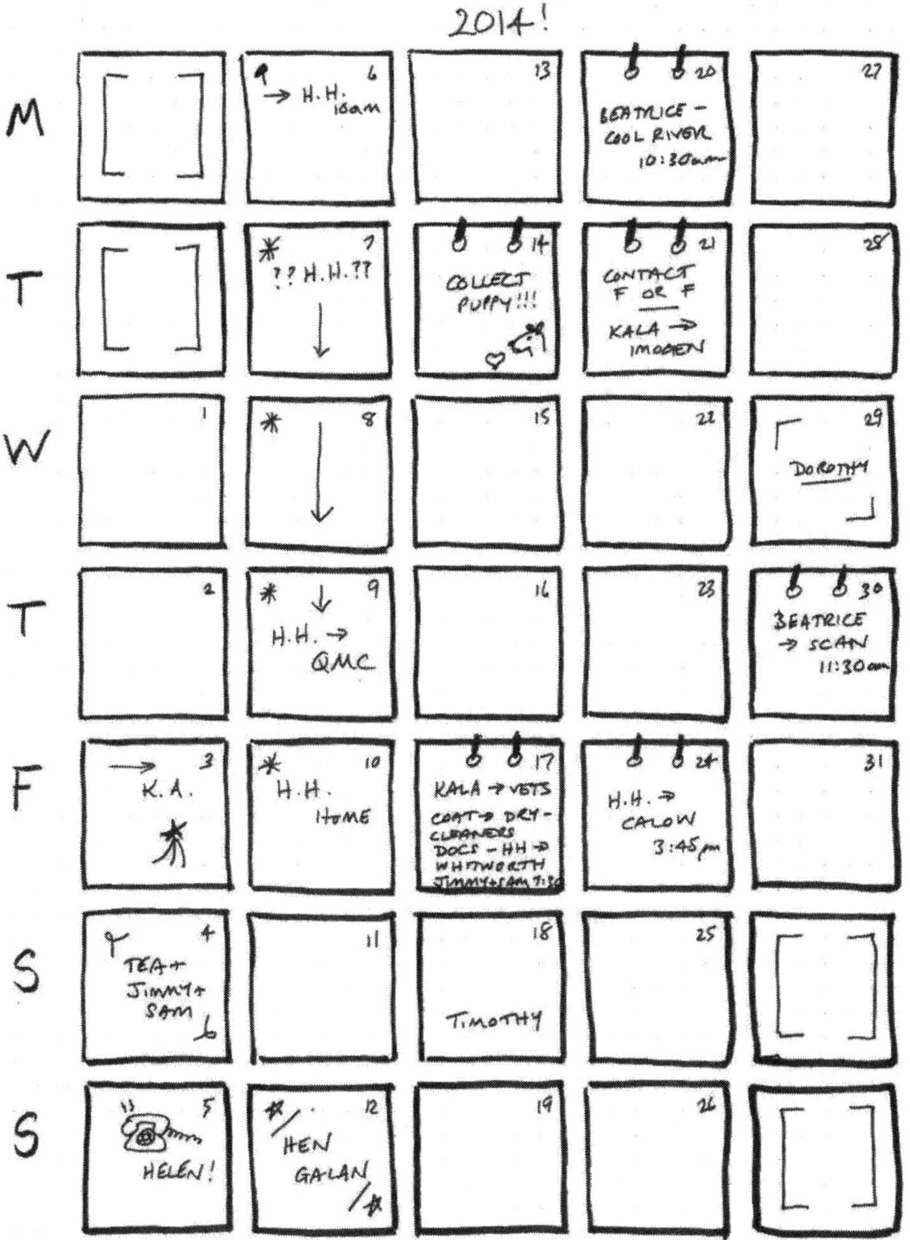
2014!
M
T
W
T
F
S
S
6
H.H. 10am
13
20
BEATRICE – COOL RIVER 10:30am
27
7
??H.H.??
14
COLLECT PUPPY!!!
21
CONTACT F OR F
KALA → IMOGEN
28
1
8
15
22
29
DOROTHY
2
9
H.H. → QMC
16
23
30
BEATRICE → SCAN 11:30am
3
K.A.
10
H.H. Home
17
KALA → VETS
COAT → DRY-CLEANERS
DOCS – HH → WHITWORTH
24
H.H. → CALOW 3:45pm
31
4
TEA + JIMMY + SAM
11
18
TIMOTHY
25
5
HELEN!
12
HEN GALAN
19
26

Wednesday 1st January 2014

1. Dorothy calls round – unannounced of course. She says she would like to take me – not Twyi for a walk – she has some things to say to me. She leaves me little choice. And it is the briefest of lulls in the weather I sense. So I agree.

2. She had been back to her Mother after the Christmas services. Trying to keep up Christmas appearances. And she had seen her Mother go round the same circles of negative thought and words and deeds as if imprisoned in a gold fish bowl. And she said she had had time to think and reflect. Upon reflection she has come to realise that she too has repeated destructive behaviours of the past. This has been a painful realisation. She behaved intemperately and she would like to apologise to me. She does not require me to say anything in response to this. Nor does she really want to spell out those habitual behaviours. But she is aware of them and she doesn't want to become like her Mother.

3. By this stage we were still in the wood squelching through mud. I mumbled my appreciation that what she had said must have been difficult, that she really had no need to apologise to me of all people – someone famously unable to make or retain friendships.

4. And then she said, "I'm sorry because I thought we had a chance and I enjoyed your company and I screwed up. And I miss you in my life."

5. With that she turned around and returned whence we came. I stood there for a moment. I turned to follow her and as I emerged from the wood, I saw her driving off.

6. I have no idea what to think or do about this. This is not my area of specialism.

Friday 3rd January

Tanushi returns.

Friday 3rd January - TANUSHI

Christmas was great. Amma made such a fuss of me. I think I slept most of the time. So tired. Back to KA. Big welcome from Jimmy who immediately starts to talk about moving our relationship onto a "new level" which is (I think) code for sex. And I just say, "Let's make no plans and keep everything relaxed, shall we? Let's see where it leads."

Sunday 5th January

1. Communion – Mrs Manifold.

Monday 6th January

1. Tanushi reports for duty. She has energy and commitment. I regret my email before Christmas suggesting we abandon the Georgian structure and apologise to her for throwing in the towel briefly. But it's a New Year and I am ready for the fight.

2. She mentions that Helen has been in touch with her about a dog asking whether she is still interested. I told her to go for it.

3. She says she is going to do the final sorting of my Mother's room. Not that much left to do.

Monday 6th January - TANUSHI

Helen in touch over the weekend about a rescue dog chucked out after Christmas. Was I still interested? She told me all about the breed and how gentle and loyal etc. NOT to tell HH the breed because he would freak out!

Went to see HH to check and got straight back to Harriet's bedroom. Still lots of smaller items to catalogue and work out if we are to keep or sell. I sense HH is not sentimentally attached to anything in this room. Open a bottom drawer of large double fronted art nouveau wardrobe (beautiful satinwood) and in the bottom is a wooden box. Too heavy for me to shift. On the top of the box is: FOR THE EYES OF HENRY HAVARD ONLY. Need to get Jimmy down. What is this?

Jimmy finally makes it down to shift the box out of the drawer and we take it round to HH. Leave it on Big Table. Tell HH.

Monday 6th January – HH cont.

4. Tanushi and Jimmy leave a box for me to look at. Busy with beetles. They seem very excited as to what it might contain. Very heavy they say. Will look at it first thing tomorrow.

Tuesday 7th January - TANUSHI

OMG – something has happened to HH.

OK – so Jane comes in early – 8.15 and notices the box opened and the contents on Big Table. There are 12 silver dinner plates. She puts them back in their tissue paper and into the box.

No sign of HH or the dogs – all day. He returned just as Ted is going home – with the dogs and said nothing even though Ted addressed him directly.

Wednesday 8th January / Thursday 9th January

He really has gone. No one knows where. He'd clearly fed the dogs and slept in his bed last night. Then by the time Jane arrived – no Henry – no Ribble – no fire lit. Other dogs upstairs. He doesn't return all day. We gathered at 6.00pm. It's been dark for a couple of hours. It's cold – not freezing but still raining as it has all day. What to do? We rang Charles and Beatrice – not there. We rang Dorothy – not there. I checked the gatehouse – not there. Sam checked all the possible places up at the farm including the cider barn – not there. We rang the police. "Wait till morning – nothing can be done right now." So, Jimmy and Sam and I camped in the house to see if he will return. No sign of him. Not light till 8.00am and then Dorothy arrived.

She suggested we check the box which we did. The only additional unnoticed thing is an open and empty envelope addressed "HENRY HAVARD ONLY." Jane said she thought she might recognise the writing – of his Father. In pencil and shaky.

So we start surmising – maybe it contained some information which upset him or told him to go somewhere or speak to someone. No sign of whatever was in the envelope. No sign of his wallet. No sign he has left the estate. Jimmy meanwhile is needing to get going – rather than over-thinking the envelope.

"Where on this estate would he go if he wanted to go missing, hide, do away with himself, just retreat into a rabbit hole?"

Sometimes asking the right question is the solution.

The Dorothy said, "Shit! I've got an idea. He might have gone up Biggle Hill to the lead workings near the top. There's an entrance you can go into."

Jimmy said it was worth a go. He collected Brook and set off up the hill. Sam followed at a distance. The weather had cleared.

Jimmy told us that Brook started barking as they approached the top and he could hear Ribble's response. Brook went straight into the cave entrance and Ribble emerged bedraggled but unscathed. Jimmy went in using his phone to guide him.

He saw Henry on the floor – unresponsive but breathing. Cold to touch on his face but his body was warm. He then noticed his hands which were thick with congealed blood. In a terrible state. No other visible injuries. Then Jimmy phoned me. "Found him alive. We'll need an ambulance and if there's an air ambulance get that. Top of Biggle in the lead workings. There's a place for them to land 75 meters further down the hill. Better than having to haul him down the whole way."

I phone 999. Tell them the exact location and the description of his condition as best I knew. I was told that Jimmy should ring them to get advice as to how to help him. Pass that on to Sam outside the cave entrance. And we wait.

Told him to keep him warm – by that stage Ribble had returned to her station of lying on top of Henry. She it was who had kept him alive thus far. Don't move him. Keep talking to him. He was now making incoherent mumblings from time to time. Sam looking out for the helicopter.

From the house, we could see the helicopter arrive and hear it land and within 25 minutes take off again.

Jimmy and Sam returned with Ribble and Brook – all are spent from their exertions. Ribble drinks and flops in front of fire. Dorothy ascertained that HH had been taken to QMC (Queen's Medical Centre) in Nottingham. It was quickly agreed that she and Jane should go.

We hovered around our phones. I made bacon sandwiches. Ted says, "It's a rum do and no mistake Miss Tanushi."

Lunchtime we get a call from Dorothy. He's going to be fine. He's awake but not speaking. No hypothermia. Hands have been cleaned and heavily bandaged. They will need x-raying when the swelling has gone down. He's going to be kept in overnight just for observation. He's just very weak – on a drip but otherwise fine. She will return with Jane later.

I opened up the box and removed one of the plates. Heavy. I check the Hallmarks. Lion – silver. Crowned leopard's head – London. "f" date letter – 1741-1742. Crowned PL – the maker's mark. At the very bottom of the box is the receipt – New Bond Street – 3000 guineas (Ed: guineas were still sometimes used for luxury items – worth one pound and one shilling) – May 14th 1972.

I waited to see Dorothy and Jane arrive back. Jane was very shaken and she needed lots of TLC. Who was going across to retrieve him tomorrow? I volunteered and Jimmy will accompany.

Hid silver upstairs.

Emailed everyone for quick meeting at 8.30 tomorrow.

Friday 10th January

First thing, Jane makes crumpets for all – Beatrice, Dorothy, Jimmy, Sam, Ted and me. Dorothy opens with a prayer for Henry. Decision needs to be taken regarding Hen Galan. I don't think Henry would want it cancelled. Even if he cannot preside. General agreement. We allocate jobs as if it is going to go ahead.

Ribble is being treated as a celebrity and is lapping that up. Sam is going to give her a proper grooming today. Her fur is a state.

Then we set off for the QMC. Jimmy and I speculate as to what possibly can have happened. Silver plates don't set off a crisis. So it's either something in the envelope or something else entirely. Dorothy wasn't around at any stage.

I am nervous as to what we will find. Will he talk to us? Jimmy not worried of course. He'll sit in the back with him and talk about pigs and cider.

I don't like the smell of hospitals. There was the inevitable wait for somebody to tell somebody else something which would enable somebody to make a decision that is then relayed to somebody else to discharge him. Quite a complex chain of communication. Eventually somebody speaks to us. He is fine. His hands will need the dressing changing. Get into touch with GP to arrange. He isn't saying a great deal at all. But all his stats are fine. He just needs rest. Should they alert the mental health team? We both say that won't be necessary. We hand over the clothes we have brought for him and the clothes he was wearing are handed to us. X-ray can be arranged locally at the Whitworth.

And then we finally see him dressed, sitting in a chair, looking a bit lost and confused. But his face is a good colour I would say. He recognises us as we enter. Mumbles something like, "Oh right. Hmm. Right. Well. Hmm. Yes. Home again, home again, jiggety-jig." He stands up on his own and holds his hands to his chest and walks slowly between us. We pause as he pauses. And Jimmy does indeed prattle on about cider, "Bet you're looking forward to pint aren't you Henry? Looking cracking is the new batch. I've put more pears into the apple and pear mix. Made it a bit sweeter. The ladies like it like that. A bit sweeter." And as they wait at the door, I get the car. Henry goes in the back and pulls his arms over his eyes – we've forgotten a blindfold. So a scarf is found for him. And he sits and hums and mumbles to himself all the way home.

Jane is there to greet him. He smiles when he sees her. The dogs cluster round. Ribble smells his bandages. He goes to pat her but realises he cannot do that without pain. So he stoops and places his head on Ribble. Jane then takes him upstairs. Gets him in to the warmest and most comfortable clothes. Ted has the fire roaring. He is sat, propped up in his chair in front of the fire. She is spoon feeding a broth she has made up

She has done this before I realise.

I leave.

Friday 10th January – TIMOTHY

Updated as to events at KA. Relayed all to Father. Hen Galan is planned to go ahead as things presently stand. I asked him what he thinks it is all about. He says he doesn't know. But he clearly has a suspicion which he won't share with me.

In touch with Tanushi – if there's anything I / we can do…

Saturday 11th January - TANUSHI

Jane slept overnight on the settee. Ted took her back home; her shift was over and Sam and Jimmy and I take over. HH is up and pottering round the room. He wants to see the silver. So I dig it out for him. Lots of mumbling. He sits down with one of the plates upturned on his lap.

"Silver...London...what's this date letter?"

"1741-42."

"PL with a crown...who's that?"

"That's the maker's mark." He knows that. More mumbling. He points to one of the bookshelves.

"Jackson's hallmarks." I go over and find the book. He indicates that he wants me to find the London makers – and who PL is.

"Magnifying glass." I hold it for him. He looks at the book and then at the plate. To and fro.

I say, "It's someone called Paul de Lamerie."

He looks at me in shock. "50,000" is all he says.

I go straight to my phone. Paul de Lamerie is the most famous English gold and silversmith ever. £50K is maybe a conservative estimate!!! OMG.

I begin a conversation, "And you knew nothing of them Henry? How come they are here?" But he shuts down immediately.

Rescue coat from the bag from hospital. We bin the rest of the clothes. They smell suitably disgusting. Hang coat to dry. It'll need dry cleaning.

We make preparations for Sunday.

Sunday 12th January – TIMOTHY – HEN GALAN

Hannah and I went across after lunch to be helpful. It was all in hand. I ventured upstairs to look in on Henry. He was gazing into the fire. He nodded in greeting. I asked him how he was feeling. He nodded again and mumbled something about his hands. He got me to read the latest Coleopterist Bulletin – page 7. It was about his discovery of a new species from Sri Lanka which is named Coptops Kirk Aeppel. Very impressive I said.

I asked him if he will be coming to Hen Galan tonight and his eyes return to the fire.

Went downstairs to help with the preparations. Tanushi and Sam are doing the pudding. Jane busy with cawl. Ted walking the dogs.

Dorothy rang Jane to ask if she is invited. Jane said, "Of course."

And so we gathered unsure of who would preside. No Henry. Mum stepped in. As the book is being handed round Henry came slowly down the stairs. He ousted Jimmy so that he can sit next to Hannah. Jane signed for Henry. The meal started and it was Hannah who fed Henry whilst telling him of her adventures in Belize. Henry asked intelligent questions and listened carefully to the answers. He has always had a soft spot for Hannah. He even admired her latest tattoo on her shoulder.

Henry stayed for the first sketch – the Parker family offering written by Father at Cambridge all those years ago. A skit on the shipping forecast. The last time – we will perform it in all likelihood and an air of loss filled the room. Afterward Henry slowly walked up to Father and stooped to kiss him on his head and then he left us to return to his domain upstairs.

The mood brightened with the music and other sketches and the excellent Bara Brith.

But it was a subdued and sober Hen Galan.

Sunday 12th January - TANUSHI

I think it was right to go ahead with Hen Galan. It just was so different to last year. HH joined us, sat next to Hannah and she spoke about her 4 months in Belize on eco projects. Just right for HH to hear all that.

Beatrice presided with headmistress authority.

When Charles did his weather sketch, it was just so painfully poignant. Will he be here next year to repeat it one more time? It seems unlikely. And then HH left us. And the atmosphere picked up a bit once Ted and Jane sang their song.

Monday 13th January

Helen has been in touch. I did not mention recent events to her. A 14 week old puppy needs re-homing. Ideally suited to a country estate. What do I think? I am so up for it. What is it? "It's a Scottish Deer Hound. They are large – in height though not overwhelmingly bulky and would so appreciate the space you can offer. And they are gentle and placid and you would love her. There is no backstory – she's not been mal-treated. Just a spectacularly inappropriate Christmas present."

"When can I collect her?!" So we talk about what I need to do and buy and when I can come across to Burnley...2 hours' drive probs.

So excited.

Pop in to see HH. I make the mistake of saying who I am – like he's senile. And he grimaces and snorts. I apologise and ask him how he is. He says he is fine. Jane is looking after him well. And that is the end of the conversation. I notice he has 20 or so Tintin books which he seems to be working through.

Go down to Jane in the kitchen and she says he always reads Tintin when he is feeling poorly. It's a good sign.

She is happy for me re the puppy and recommends the pet shop in Matlock. Head straight off to buy supplies.

As I leave the district nurse arrives. Jane tells me later that things did not go smoothly. She was there to change HH's bandages and was asking him how on earth this happened and when HH said nothing, she became more insistent at being told – which was unwise. Henry was at his mumbling "best." "Bloody...cheek...come in here...

bloody nurses...asking their questions...none of their bloody business...do your job or bugger off." She was perfectly able to handle this.

Doing the Maths – 70 (tusks) + 70 (plates) + 75 (grant) + 50 (other stuff sold off – optimistic) and we are at 265K – some way short of 350K for one roof...it really does all depend on the picture. Unless some instantly successful income generating scheme crops up. Unlikely. There are the properties in Matlock...

Tuesday 14th January

Set off at 6.00am to beat the M60 rush hour traffic. Get to the Pendle vets at 8.20am.

Met DOG!!! She is the gangliest ball of fluff. Smitten already. Helen gave me loads of advice. Feeding and treats and training and socialisation. She has a microchip of course. And all jabs. I am to call Helen with any question at all.

Head back with her in a crate. I so wanted to show her off. But she was sleeping contentedly. I need a name.

Told Sam and she popped in on the way back from school. Lots of love! She is very good with dogs and she will be my advisor I decide.

Wednesday 15th January

She is to be called Kala – it's a river in Sri Lanka. I know it's an HH tradition to name his dogs after rivers – so I thought I'd do that. She whined a bit overnight – so I went down just to show my face, tapped on the crate and said "NO!" She settled, no accidents, went out to do her stuff this morning. Haven't settled the food issue. Got a load of food from Helen that the family had bought. So OK for time being. She is so adorable!!

I will introduce her to HH tomorrow.

Thursday 16th January

First proper walk up to the House. She is a bit freaked out by the sudden appearance of 4 dogs. But she is suitably puppyish and is accepted. Already taller than Tiff! I leave her with Jane and go up to HH. "Tintin in Tibet" he says – "one of the classics."

"I have a puppy – downstairs – do you want me to bring her up? Her name is Kala – a river in Sri Lanka." He is enthusiastic. So I go and fetch Kala.

"What is she? A lurcher?" When I tell him he is shocked – "She'll be as big as a bloody pit pony." Then I pick her up and put her on his lap and Kala behaves beautifully. And he calms down and pets her as best he can.

"Mmm she's a poppet, isn't she? Kala. I approve of the name. Excellent choice."

I can see he is happy for a few moments.

Jane asks me to take Henry's coat to the drycleaners in Matlock. I wrapped it in a bag to stop it smelling the place out. Going tomorrow.

Curled up on sofa with some Shloer in front of TV with this adorable wee hound. She is going to fill this room!

Friday 17th January

Matlock first thing. Various check-ups. Get Kala signed on at Derwent Valley Vets. Weighed etc. The vet was so lovely with her. Lots of encouragement – details of puppy classes when she's ready.

Take coat to drycleaners. It does smell disgusting as I extract it from its bag and hand it over. It is one of those very heavily padded thick tweed knee-length coats/capes. The assistant shows no sign of smelling anything – part of the training I guess! Maybe it's just me. She pins on the identifying labels, searches the pockets and pulls out several sheets of paper. She gives them to me. As soon as she does, I know what it is. Or what it might be. I take them and leave.

In the car I see several damp foolscap pages folded twice. I do not read them. I put them in my bag, take them home and dry them on a radiator.

I then take Henry to the Whitworth for X-rays in the afternoon. All was peaceable. Bandages changed and cuts are healing I am told. He will have to go to Callow for results and any follow-up. He is still shut-down but engages with Kala happily.

Jimmy had to come round here tonight and Sam insisted on joining him because of Kala! A curry ordered and I am officially a dog bore. Watch a film and I fall asleep.

Saturday 18th January

I am still so tired. It's the traumas of last week catching up – and the delight of getting a dog! Get up early for Kala and then fall asleep again downstairs. Nothing on today thank goodness. Helen messages me to ask how things are going. Great!

I have not done anything apart from dry the sheets of paper. I cannot decide what to do. It might all be totally lost from having got damp. It might be nothing to do with what precipitated HH's crisis. It does not belong to me that's for sure. But it might just unlock the reason behind what happened to him.

Raise the issue with Timothy later in the day when he calls round. He says he will think about the dilemma and its ethical implications. There are no legal ramifications. A great help. I just needed someone to say, "READ IT!"

Saturday 19th January – TIMOTHY

Took Father round to see Henry and left them to it. Spoke to Jane. She is happy with his progress. I think it reminds her of the old days – looking after him as he recovers from injury.

Call in on Tanushi under the pre-text of meeting new dog. She presents me with her dilemma – to attempt to read a document which has legitimately fallen into her hands but which clearly does not belong to her – and might reasonably be assumed to be private and confidential. I said I would think further. She was clearly dissatisfied with this response.

Return to collect Father. He is easily tired. And quiet all the way back. I don't press him.

Monday 20th January - TANUSHI

Met Beatrice at Cool River in Matlock. I told her I was 12 weeks pregnant. She was amazed and thrilled and couldn't believe that she was the first person I had told in the world and she hugged me and asked me how I felt and when it was due (August 2). And how had I managed to tell nobody else not even my Mother or Sam. I have had no morning sickness which has helped.

The first scan is next week and after that I will tell Amma and Sam. She immediately volunteered to accompany me and she said all the loveliest things about wanting to support me in every possible way. She is my Derbyshire Mum – I say to her – and she cries a little. She asked me if I was taking folic acid (of course!) and generally looking after myself.

Then we discussed who to tell when – by which she meant HH. He is in no fit state to be told anything right now.

I asked her about Charles. They are trying to squeeze every last drop out of their remaining time. She is quite fragile and needs all the support herself.

Tuesday 21st January

Heard from F or F. Next filming days for me are in February and then later in March. And then when it's spring they will want some exterior shots of KA. They do not know when they will film the final scene. It depends on the experts and she (Roberta) gave nothing away – even if she did know anything – which is unlikely. Saskia has gone very quiet on me...under instructions maybe.

Timothy messages and says the honourable thing would be NOT to read the documents – if indeed they can be read. Whether to hand them back and risk a reoccurrence of the mania or simply to burn them (assuming they were the cause) – that is a different question. The loving thing to do may be simply be to burn them.

Well I suppose I respect the thought and care he has put into that answer.

Took Kala down to meet Imogen. They were just splendid together. Playful and gentle, taking it in turns to be top-dog. Andrew and Sarah so pleased. Sarah looked very intensely at me and said, "You do look so very well Tanushi." I hope she is not one of those women who can divine pregnancy in others – I've heard about them.

Friday 24th January

More storms. We are all thoroughly fed up with the weather this winter. Rain and more rain. The effect it has on HH is one of debilitation and defeat. It's as if he imagines all this rain seeping through the fabric of KA and destroying it and destroying him along with it. He continues to be taciturn in the extreme.

I take him in to Calow hospital. Yes, he has several tiny hairline fractures along the knuckles but they will heal of their own accord. Nothing can be done to assist that process except immobilisation until comfortable to use. Again the question is asked about psychiatric help which is met with a predictable response.

On the way out I meet the midwife from the Lime Grove surgery. She smiles and says, "Hi Tanushi, good to see you." Fortunately, I think HH does not hear. She responds to my alarmed look towards HH by whispering, "Sorry!" No harm done.

Monday 27th January - TIMOTHY

Tanushi messages me to say she has decided not to try to read the documents but instead to keep them in a sealed envelope – just in case HH asks about them. I think this is a reasonable course of action and I applaud her.

I drop in on HH at the end of the day. This feels a futile exercise. He is willing to talk about Tintin or beetles. Nothing else. I can't see that healing (of mind) is taking place. He is still utterly dependent on Jane. I wonder if Father can help him.

It's Father's last day on Friday. We are organising a small do after work and calling it an early retirement. There are no words to soften what is happening. And, therefore, I take my cue from Father's robust stoicism. It is what it is. I admire (and love) him so much. I have no idea of what life without him will be like.

Wednesday 29th January - TANUSHI

I am balancing my time between clock estimates, furniture to be sold off and product development – HH is in no position to think about this.

Dorothy called in unexpectedly. I was conscious that the last time she called here was not a good experience. She was clearly aware too and apologised again. She makes a big fuss of Kala!

She wanted to talk to me about HH and whether I think she might be able to help him. I have no idea. I did say that he seemed stuck in whatever state he is in and I did not think she could make things worse...she will go and speak to Jane.

Later Jane tells me that she went up to see HH. Who knows with what result?

Thursday 30th January

Beatrice picks me up to take me for the scan and I suddenly find myself really nervous. I am so glad to have someone to hold my hand. Everything as it should be. Not twins! Hadn't considered that. And I hear the heartbeat!! So amazing!! Beatrice takes a picture for me – not sure how to refer to her / him. Sprog is what Beatrice says. (I do not want to know gender – make that VERY clear). She forwards pic to me. So, I have something to send on to Sam and Amma – STRICTEST CONFIDENCE.

Sam replies - !!!!!!!!!!!!!!!!!!!!! And then – as soon as kids left the class she squealed! So pleased – due date?

Amma replies later – she is thrilled – first grandchild – it suddenly seems very, very, real now.

Return exhausted! Walk Kala up and around the house, thinking of what my child will inherit. Visit Old Oak seeking something – peace – perspective – assurance. The next Havard meets the grand old tree. Go in to the kitchen for a late tea with Jane. Kala is as good as gold in the kitchen. Ribble so gentle with her.

Friday 31st January – TIMOTHY

Mother brings Father in at 4.30 pm. All stand and applaud as he enters and he attempts to hush everyone. But they will not be hushed. He has requested no speeches except for his own. So instead a citation has been written and all have signed it. He is much loved. I know this.

And so his speech is one of generosity and gratitude. He speaks of the privilege of knowing his death is near and of having had time to prepare. Of saying all the things which need to be said. He has no regrets about how he has chosen to live his life. I can see that there are many in the office who have never heard anyone talk about their mortality ever. The one thing we absolutely know is going to happen to us, we shun and pretend it is not there waiting for us. It does release them from the guilt of naming that which all know – that my Father will soon die. That we all will die. The taboo is named and the awfulness acknowledged.

He sits and allows each person to say their piece to him. And then he leaves his office slowly and rather stooped for the last time.

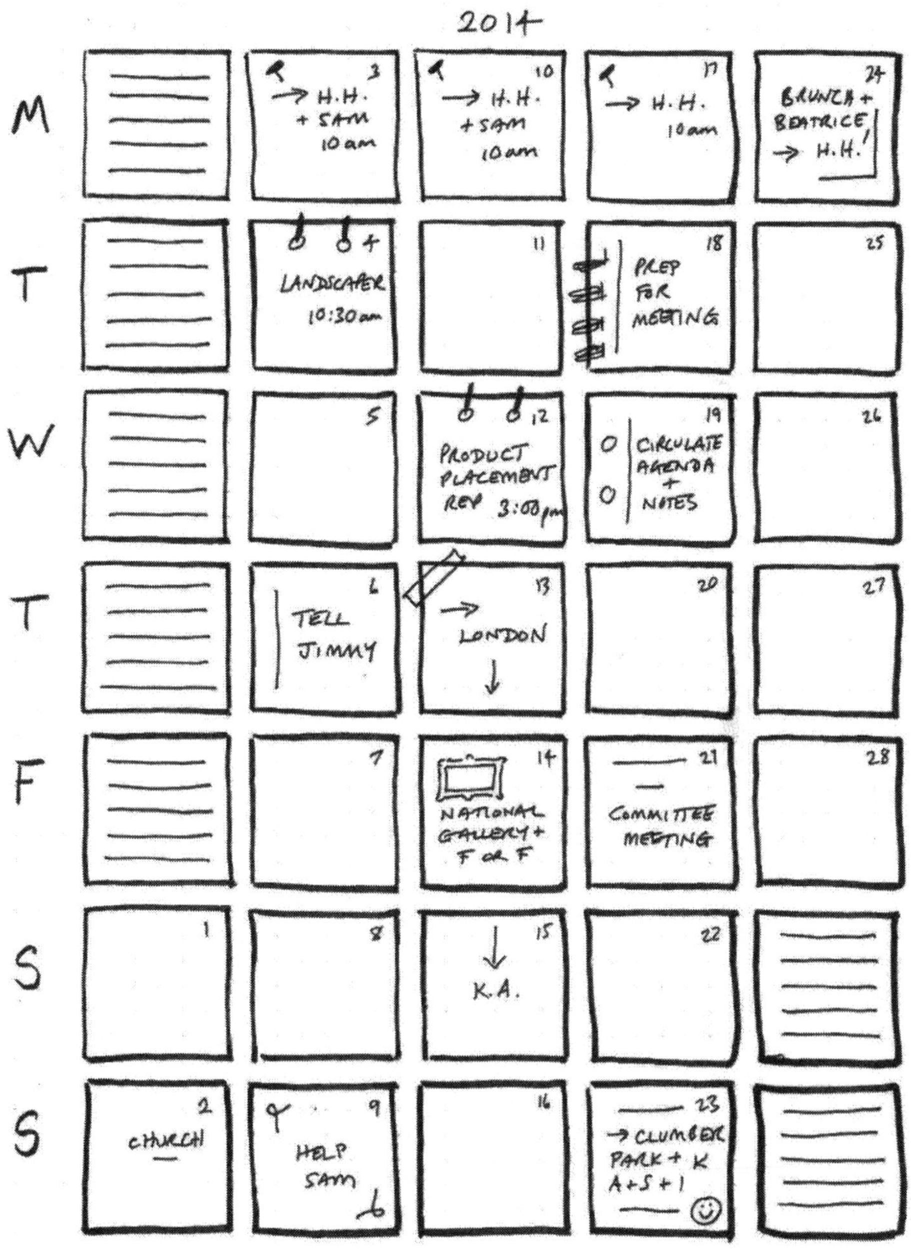
FEBRUARY
2014
M
T
W
T
F
S
S
3 → H.H. + SAM 10am
10 → H.H. + SAM 10am
17 → H.H. 10am
24 BRUNCH + BEATRICE → H.H.
4 LANDSCAPER 10:30am
11
18 PREP FOR MEETING
25
5
12 PRODUCT PLACEMENT REP 3:00pm
19 CIRCULATE AGENDA + NOTES
26
6 TELL JIMMY
13 → LONDON ↓
20
27
7
14 NATIONAL GALLERY + F OR F
21 COMMITTEE MEETING
28
1
8
15 ↓ K.A.
22
2 CHURCH
9 HELP SAM
16
23 → CLUMBER PARK + K A+S+1

Sunday 2nd February – TANUSHI

Dorothy has said she will be taking communion. I go and witness Henry's first venture out into the estate. So perhaps her visit was successful. He walks with his arms held across his chest as the monks once did. I pray for my little 14 week-old sprog knit together in my womb. I pray for HH. I pray for KA. I feel connected once again to this place as I had done when I first visited. Now I am to be part of its history – its on-going story. I try to remember back to the time my Father took me into the tree in our garden – the sacred tree and taught me about the Anuradhapura Cross – and the tree of life. I will teach my child to trace the outline on my hand as he did with me. Of course, I want my child brought up in this Christian faith.

Henry goes up to the altar rail to receive the bread and wine. Dorothy has to place the bread into Henry's mouth. He kneels and as he looks up at her, I notice a tear fall. He then begins to sob uncontrollably. He crumples on the stone steps. Jane and Dorothy rush to lift him to his feet and Jane takes him back to the house. What demons have been unleashed in this man's life I wonder?

Monday 3rd February

Sam and I go to visit HH together. I had told her about his breakdown in the chapel.

It's easier to bounce off each other in the face of silence. Sam tells him about the farm, the Aussie guy they have starting in March for 4 months – Billy – the pigs, the new cider all ready for the pubs, the first bookings for the yurts and Jimmy's progress thus far in converting the stables. Perhaps he would like her to take him up and show him the progress? He looks at her in a distant way and smiles politely.

I then chatter on about the clocks, furniture and the product development. I have engaged a landscaper to look at car park options and acquire quotations. He has by this stage absorbed himself in stroking Kala. He has long since absented himself from our reality.

We escape and Sam immediately starts asking about what I am going to say to Jimmy about my pregnancy. And how I'm going to explain that. I guess at some stage I am going to have to tell the truth...I am your girlfriend, I am pregnant and I have not been unfaithful. That should clear things up.

Collect and return the coat.

Wednesday 5th February – TIMOTHY

Parents have an excursion each day. Dad's horizons are closing in. The house, the car, perhaps a pub. I am calling round each day. Hannah is coming back from Nottingham most weekends now. He remains resolutely without self-pity, bearing the indignities and pain with doggedness.

News of on-line dating. There is no news. Two dates are spectacular mismatches.

Wednesday 5th February – TANUSHI

F or F have changed the dates to next Friday 14th. I will have to shift the committee meeting. London – filming at the National Gallery at 9.00 am. Will stay over with Amma. (Don't know whether Jimmy had any plans for Valentines.)

Attempting to start work on outhouses. Blocked by all sorts of rubbish which needs shifting. Not sure how much I should take on. What I can see are large numbers of terracotta pots in all shapes and sizes. They look weathered and beautiful. Am sure we can use them at some time in the future.

I see Dorothy clutching a book go up to see Henry. Jane tells me that Beatrice has arranged for HH to go across to see Charles over lunch each Friday. Jane insists that Henry is getting better.

Going to speak to Jimmy on Friday.

Friday 7th February – TIMOTHY

Fetched HH as arranged. He seemed superficially functioning and aware of what was happening but yet he just mumbled to himself. Maybe between them they can do each other some good. There is recognition and greeting. And we left them to it.

Certainly, on the return journey Henry was much more together. His hands are looking better. Just strapping around the knuckles. He can use his fingers to a limited extent – a spoon and a fork but not a knife I would guess.

Friday 7th February - TANUSHI

I sat Jimmy down. He kept saying, "You're going to dump me, aren't you?" I assured him I wasn't but that it was a bit more complicated than that. "I've never been dumped!"

So I asked for his confidentiality which he gave. Then I took him through the full nature of my employment at KA – and the fact that I was now pregnant. He looked at me as if to verify what I have said. He looked at my belly and then said, "Bloody hell. You're pregnant with Henry's child." I explained how this had happened and he interrupted, "Yeah, I get the mechanics of it."

He was both quite good about accepting this and quite bad. He didn't go into some mad jealous rage. He accepted the situation. But clearly it then affected how he looked at me – he didn't say this but I could tell. All talk of moving to a new level – I sense – was in the past. I tried to insist I didn't feel any different from before etc. And he kind of said neither did he. But we shall see. Maybe I'll be one of his almost conquests. A notch not quite incised on his bedpost.

Sunday 9th February

Great weekend of walking Kala and washing Kala and feeding Kala. Feel I am practising my mothering skills! Sam around. She is getting the spare bedroom ready for Billy. This involves clearing her Father's room. Much can be chucked – she uses the skip. Some clothes cleaned and put in suitcases. And much touching up of paintwork and general sprucing the place up. Jimmy will collect him from Manchester airport 1st March. Then he will work on the estate for 3 and a half months and then he will have six weeks to be a tourist.

Sam tells me of the latest letter from prison. Roger has become a born-again Christian. And he wants to start working with the disabled in a caring capacity as his way of making recompense for his crimes. I am sure they will be grateful for this – but is he suited I ask? Sam laughs...not really...at least not the old Roger...but maybe the reborn one. Where's he going to live? It has been made clear to him that he is not to live at KA. Is there some sort of half way lodging in the area – to bridge the gap? She has no idea.

Desperate to tell her about F or F... but don't.

Monday 10th February

Sam and I go to look in on HH. I think it is important to continue this regular "meeting." A bit of routine; it does however feel rather futile. HH is trying to begin work with the beetles. This will do him some good. And he has ventured out on short walks with the dogs. Jane said the first time he went, he asked about his coat – she said I had taken it to the cleaners. Each time he uses it he repeatedly checks the pockets she says.

Committee meeting delayed for a week.

Thursday 13th February

Hand Kala to Sam. She is delighted to have a chance to have her all to herself.

Travel down by train. Meet Andrew by chance at Matlock station. He too is going to London for some Navy meet up with his old chums. I am thrown and a bit garbled when asked my reason for going down to London. Talk about Amma. Anyway, we chat amiably all the way to St Pancras. They have been very troubled by what has befallen Henry and then seeing him last Sunday in the chapel. I say we simply have no idea what has happened. I say I think he may have had a difficult and lonely childhood and a very poor relationship with his parents. Andrew then talks about his experience of boarding school. It just seems such an extraordinary thing to want to do – to send your child away from home for others to instruct and shape. This will not be happening to my child!

Friday 14th February

Amma has spoilt and pampered me more in a few hours than through my whole life. She is intent on being a hands-on Grandmother!

Dress loosely. I can still easily hide my tiny bump.

I arrive at the National Gallery for 8.45 am. Early of course – Amma's insistence that you should always be early in Britain. She says she learnt very quickly that the British live by the clock.

I am ushered through to a private room into which a large portrait has been moved – Donna Isabel de Porcel. It is an utterly enchanting portrait. I know there has been some dispute about its authenticity.

In make-up I meet Fiona Bruce and she is delightful. She says she hopes that it isn't too much a waste of my time venturing down from Derbyshire. And she talks to me about KA and my role there. And then Philip (as I now call him!!) comes in and we greet.

The morning consists of Fiona and Philp talking to each other about the Donna Isabel painting and then the latest findings about Carilla and then presenting this to me and having me respond. Of course, I know it is in the nature of the programme to keep people guessing... but they do a pretty good job of just that. I get the impression they genuinely don't know what to think.

In summary, there is much on the canvas itself that is suggestive of a late portrait. The paint, the colours, the brush work, the clearly incisive psychologically convincing character that emerges. The provenance is lacking... there is no other evidence that is known of, of a daughter called Carilla. She cannot be traced in Cadiz. We have the KA account and nothing else. Nobody in the art world has ever seen this painting and there is no reference to it anywhere at all. They are working on the script on the reverse of the painting (which seems critical to me). The painting has been scanned and carbon dated and the oils analysed in every way possible. None of this has ruled it out as a genuine painting but nothing is conclusive. And we do desperately need something else.

I return to Amma in a subdued state. I have told her we are looking into one of the paintings – nothing else. That if it proves to be the real thing, it would help us greatly with restoring KA. Amma then resumes her fussing mother behaviour. Really, I have not seen her like this before! I quite like it!

Amma wants to talk about the birth itself, who is to be there as birthing partner. I do not want to think about this right now and so close down the conversation.

Saturday 15th February

Return to KA and Sam brings Kala down. I get the best welcome ever!!!!

Monday 17th February

Drop in on HH and begin to tell him of the filming. There is no point.

Friday 21st February – TIMOTHY

Take HH across to Dad. Leave them to it. It does do the both of them good. Perhaps it should be twice a week? I return with him to KA and stay for the committee meeting.

All a bit frustrating because we cannot make progress without decisions being made by Henry and he's resolutely not for making decisions.

Tanushi presents ideas and a quote for parking – up to 110 spaces primarily on either side of the avenue between the trees from the road to the Georgian house. No additional tarmac required. Won't affect views etc. Relatively cheap and at the moment 100 + cars x 2 or 3 people is plenty for what we want.

Tanushi presents product research. Again, a good potential money maker – HH mumbles. We decide to choose three of the most promising products. We need to agree on the KA picture on all produce and communication literature. A "brand identity!"

Sam says that she reckons that we could run a local fun dog show in early September. She knows who to approach locally for food stalls, dog stalls, dog competitions etc. £5.00 to enter. Start small and see how it goes. It is given the go-ahead.

Jimmy says that the accommodation should be complete by the end of June depending on how good the Aussie is in taking on pigs/glamping etc.

Once the accommodation/glamping is up and running we can think about Cider, Arts and Charity events. Tanushi will investigate permanent and temporary toilet facilities.

We then discuss what can be sold off. Tanushi shows us and tells us of the silver plates. Amazing find. Henry still holding back on tusks – these seem to have become something of a symbol of resistance. He is indifferent to the plates so we agree for those to be sold.

Update on finances.

Jane brings a grand plate of cheeses, dates, grapes, olives, biscuits etc. I notice Mother and Tanushi in deep conversation.

Friday 21st February - TANUSHI

Date for next F or F interview confirmed. In Madrid!!!! Flight from Heathrow on Monday 17th March. Exciting.

After the meeting, Beatrice and I agree to see Henry on Monday. Something needs to change.

Sunday 23rd February

I have booked some puppy training classes in Cromford starting Thursday 6.45-7.30. 6 weeks. Kala is a delight and growing rapidly upwards! And she can run so fast already. Kala's exercise restricted as instructed by Helen but this is so difficult to do!

Go with Andrew, Sarah and Imogen to Clumber Park for a big meet up of Clumber Spaniels. It is a riot of noise and dogginess. Have a great time. We could do something like this at KA.

Monday 24th February

Beatrice and I have decided to tell HH about

- The picture
- The pregnancy

And to challenge him to get his act together (in the nicest possible way) because he needs to be the Master of the estate and the Father to his child.

We gather and discuss tactics over brunch in the Gatehouse. I take Kala as a foil. We decide to speak to him upstairs away from Jane. We get our drinks from Jane and go up (tell her no interruptions). Henry is arranging his Coleopterist magazines. We say firmly we need to speak to him. He stops and looks alarmed. We sit him down. Beatrice starts.

"More than a year ago, Henry, you decided to employ Tanushi as the Preservation and Procurement officer for Kirk Aeppel. This is because you wanted to see a future for the estate that has been placed in your stewardship."

I take over: "We obviously do not know what happened to you on Biggle Hill, why you had your breakdown, why your hands were so damaged. We do not know that. And we do not know whether you have spoken to Jane or to Charles about the causes of what happened."

Tag Beatrice: "But it is important that you now decide to get over whatever it was. Now you have consistently said you do not want psychiatric help with this. Presumably because you think you can get yourself back together without professional help. Which is fine – except that's not happening right now.

Tag to me: "And the point is, this is affecting what you have employed me to do. It's undermining what you employed me to do. And it's really important you return to your duties as Master of Kirk Aeppel.

We pause. Henry is listening really carefully – for the first time since that day in January.

Beatrice: "Henry there are two things you need to know. Both are potentially life-changing. And we are telling you, because we need you back in the game. Are you going to buck up Henry?"

Henry smiled the faintest of smiles. This is language he recognised. He straightened. He looked at Beatrice fully in the eyes and then he looked at me. "Yes, I am going to buck up. Too much self-indulgence." His voice was suddenly stronger.

Me again: "Good Henry. You see I have learnt so much in this past year and a good deal of that is from you and I need you back to your best if Kirk Aeppel is to survive and thrive."

"Yes – I am sorry."

Beatrice: "The first thing we need to tell you is that the picture of Carilla has been sent off to be assessed. Tanushi thinks it may be painted by Francisco Goya. If she is right, Kirk Aeppel's future is assured. You can have as many new rooves as you want! Tanushi is now part of a Television series called Fake or Fortune? – and they are fully researching the painting and will decide whether it is by Goya or definitely not by Goya or possibly case not proven – yet. The painting is in the Fitzwilliam Museum in Cambridge and is safe. There are no guarantees though."

Henry was struggling to process all this and it was clear he had too many questions to ask and didn't know which to ask first. He paused to collect himself. He repeated "Goya? The Spanish Master? Goya? Really?" He was amazed and grateful and wanted to know when it might be decided, when we would find out. "Goya!"

Me again – I gently hold his hand avoiding the knuckles: "And the second thing Henry is that I am pregnant with your child. We are going to have an heir to this estate and I need you to be a Father to him or to her."

Henry looked away and into the fire and the tears rolled down his face. He got out his handkerchief and dabbed his eyes and he turned to me, "Tanushi, my dear Nushi – there are no words. I can't quite believe what you have said." And he waved his arms about not knowing what to do with them, so I held them lightly.

Beatrice: "So we need to get back to work Henry. We need you to take up your responsibilities to this place and its people. Do we have your assurance that this will happen?"

He just said, "A child – can it be true?" And I told him of the due date and how it has been attempt 3 (attempt 4 not needed!) And he listened and smiled and smiled.

Tuesday 25th February

1. I can type slowly and have decided to resume my diary.

2. Beatrice and Tanushi have given me a talking to. Quite right.

3. And they have told me about the baby. Nushi is 17 weeks pregnant! I can hardly believe it. Yesterday I went to the chapel and kneeled and thanked God. I am going to be a Father.

4. And they told me about the painting. Extraordinary.

5. I need to explain. Tomorrow maybe. Enough for now.

Wednesday 26th February

1. Dorothy came. I have appreciated her ministrations over the last few weeks. She has read to me.

2. Back to walking the dogs – shorter walks.

Friday 28th February

I find my life has been built on a lie. The lie was laid bare in the box with the silver plates. A document was written by my Father in the final few months of his life. In this he essentially did three things:

1. Most of the testimony was taken up with his apology to me. He said he had been a terrible Father and he knew that. He regretted many of his actions towards me and the omission of other actions. He said he felt totally ill-equipped to be a Father. He described himself as a "pervert" – and this had been made very clear to him at school and throughout his adult life. He had avoided arrest on all but three occasions. On those occasions his "class and position" had offered a measure of protection. He described something of his war experience. He witnessed and experienced the very worst of human nature. He described a little of his post-war life and choices. He regretted much. He was sorry. This was the confession of a man who knew he was soon to die.

2. He told the story of the acquisition of the silver. The criminal injuries compensation amounted to £500 – the maximum allowed. In addition the school provided £2,500 on assurance of non-disclosure. He decided to go to London to buy something of exceptional quality.

3. He said that the decision to lie to me about the "accident" was taken by my Mother and himself jointly.

- It was not an accident.

- It did not involve stairs.

- What was done to me was done deliberately with a wine bottle to the side of the head and the lacerations were caused with the stub of the now smashed bottle thrust into my neck to push me away.

- It was done by an adult – a member of staff at the school – who had demanded that I sexually gratify him.

- I had caused injury to him by biting him and refusing to release.

- He had been sent to prison for 18 months.

I find that my entire life has been based upon the lie told to me by my Mother and Father. Obviously, I still have no memory of the events described. That has been wiped, I assume, by the traumatic brain injury. I find it difficult to know how I should respond towards an unnamed person of whom I have no memory. Clearly, he did me great injury.

I do however remember my Father and Mother who perpetrated this lie and in the case of my Mother maintained it for 20 + years. I am left with no elucidation and no choices in relation to this.

I regard myself as a social cripple (I am aware that that term is verboten today but if I choose to use it of myself, I do so). How many of my difficulties, my own anti-social nature, my emotional constipation, my inability to form healthy and productive relationships are down to this event, of which I have no memory but which, it seems, informs everything.

But now there is a future and I do have a choice about what sort of Father I am to be. I do not have to be the sum of other people's choices. I do not have to be my Father or my Mother; their sins do not have to be visited on me. This is something I believe – but it needs to become a lived reality. I believe I am taking the first steps.

Of course, I am now haunted by trying to imagine, re-imagine, remember that scene in that teacher's room – or wherever it happened. I do not even know his name or what became of him. I find I cannot discern between that which I have invented, that which I have been told and that which may be a newly unearthed memory (highly unlikely I know).

How much can a man re-create himself, pull himself up by his own bootstraps? Willing it to be so, is not enough I sense. My Father wrestled with his demons, his addictions and his "perversions." How different things are now with the first gay marriage set to happen in just a few weeks. Maybe he would have been able to live at peace with himself in such a world.

I think I owe an explanation to lots of people who saved me from myself, who for some reason beyond my ken, pulled me up from the pit. I see no merit in concealment any more. This in itself may be a sign of progress.

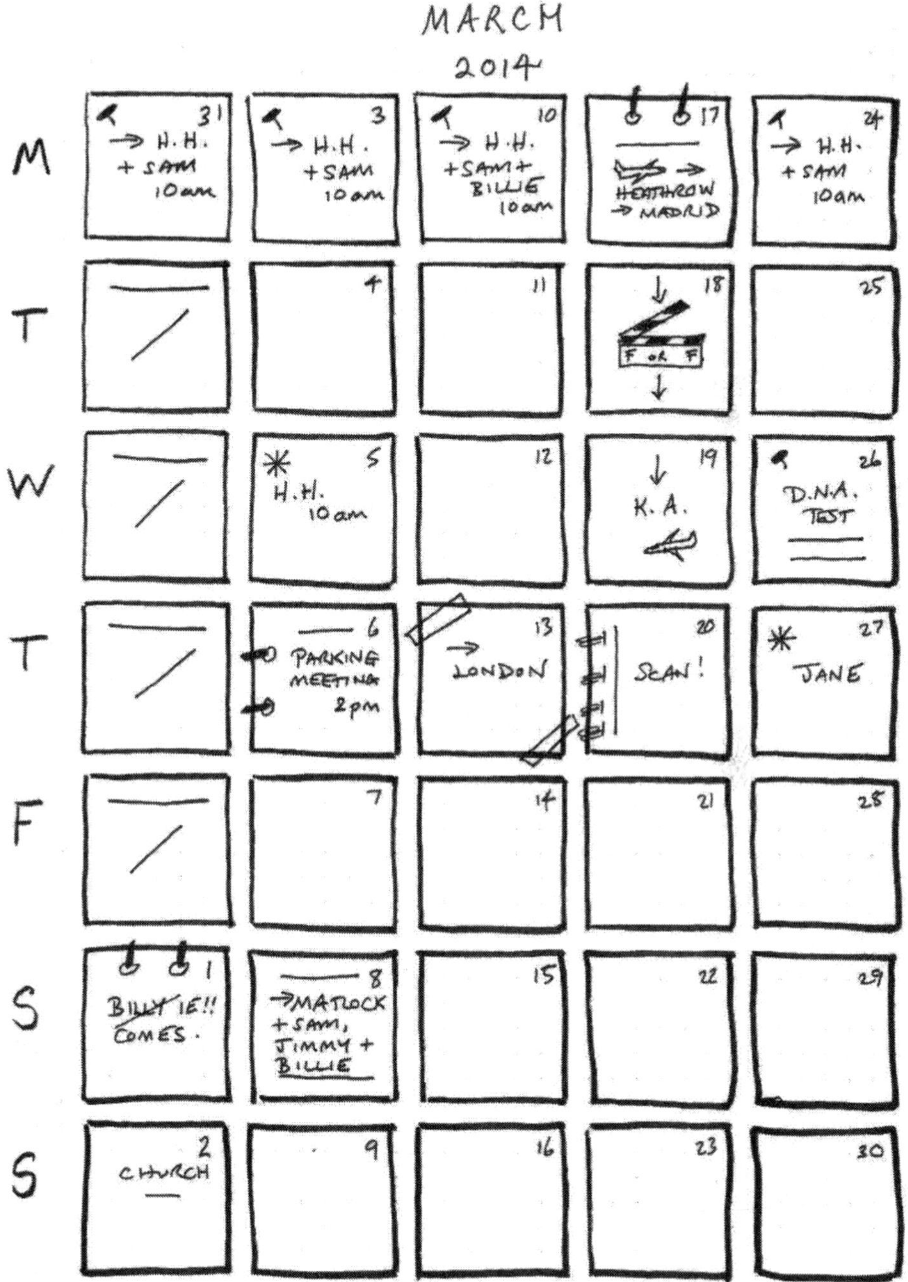
MARCH
2014
M
T
W
T
F
S
S
31
→ H.H.
+ SAM
10am
3
→ H.H.
+ SAM
10am
10
→ H.H.
+ SAM +
BILLIE
10am
17
HEATHROW
→ MADRID
24
→ H.H.
+ SAM
10am
4
11
18
F or F
25
5
H.H.
10am
12
19
K.A.
26
D.N.A.
TEST
6
PARKING
MEETING
2pm
13
→ LONDON
20
SCAN!
27
JANE
7
14
21
28
1
BILLIE!!
COMES.
8
→ MATLOCK
+ SAM,
JIMMY +
BILLIE
15
22
29
2
CHURCH
9
16
23
30

Saturday 1st March - TANUSHI

Get a message from Sam midday: "Jimmy fetches Billy. Billy is Billie and he is she. Jimmy furious." And she adds Hahahahahaha!

Saturday 1st March

1. Sam pays the rent. I am just a bit concerned by the further loan they have taken out to do all this building. She says Jimmy says, "Splash out to cash in." And she is sure it will be OK.

Sunday 2nd March

1. Communion. Dorothy presiding. Arranged to meet her on Wednesday.

2. I have decided who to tell my story to and in what order.

    - Jane – Monday morning
    - Charles and Beatrice – Tuesday lunchtime
    - Tanushi – Wednesday morning
    - Dorothy – Wednesday afternoon

    Jimmy, Sam and Ted can be informed after that by Jane.

    I sense this is going to be arduous but necessary.

3. Knuckles now without any dressings. Just scabs and scars visible.

Sunday 2nd March - TANUSHI

Communion.

Billie is very much female. Sam brought her down as part of her introduction to the estate – and she is chatty and friendly. Fussed over Kala. She realises the misunderstanding and Jimmy's irritation but she is convinced she will surprise him with her work ethic and toughness. She might be right. Jimmy does have pretty "antediluvian" views about women, I think.

Monday 3rd March

1. Tell Jane the story. She had no inkling at all. I believe her. She is horrified of course. Lots of tears. She is glad it is all out in the open. She is pleased the boil is lanced and she says how proud she is that I am facing up to this whole issue. What would have become of me without Jane?

2. Tanushi and Sam pop round. I arrange to see Tanushi on Wednesday separately. Tanushi says she will bring round some cream for my hands.

Tuesday 4th March

1. Speak to Charles and Beatrice together to begin with. Charles did not appear so very shocked. Perhaps he had worked out that neck lacerations are not a typical injury from falling down stairs. Maybe he just sensed the wrongness of the story which I had believed implicitly.

2. Charles eats very little.

3. Anyway, they too express all the usual "how appalling" etc.

4. Beatrice asks if two other items of news can be shared with Charles. Of course, I tell him first of the baby. He is amazed and delighted. His plan has come to fruition. And then about the painting. He is straight on to the internet trying to piece together a Goya timeline. 1793 Cadiz... Carilla's birthplace... Bordeaux at the end of his life when Carilla might have visited. Goya known to be in both places at those times. It peps him up having to do a bit of research. And he has always loved Fake of Fortune.

Wednesday 5th March

1. Tell Tanushi. She is horrified and disgusted on my behalf. She says she believes she has my Father's confession – recovered from my coat. She has not read it and she will return it. I have read it through quite enough.

2. She has brought round some hand cream to massage into my hands and scars (they are very dry) which she does as I am telling the story.

3. Dorothy comes round in the afternoon – for me and not just for Twyi. And finally, I tell her what happened when I was 11 years old. And she asks intelligent questions and draws me out about how I am currently thinking about the whole thing. And then she says, "You have been through the wars Henry old thing. And you need some Tender...Loving...Care...would you have an objection to me providing that?" And with that she got up, kissed me on the cheek and said, "See you Friday Henry. I'm cooking. I'll be here for 6.30." She pats all the dogs and leaves.

   I am left feeling exhausted by this whole process. It does not provide me with any sense of catharsis; I never thought it would. That was not the reason I decided to do it. There was a sense of obligation to those who had rescued me from myself. That's it. That really is it.

Friday 7th March - TANUSHI

I have been through all the arrangements for F or F. Flight out Monday 17th 12.30 pm Heathrow. Film Tuesday. Return Wednesday. I am hoping to be able to conceal my bump...I still can. Though the time is coming when I will have to tell Jane. And what of Dorothy? I am not going near there! That's for HH!!!

And then it's the second scan on Thursday 20th – busy... exciting!

Amma is coming up over Easter weekend.

Friday 7th March

1. Dorothy arrived at 6.30 pm. I had decided to tell her the news about the baby. I started to say that this may be not what she was wanting to hear – but she cut me off before I could complete the sentence.

2. She is delighted – firstly that Tanushi is pregnant and secondly that I have been honest with her (for the second time in the week) even when I could have chosen to delay any such revelation. And she acknowledged it took a little bit of courage to do that (which it did).

3. She cooked Italian – a simple but delicious fish dish with homemade focaccia and some steamed veg. And then we watched another one of those on-line movies together. It almost felt like we could be a couple – of friends who have made up.

4. I did thank her, as she left, for being there to save my life...it was her suggestion, I am told, that I might be up in the lead workings. She smiled and suddenly kissed me full on the lips. My third proper kiss. And then she was gone.

Saturday 8th March - TANUSHI

Went out to Matlock with Sam, Jimmy and Billie. All a bit awkward.

I was driving (because I'm not drinking) and when we got to The Remarkable Hare, Jimmy got the first round in. Billie said, "Why you not drinking Tanushi? You're not preggers are you?" And she laughed. And then, based on frozen expressions all round, she said, "Oh God, you are. Shit I'm sorry. You didn't tell me you were going to be a Father?" She looked at Jimmy who looked at me. Jimmy said, "Urm, well it's sort of compl..."

Sam – bless her – stepped in, "Not the best time Billie – to be fair. Can we move on?" Billie wide eyed, "Sure thing. Ignore me. I'm sorry."

Billie causing a few heads to turn.

I am aware that Jimmy has not touched me since I told him I was pregnant.

Sunday 9th March

1. Went on first full length walk. Up Biggle. Thoroughly irritated by a couple walking a Lab who keep it on the lead the whole time. What is the point of having a dog like that – desperate to run around and explore and expend energy – and keep it on its bloody lead. The dog seemed nice enough – happy to meet the pack. Couple are terrified. "Can you keep your dogs away please?" "No. They're dogs. They like meeting other dogs. They're social animals." Well they didn't like that. "Keep your dogs on a lead and under control or we'll report you."

2. Why didn't they buy a pretend dog – like a Pekinese or something? Feed and water it and put it in its cot and it's happy. But a Lab – it's cruelty not letting a dog like that run around.

3. On return journey got soaked in sudden downpour and felt suitably rebuked for my ill temper.

Monday 10th March

1. Tanushi and Sam come round first thing and bring Billie with them. She is the Aussie farm help living with them for 3 months. Could have sworn I was told it was to be a chap. She seems more than robust. She has Australian manners.

2. Tanushi is taking Thursday and Friday off to travel down to London, spend some time with her Mother and then off next week to Spain with this Fake or Fortune programme.

3. She leaves the hand cream for me to use.

Wednesday 12th March

1. First thing Dorothy sees is the hand cream of course. So she massages my hands. Then we head off on a walk. We come to the lead working which I have no desire to enter but she wants to look in. One or two bits of medical detritus still there – bits of tape and wrappings and the like. We clear it up. Ribble back to the scene of her heroism.

2. Dorothy asks me whether I remember much of what happened. I remember getting there with Ribble. But nothing of Jimmy or the helicopter. The intervening time of bedevilment, I do recollect in snatches. I wish I didn't. I wish I didn't.

3. We walk back down towards the orchard. I find we are arm in arm. Jimmy and Billie are getting the Yurts erected and ready for action. They pause briefly to allow introductions to be made. They seem happy enough.

4. We go into the chapel and light a candle.

Thursday 13th March - TANUSHI

Midday train down to London. With Amma for 4.00 pm. 100% cossetting. Special extra healthy food cooked for me. I tell her about the painting and the filming in Spain. Swear her to secrecy.

Something has changed between us. Like the slipping of a generation. I don't quite know how to describe it. It's like we're both adult women now dealing with stuff that adult women have always dealt with and doing so equally and not as Mother and infant. I like it.

Monday 17th March

Wearing suitably loose clothing. Get to Heathrow for just after midday. Already I am beginning to feel like a country bumpkin, visiting the big metropolis for the day. Weird.

Met by Tina. All goes smoothly to Madrid. Car to pick us up and straight to Jardines Boutique hotel – right in the centre. Then after quick refresh, shown to the Museo Nacional del Prado where we are filming tomorrow. Early start so I opt out of meal and just have room service.

Who knew just 12 months ago that this would be my life? With all its possibility and potential.

Tuesday 18th March

Great breakfast.

So we arrive really early. And it takes ages to set up and get the right shots and with the right painting. They show me reverentially to "The Third of May." I am told that this is so ground-breaking that it is considered one of the first paintings of the modern period. (I know all this!) I am SO happy to have my own private audience with this masterpiece and to have time to look at it closely, to look for the stigmata on the right hand, to wonder at Goya's intent – is the peasant railing at God's injustice, imploring his executioners for mercy or defying the inevitability of his fate? And the mechanisation of the soldiers and their guns – surely a precursor to Guernica? Dehumanisation. I know that if there was an altar rail here, I would kneel before this painting.

And whoever I talk to, I am trying to pick up hints... do they know something I want to know? Then by 11.00 am Philip and Fiona walk in and filming proper starts. They talk me through the latest test results – paint pigment analysis, paper chemical analysis, multispectral photography, hyper-resolution etc. All very, very encouraging. Not proof but Carilla has jumped through all those hoops with flying colours. However, the lack of any substantiating provenance whatsoever is troubling and maybe a stumbling block.

As Fiona is explaining this, I suddenly have a bit of inspiration. I interrupt her and say, "So the only piece of documentary evidence we have is the Kirk Aeppel journal written by Carilla Havard. And she says that our painting was painted by her Father. If she is correct..." at this point I feel my hand move to my tummy and for the very first time I feel it kick – for the very first time – I'm sure... "If she is correct, then her descendants are direct descendants of Goya. And we can do a DNA test. We know there are descendants of Goya. Let's see if my employer is a match. If there's a DNA match... if Carilla is related to Goya, surely that would be proof conclusive."

Fiona and Philip look at each other with surprise and Philip speaks first, "That would be surely amazing... Tanushi, what a genius you are. Of course. That would be final corroboration of the story. I think that really would be. Or on the other hand, a final disproof of all possible provenance."

And afterwards – after the filming is over, Fiona comes over and smiles and whispers in my ear, "Are you pregnant Tanushi?" I smile and say nothing but she knows; I know she knows.

Farewells to Philip and Fiona and it's back to the hotel. They are hoping it might all be settled before the summer is finished.

So we now have one further test to set up. HH's DNA.

Wednesday 19th March

Fly early and back to Matlock by mid-afternoon. Wiped out. Sam collected me from station with Kala. Such a nice greeting! I love that dog! I ask Sam if she wants to come to the hospital for my second scan tomorrow. And she does.

Thursday 20th March

1. Tanushi arrives with news of her Spanish jaunt. They need a DNA sample from me apparently. Fine. No indication as to what the outcome might be. I tell her she needs to start taking things more easily. No lifting etc. It's as if I am now an expert on pregnancy! But she takes it well and graciously. She's off to the second scan.

Thursday 20th March - TANUSHI

Off to Chesterfield with Sam. She holds my hand all excitedly as they take the measurements. Second picture for the album. All well. How fast is that little heartbeat? They ask whether I have felt it move, where would be the best place to book for antenatal classes, whether I had thought about what I wanted for the birth. I have no clear plan... hospital: definitely; pain management: everything that I can have; who present: Amma? Beatrice? Sam? Got to be Amma. So a decision is made.

Ring Amma – well of course she always assumed she was going to be there anyway! But she was pleased with the new photo – trying to guess whether it would be a girl or a boy. She needs to look properly at me when I am a bit further on. Then she'll know!

Friday 21st March

1. Dorothy takes me to the local amateur dramatic production. They had decided to tackle Ibsen – Hedda Gabler – which I think is more than ambitious. But the key characters act remarkably well. Some delightful woodenness amongst minor parts. High culture in hearty health in Derbyshire Dales.

2. We retreat to a small pub called the Thorn Tree about which Dorothy has heard good things. She thinks it will be my sort of pub. It is heaving. But we squeeze in. Lots of dogs which meets my approval. Good range of beer. Another tick. Even some real cider. No music. Real fires in both rooms. Good choice.

3. Dorothy does enrich my life – there is no question about that. This thought occurs to me as we drive home and, in the spirit of becoming more open, I resolve to say that to her on our arrival back.

4. The car pulls up and we get out and I say, "I have had a delightful evening. You enrich my life Dorothy." And she says, "Is that you inviting me up for a coffee?"

This is clearly a cultural reference too far. I say if she wants a coffee, she can of course come in to have a coffee. And she laughs and hugs me and asks if she can kiss me. I try to say, "Yes – because there is a full moon and that is clearly a required romantic parameter." But before I can half finish the sentence she has pounced. And that is very definitely my fourth proper kiss and I suppose really – given its nature and duration – it will have to count as my first proper kiss such that the previous three pale into insignificance.

5. She bids me Goodnight and drives off. I am left in the clear cold night trying to work out if I kissed correctly. I realise this is the sort of question an adolescent might ask but I was never that adolescent. Never.

Saturday 22nd March

1. Discombobulated...all day.

Monday 24th March

1. Tanushi and Sam call in as usual. It starts the week well. They prattle on about the latest scan and related issues. All well with the world. I assure her that I will not be attending antenatal classes – she said, "Oh it's a requirement Henry." And just as I am winding myself up, they both start laughing. Very amusing.

2. Receive the annual missive from Barrington inviting himself to stay – just the one night this year – over Easter. Marvellous.

3. Wander up to the farm and meet Andrew and Sarah on their walk. On the spur of the moment I invite them to dinner on Saturday. They accept.

4. In retrospect, I reflect that I have never done such a thing before. Why am I doing so now?

5. Jimmy and Billie are working hard on the bedrooms. I particularly like what he has done with the stables – retaining the partitions and stone and metalwork. Very pleasing. All on track for June / July.

Tuesday 25th March

1. Go to see Charles. Hannah is home and sits with us and holds his hand all the time. He speaks of many things. The past and the present and the future. He has been to Ashgate Hospice. He is content to die there. He praises his family and how they are coping. He asks that we toast him each Hen Galan. Whilst clearly in some discomfort, he speaks animatedly.

2. I realise I love him.

Wednesday 26th March

1. Tanushi brings round the DNA kit. Simply done. She takes it to post off. Amazing Science – what they can do these days. The future of the estate lies in that cheek tissue.

2. Dorothy arrives with some flowers for me which she puts in a vase. How extraordinary – another first. To be given flowers. Charming.

3. On the walk I apologise for not getting her something. She then explains the difference between a contractual relationship, tit for tat, and a covenantal relationship in Scripture. And we talk of Hedda Gabler and unhappy, trapped women and men. It seems she has experience, both professional and personal, of these things.

4. We reach the top of Biggle and she turns to me and she says she is happy with where we are and we kiss. (I am going to keep no further tallies.) I too am happy.

5. And we plan who is doing what for Saturday.

Thursday 27th March TANUSHI

I cannot be hiding my bump for too much longer and decide to see Jane to explain. I think this might be tricky. She is the sweetest and loveliest person but she might have old fashioned views about what we have done.

So at our normal 11 O'clock tea break, I tell her and she is utterly speechless to begin with and for some time but to give her credit – she was thrilled for me and for Henry and she wasn't at all moralistic! As if I could have imagined she would have been! And she said how nice it was that Dorothy was calling around once again. And we chat about Henry and how well he is doing in the circumstances.

Saturday 29th March

1. First gay weddings. I think of my Father.

2. Dorothy and I host a dinner for Andrew and Sarah. This seems like a milestone in some peculiar way. A delightful evening.

3. Sarah said, "So glad you are better Henry. What..." I replied, "Just an uninvited ghost from the past that needed to be dealt with."

4. I share a whisky with Andrew and with Sarah. It is some time since I enjoyed this particular treat. They are suitably impressed with the collection. Andrew tells some highly enjoyable Navy stories which mostly involve him doing something catastrophically stupid. Self-deprecation seems to me to be one of the highest virtues. I am surprised it is not more lauded – perhaps it is covered by the word humility which features in many lists of key religious / cultural virtues. A most convivial evening.

Monday 31st March - TANUSHI

Puppy training starts this week! Can't wait. I think Kala is very intelligent and very obedient and will shine! I know I might be a bit biased. Take her round when Sam and I go to see HH. He has been won over of course by Kala. But he will just keep on warning about how large she is going to get. "She's just started growing now Tanushi. Just you wait. A pit pony – you mark my words." I tell him to stop or he'll have to come to antenatal classes; he laughs out loud at this. I realise how rarely I have heard him laugh.

Overall, Henry does seem to be in a remarkably positive mind-set right now. His hands are better. He is able to attend to his beetles. He has started to do bits and pieces of manual work in the orchard as instructed by Jimmy. He can walk the dogs.

Timothy and I (and Ted) have been working on the possibility of an apprentice for Ted and we have a local youth starting on Monday 5th May. Just for 6 months initially. He's been recommended by Anthony Gell – the local school in Wirksworth. We shall see what he's like on Thursday when he comes round.

APRIL
2014

M		7 → H.H. 10am	14 → H.H. 10am	21 → H.H. 10am	28 → H.H. 10am
T	1	8	15	22	29
W	2	9 MID-WEEK BREAK!	16 MID-WEEK BREAK!	23 MID-WEEK BREAK!	30 MID-WEEK BREAK!
T	3 JASON INTERVIEW PUPPY TRAINING	10 PUPPY TRAINING	17 DEVELOPMENT COMMITTEE 3pm PUPPY TRAINING	24 PUPPY TRAINING	
F	4	11 SOTHEBY'S (COLLECT PLATES) + SAM → ITALIAN	18 BARRINGTON!	25	
S	5	12 HAIR 9:30am	19	26 GARDEN DAY	
S	6	13	20 EASTER DAY!	27 CHURCH	

Wednesday 2nd April

1. A delightful day. Dorothy and I start a jigsaw together.

Thursday 3rd April - TANUSHI

Jason is delivered as per instruction by his Mother at 2.30 pm. (She manages to privately intimate that he has been much bullied at school.) He is the wimpiest 17 year-old I have ever seen. His lack of physical stature is matched by his extreme shyness. It's a good job there isn't a goose for him to practice his boo on. At one point I thought Brook was accidentally going to reduce him to jelly.

So I am already thinking this will be a waste of time, however...

Ted took him off, showed him the walled garden, talked to him, explained his responsibilities and then returned and proclaimed, "I think Jason and I are going to make a good team!" Jason shifted awkwardly and smiled.

So instructions re May 5th given to him. Arrive 8.30 am sharp.

Puppy training classes need to be re-named: Owner humiliation (and training) classes. Kala was all over the place – had the best time but did not do anything she was told. Endeared her gangly self to all whilst doing precisely what she wanted. No amount of treats could get her to focus on the job in hand. I was mortified!

Sunday 6th April

1. I go to Communion even though it is Mrs Manifold to officiate.

2. I have been invited with Dorothy to Charles and Beatrice for lunch. Hannah and Timothy are there. Beatrice has cooked the most enormous lump of beef which she asks me to carve. I feel so sorry for Hannah – but do not say so. I am sure she does not feel sorry for her vegetarianism.

3. Charles says grace: Gratitude for the gift of life and a prayer for us not to pretend it lasts for ever.

4. Charles eats little but appreciates much. I ask him if he could take one whisky

to heaven which would it be? He smiles and he vacillates between an Islay – Lagavullin – a Lowland – Auchentoshan – a Highland – Edradour and a Speyside – a 21 year-old Glenlivet. And he plumps, surprisingly, for the Edradour. He says he feels it somehow represents him and his values and his beliefs and his Arcadian vision of heaven in that one tiny distillery near Pitlochry. Hannah cries good tears and she sets off Beatrice and the rest of us. And Charles smiles benignly holds their hands and says it is better to get the crying done early.

5. And then they talk about past family holidays.

Wednesday 9th April – TANUSHI

HH has insisted I take every Wednesday off completely. I am grateful.

Sam really strange with me when we met for coffee. No idea why.

Dreading puppy training tomorrow.

Thursday 10th April

Message from Sam. HAS JIMMY SPOKEN TO YOU?

No, he hasn't. Does he need to?

No reply

Then Jimmy turns up late afternoon looking like a pressed man – sullen and resentful. He has come to tell me that "it" – whatever "it" was – is over between us... and that he and Billie are seeing each other now and he hopes that isn't awkward for me.

I take my time.

"So, Jimmy, I guess Sam caught you at "it" – whatever "it" was – with Billie. Am I right? And that she has told you to see me to confess and you two have argued about that. Am I right Jimmy so far? Well I am glad that I am not another one of your past conquests, another notch..."

And he then launches into, "Well you're bloody pregnant with another man's child.

How weird is that? You can't seriously have imagined we had a future! You're the surrogate cow..." And as soon as he said the word cow, he stopped. He realised he had gone too far. He straightway apologised and left.

Yes, I am a bit miffed but only one glass of prosecco miffed. No more than one. I have much bigger things on my mind and in my life than little boy Jimmy Swagger.

And she'll be gone in 8 weeks anyway.

Message Sam to say he has been to see me. She wanted more info obvs.

Puppy training - limited progress – but fun.

Friday 11th April

Silver plates collected by Sotheby's. Auctioned in May.

Sam and I go out together and this means we can properly talk. Go to an Italian in Bakewell. She is so disappointed with Jimmy – more so than I am probably.

Friday 11th April

1. I cook for Dorothy.

2. It is proving a very demanding jigsaw. I had not appreciated how physically engaging a two-person jigsaw is. It also provides the opportunity to talk about:

- The visit of Barrington next week.

- The release of Roger from prison in May. He has been in touch with her. She doesn't know whether he has written to Jimmy and Samantha. He does need somewhere to sleep and something productive to do. She is working on this.

- Her life prior to ordination at the age of 37 and her vocation.

Monday 14th April

1. I ask Samantha when she arrives with Tanushi whether she has had a letter from her Father. She hasn't. Poor form. I decide to write to Roger.

2. Tanushi is showing finally. She says she can now regularly feel the baby kicking. How extraordinary. 24 weeks. The miracle of life. I realise that most people require a miracle to be that which we do not understand. I think the opposite. It is the things we do understand that are so breathtakingly miraculous.

3. She talks about going to puppy training classes. I find that most odd. What for? Puppy socialisation and training. Well I approve of puppies learning from other dogs how to behave as they would in the pack but do we really need classes? Seems completely bonkers to me. Each to their own.

4. I warn them of Barrington's arrival Friday 3.00 pm and departure Saturday 10.30 am. He likes to look around the estate – probably on the Friday.

5. Later I write to Roger pleading with him to use this opportunity to put things right with his children. A simple letter in the same tenor he wrote to me. Who knows? Ted and Jane have visited twice but know nothing of his plans upon release.

Thursday 17th April - TANUSHI

Beginning to feel really tired now. It's been OK up till now. I know I've had it easy. Coming up to 25 weeks and I suddenly feel washed out!

The Development Committee Meeting felt like a properly dull meeting. No-one seemed at their best. Still we updated progress in the various areas and identified more stuff to sell. A handful of the run-of-the-mill clocks will be sold. Told everyone the plates have been taken by the Auction House to be sold May 23rd. Estimate 45-55K. Jimmy wasn't there, so Sam spoke about building progress. I raised the issue of whether, given the figures, we were going to have to sell one or both of the Matlock properties. Just to raise the issue. No decisions needed. Or we might have to make a decision about which building to save. Henry said nothing all meeting.

Dragged myself to puppy class.

Barrington here tomorrow. Will arrange to be out with Sam in the afternoon. I would have so little patience for him right now. Jimmy has warned Billie.

Sam and I will be having a pizza night and Harry Potter fest. Jimmy and Billie will be amusing themselves no doubt.

Nothing from F or F at all. At all!

Friday 18th April

1. It is an altogether different, subdued and rather sad Barrington who arrives this year. He has been the subject of a serious disciplinary complaint and then sanctioned by the British Veterinary Association for inappropriate and salacious behaviour towards younger female staff. The modern world has finally caught up with Barrington. He bemoaned his stupidity. His dreams of preferment were in tatters. He of course tried to maintain it was all good-natured banter. But when things can be recorded so easily, he was without defence. Apparently it involved a long rubber tube.

2. He told me all this as soon as he arrived. I offer no sympathy. In truth he expected none. But it made for a dreary evening.

Saturday 19th April

1. Before Barrington left, he felt the full force of an Aussie tirade. He had ventured up to the farm to admire progress and I think he may have said something ever so slightly risqué, and Billie unleashed two barrels worth of fury. She had clearly been primed. She had her best lines ready. The phrase "little Pommie prick" was used and he took most exception to being labelled Pommie – he felt his Scottish heritage had been maligned. I almost felt sorry for him. Almost. Who knows whether he'll be back next year?

Sunday 20th April – Easter Sunday

1. Typical spring day with the weather turning on a sixpence every 15 minutes. I find my moods are erratic in like manner. I have been troubled by my plates and by haunting dreams – nightmares I suppose – for two nights now. I do not know what to do about this.

Monday 21st April – Bank Holiday

1. Tanushi arrives as usual. She wants to transport one of the rocking cradles down to the gatehouse. Fine by me. She wants to know which one I was put in. I have no idea. Choose the best I say. I offer to help but she says that Sam can help her. Jimmy?

2. I manage to dodge the showers more or less. Dogs on good form. They sense spring.

3. Dorothy arrives in the evening and she tries a back and neck massage to see if that will assist. It doesn't but I don't say that quite.

Monday 21st April - TANUSHI

Transport a beautiful 18th century high sided cradle down to the Gatehouse. I debate with Sam whether to have it upstairs or down. And we decide it is the day sleeping cradle! So it is downstairs underneath the front window. It is adorable! I need to get a foam mattress cut. Whilst measuring for the mattress, I discover a little tapestry of Havards who have been raised in it! With dates. Amazing. I will add to it – Jane will surely know how to do tapestry or needlework or whatever.

Timothy popped round on his way to see HH. He was so nice about the cradle. And he knew where I could get the foam mattress – they do it on the Bakewell market on Mondays apparently. How did he know that? Because he'd had some cushions made up for his place.

As I made him a tea, we looked out at the back garden – he offered to give me a hand in taming it. He hasn't got a garden to speak of, so he'd be happy to help. He asked me what I plan to do. I said I didn't really know except something like a cottage garden with lots of foxgloves and delphiniums. He smiled and said, "Wonderful. Perfect."

I asked him about his Dad. He said, "He continues to die slowly and graciously. It's as if he wants to show us how to die well; like he has shown us how to live well." He turned away from me and I could see him trying to compose himself. His hand clutched at the kitchen surface. I put my hand on his back and my forehead onto his shoulder and we were quiet.

Having arranged to come round next Saturday for a full-on gardening day, he left.

Monday 21st April – TIMOTHY

I feel at the stage when years are counted in months and the months in weeks. No doubt the weeks will soon be counted in days and the days in hours.

I decided to see Henry and call in on Tanushi – or maybe it's the other way round. Tanushi was really, really well. I mean she does get tired but she still looked amazing. Of course, none of this must be said or in any way indicated. 25 weeks now and she is feeling the little thing kick!

She brought me up to date with Fake or Fortune. All very exciting. All down to the DNA – possibly. She really has no idea. And she knows it is an entertainment show so suspense at the final judgement is vital. But there must be a decent chance – maybe.

She had brought down a stunning 18th century cradle. It looked perfect in the 18th century gatehouse. I offered to help with the garden. I need a break.

Wednesday 23rd April

1. We completed the jigsaw. How very satisfying. We had a pretend argument as to who should put in the final piece. She insisted I did and I insisted she did. Or should we leave it unfinished? As a reminder that only God is perfect – like the Navajo Indians weaving their carpets and including a purposed error. Perfection in imperfection. The Wabi-Sabi aesthetic. She then told me all about that – I had no idea. Fascinating. Must read more.

2. Got an email from Beatrice – they are visiting the hospice tomorrow and Charles wants me to go there with them. Fine.

3. The new PCC rota suggests far more communions have Dorothy's initials next to them.

Thursday 24th April

1. Cornish people are to be granted minority status in the European Union. How very splendid. We do seem so very concerned with identity these days. I always

imagined that Martin Luther King's dream was that content of character was to be considered important rather than colour of skin or ethnicity or gender or Cornishness or whatever.

It seems the further we give up on the idea of our identity within God – imago dei, equal and purposed, the more obsessed we become with our human demarcations – lines drawn in the sand. Still I am just a weird old white man who allies with the British clan.

2. Discuss this with Charles on the way to Ashgate Hospice. He is unforthcoming on the matter.

3. I did feel unexpectedly and suddenly nervous and hesitant on entering. But they have absolutely done everything to dispel that. They showed us a room. Wonderful, clean, cheerful, sunlit, garden views. And talked to Charles about what to expect. Charles asked me if I would visit him here in the last days. Of course. And I realised why he had wanted me to join him today. I asked whether they allow dogs and they do. One at a time.

Saturday 26th April - TANUSHI

Garden day. It is perfect gardening weather and Timothy arrives with forks and spades and the like. Even an electric hedge trimmer.

We decide where to put the compost heap. And he starts work and I encourage. He seems to know what he's doing. Even by lunch he's made a big difference. There is now a lawn of sorts – and a patio that can be used for a table and chairs.

Over lunch he asks how Jimmy is and I explain that he has hooked up with Billie now – he hadn't heard this – why should he? He says, "Oh right. I didn't know. I hope you're OK?" Is that a feigned indifference?

And he asks about the baby and if I have thought about names. And how it's going to work between Henry and me. Lots of questions which help me unpack a load of stuff about bringing up my child – our child.

After lunch he gets straight back to it. Can't fault his work ethic! He insists I do very little – tidying up at the edges. And by the end I can't believe how much we have achieved – 80% him. I thank him and say he must come over for dinner. And he says he'd like that.

Saturday 26th April – TIMOTHY

A day of work at Tanushi's. So good to get away and all the better when she told me that Jimmy was off the scene. Anyway, she may be inviting me to dinner at some stage.

Sunday 27th April

1. Back to Dorothy at communion followed by breakfast. We have prayed for Charles each time we have met. I still pray for him to be healed even though I know it will not be; I cannot help myself. The words that are used are vaguer and do not mention healing – that God would be his "great comfort and strength" at this time.

2. I am pleased to see Tanushi there taking her place at the heart of the Kirk Aeppel community – fussed over by Jane of course. Ted ever beside her – her mighty oak, speaking little but saying much. There is much to be said for community – ecclesia.

3. And into this community an infant. I cannot even begin to imagine this.

Monday 28th April

1. Tanushi, Ted and I talk about the introduction of Jason. What does he need to know, who is he to speak to apart from Ted if there is an issue, what policies have we in place to inform him of his responsibilities and us of our responsibilities to him etc. Ted utterly baffled by all this but Tanushi has it all in hand and will induct him next week.

2. Tanushi has heard nothing from the television show. Saskia in Cambridge silent.

3. Arrival of new beetles. Exciting. These are from Cardiff.

Wednesday 30th April

1. We are having a spell of early summer. Temperatures in the 20s. Wander up to the farm with Dorothy and the dogs. Jimmy is jittery – too much early growth followed by a sharp frost is terrible for the apples and pears. The glampers have been and gone. Now it's mainly weekender glamping up until half term and beyond.

2. Once we have left Dorothy says, "Those two are in a relationship." "Which two?" "Jimmy and Billie of course." "What on earth are you on about – we spoke of glamping and apples and pears and frost." Dorothy laughs at me. "Didn't you see how they were together? How she brushed past him?" I accuse her of witchcraft and she laughs some more.

3. So, I ask her if we are in relationship and can they tell. "Ah well I am talking about a sexual relationship. We are in a sexually unconsummated romantic relationship and they can probably tell – or at least she can." I was aghast. There's no arguing with her.

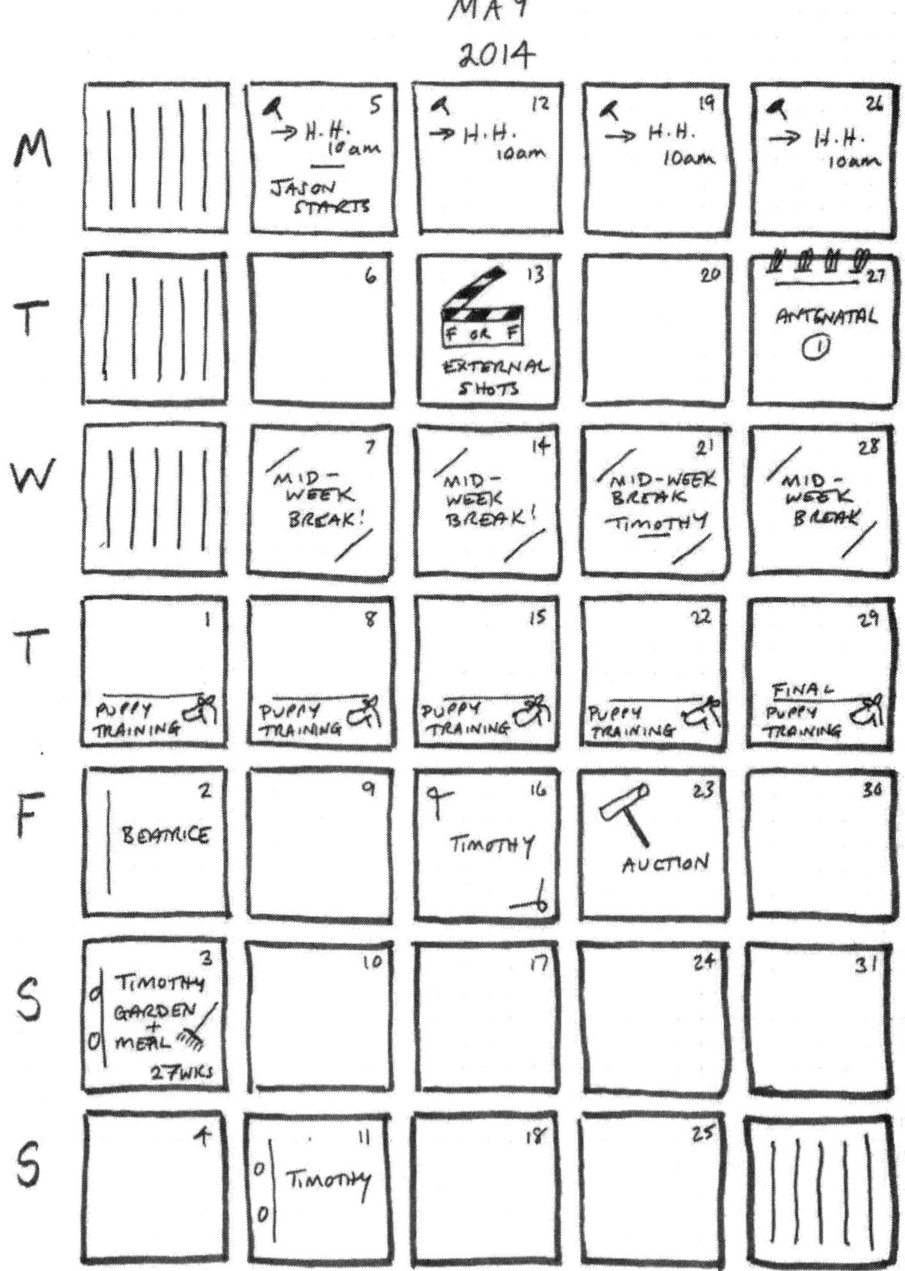
MAY
2014
M
T
W
T
F
S
S
5
→ H.H. 10am
JASON STARTS
12
→ H.H. 10am
19
→ H.H. 10am
26
→ H.H. 10am
6
13
F OR F
EXTERNAL SHOTS
20
27
ANTENATAL
1
7
MID-WEEK BREAK!
14
MID-WEEK BREAK!
21
MID-WEEK BREAK
TIMOTHY
28
MID-WEEK BREAK
1
PUPPY TRAINING
8
PUPPY TRAINING
15
PUPPY TRAINING
22
PUPPY TRAINING
29
FINAL PUPPY TRAINING
2
BEATRICE
9
16
TIMOTHY
23
AUCTION
30
3
TIMOTHY
GARDEN + MEAL
27WKS
10
17
24
31
4
11
TIMOTHY
18
25

Friday 2nd May - TANUSHI

Third trimester starts tomorrow. 27 weeks. Got a load of stuff through in the post. Details of antenatal classes, all sorts of freebies and promise of freebies, nappies etc. details of local NCT, Mother and Toddler groups. I have been assigned a midwife whom I will meet via antenatal classes. Etc.

Finally, F or F contact me – but only to say they are sending someone round to do all the external shots of KA – next week. Nothing more than that.

Timothy coming round again tomorrow to garden and have a proper meal. Asked him what he wanted to eat and he just says surprise me. Get on phone to Amma immediately!

Beatrice comes round for a cuppa and I think for some respite and time away. Charles had insisted she leaves him. It is so hard to be there the whole time and then so hard not to be there. Anyway, she doesn't want to talk about Charles but about me. And we talk babies and she tells me of her experience of having Timothy and Hannah. And I show her all the work Timothy has done in the garden. She is intrigued – and wonders what secret powers I have to get Timothy to do all that. And I blush and she smiles and she says suddenly, "I don't know what I'll do without him."

And I hold her hand and she holds my hand and I say nothing because there seems nothing to say. And then little sproglet jumps and I jump and I put her hand on my belly and call her my Derbyshire Mum. And she smiles. And that prompts the re-telling of the visit to Madrid.

Saturday 3rd May

Timothy arrives at 10.00 and works really hard. I can do little bits and pieces and so I don't feel a total spare part. So much is cleared in just two days. And we can start to contemplate what might be possible to put in its place.

He has brought a towel and change of clothes. He goes upstairs to shower. The boiler kicks in. I hear him step out of the shower his footsteps on the wooden boards. And I am doing my best to concentrate on the cooking. He comes downstairs looking and smelling good. I turn to him smack him on the chest and say, "Well that's better old chap. G and T?" And he smiles and covers my hand and said, "Absolutely old gal. Get to it."

I used too many chillies. Aaargh! (Think I used 8 rather than 4!) He manfully attempts to carry on eating and appreciating until it is too much! And we laugh uncontrollably – for some reason. And we talk and consider the future of KA. He says that he thinks that

I have made the most wonderful impact on the whole estate – everyone thinks so – he says. There is now a future he believes and that's down to me. I say, completely lamely, "You're just trying to curry favour!!" And we laugh again. (You had to be there.)

And then – after a triumph of a rhubarb crumble – he leaves. Thanks me and leaves. There's no sense he might want to take it further. I'm not saying I just expect him to want to do that...it's just that I thought he might want to. He seemed keen early on... now it's more like... I don't know. We get on so well.

I compare him to Jimmy and there's nothing to compare – Timothy is so superior in every way. He is thoughtful, sensitive, kind, intelligent, excellent sense of humour. And Jimmy has muscles and plenty of self-regard.

Saturday 3rd May – TIMOTHY

I feel knackered but happy. T's garden shaping up. And a ridiculously hot curry – she'd made a mistake on the chillies! We had a lovely, lovely time together. But I think she regards me as a friend and no more. She asked me about the online dating – I said after a couple of disasters, I was having a break. Too much on right now with Dad. And she said she understood and "maybe next time."

Monday 5th May - TANUSHI

Jason starts. There promptly at 8.30. Sit him down and go through some induction stuff. Take him upstairs to meet HH. So far he has said nothing. He sees the beetle table and lights up and starts speaking to Henry about beetles. Henry is of course amazed and impressed and explains what he is doing and the two are best buddies within 5 minutes. Ha! Who expected that? Anyway, eventually hand him over to Ted.

Monday 5th May

1. Met the new apprentice. Splendid little chap – showed an interest in the beetles. Think he'll go far.

2. Tanushi told me about the exterior filming they will be doing next week. Otherwise no news.

3. I am fretting about Roger and where he thinks he will be living when he is released – two weeks now.

Wednesday 7th May

1. Dorothy arrived saying she wanted to help me buy some new clothes. I say the current budget for clothes was zero pounds per annum and had been for some time. "Exactly Henry – threadbare corduroys and moth-eaten moleskins – they need chucking and replacing. And those shirts are terrible." Clothes shopping has been done by Jane when given specific direction once every 5 years or so. Dorothy actually wants me to go to a shop and look and try on and choose and buy. All very strange say I. "Next week I am taking you to Peak Village for some clothes!"

2. Dorothy thinks she has found somewhere for Roger – in Derby.

Thursday 8th May - TANUSHI

Get instructions for the external shots on Tuesday.

Interview with Jason at the end of his week (he is off to Buxton for formal horticulture education each Friday) – and seems happy enough with how the first week has gone... as far as one can tell. He'll be back on Monday. Ted is certainly happy.

Sunday 11th May

Invite Timothy for a cream tea to make up for the curry (sort of!) And he arrives with a Camelia to plant – a strong pink – going to be beautiful Feb / March – so kind – and he suggests the place it could be planted. It's substantial – bet it cost a bit. He says he'll plant it next time... he can see I am no position to do that. (Next time!)

He asks me for news of F or F. No news – at all. So frustrating.

He is clearly pleased to be here – he repeats that several times.

Monday 12th May

1. I have to time my visits to Charles now to coincide with peak consciousness. Too much morphine and he's out of it. It's a balancing act. He can still sit up in a chair and converse happily for short periods. And then the pain becomes too great and it's back to the morphine. He still refuses to talk about his illness. He wants to be engaged about all things exterior to his limited world. Hannah has postponed her university year and will return in January next year. It's hard for her. Sometimes we talk about all things ecological and Charles listens.

2. They are being supported by excellent charity – Helen's Trust.

Tuesday 13th May - TANUSHI

External shots take an age – but it's good weather so it should all look great – they want to get a sense of the dilapidation so I show them round the back of the house. This will be used to heighten the drama – everything hangs on this decision which it sort of does.

Wednesday 14th May

1. I went clothes shopping with Dorothy. This was a trial as expected but one with which I coped. Dorothy's unrelenting good humour and mockery of me helped. She allowed me the appearance of choice and steered me to her choices – obviously. And two pairs of trousers and 4 shirts were purchased together with a new jumper. I was rewarded with a visit to the Barley Mow at Kirk Ireton.

2. I spoke to Ted and Jane about Roger's release. Ted will collect him on Monday and take him to Derby – some church scheme for released prisoners. He hasn't, as far as I am aware, written to Samantha and Jimmy and I do not want him venturing on to Kirk Aeppel property without my explicit permission to see his family and not to attempt to get his feet in the door. Jane was clearly upset with the vigour of my pronouncement – she was imagining Sunday dinner with Roger and grandchildren...which is fine except I fear Roger will find a way of inveigling himself into the life of the estate. I forgive him but do not trust him – is that hypocrisy?

Friday 16th May

1. A thoroughly splendid evening with Dorothy.

Friday 16th May - TANUSHI

A perfect spring evening. Timothy came by after work to plant up the Camelia. Afterwards we wandered up to the walled garden with Kala. Dorothy and HH were there consuming large quantities of Pimm's as far as I could see and clearly enjoying themselves. The dogs bounced around.

And then I told Timothy something I had never come close to telling Jimmy.

When we got to Old Oak, I told Timothy about my Father and the tree in our garden and about the Anuradhapura Cross and how this tree played its part in convincing me that Kirk Aeppel was where I was meant to be. Like it knew. He just listened without judgment. He put his hand on the tree and I put my hand on his.

We walked across the stream and on up to the wood looking down towards the pond and the gatehouse. And we remembered that other perfect evening in Cambridge which had started so calamitously with me declaring my love for him!

We laughed and he suddenly said, "Tanushi, if it's not now, it's never." I didn't know what he was on about. And he became hesitant, turned away and addressed the trees, "The fact is I like you. What I really mean is I have been half in love with you ever since I laid eyes on you at the interview and now I am 100% head over heels, stupidly and irredeemably in love with you. You don't have to reply...it's just that it had to be said right now. I had to say it. And even if it is unrequited, I had to say it." He was silent still facing away from me. I pulled him round and reached to kiss him and mumbled, "Requited."

So there we were, with Kala dancing around and jumping up at us, kissing and laughing. Requited.

Saturday 17th May – TIMOTHY

I can't quite believe what happened last night. I am just so full of.... Joy! I suppose...and happiness and I can't believe that she was interested in me after all and she just said, "Requited!" I can't think straight. And I feel so conflicted going to see Dad and feeling like this. I don't know whether to tell him – in confidence… he'll be happy for me. Definitely.

Monday 19th May

1. Tanushi bounces in, "29 weeks Henry... not long now!" I don't know how she has the energy. Full of the joys of spring.

2. Jason was being looked after by Jimmy for the morning. Ted came to see me as soon as he was back from collecting Roger and delivering him to Derby. He was tired. Roger had promised again to turn over a new leaf, never to come to Kirk Aeppel without my express permission and to give his time in service to the poor and "marginalised" – yes, he really did use that term apparently. Ted had no idea what he was on about. "He's a changed man Mr 'Avard." I am sure he is – and that's how the inveigling starts. "Can he come up on Sunday 15th June – Father's Day?" I can hardly say "No" can I?

Wednesday 21st May – TIMOTHY

I go round to Tanaushi with a little card and mumble out a sort of, "Look I realise you may not feel about me what I feel about you but I am happy to take things slowly" – but she shuts me down. She's 29 weeks pregnant… all things will be taken slowly… she really likes me and she's really happy. End of story.

Wednesday 21st May - TANUSHI

Inviting everyone to watch the auctioning of the silver plates on Friday. Don't think Charles can come any more but it's all on-line. Exciting.

Timothy comes round in the evening – he brought a little card on which he had sketched – rather expertly – the cross my Father had sketched on my hand all those years ago. On the back it just had: Friday 16th May – from T to T – a perfect day – xxx

Friday 23rd May

What a day!! Oh my goodness where do I start? EVERYBODY turned up. (Apart from Jimmy and Billie – setting up for Yurt changeover day.) Everybody including Charles after all. He was showered with affection. He sat down carefully near to the screen. He whispered to me, "So pleased Tanushi... just look after him... in a few weeks he'll need you." And he pecked me on the cheek.

4.00pm Pimm's and cucumber sandwiches and strawberries and cream.

Go online at 4.25 and we're on pretty quickly. "Lots of interest ladies and Gentlemen" – blah blah blah. Full description. And then we start at £30K. Going up in £1K. We get to 41K and the internet goes down. Sam to the rescue. We all assume that it'll be over by the time we re-connect. But no – it's still going. 53 – 54 – 55 – 56 (all phone bidding) 56 – it stops... going once... 57 – 58 – 59 – 60 – 61 – are there any further bids? 61,000 pounds – it's your last chance Ladies and Gentlemen – Paul de Lamerie - 61,000 pounds. Going once and twice. GONE!!

Everyone cheers. Henry cheers with tears in his eyes – hugging Dorothy for all he's worth. Timothy puts his arm round the small of my back and says, "Well done old gal!" and kisses me on the cheek. I feel myself blush.

Jane has had a little too much Pimm's and is a bit overcome with emotion!

Friday 23rd May

1. £61,000 for the plates. Hidden away in the dark for all that time like the secrets they accompanied. Marvellous. So pleased that Charles made it. He has savoured the event with everybody. Maybe his last Kirk Aeppel moment. Drinks all round.

2. Quite exhausted. Dorothy started a new jigsaw in the evening.

Monday 26th May

1. Tanushi and Sam drop in as usual. The start of ante-natal classes on Tuesday and final puppy training Thursday. Sam will accompany her to the former. I congratulate her once again on the plates and wish her well. I ask whether they think Billie has contributed positively and they react a little oddly – "Yes she's pulled her weight... in many areas."

2. Glampers all week. Jimmy running round like a mad thing trying to keep up. Building inspectors come in a week and he needs to be as ready as he can be. I say I'll look in on the orchard if he wants to give some instructions.

3. Still not a word from Fake or Fortune.

Tuesday 27th May - TANUSHI

First ante-natal with Sam. Awkward trying to explain about the Father – would he be there? No. Was he "supportive?" Yes. Will he be coming to these classes? Never. There was a degree of judgement going on. Anyway, shown around the maternity unit at Calow. Feeling all very real now and intimidating if I'm honest – but I guess everyone feels that. Sam smiled through it all being the very best friend.

Thursday 28th May

Final puppy class. Get a certificate to say we are roadworthy. Kala has learnt to socialise – in truth she needed no help there. I have learnt one or two tricks and met some great dogs and their owners. Is Kala trained? – not really!

Friday 29th May

Drama! Billie has left suddenly and without saying anything to anyone. She left at 5.30 in the morning with all her gear, getting a taxi, we think, from outside my house – I heard nothing. Her note apparently said: "To Jimmy, thanks for everything you Pommie bastard – I have learnt loads. Look me up when you come to Oz and we can tread the grapes and fleece the sheep together. Love you, Billie xxxxxxxx"

Sam says she never really liked her. Jimmy is mortified apparently.

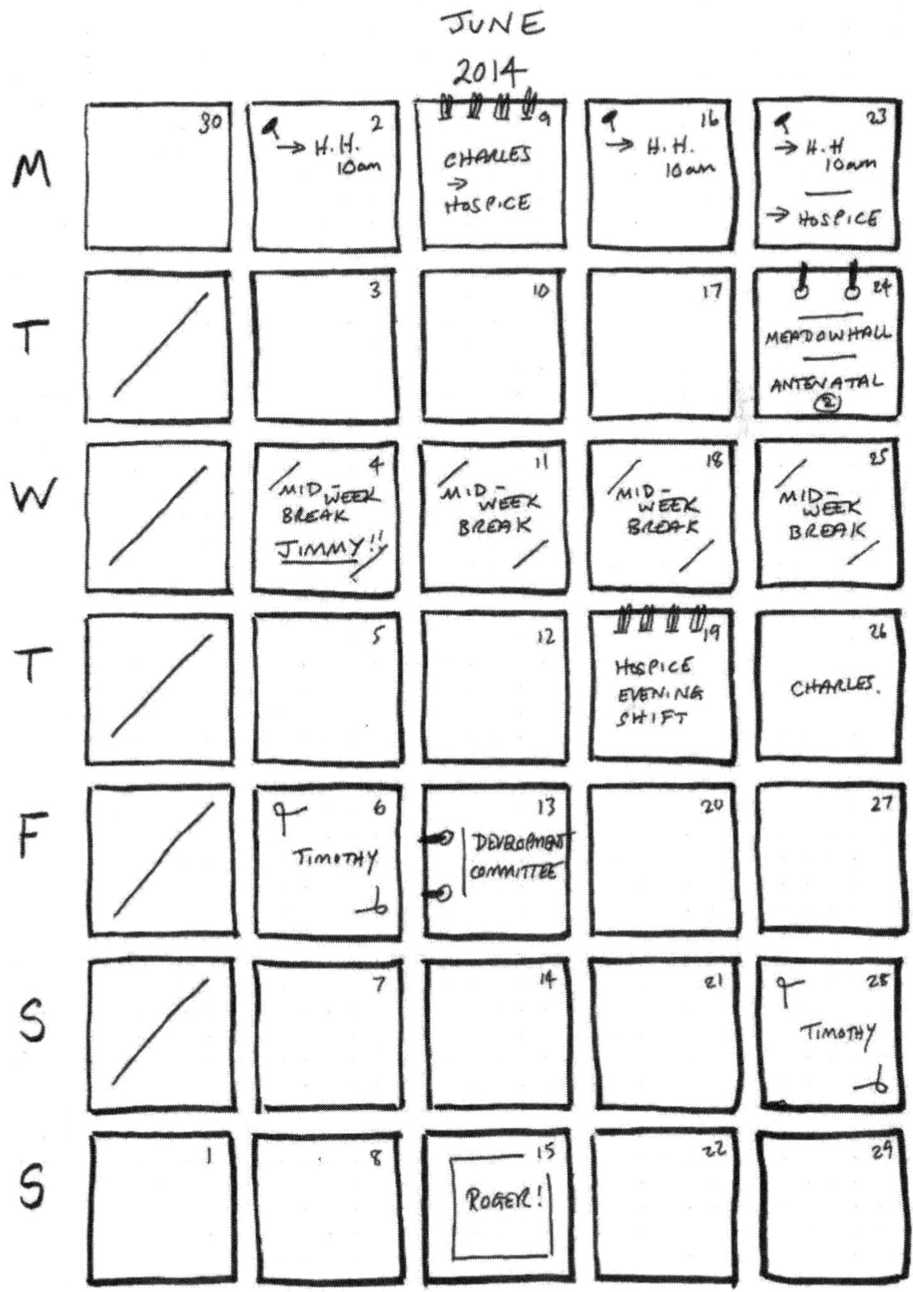
JUNE
2014
M
T
W
T
F
S
S
30
2
→ H.H.
10am
9
CHARLES
→
HOSPICE
16
→ H.H.
10am
23
→ H.H
10am
→ HOSPICE
3
10
17
24
MEADOWHALL
ANTENATAL
4
MID WEEK
BREAK
JIMMY!!
11
MID-
WEEK
BREAK
18
MID-
WEEK
BREAK
25
MID-
WEEK
BREAK
5
12
19
HOSPICE
EVENING
SHIFT
26
CHARLES.
6
TIMOTHY
13
DEVELOPMENT
COMMITTEE
20
27
7
14
21
28
TIMOTHY
1
8
15
ROGER!
22
29

Sunday 1st June

1. Communion. Dorothy. Time to reflect and draw breath. Whilst much is good and healing in my life, much is problematic. I am still plagued from time to time by potential flashbacks and nightmares and reconstructions and sometimes I still do not know which way is up. At such times my plates trouble me. Also ahead are many unknowns – the verdict on the painting which could be wonderful but could be disastrous. And the baby – I find this simply impossible to imagine – how might this impact? I just don't know. It will mean change. And then my dear friend is to die.

2. I have lived a life of pared down "security." I have committed to growth and change. I sense I am mid leap between an old life and who knows what. And it scares me. Charles would know what to say. I resolve to say all this to Dorothy.

Monday 2nd June

1. Sam tells me Billie has gone – without saying anything to anyone. I try my best to elicit what has been going on – with no success at all. Sam says, "She's got her return ticket and three months on her visa. She's done her bit here. Good luck to her!" I remember D's comment about Jimmy and Billie. Who knows what goes on?

2. Still nothing from Fake or Fortune?

Wednesday 4th June - TANUSHI

Jimmy came down at the end of the day to report that the building inspectors had picked up on one tiny thing and otherwise everything was fine. Decorating now. He is really pleased with how everything has gone. I said HH would be delighted with all he has achieved and that I would pass the news on. He lingered. He said his Dad was going to visit on Father's Day in a couple of weeks. He lingered and left.

Friday 6th June

Arrange to have Timothy over after work. Set up for drinks and snacks on the patio. Timothy is just cutting down some ivy in the far corner. Up turns Jimmy. He's already a pint or two into his evening session. At the front door he starts apologising for how he's treated me and how much he regrets it and he didn't know what he was thinking of. He trails after me through the kitchen into the garden and he sees the table, drinks and Timothy simultaneously. "What the f* * * are you doing here?"

Timothy: "Oh hello Jimmy. Just cutting back some ivy. How are you old chap?"

Jimmy takes 6 seconds and a similar number of swear words to vacate the property.

"Ah! I don't think I have ever used the phrase "old chap" in my entire life!" says Timothy and we laugh for the rest of the evening.

Saturday 7th June

A letter from F or F. Aaargh! So: the final scene at which the authenticity or otherwise is revealed, is to be filmed on Saturday 19th July. It's at the Fitzwilliam and all the timings are detailed.

Go straight to HH and tell him. Then tell Timothy. He asks whether I should forewarn them about pregnancy…38 weeks. I mull and then say I think I should. I have been the face of all this and they need me there. If we were sitting down for the grand reveal, it would be OK. Wouldn't it?

Monday 9th June

See HH without Sam. He is wondering what to do about F or F. Should he be going down? Would that be appropriate? Or just wait here for news?

Charles is to go into the hospice apparently for a few days respite care. Henry intends to visit him there this afternoon.

Messaged from the auctioneers – the money should be in our account within the week.

Monday 9th June

1. Charles in the hospice to give Beatrice a break. I visit him along with Brook and stay most of the afternoon. He appreciates Brook being there. As do I. He is asleep for a good while and at peace. He has long imagined this time. The

Chaplain visits him. We share the simplest communion. I leave a three-quarter finished bottle of Edradour – not that I think he'll drink it. Just as a reminder. I leave as Hannah arrives. She buries her head into Brook's neck and weeps a little. I say, "Be of good courage Hannah." I can think of nothing else to say.

Wednesday 11th June

1. Afternoon spent with Dorothy. There is a definite lifting of the spirits. (I have inevitably been somewhat oppressed by the visit to see Charles.) She has now completely adopted Twyi. Such a bond there between the two of them. We have said we will look after Charles on Friday to allow Beatrice to go to an outdoor concert with Hannah and Timothy.

2. She asks whether it would be appropriate to come to the committee meeting on Friday. Now that she is "back in favour." I will ask Tanushi.

3. We speak of Roger's Father's Day visit on Sunday and how to handle that. He will presumably go straight to Jane and Ted's. I will speak to Jane.

Friday 13th June - TANUSHI

Committee Meeting. Beatrice absent. (Jimmy arrived early and handed me a card apologising for his behaviour.) Dorothy back to taking the minutes after a little absence! Much chuckling and a warm welcome back to her. After reports on finance and Jimmy's progress at the farm (congratulations from one and all) we spent the bulk of the time discussing F or F. Jane and Ted joined us for this.

So, basically, they were AMAZED with the whole thing. And they couldn't believe that this had all happened under their noses without them knowing. Henry and I (and the Parkers) had kept the secret. Various suggestions. An estate day out – hire a room in Christ College and await the verdict. Or what?

We have been sworn to secrecy by the programme. No publicity – local or national until the programme is aired later in the year – in all publicity we will be guided by the F or F staff. I tried to play down the possibility of a favourable outcome. They had all made their minds up of course. Of course, it's a Goya – they'd suspected all along! Henry then said that he did not want Roger telling because it would be too difficult for him not to say anything. Jane agreed.

Friday 13th June

1. Committee – Tanushi reveals the Carilla painting secret. All very jubilant and excited. You would have thought the decision was in the bag. How to mark this? Timothy suggested an estate day out to Cambridge! Jane agreed NOT to tell Roger.

2. Dorothy and I went immediately after the meeting to relieve Beatrice. Dorothy cooked and we set up a meal for Charles. He remains as alert as he can and is appreciative of us allowing Beatrice some time off. For him it is a battle between consciousness and pain and unconsciousness and no pain. Somehow this seems a metaphor for life itself. The philosophers always chose awareness and the risks it entailed – the unexamined life is not worth living and all that. I cannot help thinking of my own newly found awareness of past events – and whether this had served some higher purpose in my life. Or had ignorance been bliss?

3. Dorothy announced that she would cook tomorrow night. "Be prepared for some surprises." I say as usual that I hate celery which I know she knows.

Saturday 14th June

1. In truth I do not rightly remember what Dorothy cooked.

2. After dinner she excused herself briefly and returned wearing the old shirt I had given her when she got wet last July and nothing else.

3. That is all the diary needs to know.

Sunday 15th June

1. Feeling invigorated by change.

2. Arranged with Jane to pop over before their meal starts. I was shocked by Roger's appearance – it was as if prison had left deep invisible scars. He was gaunt and Heepish in manner. He lumbered slowly rather than walked. He was fawningly grateful to me for allowing him to visit. Of course, I then felt guilty. "Mum has told me what a busy time it has been Mr Havard. If you ever need any help anywhere on the estate, you only need ask. Not for money mind." I ask him what

he had been doing in Derby. He says he has been working on an outreach project for some charismatic church. Very worthwhile he says. "I had it good once and I threw it all away. And this is my second chance." I wished him well and excused myself.

3. I truly hope Roger has changed and that he can build some sort of relationship with his children.

Monday 16th June

1. Tanushi now looking rather cumbersome – not that I say that. She is concerned to buy the bench and bulbs to remember Jimmy and Sam's Mother. We select the bench on-line. They have agreed the spot inside the orchard. We need to get the words right. She is hoping to do that a.s.a.p.

2. We have a conversation about parenting. I immediately make it clear she is in charge and has final say on everything. Within that it would be good if I might be consulted and that we share some sense of the priorities for him or her – a list of values and beliefs and a tradition within which to bring him or her up. She was happy with all this. We will talk more.

3. She is a remarkable young woman. I say this to her. She smiles and begins to leave and then stops. "I think our son or daughter should see us exchange a greeting on arrival and departure. I think that will be good for them to see. What do you think Henry?" I assented and so she came across and kissed me goodbye.

4. It is looking like Charles will be going into the hospice for the final time soon.

Tuesday 17th June - TANUSHI

I contacted Tina to say I will be 38 weeks pregnant when filming the final scene – perhaps seating/table can be arranged. She expressed surprise and said she would pass the message on. And then congratulated me.

Wednesday 18th June

1. Dorothy and I spent some time helping Beatrice and Hannah get ready for Charles' departure to the hospice tomorrow. In retrospect I think we contributed nothing but our moral support.

2. Beatrice is used to being organised and in control. She has attempted to apply her professional competence to the one thing outside all human control – death. Even as she checks her lists for the umpteenth time, she knows she cannot resist the unpredictability and inevitability of what lies ahead. Rotas are in place for visits. I noticed Tanushi's name next to Timothy. Dorothy told me she thought they are in a relationship. I do not argue.

3. Vicars have to be good with death. It's part of their job description. Dorothy is a reassuring presence. She knows what to do and say. I feel the very opposite about myself. Perhaps death is such a rare and professionally distanced event in modern society that all lay people feel utterly inadequate.

Thursday 19th June - TANUSHI

I have ensured that Timothy and I are on the rota together. The evening shift. When he wakes, Charles is just delighted to see us both. He says to Timothy, "Don't let her go. She is pure gold." And to me he says, "Look after this one Tanushi. He will need you. And you will need him soon enough." And then he speculates as to whether he will last long enough to hear the outcome of the painting adjudication. He doubts it and then falls asleep.

Sunday 22nd June

1. Afternoon and evening at the hospice. I take Brook. I have always thought Brook was, in the nicest way possible, something of a bruiser. However, he enters the room, looks at Charles and approaches him with the utmost gentleness, smelling his face. I push the other bed close, put the rug on it. Brook jumps up and immediately sits and plonks his head next to Charles' hand. He stays there not moving a muscle. Remarkable. He knows. How does he know? Suffused spirituality? St Francis may be right after all.

2. Charles has taken to issuing instructions. Firstly, I must look after Beatrice. I suspect he has said this to everyone. Then I must ensure that Timothy and

Tanushi marry. He gives this his most ardent blessing. (So, they are in relationship. I do not protest of course but I think this task may be beyond me.) And he tells me not to let Dorothy go like I almost did last year. "What a bloody idiot!"

3. I avail myself of the Edradour I'd left. I put a drop on to his finger and take it to his mouth. He smiles. "All those years of supping whisky together. We'll make sure this is in your coffin to take with you."

4. Hannah and Beatrice arrive.

Monday 23rd June – TIMOTHY

I don't know what I would do without Tanushi right now. It's clear that Dad really likes her and wants us to be together. She is such a support. When we go across, it's mainly she and I that chat whilst he sleeps. A relationship forged in the fire maybe.

Tuesday 24th June - TANUSHI

Head off with Sam to Meadowhall for some retail therapy and a break from the relentlessness and intensity. Buy outfit – that fits – for F or F. And I need a load of stuff for my baby!! My stamina for Meadowhall is not great. So we are super-efficient and end up at a pizza place there. Sam says what a complete idiot Jimmy has been and she asks about me and Timothy. Sam drives there and back thankfully. Feeling so tired that I sleep on the way back!

Then off to ante-natal. Who is to be my birthing partner? Mother. Why is she not here? She lives in Harrow. How will she know to be around? If your waters break, it's a long way from London! What about Father. No! Do you live on your own? Yes. Have you a supportive community? Clearly, they are not happy and make that known.

And I think of that supportive community that I have been embraced by – Jane – my dearest Derbyshire auntie and Ted who introduced me to Old Oak, Sam – my bestie and Jimmy – well some little temporary difficulties, Beatrice – who has been my constant mentor and support and sweet Charles, Dorothy and of course Henry, Andrew and Sarah – we share puppy walks! I could not have a more supportive community!

Wednesday 25th June

Timothy thinks it will be soon. He can't praise the hospice staff enough. Beatrice spending each night there with him – to catch every solitary moment of consciousness.

Charles has responded to each greeting of, "How are you?" with "Still dying – apparently."

Amma phones each evening now! So she is happy to come up and stay from Monday 21st July for as long as it takes. 38 weeks at that stage...I now have an answer for the midwife and hope that placates her. Feeling irritated by it all. Could do without that right now.

Thursday 26th June

We all go in during the day to say our goodbyes. He has rallied a little. Brook takes up his familiar position. He lies very still, very alert, looking up at Charles. I put the tiniest droplet of whisky on the cube sponge they provide to moisten his mouth and lips. Beatrice scolds me and we bicker. And Charles is most amused by it all. And we laugh along with him.

Brook – Italian Spinone

I have taken to reading to him. Winnie the Pooh seems a favourite. He loves me to read chapter 10 of The House at Pooh Corner – The Enchanted Place.

"They went on thinking of This and That, and by-and-by they came to an enchanted place on the very top of the Forest called Galleons Lap, which is sixty-something trees in a circle; and Christopher Robin knew it was enchanted because nobody had ever been able to count whether it was sixty-three or sixty-four, not even when he tied a piece of string round each tree when he had counted it."

It is, I have to confess, almost impossible to read to the end of the chapter.

I stay on with Beatrice and Timothy and Hannah into the early hours of Friday 27th June 2014 when he dies peacefully.

Timothy drives me home with Brook in the back. I take with me Charles' favourite old brogues, the laces of which Brook had habitually chewed; I put them in his bed.

At 3.30 am, I write this diary and toast my truest friend. Ribble will be allowed onto my bed – tonight only.

Friday 27th June – TIMOTHY

I open, with Mother and Hannah, the folder entitled, "When I die..." It contains every step of the process that she needs to now undertake. It is divided into sections:

Registration of death and who to inform

The Will

Finance

Funeral

Personal

All have the requisite websites/forms/phone numbers etc. And the order in which things have to be attended to.

What a man. We decide to wait before we open the Personal folder.

Friday 27th June – TANUSHI

I am messaged by Timothy with the news. I send back my love – "Call in any time. Tell me how to help you." He said he is spending the day with Mum and Hannah. Got to collect all his stuff from the hospice. He'll be in touch tomorrow.

I arranged a walk with Andrew and Sarah and Immie. None of us knew Charles very well. But we all sensed the loss to the estate and to Henry and of course to the family. It was a warm, dull day.

I invited them in for a drink on our return. Ted was in the walled garden with Jason – the delphiniums were resplendent along the back wall. I always acknowledge Old Oak as we pass. Jane was in the kitchen and busied herself with the drinks. Henry joined us. He looks tired as might be expected and he told the story of the night. And he proposed a toast to Charles.

Saturday 28th June

Timothy drops in briefly for a snack at lunch. Charles has everything in order – so he thinks they can have the funeral maybe on 11th July. Of course – even in his present state – he notices and appreciates everything I have done to prepare for the arrival. I have been busy getting things ready – and for Amma too.

Sunday 29th June

1. Communion – Dorothy steps in. We pray for Beatrice and Hannah and Timothy. And round Big Table we have the smallest of nips of sloe gin to remember Charles.

2. Later I join Andrew and Sarah with both Immie and Kala for a dog walk. We leave Tanushi to sleep.

3. I sense I am somewhat redundant and that I should be assisting Beatrice in some way but I know not how. I phone Timothy to ask if there is anything I can do. He thanks me but says they are coping.

4. In the evening I break my rule and have a whisky on my own. Or perhaps not entirely alone.

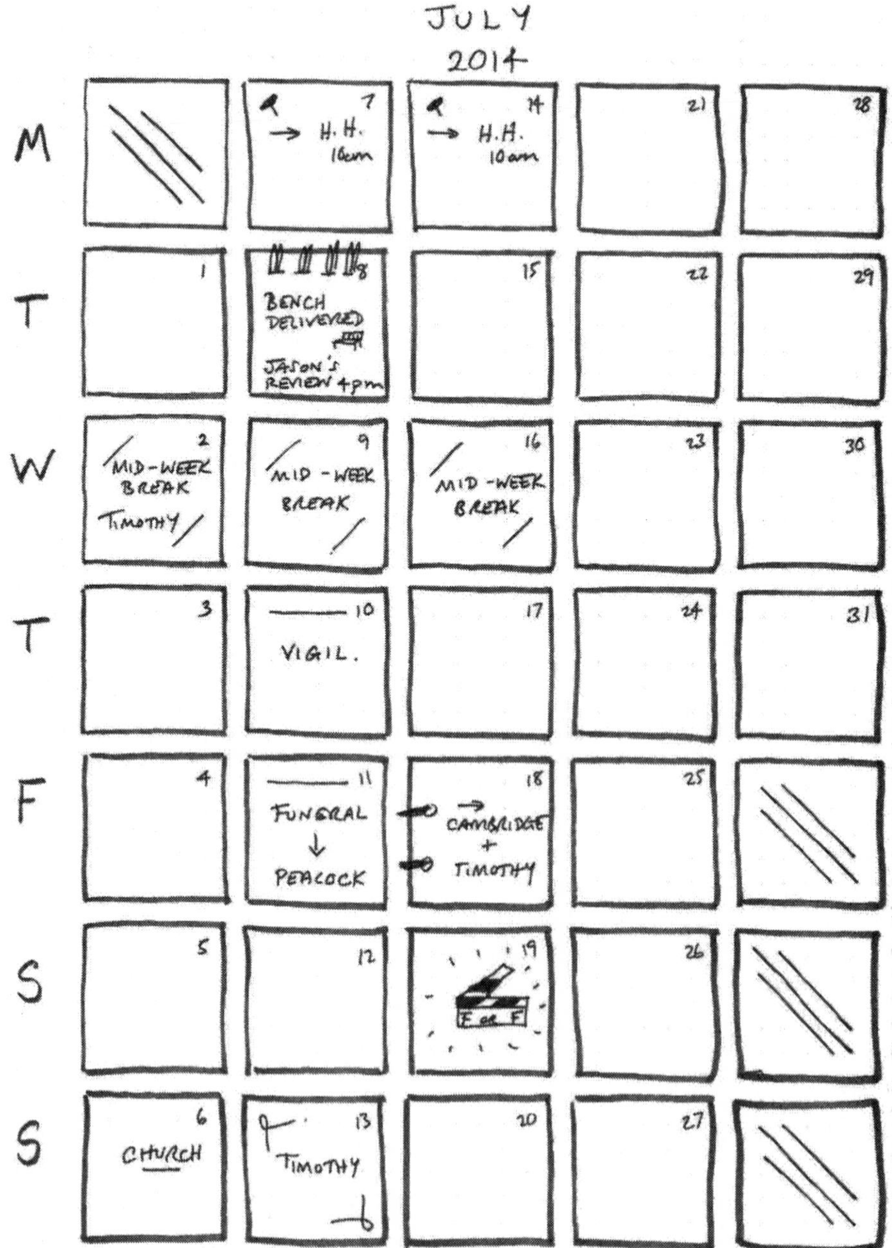

JULY
2014
M
T
W
T
F
S
S
7
→ H.H. 10am
14
→ H.H. 10am
21
28
1
8
BENCH DELIVERED
JASON'S REVIEW 4pm
15
22
29
2
MID-WEEK BREAK
TIMOTHY
9
MID-WEEK BREAK
16
MID-WEEK BREAK
23
30
3
10
VIGIL.
17
24
31
4
11
FUNERAL
↓
PEACOCK
18
→ CAMBRIDGE + TIMOTHY
25
5
12
19
F or F
26
6
CHURCH
13
TIMOTHY
20
27

Wednesday 2nd July - TANUSHI

The funeral is Friday 11th. There is to be a funeral service at St Cuthbert's for close family and friends at 10.30. Then a memorial service in the village church at 12.00 followed by the wake at the Peacock.

Timothy calls round in the evening – the first proper time we have had together since Charles died and he suddenly reminds me of his Father. I see it for the first time. A chip off the old block. Measured, generous, understated, sweet and kind, good humoured. We have a gentle time together.

Wednesday 2nd July

1. I have no idea why it takes so long before the funeral can happen. He will have had everything in order – tickety-boo. No one can settle until it happens. We all have our orders from Timothy as to our tasks.

2. I raise the issue of dogs with Tanushi with specific reference to our day in Cambridge. Jimmy is not coming. He has changeover day to look after. So the dogs can go to him. Timothy has booked the room at Christ's and the minibus. Buffet afternoon tea. She tells me the order of events. Timothy will take her down on the Friday. The rest will follow in a minibus on Saturday. Arrive midday. Room at Christs booked for 2.00 pm. We expect the filming to end by 2.30 pm. Return at 6.00 - 7.00 pm.

3. Dorothy comes round – it is a return to summer weather. We console one another. I tell her what Charles said to me about her – "Not to be a bloody fool and let her slip through your hands!" She laughed and she said, "Let's not slip through each other's hands this time."

4. She will preside of course at both the funeral and memorial services.

Thursday 3rd July

1. Beatrice came round unexpectedly and joined us for our morning drink. She brought with her a dozen or so half full bottles of malt. She's kept a couple for guests. She seemed robust enough in the circumstances. I asked her if she had requested that the Edradour be placed in the coffin. She had. It is important to me. She asked if I remembered the first occasion Charles came to Kirk Aeppel.

We had hit it off immediately. First day at Jesus. Two boys – we felt like – from Derbyshire. One grammar school boy and one public school boy. Same staircase. For me, lacking all of the confidence such a public school was supposed to cloak me in, I clung to Charles like a drowning man does to flotsam. And we became friends in a twinkling of an eye. The first week of the Christmas vacation – probably around 10th December '79 he came to Kirk Aeppel and fell in love with it as everyone does. Mother congratulated him on doing a useful degree that would earn money – rather than studying bloody bugs and beetles. She liked the sound of her unexpected alliteration. And that is how she always referred to my degree thereafter.

2. I asked her whether the coffin could be placed in St Cuthbert's the evening before the funeral to allow him to be accompanied through that final night. She was nonplussed. He hadn't requested it. He hadn't not requested it. No decision. I assured her not to let this bother her or upset her. She smiled and said, "Henry, you are a dear old stick. I know you loved him. We both did."

Friday 4th July - TANUSHI

Everything sorted re the orchard bench. Words agreed. Bench arrives on Tuesday. We shall have a little ceremony at the start of September and invite the family.

Timothy spent the evening here. We watched Notting Hill – again. Just needed something undemanding and gentle and touching.

I have never felt so comfortable with anyone ever before. It feels a bit like coming home.

Sunday 6th July

1. All join together once again for communion. Even Tanushi in her present state. She keeps insisting she is absolutely fine and that she needs no help – "It's not an affliction Henry!"

2. Dorothy passed on that Beatrice has said that she is happy for the coffin to be placed at St Cuthbert's at 5.00 pm on the Thursday but that she will not be attending.

3. Jane and Ted will decorate the chapel for the service on Friday. Ted assured me that delphiniums were his favourite flowers. Jane said, "He always remarked on the delphs, Henry – never failed. I am surprised you didn't know that."

4. I work on what I am going to say which I am convinced is the most difficult task I have ever undertaken.

Monday 7th July

1. Tanushi and Sam call in as usual. I have come to appreciate this start to the working week. I declare that if the painting is not authenticated as a Goya, I will be willing to sell the tusks. And if it is a Goya, there will be no need to sell the tusks. Tanushi is happy with this compromise.

2. We run through the arrangements one last time. Timothy is driving her down on the Friday. Staying at some hotel near the station. Early start for them on the Saturday. We will see them at Christs when they return with the news.

3. Sophie's bench arrives tomorrow. Jimmy has prepared its place in the orchard. South facing. Sam says Jimmy is really pleased and grateful that Tanushi has arranged all this. Ceremony to be confirmed on the first Saturday in September.

4. I ask Sam to prepare some of the Wassail lanterns at the front of the chapel for Thursday night.

Tuesday 8th July - TANUSHI

The bench is delivered as planned. Jimmy oversees everything. He and Sam sit there and I take a photo for them to send to their family inviting them to KA in September.

Pleased to have done that.

At Jason's preliminary review meeting, all seems extremely positive. Ted is tremendously impressed with his knowledge and desire to work hard. I think Ted might be learning a few things from Jason! And he now speaks confidently. Jason says his Mother says he doesn't shut up about KA and how he loves it here. And he's helped Jimmy in the orchard now Billie has left.

I suspect that taking him out of a bullied environment has done him the world of good. The walled garden and the orchard and the estate and Ted and Jane and Henry and the beetles and all of us have a helped a young man find himself. Type up review meeting and email it to his tutor.

Thursday 10th July – Friday 11th July

Charles is delivered at 5.00 pm and placed in front of the altar. In truth there is not a lot of space. I have arranged for food and drink. And music – some of Charles' favourite music – Gershwin in particular. Tanushi has helped with that. The magnificent delphinium display towers on the altar above him.

And so starts the evening and night. I have my diary to write and my speech to refine and Brook and Ribble for company.

Tanushi is the first to arrive at 8.30 pm. She leaves by 9.00 pm.

Ted and Jane with Sam and Jimmy arrive at 9.30 pm. Sam lights the lanterns. And we speak of Charles and to Charles. They leave.

Then Hannah and Timothy bring Beatrice. She has changed her mind. We drink and eat together. And the music plays and we remember his foibles – his punctiliousness in holiday preparation and his resolute determination not to think badly of people no matter the evidence. And they leave by midnight.

And I am here. I practice my speech. I hear him laughing at parts, turning aside at others (when he is lauded), being quietly attentive at others. And then he suggests another thousand things to mention but there is no time. How can I be content with a speech that is meant to say so much that actually says so little? And then I hear him say, "Buck up old chap, no one will ever remember a word you say!" And he laughs once again.

I hear a car pull up and footsteps I have come to recognise. Dorothy arrives at 3.00am. "I have come to keep you both company. I couldn't sleep." She kisses the coffin and then knocks on it and tells Charles not to doze off. She puts Gershwin's Rhapsody in Blue on.

And there in the dead of the night, in front of my dear friend, we decide to fulfil at least one of his dying wishes. We resolve not to let each other slip through our hands.

And Dorothy departs to ready herself. Sam arrives by 7.00 am to relieve me. Tanushi is to join her.

I take the dogs on a quick walk. Shower and prepare for the day.

I think we had looked after him well. I am content. Sam and Tanushi had cleared everything up by the time I retuned. The grave diggers had done their bit the previous day and so all was ready. Dorothy returned. She was wearing a ring on a chain round her neck which she made sure I noticed.

The funeral service and burial were perfect. We left him to his maker. Dust to dust.

The memorial service. I brought Brook along. He shouldn't miss out. And I needed him there.

Hannah spoke for the family and held it together so well. What a young woman! Timothy did the reading. And I spoke:

"When I practised my speech on Charles last night, he reminded me of a thousand things I should have included. But there is so little time and I want to say so much but have so few words. Charles told me not to worry because no one would remember a word I said."

Then my words tried to do justice to a man's life. I talked of his noble qualities and his love for Beatrice and Timothy and Hannah and of Cambridge and whisky and Islay and Kirk Aeppel and his work and his charitable concerns, his Christian faith and his friendship with me and a myriad of anecdotes. And so on. And he loved his friend Brook. I may have spoken for 5 minutes or 50. I know not.

Dorothy spoke of all she knew. That he was the bravest man she had ever encountered facing his own demise. He believed deeply in Jesus and his resurrection and this gave him the most profound hope for the future. If the measure of a man is the love that he gives and the love he elicits in others, Charles was an exemplar for us all.

And we retreated to the Peacock. I was amazed at the number there. So many stories of how he had helped people through his work. People in crisis. People who needed a friend who could sort the situation out for them.

Dorothy held my hand – metaphorically (and sometimes actually). Brook was petted. Beatrice and Hannah clung to each other. Timothy tended to Tanushi. It was exhausting but necessary. Sam and Jimmy took care of the food and drink for all.

Saturday 12th July

1. A time for recuperation and reflection. Kirk Aeppel has any number of perfect places for quiet reflection. Various people briefly dropped by to register their thanks or their support or their loss or to contribute to the Ashgate hospice fund.

2. The weather was decent and I spent the day gardening at the front of the house with the dogs. Tanushi has had Jason move some of the better and larger terracotta pots there.

Sunday 13th July

1. Dorothy dropped round in the afternoon. She has been endlessly supportive. I wanted to discuss engagement rings. She appeared happy to go along with this. I have cigar box full of rings given to me by my Mother. Each with a name tag as to whom she thought they had belonged to. I asked Dorothy whether she might want to select from that box. She said, without too much reluctance, that she was prepared to have a look.

2. There is one ring which stands out for me...and that is of course the one Dorothy choose. It is – by chance – Carilla's ring. A square of gold tops the gold band into which a square cut diamond is set. It has all the correct hallmarks. 18 carat gold. It is inscribed on the outside and inside of the band: "United hearts only death parts" and "Fear God and love me." The sizing was perfect. It seems meant. Dorothy was in raptures. She said she would be happier if we delayed any announcement given Charles' death. I agreed of course. This is all unchartered territory – and all so unexpected. I know not where I am except that I am profoundly happy to be here.

3. Tanushi and Timothy suddenly entered unannounced and she spotted the rings on Big Table within about 3 seconds of entering the room and she screamed. The dogs went crazy. There was no way to dissemble. The secret was no longer a secret. We both said that we had no intention of announcing this and upsetting Beatrice or the family in their period of mourning. Timothy smiled and hugged Dorothy and said, "You both know don't you that nothing would have made him happier than to see you two engaged."

4. I corrected him – I can think of one thing that would have made him happier. They both blushed and we laughed.

5. They agreed nevertheless to be discreet. I put the cigar box away. Dorothy secreted the ring in her purse.

Sunday 13th July - TANUSHI

We (Timothy and me) walked in on HH and D selecting an engagement ring! I screamed! All hush-hush. Dorothy had chosen. Very distinctive and weirdly familiar – square set diamond. Carilla's ring.

I am going to have to tell Sam...but I am sworn to secrecy. 54 years old and getting engaged for the first time! There's life in the old dog yet – or whatever the phrase is. Soooo pleased for them. If Sam visits... I must not blurt it out!

Monday 14th July

Sam and I look in on HH just to confirm that Jimmy will come round to collect the dogs first thing on Saturday.

It all feels very weird not telling Sam. Henry is absolutely his usual self – not betraying anything.

He talks about the possible outcomes. If it is a Goya, we sell and do both rooves obviously. If it is not, we sell the tusks and sell one of the Matlock properties – and get one roof done. This should leave us with some cash to develop car parking and public facilities maybe. If it's a "maybe" judgement...I think we have to accept it's not a Goya and there is no possible realistic chance of it being accepted as such. Adopt the latter strategy. I cannot believe that Henry is talking in such terms as "public conveniences" so readily. What has happened!

Wednesday 16th July

1. Dorothy comes round sporting the ring just for me to see. It is quite a distinctive ring. Not to be easily concealed. She is thrilled by it. I imagine Carilla showing it to the Duchess of Devonshire at one of the Chatsworth soirees she attended. (She then puts the ring away.)

2. We talk inevitably about Saturday. I have reached a place of peace in that I know either way what will happen. The estate is on a firmer footing than one year ago just prior to Tanushi's start.

3. And we inevitably talk of the funeral and memorial service. And Charles. He would have loved to be there on Saturday. I say that Dorothy had spoken so well and allowed Charles to speak so well about his beliefs and his hope.

Friday 18th July – TIMOTHY

Here at the Ibis once again. The stakes are higher this time!

Leisurely journey down. Tanushi slept most of the time. Stopped twice for loo and once for afternoon tea at her request. Arrived at 4.30.

We had a brief outing to "Sallies" just for old time's sake. We decided not to re-enact the scene where she attempted to propose to some old boring guy. Tanushi was consumed naturally by what might happen tomorrow. She said she wasn't exactly nervous (she was) – just that it was such a big deal and it obviously didn't rest on her. She didn't have to do anything. But what a difference this will make to her child.

Saturday 19th July

NO DIARY ENTRIES

Sunday 20th July – TIMOTHY

3.35 am Addenbrooke's Hospital

If I live to a thousand, I will not live through such day. Where to start?

Tanushi had said she'd slept as well as she does normally (which did not seem that well to me). Still, we had breakfast and got an Uber to the Fitzwilliam for 7.30 am. All fine. Tanushi really excited. Introduces me to Saskia. Lots of setting up and preliminary shots of the painting, followed by more questions with Tanushi – she was sat down as requested. She seemed on really good form taking it all in her stride. Morning break. I hovered and helped Tanushi. Back to it. Fiona and Philip arrived. They were delightful to Tanushi. So thrilled and caring. Fiona said, "I knew it Tanushi! I knew you were pregnant!"

Finally, to the filming of what will be the final scene. I genuinely think the presenters had no idea what the outcome would be. They seemed to make encouraging noises but, "We have been here before! To what extent do you think it all hangs on the DNA result? Provenance is vital – we know that."

Tanushi sat between Philp and Fiona. The director pulls out a large, thick manila envelope. It was given to Philip. He paused, inspected it and brandished it. "This is it then!" Pause. He opened it slowly and deliberately. The large black portfolio of documents spilt out. The first entitled: The Verdict.

He opened the first page and skim reads aloud: "These are the tests undertaken by The Prado Goya validation committee – list of tests – we mostly know about these already. The full display of the results are in the accompanying documents – etc. etc. Having analysed all the results, we were keen to see the DNA outcome to assess the reliability of the provenance narrative."

Next page – "The DNA shows conclusively that Henry Havard is a direct descendant of Francisco Jose de Goya."

Next page – "Therefore – taking all the evidence into consideration, we can confirm that we are happy to authenticate the Carilla Havard portrait as a genuine Goya masterpiece!"

Tanushi squealed for joy and the two presenters went into overdrive. I can see they are thrilled too. What a story for them and the programme. Some final questions – What does this mean? What will you now do with the portrait?

And then we are free! How amazing! Tanushi thanked everyone again and again. Yes, there can be follow up filmed at KA.

xxxxxxxxxxxxxxxxxxxxxxxxxxxxxxxxxxxxxxxxxxxxxxxxxxxxxxxxxxxxx

I need to say at this stage that Tanushi was absolutely fine. She had not been standing too much. She had had plenty of water to drink. She had eaten snacks through the morning. She was fine. I went over to kiss her and congratulate her and said I would order an Uber to take us to Christs. She said, "It's only 10 minutes' walk! What are you thinking? That we have money to throw around!" She burst out laughing. She wouldn't hear of a taxi. Quite happy to walk. It's half a mile. No more. Whichever way you go. We cut up Fitzwilliam Street and left onto Tennis Court Road and then right onto Downing Street and left onto St Andrew's Street. It's the quickest route. It's half a mile.

She was so happy. Just on cloud nine. And we walked carefully and slowly but there was no stopping her rabbiting away and then just on

St Andrew's Street she stopped and said, "Now how are we going to tell them all? Mustn't give it all away when we arrive because of the expressions on our faces. Let's look sombre and then I tell them." So, we agreed.

We entered and were shown to the interview room where I first met Tanushi over a year and a half ago. We went into the room with our best serious faces on. They were all there: Henry and Dorothy, Ted and Jane, Sam, Andrew and Sarah, Mrs Dias and Tavesh. There was a hushed silence. And she said, "I am here to inform you… that the painting… has been… authenticated as a genuine Goya masterpiece… price – very roughly 25 – 30 million pounds!" Everyone went bonkers. Jane was in tears hugging me like she won't ever let go. Dorothy has hold of Henry. Ted did a little jig – "no more talk of turning us into a theme park Timothy." Andrew and Sarah were just congratulating everybody over and over.

And the noise elicited a visit from a Porter who disappeared once he sees we are not destroying the place and I suddenly noticed Tanushi in that chair – that very chair next to the cast iron radiator – where I had first seen her. Stunning in the sari, waking up from a night of carousing at Selwyn Snowball. She suddenly looked not right. Flushed. Over-hot. Holding her belly.

Others have now spotted her. Mrs Dias was down by her side. I called an ambulance. Mrs Dias went with her in the ambulance. Tavesh and I went back to retrieve my car and we drove to Addenbrooke's. The party ended abruptly and I guessed they return to Kirk Aeppel.

Except an hour later Henry – looking utterly lost and dishevelled, found his way here with Dorothy.

xxxxxxxxxxxxxxxxxxxxxxxxxxxxxxxxxxxxxxxxxxxxxxxxxxxxxxxxxxxxx

And so we have occupied this corridor for 15 hours now. Mrs Dias has been largely by her side. She it is who relays the news from the doctors.

They don't do comfort anymore – doctors and nurses. Someone somewhere has decided – probably for insurance reasons – that medical types shouldn't say things like, "I'm sure it's going to be fine" or "She'll be as right as rain in no time" or "We see this all the time – really, there's nothing to worry about" or "We'll have this all sorted in a jiffy." They don't do reassuring at all. They spell out the risks brutally – "this could happen…another possible complication is… at this stage we just don't know if. Are you the next of kin?"

At 11.30 pm they performed an emergency caesarean.

I do not know which way to turn and so I pray. I find my way to the chapel and I pray. I have never prayed in my life before – not really. I pray because it matters so much I cannot not pray. And I wonder if Dad has got any sway up there – a bit early perhaps – I don't know the protocol. What would Dad have done? Remained calm, believed in hope, trusted to love, prayed.

There's a sculpture of a large mother hen with her chicks taking shelter under her wings. There's an explanation underneath – apparently Jesus compared himself to a hen wanting to shelter and protect her chicks.

xxxxxxxxxxxxxxxxxxxxxxxxxxxxxxxxxxxxxxxxxxxxxxxxxxxxxxxxxxxx

10.15 am Addenbrooke's Hospital

At 6.30 am we were allowed in, briefly in pairs, to see Tanushi. She smiles and I blubber and hold her hand and she's going to be fine. She's going to be fine. She is just anxious to see Evie – for it is Evie – the first Mistress of Kirk Aeppel – she is in the special care baby unit. SCBU they call it.

Mrs Dias – Kia – has been down to SCBU – 5 pounds 14 and a half ounces – and doing well. No need for any interventions. They are just keeping an eye on her.

I hug Kia; I hug Dorothy; I hug Henry; I hug Tavesh.

xxxxxxxxxxxxxxxxxxxxxxxxxxxxxxxxxxxxxxxxxxxxxxxxxxxxxxxxxxxxx

Sunday 3rd August - TANUSHI

I am reminded by my phone that I have been here at Kirk Aeppel for one year now.

From my room I can look up at Old Oak and the house. I took Evie up for the first time to meet our tree. All is well and all manner of things are well.

Amma has left today. She has loved being here but the time has come. She approves of Timothy. (I never thought I would hear that. Lawyers are only one rung down from doctors and engineers I am told.) She has learnt to cope with Kala – sort of. And she dotes on Evie of course.

Henry is learning how to handle a baby! He is not a natural at it but if love was the measure, he is more than coping.

Dorothy wears Carilla's ring (as painted by Fran. de Goya!) with girlish pride. She has been inordinately kind to me.

Sam has been closer than a sister. I love her.

Jimmy has moved on. He sits now with Bella on Sophie's bench talking of his apples and pears.

Beatrice and Hannah have visited the grave most days and sometimes drop in on me and Evie on their return. Blessings on them.

Andrew and Sarah think they have landed in some idyll and are fully Kirk Aeppel folk now; they walk Kala with Immie for me. Kala begins to resemble a pit pony (in size).

Jane finds any excuse to venture down to fuss and cluck over Evie. And dear Ted was of course there when I introduced Evie, the new Havard, to Old Oak – "Listen! Hear that Miss Tanushi? I think she's pleased to meet little Evie."

Timothy stands true.

And Evie, my Father's first grandchild, takes it all in her stride.

Sunday 3rd August

1. Communion. Dorothy. Order restored. Familiar rhythms. Death and birth. Kirk Aeppel continues with precious Evie.

2. Concerned about Samantha's plans for the family fun dog show in a month's time. Must talk to her tomorrow.

Ribble

8/04/16 – 15/12/21